TERMINAL ISLAND

TERMINAL ISLAND

A JACK LIFFEY MYSTERY

John Shannon

An Otto Penzler Book

CARROLL & GRAF PUBLISHERS
NEW YORK

For my father, Herb, a Depression child,
combat cameraman in the last just war, journalist,
a man of great integrity, and nothing like anyone in this book.

TERMINAL ISLAND

An Otto Penzler Book
Carroll & Graf Publishers
An Imprint of Avalon Publishing Group Inc.
245 West 17th Street
New York, NY 10011

Copyright © 2004 by John Shannon

First Carroll & Graf edition 2004

Library of Congress Cataloging-in-Publication Data is available.

ISBN: 0-7867-1337-2

Printed in the United States of America
Distributed by Publishers Group West

AUTHOR'S NOTE

Thanks to Chris Cole, Russ Buchan, Tommi Aguallo, and many others for showing me around and reacquainting me with my hometown. Among many printed sources, including the archives and oral histories of the Japanese American Museum in Los Angeles, I have to acknowledge especially the books *No-No Boy* by John Okada, and *Hagakure* by Yamamoto Tsunetomo, translated by William Scott Wilson.

Whatever is unnamed, undepicted, in images . . . whatever is misnamed as something else, made difficult to come by, whatever is buried in the memory by the collapse of meaning under inadequate or lying language, this will become, not merely unspoken, but unspeakable.

—Adrienne Rich

One

Doctor's Orders

Lieutenant Ken Steelyard took a sip of Calvados and bent over the lovely 4-8-4 GS-4 Daylight locomotive in its Southern Pacific colors (he had an identical one in the more austere black and graphite "war baby" colors from World War II). He adjusted his grip minutely on the penciltip soldering iron as he silver-soldered a tiny grab bar onto the cab. The western half of his HO layout was all steam era, but the eastern half—colonizing the rest of his immense basement—was so up-to-date he'd had to repaint all the AT&SF diesels to say Burlington Northern Santa Fe after the merger. The tracks all joined up at a sort of surreal fold in time, which occasionally sent a sleek diesel rocketing out of a contemporary suburb and through a small stretch of grazing chaparral into an Old West town. Such anachronisms didn't bother him in the least. The trains had already cost him two wives and a lot of random grief at Harbor Police Station, so a little more annoyance suited him fine.

His cell phone hooted its pale imitation of a two-note diesel air horn from where it lay on the workbench. He scowled.

"Steelyard."

"Detective, sorry to interrupt there. I know you're probably about to come around Deadeye Bend on full steam, but the sheriff's

1

guys got some bad kid trouble just over the line in PV. They're saying, like a two-oh-seven. They're goths, you know, those high school kids who all try to look like Count Dracula."

"Let the county guys sort it out."

"The missing kid lives in town. In fact, all of them do, so Higher thought we ought to take it."

He got the location and hung up. No sense moaning about it. His partner Gloria was off sick, too, getting a benign lump cut out of her breast, and he'd have to open the book by himself. He finished the Calvados before unplugging the soldering iron. Once it was poured it was spoken for.

Jack Liffey opened one eye from his nap, took a moment to wrench himself bodily out of the baffling foreign city that had sucked him down into its confusion and guilt, almost hearing a pop as he reemerged into his ordinary bedroom. He glared at the green oxygen cylinder by the bed. He had come to hate it for what it reminded him of, but he reached for the mask and cranked off a whiff. He was short one lung for now, and a gulp of pure O_2 was like a quick pick-me-up of single-malt scotch. Though the comparison was merely a memory. He hadn't had a drink in years.

"Hon, you okay?"

"I just had one of those energy flags. How long have I been down?"

"Almost an hour."

"Really?"

Rebecca Plumkill lowered herself gently beside him and ran her fingers lightly on his arm. "You've got an appointment with Auslander at two."

"Can I have a wisdom tooth out instead?"

She chuckled and ruffled his hair. He closed his eyes and pressed his head against her hand like a pet.

"I really appreciate you, Beck."

The calamity that had left him with a collapsed lung and as weak as a kitten had also reinforced what seemed to be a slow-burning nervous breakdown, and he was astonished Rebecca had stayed with him through it all. Dicky Auslander was a shrink, and Jack Liffey didn't get along very well with him, but he was an M.D., too, and the only access to the pills that kept him from a lot worse. His normal life, for whatever that phrase was worth, was tracking down missing children, and he hadn't been able to get back to that for several months now.

"You're still pretty good in bed, even if you're not much good for anything else."

"I can make a farting sound with my underarm," he boasted.

"And you still make me laugh," she said. "No woman asks for more than that."

"A lot have, believe me."

The phone on the bedside table rang, and Rebecca Plumkill answered it. She made a long face, reluctantly divulged that Jack Liffey was there, and then listened for a while with a dubious furrow across her brow. He gave insistent tugs on her skirt until she offered up a fatalistic shrug and handed him the receiver.

"Do I ever deny you?"

"Jacko, it's Art Castro. How you doin', amigo?"

"Every day a little better."

"Better than what?"

"That's the question, all right. Better than a big hole in the ground. You know the Rule of Holes, Art?"

"Nah."

"When you're in one, stop digging. How about you? You back in the good graces?"

Art Castro worked for Rosewood, the big detective agency in town, and he had gotten in dutch with his bosses, basically for helping out Jack Liffey on a job that had slumped abruptly into a terrorist quagmire, bringing down a lot of guys in dark suits on the Rosewood offices.

"They had to let a couple operatives go, you know, for multipurpose ethics and stuff like that, but I finally have my old office back. I can see the outside world again. And I even get a visitor's chair."

"That's great. I felt a bit guilty." Jack Liffey noticed Rebecca Plumkill's eagle eye on him as he talked.

"A bit? That's rich, *compa*. You had me in the FBI office three times explaining why my third cousin once read a book about Ali Baba. But hey, what's a little hard time between friends?"

"That's the attitude."

"Fact, I've got an absconded kid for you if you want the job. You're always good with the ones off on a religious bender."

He wondered if Rebecca could sense any change in his expression.

"This time it's Satanism, and the parents want to pay somebody to duel with the Old Serpent for the kid's soul."

"Most of that's just adult hysteria, Art. A kid draws a grinning devil on his schoolbook and the mom freaks."

"In this case the kid really seems to have joined up with an honest-to-God Church of Satan, with some antipope up in San Francisco named Mad as Hell."

Jack Liffey laughed. "Sounds more like performance art. Can't do it, Art." He caught Rebecca's skeptical eye. "The powers that be say I'm not ready for work yet."

"Sorry to hear that. But I can dig it. Lately you seem to be leaving a big chunk of you behind on every job."

"The lung's just collapsed temporarily. It's having a little rest." But there was also a metal plate in his head, a rib with a titanium peg in it, a star-shaped scar on his shoulder, and a bad Frankenstein stitch down one leg. "Thanks for the offer, though. If you get any tickets for the Pasadena Penguins, let me know."

It was an old joke between them. Jack Liffey pretty much hated all professional sports, and referring to the nonexistent Penguins was his usual way of changing the subject.

"It's off-season for the 'Guins. Take care, Jacko."

"Thanks."

He hung up the receiver delicately with two hands.

"But you really wanted to take the job, didn't you?" Rebecca said huskily. She bent close to play erotically with a slight protrusion under the covers.

"What if there were no such thing as rhetorical questions?" Jack Liffey whispered in her ear.

December 13
Darkness before and darkness after and this pain in
between. Why keep a journal, why record what I am belat-
edly learning? I only know others have done so and it is
from them that I have learned how to take up the bow
again. And how to act wholly within a code.

Father, to honor you finally I must become chiseled down.

I can see now that worthiness gradually wanes from the
world, the slow decline of men's capacities. As the gold is
used up, men settle for silver. And after the silver . . . what?

All those who know what I know and have been where I
have been will be dead in another thirty years. Perhaps that
thirty years is the limit of one historic period of moral stillness. I long for the stillness, the way I knew it once, night
after day, within a forest blind, on a ridge overlooking paddies, braced in a tree beside a trail. All this comes back now
as distraction, nostalgia, pointless wish. Yet—the smell and
feel of the tropics, that mildewy undertone to all sensation,
like a damp inbending of time and space to enclose one in
calm. I miss the inner calm.

I know I have lost my edge. I must substitute a new code of
being for the discipline of danger. No, *substitute* is not the
word. The code will undergird everything, complete and
define and perfect. My strength may not be sufficient, but it
still buoys me above most of the pain.

Honor is all. Honor is salvation.

Before the first act today I did five hundred push-ups and
tested my capacity for watchfulness for two hours, fifteen
minutes. My *dozukuri* was only partial. Thoughts came to
me unbidden, distractions. I must eliminate one comfort

from my life to see if I can get back some of my stillness. What should I give up? The bed, perhaps. Sleep tonight in the warehouse, on concrete, and sleep only half the night. No, better: tonight I will not sleep. I will find a place in the midst of distraction and remain mindful only of my breathing. Strength. Loyalty. Justice. Bravery.

Father, I know honor is all, but the pain is so great.

It was one of the World War II gun emplacements above the Palos Verdes cliffs, looking out southwest over the green-blue Pacific. A broad gun slit facing the water, much of the concrete unearthed now by erosion with a steel trapdoor rusted open above and a number of connecting tunnels to other bunkers. It had been built in the first flush of hysteria after Pearl Harbor, and at least three generations of San Pedro children had played war in the emplacement during the daytime while their older siblings built campfires and canoodled in the bunkers at night. In between somewhere, the graffiti artists had had a field day on the concrete of the picturesque nuisances.

Steelyard came toward it along the dirt road that had been a farm access track for the garbanzo bean growers of his youth. He had hiked here, alone, at fifteen, a bit fearful that one of the Japanese farmers might confront him, and there was a great deal of uneasy melancholy in that recollection. For twenty years after the war, Japanese Americans had had to lease back the fields that they had once owned as their truck gardens. Not to mention the fact that for Ken Steelyard, it had been a very unhappy period of his life. But that was then.

"This is five Henry fifteen. I'm going code six to lend a hand to our beige brethren. Out."

There were no garbanzo beans here now, he noted, had been none for years. As a boy he had no idea at all what the little gnarled brown fists were used for, or who ate them, and now that he knew, he thought of those old bean fields every time he ate in a Greek restaurant.

He headed across to where all the activity was concentrated. Two sheriff's Crown Victorias had plowed right across the harrowed-up field, and he hoped they'd be able to get them out again without a tow. Three kids dressed in black were sitting with their backs against the exposed side of one of the bunkers. They looked pretty miserable.

"*Hola,* gents. Detective Lieutenant Steelyard, Harbor Division."

The sheriff's deputies introduced themselves and they shook hands politely all around. They were only patrol units. The county hadn't sent any of their detectives, so it seemed there wouldn't be any dick-waving about jurisdiction, even though they were a good mile into Rancho Palos Verdes, which contracted with the county for its police and fire.

The deputy with the biggest mustache handed him an evidence Baggie with a playing card in it. The back was a big-eyed pink kitten of vaguely Japanese aspect, and the front was the two of spades, though each spade shape was actually a reproduction of some other overcute animal. The card had been struck with some kind of Japanese rubber stamp that showed curlicued letters, and beneath that two words were written in felt pen: *Stay down.*

"The kids say they exited the bunker pursuant to some form of ritual and they only left their friend alone a minute. When they went back inside, the card's all they found, taped right where the kid had been. They're sure it wasn't there before."

"Thanks. I'd appreciate it if you guys would code four on out of here now. If I have to call in a CSI, we don't want the ground too walked over."

"Sure thing, sir."

The kids all watched as the sheriff's cars backed and humped and spun dirt, but they had pusher bars like CHP units and managed to push each other back out to the hard-packed dirt road.

Steelyard squatted in front of the kids. They were in black jeans and leather and shirts of something shiny like satin, with bits of whitish makeup here and there and long black fingernails. He hadn't had any children of his own and wasn't good with them, even the normal ones, so he always overcompensated. He chose the one who looked the brightest.

"Your name?"

"Chuck Marks."

"Chuck, I'll get all the particulars later, but right now time is important. Show me where you last saw your friend. His name?"

"Vin Petricich. He called himself Turtle."

"Let's find Turtle's trail if we can."

He unbelted his big three-cell Maglite, and they climbed atop the bunker. The rusted metal hatch door exhaled a cool wind, and Steelyard was first down the old rungs that had been cast into the cement wall. The bottom was a litter of dry leaves, fast-food packaging, and condom wrappers, the dim room offering a brew of indefinable rotten smells—burned wood, marinating leaves, layers of semen drying out over decades. A long bright rectangle showed the ocean far out, greenish and dotted with whitecaps in the wind. A waist-high concrete pillar in the middle of the big room might once have mounted an armor-piercing .50 or maybe just a telescope to watch the sea. One dark tunnel led off the main room, straight inland, and another paralleled the cliffs.

"Where was he?"

The boy pointed to a stained mattress. "Honest, we were only outside a minute."

"Count out the minute you remember and tell me when it's over. Go over in your head everything you did in that time."

The boy looked a little confused but tried. "One . . . two—"

"*Silently.*"

Steelyard used the time to run his light carefully over the floor. If nothing jumped out at him, it would be quite a job for CSI. He knew he wasn't Sherlock Holmes. There were crushed beer cans and an empty clove cigarette pack, which he left untouched. He checked the back tunnel but it ended definitively in a dirt fall and collapse. The flat walls had been layered by generations of graffiti, mostly big puffy initials but through the tangle here and there he could see something more ambitious, a bit of an Aztec mural maybe. The topmost layers were mainly obscene comments, erect penises, and hairy vaginas, men's room stuff, not breaking any new ground.

"Now, sir."

"Okay. In that time he could have wriggled out the slit."

"We'd'a seen."

"Or gone down the other tunnel." He frowned at the dark orifice. It was pitch dark because it zigged and zagged as per military protocol, protection against blast and gunfire. He'd only been an MP in 'Nam, but he knew this was where they'd call in the tunnel rats who liked this sort of thing, feeling ahead of themselves for tripwires and booby traps.

He was pretty sure from his own explorations as a boy that the tunnel connected to another bunker about thirty yards west, but he was tall enough that his hair teased the ceiling and he didn't like the sense of narrow enclosure one bit. "Stay there. Did you call in the sheriff's on a cell?"

"Uh huh."

"If I don't make it out, call nine-one-one and ask for Harbor Division detectives. My name's Steelyard."

"Break a leg."

"Huh?"

"It means good luck."

"Thanks."

His flashlight showed about twenty feet ahead, to the first zig. There was a little less graffiti here, more smell of damp. After the bend, the floor was chock-full of used rubbers, as if there were always kids sneaking out of sight of the main party for their fun.

After the third turning, he came to a halt with a chill. A perfect little B&O boxcar rested in a cleared spot on the floor ahead of him where his oval of light wobbled. It was HO scale, lovingly detailed, identical to three of his own. He came closer and saw that another one of the pink kitty cards jutted out of the open boxcar door. He knelt and looked it over carefully. There were no wires visible, no extraneous objects. He knew he shouldn't touch things, but he had a surgical glove in his pocket and he tugged it on resignedly. Gingerly he took a pinch grip on one corner of the card. That was his mistake.

The flash-bang went off in his face and knocked him flat on his ass. Blinded, at least temporarily, his ears howling with pain, he lay back and cursed himself. *You big dumb shit!*

* * *

Jack Liffey parked the old VW in his allotted space in his condo's lot and sat in it for a while after the noisy engine died, trying to recover some good cheer. The condo workers had just installed the usual Christmas lights over the entrance, but that hadn't helped his mood much. Dicky Auslander managed without fail to annoy him to the edge of mutiny with a kind of sanctimonious goodwill that played off the therapist's own obscure needs and theories and seemed to have little to do with him.

Becky's Range Rover was gone, of course, off at school. She was headmistress of a private academy for girls called Taunton and even on Saturday had to show her face. In theory he disapproved of private schools, but he did not make a big deal about it, since the relationship was so delightful and everything else in his life—barring the love of his daughter Maeve—was so fragile or so plain gone.

"Yes, Dicky, I have my gloomy stretches. You know, in many eras of history philosophers used to cherish their dark moods."

"No, I've never wanted to think of you as my father confessor figure, whatever cute name you give it."

"My father's death is none of your fucking business."

"If your potted fern brushes my ear one more time, I'm going to incinerate it."

He wasn't sure the therapy was even necessary. If only he could get a good, deep breath, he felt he'd be on the way back to 100 percent, but some other doctors he was stuck with had their own ideas about letting it refill on its own time. It took a great deal of strength to keep illness like this from seeping into the soul. But his spirit lifted all at once when he saw his daughter's little top-heavy car in a visitor space. Her mom had given her an ugly, but probably quite safe, brand-new Toyota Echo. The sight of the car got him moving, and he collected the mail—only bills—and went in.

"Hon?"

She came running and hugged him. He tried not to be aware of the pressure of her breasts. "Daddy, you're looking much better!"

"That's because I *am* much better. Rebecca takes good care of me, in all the ways it's prudent to talk about."

"To talk about with me, you mean."

She held him back at arm's length, a sixteen-year-old solicitous great-aunt, almost his own height now. He wondered if boys her age had the sense to desire and cherish this precious bright being, and then part of him decided he was quite happy if they were stupid as dirt and left her alone and went for the blond cheerleaders.

"I'm surprised you two get along so well," Maeve said. "She's not really your type."

"What's my type? A meddler like your mom?"

"I'll make you some tea."

"Thanks." He followed her into the kitchen, grinning, to let her fuss over him, a smaller, much more chipper version of her mother.

"I figure your type is somebody a little less hoity-toity than Ms. Plumkill."

"Nice," he said approvingly. They teased each other with old slang. "Her school's hoity-toity for sure, but somehow she's pretty down to earth."

"Uh-huh," Maeve said skeptically. "Caff or de? I'll bet you were crazy about going to *Swan Lake* last week."

"I'm willing to try new things, hon. E.g., you can make me some of that plum mango pomegranate persimmon watermelon perfume tea you love. Rebecca said she'd get you a scholarship to Taunton for your last two years if you'd like a close look at how the other half lives."

"As if. Dad, it's an all-girls school."

"That *would* be one of the selling points, yes."

"Not to me. And it's only orange mango zinger. I don't know if I'd like rich girls, but I know I couldn't keep up with them. Too many yachts and trips to Sun Valley. And they've got some attitudes I don't think I'd like, either. We've got some pretty rich kids at Redondo and they can be okay, but there's always a sticking point."

"I'm listening."

Maeve screwed up her face and it was a pleasure to watch her think in pantomime. "There's just a way rich kids have. It comes out when you're least expecting it. It's like looking at all those huge ads in the front of *Vanity Fair* for ten-thousand-dollar watches.

There's a kind of feeling that they deserve every bit of the good stuff in the world. Not just want it and can have it because they have money, but actually *deserve* it. Like a birthright."

"A sense of entitlement, I think it's called," he said.

"It's not that it makes me think of the poor or anything. Though sometimes I do. It just aghasts me."

"I don't think that's a transitive verb, hon, but I know what you mean. A world of *stuff* can end up making you pretty shallow, even the richest stuff. That's definitely why I've always kept us poor."

She put the refilled pot on the burner and hugged him again, sensing the irony. "You give me the riches of your accumulating personhood. What could be nicer? I just hope Ms. Plumkill is *really* good to you and you stick it out a while. You don't have the world's best record for lasting, you know?"

"Ouch. By the way, what's become of your Persian boyfriend?" Fariborz Bayat was one of the boys Jack Liffey had been hunting down when he'd got caught up in the terrorist bombing that had collapsed his lung. Fariborz had helped him foil the plot and he liked the boy a lot. He had a kind of earnestness to do the right thing.

"He's going to visit relatives in Iran. He wants to try living with less of what he calls 'Hollywood capitalism.' I understand—it's that same business about *stuff*."

"And a flight from individualism, I'll bet. I think I know Fariborz. He's looking for that peace that comes with . . . whatever you want to call the opposite of our dog-eat-dog life."

Speaking of dogs, Loco wandered in, saving them from sinking further into philosophical piffle. The animal was half coyote but had recently given up his pretensions to the call of the wild and seemed to be settling in as a loving pet, particularly with Maeve, whom he now rubbed against. He cranked his neck up to wheedle her with his weird yellow eyes. She stooped to give the animal a big hug.

"Hi, Loc. Old reliable."

"Reliable? What world do you live in?"

"He's changed. You just don't give him any credit." Maeve reached into her shirt pocket and brought out an index card, as if it were a sudden inspiration, and showed it to him. It said MEDB.

"That's interesting," he said dubiously.

"You and Mom screwed up."

"That's for sure. Oh, indeed we did. I cop. Guilty."

"Stop it. We've got an Irish exchange student this year and that's how my name should really be spelled, or 'spelt,' as she says."

He chuckled at the downright implausibility of Gaelic spelling. "Would you rather we screwed up, or would you rather spend the rest of your life explaining to surly DMV employees that you are not actually called Meddub?"

She pocketed the card again. "Maybe the real thing'll be lucky for me."

The phone rang and he decided to take it in the bedroom, away from prying ears. Loco stayed with her.

"Hello."

"Is this Jack Liffey, from San Pedro High, summer '63?"

It gave him a jolt. It was a man's voice, but he didn't recognize it, and there was a faint honking in the background, as if the call were being relayed by a failing satellite.

"The Majestics," Jack Liffey heard himself saying. Why do we remember crap like that from so long ago? He could still see the ugly chartreuse cardigan that had been their senior class sweater, and the loopy little cross-eyed king that had been embroidered on it as their logo. He doubted they did that sort of thing anymore. The last gasp of the fifties.

"This is Dan Petricich. We were in Mrs. Felder's English together, but I was in the winter class."

Back then there had been two graduating classes every year, the big one in the summer, and a smaller one each winter, probably something to do with the baby boom. He bet they didn't do that anymore, either, unless year-round schooling had brought it back.

"I remember you. You used to argue back with that history teacher, the right-wing one."

"Mr. Gianelli. What a shithead."

"Give him credit, he never took it off your grade if you disagreed with him."

"Still a shithead. I hear you're a detective now, Jack."

"Not exactly."

"I've got a business card here that says you find missing children." There was a real quaver of apprehension in his voice.

He winced. A former woman-friend had printed up those cards for him and even put a big eyeball on them. He did his best not to spread them around. "I seem to be in a retirement phase at the moment. Some health trouble I've had."

"Suppose we just talk, Jack. I need something, some help or I don't know what, maybe just the benefit of your experience. My kid is okay now, but somebody in a ninja suit snatched him yesterday and taped him all up with duct tape and I'm afraid they're going to come after him again. The cops don't have a clue."

There were other voices in the background, speaking in Spanish, and he could tell Dan was calling from somewhere busy.

"I really can't, Dan, I'm sorry. I'm under doctor's orders. Where the hell are you?"

"I'm on a fishing boat. Just come and talk to me, please, Jack. You can't be that gummed up you can't drive down here for a visit. For old times." He seemed about to run down and then hurried on. "My kid fancies himself a goth. You know what that means, I'm sure. I'm not crazy about it myself, but it's really pretty innocent. He's a good kid, but who knows what some idiots think these days? Maybe they get the idea that because he wears black, he's got a bunch of sawed-off shotguns and is laying plans to attack the school like Columbine or something so they've got to get him first. I just don't know. He's a mixed-up kid but he doesn't deserve somebody dogging him."

Jack Liffey stared at the mussed bed where earlier Rebecca had sat to glower suspiciously at him as he'd turned down Art Castro's job. He could still see the impression of her rump in the sheet, and he wished he could fondle it right now. He figured this was just a way of distracting himself from the decision he knew he was making.

Two

The Home Tree

"Toot-toot there."

"I *think* I can, I *think* I can."

It was vice detectives named Cole and Buchan, sauntering languidly past his desk, and he didn't even bother to give them the finger. Buchan made a little choo-choo alternate rotation of his arms as the two of them passed out the door toward the lunchroom.

The wounded B&O boxcar sat in the middle of his green blotter, not just *like* one of his rolling stock, it *was* one. He'd found the telltale KS he always engraved on the potmetal undercarriage. Somebody had broken into his home without leaving a sign, and now he didn't even know whether *he* was the target of the perp or the Petricich kid.

The missing boy had been right there in the next bunker, trussed up like a rib roast with silver duct tape and beginning to go panicky at his immobility. All the boy could say about his assailant was that he was a small man but extremely strong. The guy hadn't said a word, just come down on him out of nowhere in a black jumpsuit. The kid kept insisting it was like some graphic novel, or Japanese *anime*. What was left of the second pink kitty card, a bit frayed by the flash-bang grenade, revealed it to be the three of

15

spades. It had the same Japanese ink stamp and the words *Don't get in the way*. Steelyard didn't like the way the cards had progressed from a two to a three. It implied there were a lot more in store, and probably a few pretty nasty surprises waiting up around the ace.

"How you feeling, Ken? *¿Qué tal?*"

He felt a strong hand on his shoulder and looked up to see Gloria Ramirez, a little pale but looking fine in a navy blue business suit. She was a fairly new detective, a D-1, and he was her training officer.

"How you doing yourself, kid? You were the one under the knife."

"You know how it is these days with the HMOs. If you can walk, you're outta here."

"Don't fuck around. Tell me."

She sat at her desk, which back-to-backed his. "They don't know for sure, but they think it's okay. There's always more tests."

"Let's hope. You shouldn't be back at work yet."

"I'm going to do half days. You had a bit of an ER trip yourself."

"It was just one of those stun grenades, like SWAT uses, but I was sitting right on top of it like a moron rookie. I got all my senses back eventually."

She pressed her palms in front of her chin, like a Hindu set to pray, and made a face. "Ken, I know you like to be this *pinche* loner and head off on your own private tangent, but I'd like to learn something on this case. Even at half speed."

He tossed her the two cards, out of their Baggies now as the perp had wiped them down so carefully they hadn't yielded even a partial print.

"Nutcase," he said. "He's leaving them in order."

"Could be warnings," Ramirez said. "Could be somebody trying to set up a treasure hunt, I suppose. *Stay down.* You were in a tunnel complex, and the boy was tied up down there, too, in the next room. Could have been a clue to finding him."

"You *have* been keeping up. The trey isn't much of a clue, though. *Don't get in the way.*"

"How did he get in your house to get that train car?"

Steelyard sighed. "You don't think I haven't been banging my head on that? I've got an alarm system. I've got a big, bad dog. I've got real Mannlicher deadbolts. How did he even know I had a train layout in the basement? How did he know it'd be me scrambled on the kidnap?"

"How do we know it's a he?"

"The boy thought it was. Short and strong as an ox."

"That's something."

"Uh-huh, we've eliminated half the human race. More if you eliminate tall quadriplegics, infants, Nepalese."

"Why Nepalese?"

"They don't live around here much."

"I think the key is you," she said. "It didn't matter whether you were going to show up there or not. The boxcar would trace to you eventually."

For some reason he didn't like her stating that. "How is your boyfriend taking the operation? I remember he was a bit squeamish."

Her face darkened. "Let's just let that go, okay?"

"Sure. Sorry. If you know any Japs you might ask them to translate that ink stamp."

"It's called a *hanko,* and the preferred term is Japanese Americans."

"Fine, whatever."

"Tell me about goths, hon."

Maeve was inserting a Pop-Tart into his old toaster. It was not a food item he kept around much, and then he saw the fresh box she must have brought with her.

"Those things are made out of petrochemicals and steer manure," he admonished.

"They're my one lapse into junk food. I can't help it. Brad and Mom have built a whole cuisine out of Pop-Tarts. Pop-Tart au gratin, Pop-Tart mousse, Sauerkraut and Pop-Tarts. Anyway, you eat Big Macs."

"Only when I'm traveling. You know why I go into McDonald's on the road, don't you?"

"It's quick and predictable?"

"I suppose that's part of it, but here I am, in Lodi, sweaty and road-weary because the car hasn't got an air conditioner. I'm disappointed because some runaway kid has eluded me or cursed me out or waved a gun in my face, yet my spirit lifts because I know with absolute certainty that I can stroll into this McDonald's and for a few bucks I can purchase thirty seconds, maybe a full minute, of politeness from a teenager."

She wrinkled her forehead a moment, as if she'd lost her sense of humor somewhere, and then laughed softly. "It's true, isn't it. But if it's politeness you want from us, you'd better avoid goths. The whole getup's supposed to be a thumb in your eye."

"They take it all seriously?"

"Some do. You were a beatnik, weren't you?"

"I suppose so, but I wouldn't have liked being *called* one."

"I don't think they mind the word at all. It's a style. There're maybe twenty of them at Redondo High. Some play Dungeons and Dragons, some go to the raves and listen to death metal or speed metal. Mostly they seem unhappy and kind of lost, but they read a lot, even good stuff, though mostly with dark themes. Dostoevsky, Baudelaire, Blake. There're even a couple of Latino goths. It fits right in with all that Day of the Dead stuff in their culture."

The toaster chirped and a brown Pop-Tart, leaking red, rose slowly like a ghoul from its grave. "Want half?"

He made a face. "I haven't had one in fifteen years and I still have a distinct memory of the taste. It was like sucking chrome off a bumper."

Cops with fizzing flares were funneling the traffic at the bottom of the Harbor Freeway into a creeping clog and by the time he neared the offramp at Channel, he could see why. Two immense belly-to-the-ground pigs were glaring and snorting at a ring of blue-clad cops who were trying skittishly to pen them in. One cop even had his pistol out.

Freeze, motherfucker! Jack Liffey thought.

Pigs always turned out to be a lot bigger than you thought, and these looked huge, prehistoric, the size of his car. Just as he angled down the ramp, both pigs squealed on some unheard signal and charged, setting off a panic among the retreating cops, but he didn't get to see the sequel.

Then he was coming up Gaffey through the gap in Goat Hill into San Pedro proper, toward the old downtown that had defined his youth: the Warners Theater, the war surplus, the hobby shop, and only two blocks farther down Sixth Street, the harbor itself, which had once had a ferryboat across to Terminal Island. Then there were the shipyards and the dark glamour of Beacon Street, the tattoo parlors and mission hotels and a bar named Shanghai Red's, where men had once actually been shanghaied. Urban renewal had knocked down a lot of it before the fashion had shifted in the nineties to trying to preserve a cardboard cutout of the past. Pasadena had started the trend by pouring new boutiques and Starbucks and all the ordinary mall stores like Banana Republic into the historic storefronts, as if repopulating the world from outer space.

He tended to avoid San Pedro as much as he could. It was a great place, one of the few LA districts with real character, but there were just too many of his own ghosts, too many spots where he'd messed up a young love or lost a friend or stepped on some Latino's spit-shined shoes and had to run for his life. They didn't call them gangbangers then, but they were. The Latinos in gray checked Pendletons buttoned to the neck and the Yugoslavs in gray felt carcoats with names and designs, just like the Pharaohs in *American Graffiti*. It had been a working-class town for the most part—longshoremen and fishermen and shipyard workers.

There was a pang in his heart as he passed the building that had been Macowan's Market, now a 99-Cent Only Store scrawled with Christmas designs. Two or three times a week, after junior high, he and Billy Engels would hunker down behind the magazine rack with a bag of Bell Brand barbecued potato chips and big RC Colas—sixteen-ouncers—and read the science fiction comics one after another. Once he'd read for so long that his legs had gone completely to sleep and in trying to stand up he'd fallen flat on his face, astonished by his rubbery, numb appendages. The clerk knew

they were there, of course, but he had let them read their way
through his comics for free on some kindly impulse of a bygone era.

He tried to stay numb to all that nostalgia as he motored past the
ferry building, which had been turned into a maritime museum,
and then through the seemingly endless square miles of lovely old
California bungalows that spread over the rolling hills above the
harbor. In fact, as he parked the VW, the bungalow that waited up
a scabby lawn looked eerily familiar to him, and he wondered if
he'd been better friends with Petricich and his family than he
remembered.

"Your house looks awfully familiar," Jack Liffey admitted, sipping the
wonderfully strong black coffee Dan's wife had poured out for him.

"Sure, sure," Dan Petricich said. "Everybody thinks so. We
rented the place out to Polanski for *Chinatown*. Remember Curly's
house? Three days of shooting, and it made us more than a good
month of a tuna run in the old days."

They sat around a big scarred-up oak table, having a hearty late
breakfast because Dan's boat, the *Sanja P.*, had been out squidding
all night and had just come in and offloaded. Dan looked suitably
spaced out by exhaustion, his hair awry and radiating a certain
fishy pung into the room, but it didn't stop him shoveling down
fried potatoes and eggs and sausages, which were regularly replen-
ished by his plump blond wife, Marin. She hovered over them,
having been introduced to Jack Liffey as "my damned Swede." A
fantastically leathered old man sat at the end of the table, competing hard with Dan for all the food he could spear. Ante Petricich,
the patriarch and original owner of the *Sanja P.*

"Fishing was always this big fight between Yugoslavs and Ital-
ians," Jack Liffey said. "All my youth. I knew kids on both sides—
Mardesiches and Pescaras."

"You remember wrong," the old man put in in a harsh croak. "It
was Croatians and fuckin' Sicilians, what it was, in fact. Know how
you can tell a fuckin' Sicilian boat?" It was a rhetorical question, and
Jack Liffey had no intention of answering. "They got a big open
bridge so the fuckin' hotheaded Sicilian captain can stand up there

like some puffed-up godfather all day cursing and swearing at every-body. Croatian boats got a nice professional closed wheelhouse."

"The tuna's gone, isn't it?" Jack Liffey said.

The old man shrugged. "Fuckin' longline boats out of Japan. Ten miles of hooks. It's like nuking the sea. Tuna was a real man's fish to catch. Squid is for sissies. I quit when we started using lights."

"It pays the bills, Pops."

The old man gave a snort. "They shine these big lights into the water to pull them up like magnets. It's no better than jacklighting deer."

"The tuna didn't have much of a chance either, did they?" Jack Liffey said. "I always figured the only fair fishing would be if you gave the tuna automatic weapons."

Dan Petricich laughed. "We got so much sonar and GPS stuff and spotter planes these days the squid are sitting ducks."

"Wouldn't you like some eggs and sausages, Mr. Liffey? I can make fresh."

"No, thanks. I already ate." He tried to remember a Swedish Marin in his class but could only recall a Swedish Carol who had grown great breasts prematurely and had everybody lusting after her. Carol'd had large buttocks, too, and he and a friend had pri-vately named her MNA, for magnisimus novisimus agmen, which was as near as their crude Latin dictionary could get to "greatest rear," though in fact it meant greatest rear platoon, or, quite liter-ally, "greatest newest line of march." He was amazed that after so many years, stuff like this was still banging around in his head.

"It's here if you want it," Marin said, turning away in tight pedal pushers to show a fairly nice newest line of march herself.

"The kid is sulking," Dan said. "I won't call him out right now, he'll only clam up. You take him away from the house and see what you can get out of him."

"I'll be happy to."

"And get this"—he waved a fork with his mouth full. "You're not going to believe it, it's old home week. The cop on the case is Ken Steelyard."

That rocked Jack Liffey back in his chair a bit.

"Not the one from Seventh Street School?"

"How many you think there are in this town?"

Ken Steelyard was the most unlikely person from his grade school days to turn cop he could imagine. They had still been fairly close friends for a while at the beginning of junior high, but the last Jack Liffey really remembered of the tall, skinny, sad, and troubled boy was when he had secretly piled all of his possessions, including an ungainly hi-fi console, onto a Greyhound bus and taken himself off to Fresno by himself at age fourteen. When his mom and new stepdad found him, they dragged him home, but for some reason he and Jack Liffey hadn't stayed close after that.

"I'd figure him for the guy who goes up on the roof with a high-powered rifle and starts shooting innocent pedestrians."

Dan chuckled. "He straightened up, I guess."

"I guess I ought to go to some class reunions, but I can't bring myself."

"I went to one ten years ago. You get to know what the guys are up to."

"Yeah, I want to see a reunion, but only through about ten panes of one-way glass." How many times could you stand to explain how you got laid off from a nice aerospace job all of a sudden, in the middle of a normal life, and then got drunk a lot and lost your marriage, and in trying to dig yourself out, you fell into hunting down missing children as a living? It was probably a lot easier to introduce yourself if you were a success of some kind.

December 14

When the world around you is in decline in every respect, to excel becomes much simpler, sometimes no more than a basic *kata*. Last night, after the task of the day, at midnight I con-structed a private willed space. I stood against a closed metal grate in the entry of a cheap souvenir shop on Hollywood Boulevard. I remained there until dawn, passed by hookers, by waifs, lost runaways, drug dealers, by pimps and under-cover police. For the first time in thirty years I rediscovered what it meant to be both aware of your surroundings and unaware at once. The pain was lessened somewhat, too. I

simply was. I was aware of what passed as nothing, as ghosts
of this sad underlife. Almost no one saw me there, enfolded
in stillness, and the few who did went on quickly.

The right and wrong ways of behaving are both contained
within the trivial. At first, there were distracting thoughts.
Then I found the place, on the outer margin of the world,
above an infinite cliff. I could have grabbed bullets out of
the air with my bare hands. Readiness. I knew: All movement is ritual. Like a new kind of breathing, almost peace.

Father, my obligation to you is heavy. Honor is everything.

I am completely at one with your memory and will serve
you as if I, too, am already dead. I rush to my death freely.
I must act again, for you, according to the code. I will keep
ahimsa in mind. Hurt no one who does not hurt me.

Be sincere and hard and quick. Loyalty. Justice. Bravery.

Honor holds off darkness.

The disease of secrets, Jack Liffey thought, the disease of private
pain. The boy sat sullenly on a plastic bench at Hugo's Tacos, while
Jack Liffey brought him a couple of nondescript crisp tacos and a
Coke from the take-out window, ordering for himself a bad coffee
and a cardboard tray of French fries.
    "I already talked to the fucking cop."
    "This isn't really your hangout, is it?" Jack Liffey said, ignoring
the undirected venom. He had suggested going someplace where
the boy felt comfortable.
    The boy shrugged slightly. He'd no more take an adult into his
world than put on a Hawaiian lei. He didn't touch the food. Ants
made a line up one of the legs of the concrete table, across a corner
to a puddle of catsup, where they milled and gorged before heading
back down again.

"I went to San Pedro High, too."

Jack Liffey might as well not have spoken. He continued, "I wasn't very popular. Before I left, I wrote 'Fuck the Knights' on the base of the big pirate. I wonder if there's any trace of it."

The kid smiled at that momentarily.

Jack Liffey hadn't done any such thing, but he understood what it meant to be pissed off enough to want to. "Do you want to be called Turtle or Vin?"

The boy shrugged again.

"Are the Knights still around?" This exclusive fraternity of suck-ups and student council types had, in Jack Liffey's day, colluded with the jocks to lord it over everyone else.

"They leave us alone."

"I imagine since Columbine the school's a bit on your ass, frisking you for shotguns and such."

"We can't wear trench coats to school anymore. No big deal. What *was* Columbine?"

He let that alone. He knew the kid knew. "Pedro have metal detectors?"

"Uh-huh."

"Do the campus cops hassle you?"

He shrugged, which might have meant anything. There hadn't been any real security in Jack Liffey's time. It had been an open campus and you could come and go at will. You could play in the parks at night, too. Now it seemed to him as if there'd been a universal toxic spill of some chemical that had etched the comfortable edges off everything in the world.

"You prefer to be left alone, I take it."

"Uh-huh."

"I'll do my best, but I promised your dad I'd talk to you about what happened."

"Don't do me any favors."

"How about you just tell me who your natural enemies are at school. Every food chain's full of them."

The kid looked at him. "Huh?"

Jack Liffey wondered how much of Western civilization he

shared with this boy. "You know, each one eats the weaker, catsup, ants, me." He squashed a few ants with his thumb. "Worms eat the pond scum, birds eat the worms, coyotes eat the birds, bears eat the coyotes, we eat the bears. Somewhere in there, there's something that wants to get you. Surfers? Gangbangers? Jocks? Schools are always like that."

The boy just looked away for the next few minutes, and Jack Liffey got nowhere with his questions.

"Did you ever have a fight with anybody?"

The boy sighed and finally ate a bite of the congealing taco. "I was at a party in PV last month and some vamps got in my face."

PV he knew. There had never been any love lost between the working-class town of San Pedro down on the flat and the horsy Palos Verdes hills above. In fact, there were several layerings of new-money towns up there, Rancho Palos Verdes, Palos Verdes Estates, Rolling Hills Estates, and then right up on top, the gated community of Rolling Hills that he'd read somewhere had the highest per capita income in the country, probably the known world. But the word *vamps* didn't register.

"Vamps?"

The boy took a moment, then answered reluctantly. "Vampire goths. They wanted me to drink some blood with them and I told them to fuck off."

Vampire goths. Jack Liffey was not going to betray his surprise. More weirdness. Generally he liked weirdness, but something about kids playing vampires was just sad and pitiable. "You go to parties with vamps a lot?"

"Some."

"You remember where this was?"

"Somewhere up on Bridlewood."

That was PV, all right. It was something. But if he decided to take this case, it looked like he was going to need garlic and some silver bullets. They talked for another half hour as the boy finished the aging tacos and then the fries, but Jack Liffey got no more useful information out of him. In the end he tucked his card in the boy's shirt pocket. "If you think of anything else, call me."

That would happen right after the boy got a button-down shirt and ran for class president, he thought.

Before heading home, he detoured to the far side of town toward Averill Park, where he'd spent about half his childhood. The park had been a WPA project back in the thirties, but to him, growing up nearby, it had just been a park. It had an artificial waterfall that fed a stream running two blocks between rock retaining walls, and above the stream, trees and then rolling grass hills—the most beautiful urban park he had ever seen. Not a stream, in fact, but a series of long ponds that flowed over stone weirs on and on to the big pond at the end at Thirteenth Street. In the middle was a longer pond with an island and a hump bridge, and just over the bridge, the Big Tree. The Big Tree, the Home Tree, had been home base for a million games of hide-and-seek, and it stood there in his psyche as the anchor point of his childhood. Maybe even where it had all gone wrong. If he could get back to the Big Tree, he thought, maybe he could find some way to set off again, the right way this time. He wondered idly what sort of tree it had been. He remembered gnarled and gray, branching at head height and easy to climb. He hadn't been into botany much then, like most kids, or the scientific names of things.

He found a parking spot behind a bunch of shiny old cars with pom-poms that were spilling out a big overdressed Latino wedding party onto the high grass, where they were posing for photographs. The park below was pretty much as he remembered—along the stream, rustic railings made of concrete molds of the same log, repeating the same knots and sawn-off stub over and over again. At the crest of the bridge he started to get a bad feeling. He stopped and stared. There was no Big Tree at the far end of the bridge, not even a stump where the Big Tree had been. About twenty feet away there was a pepper tree, but not as big as the Home Tree and split in a different way.

For a long time he stood there trying to reconcile his memory with what he saw. They couldn't have eradicated his tree so thoroughly. And this other one, it looked so old and so close to where the Home Tree should have been that their roots and branches would have interfered with one another had they coexisted. Could his recollection be that far wrong? He felt bewildered and disoriented, betrayed in some fundamental way.

Suddenly he was having a little trouble getting his breath, a nasty reminder of his collapsed lung. After a while he found himself on a rock bench set into the wall beside the water, staring dully at the ground at his feet. It was as if he'd never find his way home now. He wiped away a single tear.

Three

Soo Busted

"Jack Fucking Liffey."

"Ken Fucking Steelyard."

They examined one another from opposite ends of the short bleachers, like two tomcats not sure there was enough food set out for both. Steelyard had filled out a lot and his hair was combed back in one of those looks that made him seem even older than he was. He wore an atrocious brown suit and a tie with a gravy stain on it.

"So have a seat," Steelyard said. "It was you wanted to meet in the great outdoors."

"I sure didn't want to troop through a police station."

But Steelyard had suggested the location. The bleachers were just upchannel from the old fireboat house, and they faced an open area next to the water where somebody was building a full-size reproduction of a square-rigger, the wooden ribs lashed together now like a whale's skeleton. There was apparently no hurry to complete it, as only three men were working there at the moment, and they seemed to be moving at half speed.

The two former classmates approached one another warily along the bottom tier of the bleachers until they were close enough to shake hands. Then they sat at uncomfortable angles on the bench so they could see one another to talk. "I would never have figured you'd become a cop. Never."

"You were the brain. I sure didn't expect you to become a private dick."

"You've been checking up."

"You were in the papers quite a bit last year." Jack Liffey had more or less accidentally thwarted a terrorist attack, exposing himself to a lot of what he had thought was plutonium powder but turned out to be harmless granite dust. Still, it had shut down one of his lungs—hopefully, only temporarily—and earned him a Citizen's Medal of Outstanding Valor, plus a lot of free publicity that had done him no good whatsoever.

"I'm not really a detective, you know. I worked in aerospace for a while and got laid off, and I just sort of fell into tracking down missing kids. It's more satisfying than making pizza."

Neither one of them spoke for a few moments.

"So how did you end up a cop?" Jack Liffey asked after a while.

His companion waited some more, probably out of habit, Jack Liffey thought, since he was trained in interrogation techniques. "It all came to me when I was watching *Star Trek*."

Jack Liffey laughed for a moment but cranked it down and shut it off when he noticed that Steelyard seemed quite serious. "Was it the pointy ears?"

"You know, Jack, it wasn't. I saw all these different folks working together on a team to do good in the world. I wanted to be on a team like that. Since the United Federation of Planets or whatever didn't seem to be recruiting, I settled for the LAPD."

His tone was hard to work out. "You did pretty well for yourself if you made detective."

"I do my job."

The silence lengthened out.

"If we're through waving our dicks at each other here, I'd like to talk about the Petricich kid."

The cop grinned a little now, but just for a moment. "Gotta stay in practice. It's good to see you, Jack, really. You were good to me in a really bad time in my life. Remember when we used to make play ghosts with a golf ball tied into a handkerchief?"

The memory gave Jack Liffey a bit of a chill. Even now, he had no idea what they'd been playing at back then. Once in a while, much later, when he knew about things like that, he'd wondered if Steelyard had been gay and struggling with it. "Yeah. I just had a stroll through Averill Park. What a great town this was to grow up in. Barring other problems, of course."

"I had the other problems, as you know. I didn't get along with my stepdad. Back then, I was the only kid I knew with divorced parents. Now everybody's doing it."

"Different times."

A brisk argument was going on up on the scaffold inside the boat's skeleton. The second carpenter had come up and apparently was trying to put back something that had been hammered off. Jack Liffey caught a few of the words wafted into the bleachers against the prevailing breeze, including *shithead* and *pendejo* and *cabrón*.

"Are you working for Dan Petricich?" Steelyard asked amiably.

"I'm really just looking into it as an old friend. Dan was right behind us in school. The kid's pretty screwed up. Dan's afraid he's attracting trouble like a lightning rod."

"I can't really figure out these goths or whatever they are, but I'm the last guy to start sneering at kids in trouble."

"Yeah." They talked of their own divorces for a while, and a big green container ship came up the channel, hooting now and then as if in pain from the tugs pushing it around. As it passed, Jack Liffey noticed an endless stack of containers identical to the ones it was carrying to Terminal Island.

"What can you tell me about what happened?"

"We're not sure the kid is even the target, but the perp left two playing cards out of some Japanese deck, the two and three. The trouble is, that leaves fifty more chances for mischief. There were also pointless messages written on the cards, along with a Jap rubber stamp with a funny name."

"A *hanko?*"

"I think that's what my partner said."

"It's usually a signature. Could I see the cards?"

"Are you officially working for Dan?"

"Not yet."

"I think I've got to cover my butt, then, unless he gives me a release. Sorry, Jack."

"I understand. I've got to think about this whole business. I'm under doctor's orders to take it easy, and I know my daughter and womanfriend will both kill me if I decide to do this."

"You got a daughter. That's great."

"Sixteen going on thirty-five. She's a wonderful girl. Really, some days it's just her energy and brain and her good heart that keep me going."

The second ship carpenter now muscled his way in and started hammering the piece back together while his partner pointed and protested. Jack Liffey hoped it wasn't a critical part. It would be disconcerting to set out to sea one day and have the stopper come out. But then, what did he know about boats?

"I had a daughter, too. She got in a lot of trouble and I couldn't stop it."

"It takes a lot of strength to keep that stuff out of your soul, but you seem to be doing okay."

"You don't know me well enough to say that."

"I guess I don't. I'll be in touch."

They shook hands again, just a touch, and Jack Liffey walked away.

Steelyard watched the man walk back toward a beat-up old VW, and he couldn't help entertaining a number of might-have-beens. For his money Jack had been the smartest boy in the senior class and might have done a lot better for himself, but he'd always had a malcontent streak, maybe even a self-destructive one. He remembered vaguely that Jack had refused to give the valedictorian's address at graduation. Or, rather, the school had refused to let him give the one he'd written, which reportedly had been a little too fiery. Steelyard grinned. Burn it all down. The times had been like that, and here they were now, both of them uneasily on the side of order, more or less. Maybe one day he'd show him the trains.

* * *

"You're avoiding talking about your father again. He's like the five-hundred-pound elephant standing there in the corner."

"He's not even in the room anymore. Let's leave it that way."

"You know what reality is?" Dicky Auslander said, making a little tepee of his fingers.

Dicky's consultation room gave Jack Liffey the creeps, and he made a face. Auslander was full of theories, none of them very profound, and Jack Liffey wasn't going to touch a sucker line like that.

"It's when you pretend the thing isn't there that it sneaks over and kicks your ass."

"That's a super theory, Dicky. I hope you get it published."

If Jack Liffey didn't show up weekly, he lost the regular stipend some victim's legislation was granting him for a while. But his goal was to keep the sessions brisk and empty because he didn't trust Auslander. There was a new painting on the wall now, where an earnestly restful seascape had once been. He was glad the old painting was gone; it had been done by someone who'd obviously never looked very closely at the sea, probably sitting in a warehouse in Kansas copying the same photo over and over. The new one was an abstract with a lot of fiddly little markings creeping over it like insects. It seemed more authentic in some way, though it was also more disturbing and left him edgy.

"How's the relationship with Rebecca?"

"Great. We're still going slow on it. I stay at her place sometimes and then she takes a turn and stays with me. More often at my place, really, so Maeve knows where we are. Becky's just great—solid and funny and affectionate. I can't believe my luck."

"Why would you say that, Jack?"

"Oh, come off it. You don't have to leap on everything I say."

"Do you think you're good for her?"

"I'm good *to* her. I may not be fit to judge the other. We're doing fine."

"Have you had any of your bad spells lately?"

"Yeah, some."

"I'm going to ask again: Have you ever thought of trying one of the new antidepressants? Sometimes all it takes is a bit of a chemical nudge to jolt you right back into the groove. I've seen them work miracles. Don't keep dismissing the idea out of hand."

"I gave up drinking, Dicky, to show myself I could. I'll use your tranqs from time to time when the anxiety starts getting the best of me—but that's all. It's my belief that my natural mental state contains something of value to me, and I'm not inclined to use those big, blunt tools to hammer at it. What's really wrong is I'm going nuts sitting home reading. I need to get back to work."

The small house that contained Auslander's clinic vibrated with some new equipment in the physical therapy room next door. The year before, Liffey knew they'd done a lot of anger work in there—people boffing each other with those big foam-tipped cudgels—but that approach seemed to have gone out of fashion.

"What does your lung man say about that?"

"He'd probably tell me to wait, but I don't think I'm going to ask permission."

"So why are you asking me?"

"I guess I'm just thinking out loud."

"For the record, then, I disapprove. I think your mental state is too fragile for anything very stimulating."

"I'll keep that in mind."

Maeve showed up just after he'd pulled in, and he made a point of not asking where she'd been as they walked to the condo. At a certain point you either trusted your offspring, or not. Maeve made a beeline for the answering machine, as if there might be a message for her that needed to be censored, but the only one was for both of them, and she cranked up the volume.

"Jack and Maeve, I'm sorry but I'll be stuck hovering over the parents setting up for next week's school pageant so I won't be able to make it home by dinner. I'll see you later this evening. My cell is on the blink, but my pager works. Love you both."

"Pageant," Maeve said, rolling the word around in her mouth like an exotic food.

"I guess rich schools still do that sort of thing. Fly in some camels and rhinos, dress up the girls like Schehcrazade."

"Funny, I know that name but not who she is." He always marveled at her unself-conscious honesty. Maeve went to the fridge and took out a flavored iced tea with some goofy name, the only thing she drank these days.

"There was a sultan who believed all women were unfaithful, so he vowed he'd marry a different bride every day and strangle her the next morning. But Scheherazade was too clever for him. She started telling her elaborate tales, then every morning broke off right at the crucial moment."

"*The Thousand and One Nights?*"

"You got it. That's how long she had to tease him with her stories before he changed his mind."

"I forgot that you know everything."

"Far from it. For instance, I don't have a clue why you pay four eighty-nine for a few bottles of iced tea that we could make for a quarter. In fact, I don't know much of anything about the world you're growing up in. It's not like mine."

"What do you mean?"

"I'll bet there are things that go on at your school that would astonish me." He nodded at her encouragingly. "Go on, astonish me. I'm not prying, it doesn't have to be personal."

She screwed up her face. "I have to think about it because it's all normal to me." She swigged her tea as he went through the mail. Mostly bills, but none of the bright red ones that you really had to pay right now or go without something important.

"Okay, here's something that'll seem pretty strange to you, but first, I don't do this, okay?"

"I believe you."

"There are these hook-up parties. Not everybody goes, but a lot of kids do. They go to meet somebody just to have sex with, but no emotional attachments, just sort of like calisthenics. They go off and do it and then just leave. Hooking up."

"In the era of AIDS?" He was dumbfounded. The very idea of high school kids sex-swapping like a fifties daydream of the idle rich cranked up his free-floating anxiety another notch.

"I suppose most of them are careful. I don't know."

He was quiet for a while. "Okay, you did it. You flabbergasted me."

"Was all this leading up to something?"

"You know me too well," he admitted. "What do you know about vampire goths?"

She came across the room and tugged his collar open a bit to peer closely at his neck. When he got the joke—a little tardily—he chuckled. "I get a chill every time I pass garlic in the supermarket."

"Ha-ha. There are a few of them at Redondo. But I think they just play at it, dressing up for parties. I've heard they do body piercing and lick the blood off the needles. Gross."

"Do you think you could get me some names, from up in PV?"

"Dad, are you on a case?" Maeve glared at him.

"Not officially."

"Oh, great. So if your other lung just *unofficially* collapses, everything will be fine."

He gave an elaborate shrug. "These vamps, I can't believe they're enough of a threat to do me any harm."

"We'll see what Rebecca has to say when you tell her you're going back to work. You're going to be *soo* busted."

December 15

A practical note: This evening I located and unburied my weapons kit on the island. A certain number of paces due east of a certain object on a certain road, then due north into an oil sump wasteland. I had left it only two feet deep in unpleasant soil, but any random disturbance would have ignited a fourteen-pound satchel charge of C-4. One needed to know how to disarm the mechanism. I took out the old Franchi SPAS-12 shotgun that I used to use incountry and that I had taken the trouble to disassemble and ship home in five parcels. Stripped, wrapped in Saran, the firing pin and trigger assembly soaking in cosmoline. A patient old friend, it must have awaited me with great serenity, like a sheathed *kenjutsu* that rests on a shelf uncomplainingly for centuries for the spirit of Justice to draw it forth again.

Unusual sensations. I must admit this to myself as I reassembled the automatic shotgun. I must admit. The rush of a *ronin* who has learned that his master may not be dead after all. It fits the description from that other journal: at last I am drawing the bow back in stages, *hikiwake,* the samurai call it. The god of war is by my side, in modesty and respect and comradeship. I am quite certain that this is the path, the virtues are self-evident. I can hear my blood coursing through my veins. Holding the Franchi again fills me with radiance.

Honor is salvation. I serve you, Father, as if I am already dead.

The act itself was hardly worth writing of. It was swift and sudden, as it should be. Break through to completion in one step. The boat sank there. No one saw me, no one was harmed.

Loyalty. Justice. Bravery.

He opened his eyes from a lucid dream in which he had willed himself fluent in Spanish, even if it still hadn't done him any good. The two Latinas he had been dreaming about had whispered too softly, though definitely about him—and then there she was, real, undressing in the dark bedroom in silence. "Ahh. One of life's great mysteries," he said.

"Which one?" Rebecca asked, swiveling her bra clasp around to the front to unsnap it. She looked pretty worn out.

"God, so many. Your body. You returning to me like some demented swallow. Your body. Ah, yes, your body."

She crawled onto the bed and then over him like a skinny animal. Her limbs were very slender, and gravity accentuated her small breasts. "You should go back to your beauty sleep," she suggested, but not seriously.

"With an eyeful like this? You're kidding."

She lowered herself gently upon him and they made love much more tenderly than usual, missing some of the urgency she usually inspired. Afterward, she apologized for getting caught up in the pageant preparations for so long, something about a mock medieval castle some of the more competitive fathers were building across the school's back lawn.

"What time is it?" He could barely keep his eyes open, but it seemed terribly rude to go to sleep right after sex.

"Almost two."

"So you didn't see Maeve?"

"I think she was on her laptop when I came in. There was that blue glow, but I didn't disturb her."

So he wasn't busted yet, he thought. "You know, I think I've come to the conclusion that I'm going stir-crazy. I don't know how much longer I can be expected to sit home days watching *As the Stomach Turns.*"

"Uh-oh. I've had enough naughty kids stand in front of my desk to know that tone."

"But you like me naughty."

She ran a finger over his lips. "There's naughty and then there's naughty. This one is about breaking the cookie jar."

"I agreed to do a guy a favor, but it's nothing very strenuous. A boy got tied up as a prank by somebody. He's already back home. It's not like he's missing. I'll just look into who did it and why." He'd already called Petricich and asked for a token retainer to make it official and told him to inform Steelyard so he could get a peek at the evidence.

"Have you told the gentlemen from—where is it?"

Just outside Bethesda it was, the home of the Armed Forces Radiological Warfare Institute. Technically they were still monitoring his condition, what they called a sentinel case—but in fact, his doctor was just a local lung man with whom they consulted. "I'll tell Massoud when I see him. I told Dicky Auslander today. He wasn't happy about it, but I'll take it easy. I promise no gunplay or slapping people around."

She pinched his ear, quite hard. "What am I going to do with you?"

"Ow. You can help me is what, with information. This may have to do with vampire goths."

"Taunton doesn't allow them. Too lower-class."

"I think I like them better already."

Four

To Be Too Conscious Is an Illness

"Hell, I let you drive the Crown Vic. That must put me at least an inch to the good side in the male chauvinist pig league."

She did her best to ignore the irony he larded up around himself. She didn't really believe he was what he so often made himself out to be, but she also knew it was hard being a cop without flaunting a little aggressive malice to each and all. Your fellow cops would make you pay dearly for any signs of kindheartedness.

"Nobody uses that language anymore," she said. "It almost makes it worse."

"Uh-oh. What do you say now?"

"*Insensitive* will do fine."

"Whatever."

There were two ways to drive from the station to San Pedro Slip, where the commercial fishing boats docked: straight down Gaffey or Pacific and then hard east on Twenty-second Street and back along the water, or you could come in on Harbor, paralleling the ship channel, then through the huge parking lot of Ports o' Call Village and past Cannetti's Cafe. This last was her choice, the scenic route, and she went fast, but not code three.

It was clear that the deed was over and done, so there was no hurry. She skirted the tour boat dock and approached the space beside the fireboat dock where they were building the square-rigger. She noticed that Steelyard's eye was drawn to the boat hull under construction.

"I met an old high school friend here yesterday. Man, that took me back to some pretty bad times," he explained.

"Unhappy childhood?" He never talked about it.

He shrugged. "Broken home. Dad drinks, Dad hits Mom, Dad hits kid, Dad leaves. Stepdad is worse. Same old story."

"Try being a Paiute kid who gets adopted by a couple of old Latinos who tell you day in, day out that Indians are drunken scum." She didn't talk about it either, but since they were confiding . . .

"Shit, I never knew you were an Indian. *Ramirez* and all. You got a real name like Red Bird or something?"

"Wilson. I was twelve when I found out who I was."

"That's blunt. Did you ever try to find your birth parents?"

"My mom was a wino whore, Ken. Not that that means she should be banished from the human race. But she died outside a saloon, literally in the gutter. They said it was hepatitis C, and after a life of needles and drink, that's no surprise. I don't know what it would have done to me to find her. Maybe I'm better off."

He puffed out a slow breath. "Sorry. I had no idea."

"It's okay. Once in a while a window sort of clears between us and I see you're not the troglodyte you pretend to be."

"What's a troglodyte?"

"Literally, I think it's a caveman or something. One of those cops like Eddie Rafter who thinks the answer to every problem is a curse and a nightstick."

Steelyard laughed softly, and then seemed to readjust his whole being in some strange movement that she had never seen before, almost a schizophrenic's body English. "Glor, don't think I haven't seen you get right down to work and smooth out a bad situation with a few calm words. You're a good cop. Maybe that's what makes women good cops—*when* they're good, which happens now and then. But I think we got to have the warriors, too. It's bad news times two out there. I've seen Eddie back down a whole gang of angry perps."

"And I've seen him turn them violent when they were only scared and upset."

He settled back and thought about that. In glances away from the road, she could actually see him considering what she'd said, thoughts crossing his face like a Times Square news ticker. "Funny," he said finally, "the way a little thing can make a big difference sometimes." There was a pause and then a tentative voice, odd for him. "What you said hits me deep, Glor. I can think of times it would have been better to soothe."

But there wasn't much more thoughtful time. No question where the problem lay. She pulled the big car directly onto the dock and gunned it over a discarded hawser to brake hard where the semicircle of people stood staring down into the water. He locked the shotgun into its vertical mount by instinct and got out to a chorus of "over here"s. At the heart of the mess he recognized Dan Petricich in a trench coat apparently thrown over floppy pajamas. Beside him was the ninety-year-old grizzled paterfamilias he thought was named Ante, who was cursing softly in Serbo-Croatian.

What they were all staring at was the mast and crow's nest, plus a bit of the stack and wheelhouse of a big fishing boat that was all that remained visible sticking out of the oily water in the slip. Apparently speechless, Dan Petricich pointed at the stub end of a mooring line that looked like it had been axed.

"Good they cut it," a voice said. "Whoever. Would have torn the davits off the deck going down."

The younger Petricich swore a bit in what must have been Serbo-Croatian, in imitation of his father.

Steelyard had his pad out. "Anybody know when this happened?"

"Marco Trani on the *San Giovanni* saw it sunk when he came in at six. He usually ties up on my port side. I'd'a been out last night, but we got electrical trouble with the power block and the guy couldn't get to it until today."

"Now you got electrical trouble with everything," a short man said, but nobody acknowledged him.

"And look here," Dan Petricich instructed Steelyard.

Dan and the old man took the two cops over to a wooden sea chest that was bolted to the dock near where the boat's stack stuck out of the water. A playing card was stabbed fast into the chest with some kind of serrated throwing knife. Sure enough, it was the four of kittens, or whatever they called their suits, and it had the same round Japanese stamp on it. The message read: *The sin.*

"A little Nip in the air," the old man said.

"Japanese American is preferred," Steelyard said.

"Don't be no *cafone*. I knew your dad."

"Dad was the *cafone*—whatever the fuck that is. Drinking, feuding, and bopping women—that's all he knew."

The old man was grinning. "I liked your dad. A real man."

He turned away from the old man. "Glor, can you call the Harbor Department and see if they'll send a dive team?"

Dec 16 AM

I don't know why I waited so long to read the classics. They make so much sense. I know now that Bushido contains two levels of belief. The first level is called *hagakure,* or life in the shadow of leaves. Dappled, maybe. So lovely and so Japanese, so obvious when you are tuned to it. Warriors addressing themselves to ordinary principles of gentlemanly self-respect, such as bathing and grooming, being courteous to all. Practicing reading and calligraphy and the arts.

Only after that: weaponry. One must learn to master every weapon, beyond even the thinking of it, so it becomes an integral part of the warrior's body. This is all basic, all to be learned in times of peace.

Then, level two: emergency principles, the warriorness of warrior. A platform of theory, encompassing soldier thought and combat thought. Soldier thought entails the willingness to set aside all comforts and customs of peace in an instant. No questions, no hesitation. Beyond the readiness to die, into the acceptance of imminent death. Dappled again, by the grandeur of sacrifice.

And, after all else: combat itself. Maneuver and disposition, feint and misdirection, direct assault, scissors, assault of the cat and assault of the worm, breakthrough and attack in depth. Here the wholehearted spirit of combat rules the mind, courting death. There is no longer "when my time comes," only now.

Of course, I am not naive of combat. I discovered much of this on my own, impractically, brokenly, clinging to trees. But until reading the code, I knew nothing of combat's hierarchy, its history and its necessity.

Bushido now explains it all, validates it. Honor is all. Father, when your own heart asked, how did you respond?

I performed the next act in full daylight and in the face of a formidable alarm system, and I succeeded. *Ahimsa* has been preserved and no innocent one was injured. I know it's self-delusion to think this can be made to last forever. I must learn to welcome the deaths of others, if they come, as I welcome my own. Father, another step in the settlement.

"You got us all wrong, you know?"

Jack Liffey didn't reply. The Muddy Cup was one of the coffeehouses in Redondo, full of old sofas and not all that far from Maeve's school. She was waiting across the room as promised while he talked to Hal Englander, a kid who was at least six-six and lying so far back in his chair that his body nearly made a straight line. He had several piercings in his ears and what looked like a pterodactyl tattooed on his forearm.

"No, I'm sure you're all reading Earnest Dowson and Oscar Wilde."

Maeve was doing her best to eavesdrop on the conversation, though she was pretending otherwise.

"Wilde I know. Who's that other one?"

"A poet of the fin de the last siècle, famous for his world-weariness."

"No shit. I'll have to look him up. I'm into Poe, of course, and Dostoyevsky. This black is just a homage to the tragic essence of life. We all die, and all that. You oughta honor us for being the last saviors of the humanities."

"What makes you think I want to save the humanities?"

The boy shrugged, no easy task at his steep angle. "Whatever."

"What I want is to know about Turtle Petricich and any trouble he had with your friends."

"Yeah, I remember the guy who wanted us to call him Turtle. He was sniffing around one of our parties, so we decided to have a little fun with him. We made him sing the words to 'Bela Lugosi's Dead.' My friend Preston has fang caps on his incisors and he's good at yanking your chain. There probably are some twisted vamp goths somewhere, actually into weird shit like biting and drinking blood, but I don't know any of them."

"Where were you two afternoons ago?"

"I was at a poetry slam at Beyond Baroque in Venice."

Out of the corner of his eye, Jack Liffey saw another goth kid stop and say something to Maeve. Then he ambled in their direction. He was a bit shorter than Hal and there was something strange about his face. Jack Liffey realized he'd shaved his eyebrows. He sat down next to Hal and deposited on the table what looked like an ordinary lunch pail painted dead black.

" 'To be too conscious . . .' " he offered.

" '. . . is an illness,' " Englander finished for him, like a password.

Notes from Underground," Jack Liffey said. He could have explained that Dostoyevsky had actually been poking fun at all those gloomy, self-absorbed rebels, but they probably wouldn't believe him.

"This is Preston Rivet," Englander said. "Jack Liffey, some kind of detective." He raised an eyebrow, trying for a camp effect, but didn't quite pull it off. "Remember that weekender who latched onto us at Meg's house? Wanted to be cool but was pretty clueless?"

Preston Rivet, if that was actually his name, smiled tightly, just enough to reveal the pointed teeth Hal had mentioned.

"We had him going a mile a minute. He'd have stripped down and sucked his own cock if we asked."

At this exciting moment, a waitress arrived wearing a form-fitting black rubber wet suit with a tightly laced corset over it, and a big silver cross. Her hair was the red of a fire truck. Jack Liffey couldn't remember ever having waitresses at coffeehouses. You always went up and got your own.

"What can I do you?"

"A double," Englander said, and he showed the flat of his hand on offer to the others.

"Americano if you can," Jack Liffey said. "I'll get this round."

Preston Rivet sighed. "Got any O-positive?"

"Eat me, Pres."

"Name the time and place."

"Catalina, twelve fathoms down."

Rivet laughed good-naturedly. "Latte, with nonfat."

The waitress wandered away, and Preston Rivet's eye caught on Maeve. "Man, that chick is something. Smart, too. We traded thoughts on Poppy Z. Brite. I can just imagine being bitten by those big ivory whites."

Jack Liffey's hands were getting restless, as if they wanted to strangle someone. "Finish telling me about Turtle."

Before he started in, Preston Rivet made a big show of lighting up a slender brown cigarette with a kitchen match struck on his shoe. Jack Liffey sniffed the air and got a strong whiff of clove.

"He was just a wannabe. It was nothing, man. We made fun of him pretty subtly at first, then got into it a bit. The woman who lives there is into community theater and she had a whole pint of stage blood, so I pretended to bleed my vein into a shot glass and wanted him to drink it. He freaked. He almost did it, though, but even jerks like him get it right once in a while. He just put the shot glass down and ran."

"No threats?"

"Nah."

"Tell me about your fangs."

"These? It's a joke. No, I do not think I'm an actual vampire. It's just something that always fascinated me, pointy teeth, like a tattoo or something. I'll probably have 'em knocked off when I get as old as you, heaven forbid."

"And those welts I see on your arm?"

"I used to do one a night with a soldering pencil. Mind over matter. Man, the pain really focuses you. Makes the trivial just *go away*."

"Puts you in touch with mortality," Englander tried to help out.

Jack Liffey had only the one lung functioning, a metal plate in his head over a crushed spot in his skull, and a blood pressure he could sometimes feel pounding in his forehead. Mortality was not something he had any desire to invite on in. But he didn't really think these last-of-the-breed self-conscious romantics had had anything to do with tying up the poor Petricich kid with duct tape. They were just working overtime trying to make themselves seem interesting to themselves.

He left some money for the waitress. "Gotta get my girlfriend and split," he told them.

He gave Maeve an ambiguous kiss on the forehead and took her out with his arm over her shoulder.

"That's supposed to be the steepest street in the whole city of LA." He'd pulled off Pacific in San Pedro and stopped the VW, looking up Twenty-second Street. It was pretty impressive, with the houses on both sides seeming to cling for dear life. "But I don't believe it. There's a street in Echo Park that gives me the heebie-jeebies. I had a friend over there and every time I visited I went miles out of my way to avoid it. Baxter, that was the name. From the top you couldn't even tell there was a street below you. It was like driving off a cliff."

She eyed the hill with polite interest. "That would be something on a skateboard."

"That would be suicide on a skateboard."

He'd already shown her the Point Fermin lighthouse and the spot out the Palos Verdes peninsula where the beached Greek freighter *Dominator* had sat on the rocks all his youth, rusting away. It was gone now, utterly, another little tweak to his nostalgia gland, which seemed to be acting up.

"How come you never bring me down here much?" Maeve asked. "It's your hometown."

"I guess there're just too many ghosts for me. I wasn't at my happiest then, hon. I'm amazed you seem to like high school so much."

"It's not bad, but nobody expects me to play football or run a six-minute mile."

"Ah, you know my secret."

"It's not very secret."

"I'll try not to rant about sports. But I just can't see all that noise and spurious loyalty devoted to moving balls from one place to another."

"The Aztecs killed the losers in their ball games," she said, as if trying to establish some sort of moral superiority for modern sports.

"That would be an improvement," he said. "From my point of view. Look at this."

A middle-aged woman had pedaled a bicycle right past them, hooked up to a lightweight homemade trailer full of bags and cans and discarded cooking implements, the kind of stuff that all the schizophrenics wheeled around in shopping carts. What had caught his attention were the big wooden tail fins coming out of the bicycle that were alight with spangles and reflectors and dangling fluorescent tassles. The woman stopped at the curb just before the street sloped up steeply and began unpacking the trailer onto the curb, speaking sternly to each item. She was wearing too many clothes, layer on layer.

Maeve took his hand. "It makes you want to do something for her."

"Yes," he said. "Like reopen the asylums we shut down on them, or open the community clinics they were promised but we never built."

"You always think in the big picture. I want to do something for *her*."

He nodded. "I bet she's built up a pretty grand imaginary world around herself. I'm not sure you could penetrate it to do much, hon. She looks pretty clean, so she's probably got a place to stay somewhere." He handed Maeve a five. "If you really want to try spooning out the ocean, give her this."

Maeve took the money, and he could see her plucking up her courage before stepping out to approach the woman. The woman looked quite startled to be addressed. She glared at the money suspiciously, and the two of them talked softly for a while. He watched carefully, but Maeve seemed to be okay. He was actually proud of her willingness to approach someone so obviously around the bend. He did the same on principle now and then, but he had never found it did much good for anyone.

In the end the woman took the money, and Maeve came back a bit chastened.

"How was it?"

"Well." She paused and took a deep breath. "She's into, like, visitors from other dimensions, and even has a name for where *I* come from, really strange. Bagnidor-grizzle, or something like that. I wonder if it comes from TV." She took another deep breath and rested her head against his shoulder. "Can't they do anything?"

"Hon, she's out in the fresh air. She's living in whatever world she can make for herself, instead of some miserable institution. I can't even begin to work out the moral ambiguities. Can I borrow your cell?"

He'd forgotten his promise to check in with Steelyard, and he owed it to him to report his belief that the local goths were pretty unlikely perps. A recorded voice at the number Steelyard had given him referred him to another number.

"Steelyard."

The policeman's voice sounded strangely subdued, as if he'd just gone a dozen rounds with somebody a lot bigger than him. "This is Jack Liffey. You asked me to call, and said maybe we'd swap information." He told him about the goths, and Steelyard took it all in without comment. "Do you any good?"

"Jack, you're two cards behind. Can you come to Ellery Drive?"

"I'm five minutes away." He remembered that that was Steelyard's mother's address, on the very flank of the hills and not far from Averill Park, real middle-class territory. He wondered if Steelyard still lived there. "I'll be there." He himself had grown up only a few blocks closer to the water, as the crow flies, but then his family had moved farther down on the working-class flats, into another world.

"Whoever the fuck this guy is," Steelyard told him, "he's hit Dan and me both now. Hard."

F i v e

Come Home to Roost

They drove up just as three technicians in white smocks, and laden with bags and boxes, bustled out of the house and headed down the grass toward a big panel van that said CRIME SCENE UNIT in letters so big it looked like they were trying to sell it. Jack Liffey wondered, not for the first time, how it would feel to see something like that parked in your driveway. It would certainly perk up all your neighbors.

"Should I wait out here?" Maeve asked.

"Don't tell me you're not curious."

She made a face. "I may be, but the last time I got caught up in one of your cases, mom grounded me for twenty-to-life."

"Mea culpa. That was a mess. But this one shouldn't come home to roost."

It was what she wanted to do anyway, so she followed him up the lawn toward the big Norman-style house with its parabolic front window, thick stucco walls, and steeply pitched roof—waiting forlornly eighty years or so for the Norman snowstorms to reach San Pedro. It really belonged in Beverly Hills, he thought, with all the other rich men's fantasies, although this was almost into the local hills, where San Pedro's doctors and lawyers retreated at night if they didn't actually drive into the hills. The heavy wood door stood open, but he knocked and shouted hello as precautions.

Eventually a stocky Latina with a police badge on a chain around her neck showed up.

"I'm Jack Liffey. Ken asked me to come over."

She nodded. "I'm Detective Ramirez, his partner. He's in the basement."

He introduced Maeve, and they all walked inside on a noisy paper runner on the floor, and then down steep stairs. It was one of the few houses he'd ever seen in LA with a full basement, obviously built well before the dread of earthquakes had set in. Maeve hung back a bit, but he figured her pluck would catch up with her before long.

A faint smell gathered as they came down, like an electrical circuit overheating, and then they emerged into a tiny universe laid out before them at waist level. It looked like a model of something from the 1880s, with dusty western one-street towns, picturesque buttes, wooden trestles, and even a tiny herd of cattle. A fair-size city ran right up against the far wall, and all of it was lashed together by model railroad tracks.

The real situation, however, seemed to be on the far side of the room, where Steelyard stood at the rim of his tiny universe, glaring down at its other half, which apparently had suffered a nuclear strike. Enough remained to suggest what had been houses and the tangled wreckage of taller buildings. Every single structure was crushed, right up to some arbitrary dividing line through the middle of the room, but it was clearly not meant to be that way.

Jack Liffey looked at the room's owner.

Steelyard nodded glumly. "Twelve years of work." Something looked a little funny about his eyes, and he kept rubbing his shoulder, as if he'd wrenched it. "All from scratch. Even the rolling stock. No kits. No fucking kits."

That seemed to matter to him. "Why does the destruction stop in the middle?" Jack Liffey asked.

"It was an idea. That half of the layout is nineteenth-century and steam. The part over here was modern, diesel-electric. It's all HO scale and you could still run from one century to the other. It was just an idea," he concluded glumly.

"Why do you think the old stuff was spared?"

His eyes came up, reddened, flattened from within like the eyes of a big wounded dog. "Do you think I have a fucking clue?" He went straight up the steps, and the policewoman watched him go, then turned to Jack Liffey.

"Please pardon him. This was his baby."

"No kidding."

"I mean it was *really* important to him. Somebody figured out how to make him hurt. There was no sign of forced entry, and the alarms were all bypassed, we don't know how. Oh, there's a chair missing, too. He used it as his Engineer Bill chair over there. Nothing special, just a beat-up old ladderback that he's had for years."

"Was there one of those Japanese playing cards?"

She nodded. "The five of whatever little girls call those suits. I think you haven't even heard about the four yet, Mr. Liffey."

"Jack, please. I haven't."

"It was presumably the same perpetrator or perpetrators who sank the Petricich fishing boat last night, right at its dock. It was a wooden vessel, and the police divers said somebody just went down into the engine room and shot a big shotgun hole clean through the hull. It probably took half an hour to go down, plenty of time to get out. The perp stuck the four to the boat's dockside locker with some kind of Special Forces throwing knife."

"And the five?"

"It was over there by the train controls, pinned to that little park lawn with Ken's own X-Acto knife. Crime Scene has both the card and the knife now."

"What did it say on the card?"

"The battle is engaged."

"Ah."

She scowled into a coffee cup. "Could I get you some coffee? This has gone cold."

"No, thanks. But suit yourself."

She trudged up the stairs as Maeve bent over to inspect the wreckage, her hands behind her back as if avoiding leaving fingerprints. "Some of it was crushed downward," she said, "like with a big mallet, and some of it was swiped off like with a baseball bat."

"We probably won't be able to outdo the cops in the clue game, hon, but that's all right. You can keep looking." He studied the devastation himself. It disturbed him somewhere deep inside—it was like seeing the effects of a terribly unequal barroom brawl, some defenseless midgets collapsed against a bar with shiners and torn shirts.

"Isn't it a bit odd, a grown-up man putting so much time into model trains?" Maeve suggested softly.

"He had a really troubled childhood. I knew him in school. And he has a job that's probably always threatening to spin out of control on him. I'd guess he found one corner of life where he felt he had effortless control of things. Or so he thought. That may be partly why it's hitting him so hard."

Detective Ramirez came back down the steep concrete staircase with a fresh cup of coffee and a can of 7UP that she handed to Maeve.

"Thanks."

He could tell Maeve didn't want the sugary soft drink, but she took it politely. Recently she'd been drinking mainly those peculiar herbal iced teas. She was trying to keep her weight down. If her waist stayed small and her breasts got any bigger, boys would be following her around with their tongues hanging out. He remembered being that age.

"Detective Steelyard is resting."

"We went to school together. I think I can handle the name Ken."

"In that case, I'm Gloria. Were you close to Ken in high school?"

"No. We were very close in grade school and a bit in junior high. Then his family started . . . going to hell, and he went away for a while by himself. Did he ever tell you about Fresno?"

She shook her head, no.

"We just never really picked it up again when he came back, I guess. I feel a bit bad about it. I'm stunned he turned out to be a cop, if you want to know the truth."

"He was a bad boy?"

"Not at all. He just didn't seem to have . . . what would you call it? Maybe a sense of authority. But that was then. He's changed."

"He's tough, he works at it, but he's a little more fragile than he thinks, like a lot of cops," was all she would admit to.

"Aren't we all. When I called, I told him that the goth angle looks like a dead end. I don't see how they would connect to this train business anyway."

Gloria Ramirez was looking over the devastation thoughtfully. "There's one pattern Ken didn't want to see."

She waited, but he could see she was going to tell him, whether he encouraged her or not.

"The cards have come in sets. I think the first card in each set marks a kind of warning shot. The Petricich kid was tied up—that's where we found the two of whatever it is, call it spades. That's the warning. Then Ken's boxcar was trashed with a flash-bang, the three of spades, another warning shot. The next two were second cards. They sink the Petricich fishing boat on the second Petricich card, and they do *this* to Ken on his second card. It might be just a coincidence that the sets overlapped; I don't know. In the Petricich case, it looks like the real target was the father. What do you know about Ken's father?"

"Long gone. He abandoned Ken's mom when Ken was about thirteen, after slapping her around a lot. I don't remember much about him except he seemed cranky and old. I mean, older than the other baby boom dads. I'm sure he's dead by now."

"Can you think of anything special that happened in high school? You and Ken and Dan Petricich were all there together."

"The football team beat Banning once." He almost laughed, amazed that he remembered that, but he shrugged instead. "It was before the antiwar era, so I can't think of any demonstrations. That stuff came after us. High school was all so personal, full of the usual dreadfulness of adolescence. I assume we each had a share of the horrors, but it's a pretty solitary time and everybody thinks he's going through it alone. You hardly notice anybody else's troubles."

"Think about it, will you? You might have the key to this and not know you know it."

"I'll try. Did you find out anything about the ink stamp?"

She nodded. "It says 'no no.' Two distinct 'no's, not a single word like the English no-no, you know, for a taboo. We had an expert on *hanko* look it over and he didn't recognize it. He said it was odd, though it might just be a nickname. Most *hankos* are used as a kind of signature. We faxed it to the Tokyo police and asked for their input."

"The symbol isn't part of the card?"

"No; we bought a couple sets to look them over. Anyway, it's in a different place on each card. He's definitely stamping the cards. He means it to be the kind of clue that drives you nuts. I really hate these puzzle cases. You've got some geek out there who feels compelled to outthink you, and, of course, he's got all the advantages. All the aces, if you like. To be literal, I'm worried about the ace. It's got to be something big."

"Let's hope you get him long before that. He hasn't really hurt anyone yet."

"Jack!" Steelyard's voice skirled down the open stairwell and seemed to ricochet a few times around the concrete-walled room. "Get up here!" It was so peremptory that he glanced at the woman, but she only shrugged.

"Hold the fort," Jack Liffey suggested as he climbed up out of Tinytown.

Maeve was a little embarrassed to be left there alone with the policewoman and didn't know quite what to say. "What do you think of all this?" Maeve asked, which allowed enough latitude so that almost any answer would do.

"The toy trains, or the destruction?" Gloria Ramirez replied.

"I guess I meant the trains. It's just not a girl thing."

The woman looked around the room. She wore a severe navy blue suit that was at odds with her lovely rich skin and thick jet black hair that she had tied back. "You and I would probably have a lot more sympathy if it were a collection of heirloom quilts. It sure meant a lot to him."

"I guess a lot of work went into it," Maeve conceded.

"I think he said once his dad started it, but that doesn't seem likely, does it?"

The conversation kept threatening to wind down to nothing, but Maeve sensed the woman looking at her with sidelong glances, maybe just out-of-ordinary curiosity.

"I don't think I've ever talked to a policewoman one-on-one," Maeve offered. "Oops, can you say 'policewoman'? It's not 'police person'?"

" 'Officer.' " She smiled. "In my case, 'detective.' That's gender-neutral. Is your family still together?"

"That's a funny question," Maeve said.

"It's just that it's so rare these days. Let me guess: you live week-days with your mother and weekends with your father."

"Something like that. That must be police training, to look for stuff like that."

"I think it's female training. Ken would always prefer to avoid asking about family if he could get away with it." She set down her coffee cup and leaned against the edge of the huge train layout, looking across a trestle and a low mesa at Maeve, still watching with something that struck Maeve as beyond normal interest.

"You're not drinking your 7UP."

"I usually stick to diet. The chemicals will kill you in the end, but you'll have a nice, skinny corpse."

"I wish I had the motivation to take better care of my body." Just as Maeve thought, the conversation was spiraling down toward stasis when suddenly, the woman's expression registered discovery. "Something's been teasing my memory. Aren't you that girl who saved her dad in the riots a couple years ago?"

Maeve felt herself blushing. "You have a good memory."

"It was in the papers a lot. And I remember the papers saying your father was a detective."

"Dad always says he just hunts for missing children; he's not a detective. He's sensitive about that for some reason."

The woman looked upward, as if she could see through the ceiling to the two men upstairs. "They take a lot of care and feeding, don't they?"

Maeve grinned. "Why do you think they need so much tending?"

"I don't know. But some of us have got to have the homely virtues, or the whole world will end up a pissing contest. Pardon me. I'm not really antimale. Some of my ex-boyfriends haven't been so bad."

"My dad isn't so bad, either." She wasn't sure she wanted to tell this woman any more about her dad. It felt like disloyalty.

"Detective Ramirez, if your boyfriends weren't so bad, how come they're ex?"

"Please call me Gloria. It's impossible to stay together with a cop, from either end. I mean for women or men married to cops. Ken's been through two wives. The job just takes too much of your soul, dirties you somehow, leaves you with too much baggage you can't share."

"In my dad's case, he just keeps picking wrong, I think. I liked his last girlfriend a lot better than the current one. She's too snooty for him. I'm sure it won't last."

"I bet she's attractive."

"He seems to think so. The last one was a Latina, like you, but she ran off with a guy in her church. They were sort of fundamentalists."

"I'm not actually Latina," the detective said with her head cocked to the side, as if listening to music only she could hear. "I'm a full-blood Paiute."

"Wow, really?"

She laughed. "You're practically the first person I've met who's actually impressed by it."

"I think it would be *great*. All that wonderful heritage. Do you have a . . . is it okay to say 'reservation'?"

"My mom came from a *rancheria* up in the Owens Valley. That's what they call them when they're tiny. I was fostered out, though, so I don't know much about it. Alcohol is killing us faster than the palefaces ever did."

"I'm sorry. That's so sad. Are you in touch with your mom?"

"She died in a gutter long ago."

Maeve was distressed. "How can you say it so coldly like that?"

"She expired horizontally in the open air in the street in front of a tavern. Does that help?"

Maeve shook her head.

"I'm sorry if I can't work up much sentiment about my mother. She took money for sleeping with men, too. I won't trouble you with that other word."

"How were your adopted parents?"

"Not so great. They hated Indians and tried to make me do the same."

"That's *awful.*"

"I went pretty bad for a while, up in East LA. Then, long ago, a police officer plucked me out of my craziness and I decided he'd be my role model. It leaves you with a certain independent perspective on life and lots of inner strength—if you survive it all, of course. I'm lucky, really. I'm me. I don't crave to be anybody I see on television."

Maeve cocked her own head in imitation. "You don't want just a tiny little BMW?"

The detective laughed. "I already drive a big black-and-white V-8 with more power than I know what to do with. Are you driving yet?"

"My mom gave me her old Echo. It's reliable and, if you squint, it's almost cute."

"Maeve!" It was her dad's voice, invading the basement in a tone of apprehension she hadn't heard in a long time.

"You need me?"

"Come on up, please."

"It was nice to meet you," she said politely to the policewoman.

"Yes. Hold on, hon." The woman dug something out of the patch pocket of her coat, and as Maeve came around the layout, she handed her a business card with an LAPD badge printed on it. "If you need anything, you can reach me there. Or if your dad needs anything."

Maeve looked it over neutrally.

"I have a hunch you're a pretty good caretaker, yourself," Gloria Ramirez said.

* * *

Jack Liffey stared balefully at the address Ken Steelyard had just written down for him. He knew it, of course, a ramshackle bungalow on the flats overlooking the harbor, down in gang territory. He hadn't been there in twenty years, by choice and by . . . something else.

"You want some time with him?" Steelyard asked.

"I guess so. Shit."

He heard Maeve's steps coming up briskly. There was something so trusting in the eagerness of the young; it showed in every movement they made. It felt so monstrous to betray it. He had no idea how she was going to react. He had just promised her that the case wouldn't come home to roost, and now it was going to, after all.

"What's up?"

Steelyard was watching as Jack Liffey led his only daughter outside without a word, toward the old VW. "I don't know how to tell you this."

"Is Mom hurt?" She froze in place on the grass.

"No, no, no. Not at all. Nobody's hurt. Come on."

She seemed to consider throwing a tantrum, but then trotted after him. He gave a big strange sigh that confused her further.

"I've been keeping something from you all your life, about one thing. Protecting you, let's say."

He could see a real terror forming on her face. There was nothing he could do but plunge on.

"You have a living grandfather," he blurted.

"No, I don't. Mom's parents died five years ago and your dad died the same time as your mom."

He shook his head. "I used to admire him, I think, but he changed. Something changed him as he got older, and it really accelerated after Mom died. We haven't spoken since I married your mother. She thinks he's dead, too. We cut each other off like the Hatfields and McCoys."

"I can't *believe* this."

"You'll see why soon. If you want to meet him."

"Of course I do. Dad, this is really *rank*."
"I know."

Dec 16 PM
Today I issued the third warning. The future is never contained entirely in the past. This one may entail a new train
of consequences. I am not worried about the police and
their pathetic resources, but this man is the father of a
detective who has a certain renown in this city. He is, perhaps, a loose cannon, but he is also a veteran of my war. It
may not matter in the long run, but I must not underestimate his attendance at the dance.

On July 14, 1789, the day the Bastille was overrun, which
marked the beginning of the end of the feudal world in
Europe, perhaps the last year in which honor still counted
above all else, Louis XVI wrote in his journal only one
word: *rien.*

Was this bravado, or utter ignorance? I cannot allow either.

Six

Declan Liffey

He pointed out a view of the harbor and the sweep of the Vincent Thomas Bridge as they headed down Ninth off the flank of the hills, but Maeve was too busy feeling resentful to look. She kept her eyes furiously ahead. He stopped for the light at Gaffey, where even she couldn't ignore the young man who strode in front of them in an ankle-length duster coat that was completely covered with light-bulbs. The bulbs didn't seem to be wired to light up, just sewn on as ornaments.

"One point?" he offered.

She watched grimly.

"That has to be the world's most fragile body armor," he pointed out, encouraging a response. His daughter remained silent.

Just before the man mounted the sidewalk, he spun once and the coat rose with centrifugal force and then overswung and swayed back as the bulb man stopped and gave them a small bow. You could imagine the sounds of all the bulbs rubbing and clattering against one another, but the VW idle left nothing to the ear.

"There's something not quite right with giving points for that," Maeve finally said.

"Too self-conscious," he agreed. By consensus, their spotting-oddities game worked best when what was pointed out was naively peculiar, intensely self-absorbed, or else some public anomaly that generally went unnoticed. He still favored the dapper mounted John Wayne sculpture up on Wilshire with the horse under him running about two-thirds scale, like a really big Great Dane. Circus acts or what were probably schizophrenic exploits, like the bulb man's, were just too easy.

"What's your dad like?"

"You don't want to make up your own mind?"

"You could give me some background. Like, if he's got two noses or something."

The light finally went green and he motored on with a smile. "Declan is his name; his own dad, Seamus, was the one who actually left the auld sod, and he sometimes makes a big deal out of being Irish, which is one reason I don't. He fought in Korea, and then worked as a longshoreman for a time. He should have kept the job. It's an unbeatable union. It turned out to be one of the best jobs in the country after Harry Bridges got through terrifying the shippers into giving his workers a guaranteed annual wage. But Dad quit to go to a community college and study philosophy.

"By some accounts he was thrown out of the JC. Alternately, he dropped out when the teachers didn't honor his work. Then he did a lot of odd jobs like clerking at the war surplus store, most of which he felt were beneath him. Of course, he's on Social Security now. We lived back up near Steelyard's place when I was little, in one of those boxy little tract houses they built out at the rim of civilization in the early 1950s, but he moved down here after Mom died."

"And then you cut him off."

"It's not that simple."

"I can't imagine ever cutting you off, or Mom."

What could he say to that? It wasn't like every crossroad offered you a choice between a glorious rising path toward the Right Thing and a clearly discernible craggy descent toward Shame and Ignominy. Sometimes all the paths were bad and all of them led downward.

"There's going to be some things about your granddad that you aren't going to like, hon. Feel free to object, but prepare yourself a bit because I don't think you're going to budge him. Lord knows I tried."

Her head came around to confront him with a glare that was suddenly more curious than angry. The house was just off Centre and Fourteenth, a little clapboard bungalow that badly needed paint, the biggest eyesore in a neighborhood that had more than its share. Half the original buildings here had been knocked down long ago and converted to stucco apartments that now sported a lot of sprayed-on graffiti. Some even had Christmas lights. The curbs were packed with big, scarred 1970s Chevies, and a couple of very old boxy ice cream trucks that offered their wares exclusively in Spanish.

The only place to park was on the next block from his father's home, and they walked back to the accompaniment of radios thudding out *ranchera* and *banda* music. He could sense her trepidation, but this was something she was going to have to confront in her own way, with her own peeled-back nerve endings.

Yellowing weeds were winning the battle with the bungalow's lawn. There were a few Christmas decorations up and down the block, but none here. The button for the bell didn't seem to work, so he rapped twice by swinging the big Celtic cross knocker. In a few moments the door came open suspiciously on a chain, and an old man's eye peered out a narrow slit. Then, as no threat materialized, he closed the door to release the chain and slowly opened the door. Jack Liffey thought he'd prepared himself for the effects of age, but he hadn't. The man had shrunk to a raisin state and wore a dirty T-shirt, plaid wrestler's pants, and rubber flip-flops on his bare feet.

"It's Jack, Declan. And your granddaughter, Maeve. Detective Steelyard sent us over because of your troubles." He put a hand protectively on Maeve's shoulder as the old man looked them over like people he was sure wanted to take something precious away from him.

"You poisoned her against me?" the old man said.

"No, sir. I thought I'd leave that to you."

There was a repetitive grunting sound from deep within the

man's chest that might have been a private bronchitic laugh, and he backed away to beckon them in. "I'm pleased to meet you at last, Maeve Liffey."

He held out his hand, and she shook it formally.

"Nice to meet you, Grandfather."

The room was a shock, too, like the nest of one of those hoarders with a compulsive disorder that you saw on the junk news shows, but Jack Liffey knew better. Chest-high stacks of magazines and books and catalogs made up a maze that left only narrow passageways through the small house. None of the magazines looked quite familiar, and on top of the nearest pile, Jack Liffey nosily peered at a drab, academic-looking journal in buff covers titled *Modern Eugenics*. He could guess.

On the wall over an old sofa there was a photo of a mossy Celtic graveyard cross, and Jack Liffey had a vague memory that it had been in the den of the family house, and marked some ancestor's grave near Ballymore. There was also a small limp flag flat to the wall above a desk with a similar cross in a black circle. This one had nothing to do with Ireland. There were no mementos of his mother visible, but he did recognize a lopsided cabinet with big metal Chinese characters for drawer pulls that used to sit in their dining room to hold his mom's good china and silver, which they almost never used.

"Best we'd all promenade out to the backyard, where there's some room," he offered. "I'm not rightly set up for entertaining. And the backyard is where the trouble is at."

His rubber sandals flap-flapped ahead of them, along shiny bald paths worn into the carpet. The old man had to shoulder open a French door, but when they walked out, the backyard was a bit of a surprise, in contrast. An artificial waterfall, the cheap plastic kind you bought at Home Depot, dribbled softly into a plastic koi pond. The grass there was just as dead as the front lawn, though, and there were four unmatched lawn chairs, undoubtedly salvaged one by one on trash night.

Maeve stood next to the pond, her eye obviously caught by the single big mottled red-and-white fish that was out of the water beside the pond, stabbed right through, along with a playing card, by a long kitchen knife.

"Oh, that's terrible."

"The cops said not to touch. They think it's some Jap doing this, but that sounds wrong to me. Japs love koi. The Mexes around here, now, I could see that. Probably try to cook it up for a taco."

He pronounced it tay-co, though Jack Liffey was quite sure he knew how to do it right. He had seen Maeve stiffen from the first "Jap."

Jack Liffey squatted to look at the fish without touching it. "This has nothing to do with eating your damn goldfish. It's a warning shot somebody sent to scare you. And you're not the first in town to get one." On the way over, before descending into her angry funk, Maeve had told him the detective's theory about the cards coming in pairs.

"Sit yourselves. Can I get you some Postum? It's the only beverage in the house. 'Cept water."

"I'll pass."

"No, thank you, sir."

"Would you try out 'Gramps,' Miss Maeve? See if it works for you. Always thought that would be sweet."

"Sure, Gramps."

The old man gave a brief smile and wandered back into the house, apparently to get his own Postum.

"Did he actually say 'Jap' and 'tay-co'?" Maeve whispered.

Jack Liffey waited a moment, considering. "That's an appetizer."

"He must know it's offensive."

"Being offensive is kind of a point of honor for Declan. The closest thing I can think of is the sentiment behind that old bumper sticker 'Speak Truth to Power.' But, of course, he's punishing the weak, not the powerful."

She looked back at the fish. "You think race has something to do with these incidents?"

"It's had something to do with almost everything that's happened in this country for four hundred years, so I wouldn't be surprised."

He heard an engine revving in the neighborhood—a good old souped-up American car by the sound—and then more Latino

music. A high fence kept them from seeing into the other back-
yards, but a couple of two-story apartments rose above the fence,
the kind with aluminum foil in the sun-facing windows. Maeve was
brooding on something. In a while, his father wandered back out,
cradling a steaming mug, and settled into one of the chairs.

"I didn't know they still made Postum," Jack Liffey said pleasantly.

"What is it you want from me?" the old man croaked.

Jack Liffey did his best to hold his temper. "I'm trying to help the
police on this case, and maybe help you now. There's somebody
who leaves those cards behind as a trademark. He's gone after the
Petricich family already, and one of the cops. Maybe you remember
the kid Ken Steelyard I hung out with in grade school? Skinny then
with big, sad eyes. Can you think of any connection between you
and those families?"

The old man sipped, found his beverage too hot with a wince,
and set the cup back down gingerly on the arm of his chair. "Don't
know 'em. Don't know many people anymore. I didn't have enough
money to stay in the white part of town no more."

Jack Liffey could see his daughter make a slight face to herself.
In fact, the part of town between Gaffey and the channel was pretty
thoroughly integrated, but it was also pretty much poor and
working-class, whatever the color, and maybe that was enough to
relegate anyone to his dad's out basket.

"Dan Petricich doesn't live very far from here, if you consider
Croatians white. It was his family's house. His father, Ante, is still
living there. Did you know Ante?"

Declan Liffey seemed to chew that over in his mind. "Damn, I
think my dad knew an Ante. Seamus Liffey was in that big war, you
know, back before they started giving them numbers. He was
drafted in '18, two years after he emigrated, and back then I
think you had the choice of skedaddling back where you came
from or accepting the draft and becoming a citizen. So he became a
doughboy for ol' Blackjack Pershing. Lucky he missed all the
poison gas stuff. I think he was discharged before he had to fight
much at all. When I was a boy, he used to hang out at that American Legion hall up on Pacific and tell tall tales the way some

professional Irishmen do. I think that's where I remember an Ante. It was a long time ago."

Jack Liffey perked up. This might be the first real link. "You think there was a Steelyard in that gossipy group, too?"

"Don't know. Say, you're a detective these days, huh?"

"I look for missing children and try to bring them home. I got a call about the Petricich boy."

"And Kathy's okay?"

"We're not together. She remarried. She's fine. Thanks for asking."

The old man had never even met Kathy, but he'd remembered the name. His eyes went to Maeve, who, uncharacteristically, was being very quiet and doing her best to keep her head down, but still watching everything like a hawk. "Are you good in school, Miss Maeve?"

"Yes, sir."

"She gets all A's except math," Jack Liffey prompted.

"Try saying 'Gramps' again. I like to hear it."

"I work hard at school . . . Gramps. I want to go to college and study anthropology."

This was the first Jack Liffey had heard of it, but her intended major changed every few months—marine biology, photojournalism, political science, English. Now, anthropology.

"Anthropology." The old man chewed the word around as if it might become something more palatable with a little efficient mastication. "I suppose they teach that guff about the African genesis in the Rift Valley and all that, Lucy's bones, instead of the glorious history of the northern races."

Maeve's eyes were laser beams now, watching her grandfather's face. "I don't know."

It was the first time Jack Liffey had ever seen his daughter back off, and he could tell there was an agenda simmering away.

"Well, you come see me sometime without his nibs here to butt in and we'll talk about it."

"I'd like that, Gramps."

He hated the idea of turning the old man loose on her, but it

didn't look like he'd have much choice. She had her own car, and
her own ideas, and anyway, he was pretty sure he could trust her
judgment. But in the end she was only sixteen, and it was hard to
know what it took to send someone spinning off the merry-go-
round of adolescence into some goofball hermetic ideology that
would stick with her for years to come.

"That's fine with me," Jack Liffey said falsely, just to establish his
general evenhandedness. He thought he'd try the word "Dad," see if
it stuck in his throat. "Dad, there's something else. This thing with
the carp is just a warning shot. In every case so far, the guy has come
back and done a lot worse. I mean, a *whole* lot worse." Here, now,
was the worst part. "I think you should come up to Culver City and
stay with me for a while for protection. Until this blows over."

The old man eyed him strangely. "I don't see hide nor hair of you
for twenty years and now you show up, all of a sudden, and want
to take care of me."

"We are flesh and blood."

"That's out of the question, boy. This is my home, and if I left
this place unguarded for so much as a day, the niggers and spics
around here would break in and steal everything I got."

At those potent words, Jack Liffey could see Maeve stiffen and
fidget and almost speak out, but once again she subsided and kept
her own counsel.

"I thought you might feel that way. For your own sake, if there's
something you really value in the house, I mean really, Dad, you
should give it to me now to keep safe or put it somewhere you trust.
Whoever he is, he's coming back. I imagine Steelyard and the cops
will be watching over you, but it didn't do *him* much good in his
own home. This guy who's doing this stuff, whoever he is, is something else. He's mean and he's smart."

"I'll note that, Mr. Detective. But I got ways of protecting
myself."

"Okay, Dad, you've got a gun. Great. So did Steelyard, and the
guy disabled two sophisticated alarm systems and two locked
doors."

"What we got here is a battle of wits, then, and I don't figure there's enough wits in the whole world of mud people to catch me with my drawers down."

Maeve was almost catatonic with suppressed indignation now.

"Might be an angry white guy, Dad. You never know."

"I'll take my chances."

They all tried to be pleasant for a while longer, talking about how the lower part of the old downtown had been hammered flat by urban renewal, and later, how artists had moved into the lofts and storefronts of some of what was left.

Finally the police phoned, announcing their imminent arrival, and Jack Liffey used it as an excuse to start his drift out.

"I'll call you, Gramps," Maeve said.

In front they saw a police plainwrap across the road, and he waved to Gloria Ramirez. He strolled over and told her that the prewar American Legion Hall might be something to look into, and suggested she ask Steelyard if he knew any legion connections with his own father.

"How's Maeve?"

She was waiting over by the VW.

"A little dazed by the old man's up-front nastiness, but she's offered to come back and see him on her own sometime. Probably plans to get him to join the NAACP, but she doesn't know the half of who he is yet. He didn't mention his project or his pals. I assume the whole of San Pedro knows who he is."

She nodded. "Maeve is a fine young woman."

"Thank you. I sure think so."

"I asked her to call me if she needs anything. I hope you don't mind."

He smiled. "I've met my share of good cops. Thanks." She patted his hand lightly where it rested on her window, which gave him a little charge for some reason.

Maeve was hugging herself beside the VW, waiting for him to unlock it. "Wow," she said. "You warned me."

He had to fight with the key. Something about the old door lock was going bad, just a minor irritation, but it set off a whole wave of irrational annoyance at Declan. Feelings he stepped on hard. He got in his side and then reached over to let her in.

"There's a lot more about him you don't know, hon. But I won't step between you. What do you feel like for lunch?"

"Is there someplace quaint in town?"

"Quaint." He mulled it over. "San Pedro invented quaint. The fishermen tend to go to a place called Cannetti's, which is a cafe over by the canneries and fish buyers, or there's a nice little dive with an outdoor beer garden right at the head of fish harbor called Utro's, where you can see the boats. Just burgers and stuff."

"Let's see the boats."

He drove along the outer reaches of Ports o' Call, a strange failed tourist attraction of the 1970s, an ersatz New England whaling village full of trinket shops, half of which were now standing empty. Though the place was dying, there was a seedy magnetism to it that tugged at his heartstrings, like old sideshows and Tilt-A-Whirls and giant roadside Paul Bunyans.

Out of the corner of his eye he noticed that some kids were racing radio-controlled cars in the half-empty parking lot. When he looked closer, he saw the cars were on fire and they were trying to leap a ramp into a big tub of water. He wasn't in the mood for oddity points.

"What happened to set your father off?" Maeve asked.

"I wish I knew." He realized she deserved more than that. "Maybe in some people, as they get older, they just get a kind of rash when they're confronted with the complexity of the world. After the rash, they have this overwhelming need for things to be straightforward and comprehensible. And if there's one thing human beings never have been, that's it."

He had to stop at a stop sign for an eighteen-wheeler that was stuck and trying to back around on the two-lane road. Apparently it had taken a wrong turn.

"My dad found his simple answers in race. It started with national stereotypes—the British were stiff-upper-lippers, the French were sex maniacs or something like that, the Germans were humorless control freaks . . . all that guff. But for Dad, it wasn't long before it morphed into something more serious."

He'd meant not to tell her any more, but he had to give her at least an introduction of sorts.

"Somewhere he latched onto all those northern European scholars of race, if you can call them that. Danes and Norwegians and Germans, they're the ones who wrote those pseudoscience articles about racial types and purifying the races, all the crap that inspired Hitler. You'd think they were long gone, but strangely enough, they never went away. Their heirs are still publishing these unreadable, footnoted articles about the pure Nordic stock and the Alpine stock and whatever. Dad got sucked into it when he went back to junior college and he never found his way out of the woods."

The eighteen-wheeler finally got itself around, and he started up again. He was happy to concentrate on driving and not see the pain in Maeve's face.

"Recently the question of IQ has been one of the big things. They're using it to prove how great we white folks are." He smiled. "Though they conveniently forget that the Asians beat our pants off at our own tests. Blacks don't do as well. Personally, when I look at a whole group of people who've been kidnapped from their homeland and enslaved and had their families destroyed and are forced to grow up in the middle of a society that basically assumes they're worthless, I have no trouble understanding why some of them don't do well on the intelligence tests we make up for ourselves. Maybe if the IQ tests measured the ability to improvise music or clever English idioms or manufacture social confidence, the blacks would beat us blind, but the tests never will." He glanced at Maeve.

"Frankly, I'm a little worried about turning Declan loose on you, hon. He's not a dummy, and you're such a sympathetic person you always give people the benefit of the doubt."

"I'm blood sisters with Ornetta, remember?" she said. Ornetta was a smart, spirited African American girl two years younger than Maeve. The pair of them had helped save his life in the riots, and she was his unofficial niece now. "I'm cast iron against that sort of argument."

"Cast iron is brittle, hon. I've seen worldviews crumble in a blink, up against a really persuasive talker. In any case, I'd really rather you waited a while to see Declan. Right now he's a target. This playing card wacko is going to come down on Dad again, I'm afraid."

"Uh-huh."

"Give me your promise."

"I promise. I'll wait a while."

"Thanks, Maeve. Basically, I trust you, but there's just too much physical danger right now."

He pulled into a space in front of Utro's, and already her eyes were going crazy taking in the scene, glancing around at the fish harbor stretching away with its piles of nets and the slowly bobbing masts of the big fishing boats. What he noticed was a flash of the yellow police tape on the far-side dock, defining the place where the *Sanja P.* had gone down. The hulk was hidden now by two nearer boats.

After dropping off Maeve, he did something he almost never did and went into a coffee shop by himself, ordering a dark roast that he nursed in a corner. It was a Starbucks, the ubiquitous Seattle company that had taken over the wonderful old Ships Coffee Shop in Culver City after it had died, as they seemed to annex any commercial space left vacant more than an hour or two. Basically Jack Liffey didn't like to go into any kind of eatery alone, since it made him feel like one of those codgers who end up downtown, talking earnestly to their fists or living in refrigerator crates. When you weren't actively paired off, you had a hard time in a world built for twos. He was paired up, of course, but he was beginning to worry about Becky. He was crazy about her, yet Maeve's doubts meant something, because she was so often right about him.

He glared at a pine bough with a red bow and two ornaments on the wall. He hadn't bought a single Christmas present yet. And he was having a little trouble catching his breath, too. He'd have to get the collapsed lung pumped up again soon or go on oxygen. Something was bonding all his doubts and frailties into one big snowball of fretting. Seeing his dad again hadn't helped. He had no idea what to do with a close relation who goes so far off the human rails, but flesh is flesh, and he knew he should have done *something* long ago. It takes a great deal of strength to keep winter out of the soul, even in Southern California. All the Christmas decorations just made it worse.

Dec 16 Late

Am I a *ronin?* Is the concept right for my situation? Not all masterless warriors are *ronin;* some are merely brigands. I fought for years for a country I trusted implicitly, and I fought with ferocity as I should have, without regard for my own life, yet everything I discover now suggests that my fight was worthless. I killed innocent Asians to no purpose. Tsunetomo writes that you must be a *ronin* seven times over as a test in life. Maybe this has all been a test.

Of course, there is nothing to be done about the past. I can only look forward. Father, I am requiting your life.

The last test of a *ronin* is always against a nemesis. I wonder if I am acquiring one. I am not referring to the pitiable policeman whose house was so easy to violate, but to the solitary, this puzzling detective. I know he has been in the war, my war, and he seems to know the deep sadness of accomplished men. And like me, he has no master. I can't hope for an equal in skills, but I can hope for someone who has lived and still lives on the same field of honor.

Seven

The Ghost Dance

"Tony! Watanabe! Hello out there!"

Jack Liffey waved to the man and then crab-walked cautiously down the steep rough slope, using both hands to grasp at roughened outcrops in the concrete. He'd been directed to what one of the secretaries had called a creek, but it was really just another of LA's concrete flood control channels, the bottom punctuated with trash and a few shopping carts, justified by a trickle of rainbow-hued water down the center. He'd searched several places where roads crossed the "creek" and found Watanabe at last, fifty yards north of the Jefferson Street bridge, dipping a little bottle into the effluent that was dribbling out of a barred orifice on the side of the channel like the exit of a secret grotto.

Tony Watanabe semaphored once and called "Kelly Le Brock!" to him between cupped hands, and Jack Liffey laughed. It had been a long time. They'd lived in back-to-back cubicles at TBW Aerospace, with two other tech writers on the kitty-cornered walls, and one afternoon a voice had asked out of the blue for the name of the luscious British star of some teen film. "Julie Christie?" he had tried. Others had suggested Helen Mirren and Jane Birken, and then a supremely scornful voice laid the hunt to rest with the words

"Kelly Le Brock." And so, for a time, her name had become the general-purpose answer to all their over-the-cubicle questions.

Who was it wrote *The Rime of the Ancient Mariner*?

Kelly Le Brock!

What's the difference between a secant and a cosine? I can never remember.

Kelly Le Brock!

Tony Watanabe stood erect and smiling. The man defied several racial stereotypes. He was six-two, and, with his shoulders, he could have played a creditable interior lineman, at least at the college level. He sealed up his little vial of effluent water and stored it in a plastic eggshell crate with dozens of others.

"Good to see you landed on your feet after the layoff," Jack Liffey said. They shook hands heartily. "It's a pretty good bet working for the EPA won't kill babies."

At TBW they had divided the products the company developed into those that killed babies (satellites for targeting nuclear weapons) and those that didn't (in-flight entertainment systems). Some of the tech writers hadn't minded which ones they worked on, but he and Watanabe had.

"How'd you find me?"

"Your office said you were tracking down some heavy metals leaching into Centinella Creek."

"And thence Ballona Creek and thence the bay. There's a lot of light industries that feed into this tributary, and I dig it I get to track down the polluters. It's almost like being a cop, but I guess that's your field, too."

"No, I have a certain talent for chasing down runaway kids, that's all. Some might call it copwork, but cops tend to be a little too wedded to a world of order. Runaway kids can smell that."

As if to illustrate his point, a couple of small boys on banana bikes came very fast along the bike trail above the creek, now and then daredeviling a few feet down the steeply angled wall of the channel and back up. It made the hair stand up on Jack Liffey's neck.

"Jayzuz," Watanabe commented. "Kids today."

"How's your family?"

"Just great, Jack. The kids are both in middle school, getting good grades, and Masako has them going to Japanese school one day a week." He smiled with a mischievous undertow. "They hate it, of course. They're normal American kids, and, all of a sudden, they have to gear down and be polite to some old guy in a kimono who's teaching them stuff like the tea ceremony. Did you know even boys have to learn that?"

"What I know about Japanese culture you could probably put in one Toyota door hinge."

"The kids didn't know much more, but they're learning, even some of the spoken language. It's far too late for them to learn written Japanese, but Masako says she doesn't want them to forget who they are."

Jack Liffey thought of the Xerox of the Japanese playing card he had in his breast pocket, with its rubber stamp runes, but he held off for now. "You know, I can't imagine my folks shipping me off once a week to learn stiff-arm tap dancing and Gaelic."

"You don't have to worry about your heritage as much when you're part of the dominant group."

"I never thought of micks as the dominant group."

A small dog charged abruptly around a bend in the creek, and they both glanced over as it yapped angrily at them. The dog had a collar and a leash dragging behind as it made another mock charge.

"I already called animal control. He won't let you close enough to catch the leash. I'm not really complaining about the race stuff, by the way. Nobody ever beat me up for being Japanese."

"You're too damn big to beat up, man."

He started packing up his equipment. Canvas flaps folded up snugly over the plastic tray of vials and snapped into place, and the whole structure went into a backpack.

"Was this once really a creek?" Jack Liffey asked.

"You know, you take a big floodplain like this and the rivers and tributaries change their course all the time. Until we decide to stop it. It's frozen the way it was when the army Corps of Engineers decided to channelize everything in sight. Sort of like that Fukuyama thing, *The End of History*."

"I kind of like history," Jack Liffey said.

The dog made another false charge, but this time changed its mind and turned up the cement toward a group of kids who were tagging a warehouse wall just outside the channel fence. The kids ignored the dog. They weren't doing anything fancy, just the zigzag letters of their tagger names. *Zuko,* one clearly said.

"I wonder if you feel any more immortal after doing that," Tony Watanabe mused.

"All kids feel immortal. There's a bit of sidewalk in San Pedro that's got 'J. L.' incised into the cement, immortal until the ficus tree roots bust it all up."

The taggers ran off laughing, banging their own legs with their cumbersome cans of paint.

"You ever go back and look at it?"

"I was back there just two days ago, and I forgot to look up my initials. Ironic, isn't it? I just up and forgot about my immortality." He laughed. "The lizard brain wins."

That was something else they'd nattered about a lot at TBW, somebody's theory that what the Buddhists had done was fixate on an ancient part of the human brain that didn't know past or future, only the now.

"You didn't hunt me down to talk about the lizard brain."

"No. There's a guy down in San Pedro who's committing a series of crimes. Spiteful, really, but nobody's been physically hurt yet. You know about Hello Kitty?"

"I haven't been on Mars for the past few years."

"Okay, it's like that. He leaves Happy Kitty playing cards at his crime scenes with a—whatchamacallit, a *hanko*—stamped on each one." He took out the Xerox and showed him.

"I can't read *kanji,* Jack. You have to master five thousand of these to be considered literate. There're also two phonetic alphabets the poor Japanese kids have to learn, plus our Roman alphabet."

"Jesus, I had no idea."

"They say it takes seven years of pure memorizing to master written Japanese. It's no wonder the schools have the reputation of being stuck on rote learning."

"I guess so. That stamp says 'no no.' I already know that, but it doesn't help me much. I thought it might mean something to you."

Tony Watanabe took the Xerox from him. "Uh-uh, but Masako is a lot more into the culture, and I could ask this Mr. Japan teacher the kids have. You want me to try?"

"I'd be delighted."

He'd found a note from Maeve at his condo that she was going to spend a couple of days at her mom's, which was mildly suspicious because she rarely went back there willingly before she was due. But he let it rest and called Rebecca's voice mail at school to say he'd be at her place tonight and he'd make dinner. They tried to take turns on houses, but more often they ended up together for stretches at one place or the other, and when Maeve wasn't around, it was often Rebecca's place.

He bundled Loco into the car and shopped at a fancy market in Larchmont to get the fixings for a sun-dried tomato pasta, only wincing a little when he noticed at checkout that everything was about three times the price of Trader Joe's. Her place was relatively modest, all things considered, a small and finely restored Cal bungalow on the outer edges of Hancock Park. Or, as he and Rebecca pointed out gleefully to one another when they found real-estate flyers rubber-banded to the doorknob from time to time, "Hancock Park *Adjacent*." Hancock Park was old-money LA, full of true mansions, like great out-of-place Tudor baronials, but you could tell exactly where even *adjacent* ended. Three blocks east of Rebecca's house you were into Latino apartment houses, the streets jammed with Chevies and junkers, and the brand-new high-density Korean high-rises, with a lot of angles and earth tones and balconies the size of postage stamps.

Taunton School, where she was headmistress, was only a short drive away—in Hancock Park *proper*—but he knew she would probably be late home. There were always problems to attend to, it seemed. He had trouble mustering very much sympathy for the problems of very rich young girls, and he occasionally wondered aloud what these unspecified problems could be—an unexpected rumple in the Armani skirt, a drop of a quarter percent on a stock certificate. He thought of his father, and realized that his own prejudices against the relatively innocent children of the rich were parallel to his father's against people of color, at least in the sense that they both relied on stereotypes. But all in all, he just didn't feel that guilty about resenting the affluent and comfortable.

He let himself in Rebecca's handsome front door, which was varnished white oak below and leaded glass above, a bright design of a spreading fruit tree. Rebecca said she had heard that the place had actually been designed—first draft, anyway—by the great Charles and Henry Greene, though taken over and completed by an apprentice. Inside he was struck as always by the resonances of money—the real Kandinsky over the mantel and the little Goya drawing beside it. He didn't like Kandinsky all that much, but you couldn't help being impressed by what it meant, a single oil painting worth more than all the money he had earned in his lifetime, all the way back to his newspaper route as a boy.

It was her family's house—her father had been some bigwig at a film studio—and she was an only child, so she had inherited it all: real Persian carpets, Picasso litho in the bathroom, signed Edward Weston print of a gnarled green pepper in the hall, and even the Lipshitz bronze on a granite pedestal. The only thing she had that he really and truly loved was a portrait of her father on the steps of Angel's Flight by Millard Sheets.

No, he thought, there was another item he loved, tucked away and forgotten in the unused guest room. An LA surrealist piece from the 1960s by Joe Steuben, a kind of kiosk that portrayed an immensely sad view out the back window of a forlorn little house, seen through torn lace curtains. If you plugged the kiosk in and activated it, the taillights of a car passed from time to time in the alley, in some kind of inexplicably heartbreaking depiction of loneliness. It prodded a finger at something deep inside him.

He chopped leeks and sautéed them in olive oil, then added sun-dried tomatoes, a bit of cooked chicken, garlic, and mint. Finally he set the penne boiling. The nice thing about the meal was he could put it aside and the microwave wouldn't wreck it on reheating.

In the living room, he sat in the leathery mission-style chair and started to read a Cormac McCarthy he was fighting his way through. But he found he just wasn't in the mood for that dense, fierce prose, and he let the book fall and sat with his eyes closed, listening to the rattle of the fridge shifting itself into some other mode. Maeve's doubts about Rebecca were hard to shake, and his mind turned to the dissimilarities between them.

They'd gotten past the newness and the excitement of exploring one another, and now he'd begun to notice that the differences were starting to matter more. He'd never paid enough attention to some of the ones he'd had with Marlena, thinking they were both far enough along in life that they could just live them out. But the differences had crouched there, murmuring like poisonous gossips, until she had found a guy on the same astral wavelength as herself, awaiting the same imminent touchdown of the Lord.

Now it was wealth itself—ballet, season opera tickets, fragile china and crystal, plus the regular tidying excursion through his fridge that disappeared his plastic lemon and his off-brand sauces. At dinner, both exercised control over their conversation, and Jack Liffey couldn't help wondering if she thought LA's rich and powerful—many of whom she knew—could overhear his wisecracks about them.

Now and then she gave little yelps that suggested she wanted to free herself from the burden of all this—which touched him in a confused way, as if he'd come in just a little too late after the main titles of her life—but he didn't know how to help. He didn't know, either, how he was going to deal with these things in the long run, but it didn't bear thinking about just then.

Loco snuggled up to his legs, and he focused on a white section of textured stucco and on the curious, lopsided sensation of breathing through one lung. Loco's old coyote nature was giving way more and more to an affectionate petness, and the animal warmth, the general mindfulness of the moment, all his chores done, bathed him in a wonderful nothingness. He wished he still drank, to crystallize the moment that way.

In that state he heard her new car, a Lexus IS, pull into the driveway. Some boyfriend had long ago taught her to gun an engine once and switch off as it was revving down, an old trick from the days when powerful cars had big carburetors and it was advisable to empty the carb barrel when you shut down. But he liked hearing the brief, powerful whoop and had no intention of disabusing her about fuel injection. Not the man who drove a VW 1600 with one Rust-Oleum fender. Loco was up and standing erect at the window, like a Peeping Tom.

"Good work," Jack Liffey said. "Several million years of adaptation to hunting and only a few hundred to window glass."

She came in the side door with a couple of large store bags that meant she'd probably been Christmas shopping.

"Hello, Jack. I smell mint, mmm."

He got up and kissed her. They were still new enough so it wasn't perfunctory, and her body pressed against him.

"That's even better than the mint. How was your day?"

"Entertaining." He plucked at one of the bags to help her. "It looks like I may be too late, but I've been wanting to say something about Christmas."

She held on and set the big bags beside the hall. " 'Bah, humbug'?"

He laughed. "Something like that. Do you think we could keep it simple between us, maybe just one present each and even that more a token of affection? Whatever that means. I can't keep you in the style to which you were accustomed, Beck, you know that. I can't buy you anything new from Prada on this disability they're allowing me. And I may even lose that if I start working."

She kissed him again. "Don't worry, these are for a couple of aunts and some nieces and nephews in the Midwest. Tell me about your adventures while I strip down to something more comfortable."

"We may never get around to dinner if you use words like that."

"I'll try to stop somewhere between pricktease and serious come-on."

He was actually a little shocked. "I didn't know you knew a word like 'pricktease.' "

"Jack, really!"

"Okay, sure, you deal with overheated teens all day. You know words even *I* don't."

"Fisting took me a while to work out," she admitted.

"Oh, Lord."

They had one last smooch. "You know how to please me heaps," she said. "That's better than words forever and ever."

She went into the bedroom and changed into loose sweats while he made her a Campari soda and got himself a diet ginger ale.

"You're weasling out of telling me about your new case," she called. "I know you're on the job. I can sense it."

He told her a bit about it, the man down in San Pedro challenging and taunting the police with his planted clues. "Actually, you don't know me well enough to be surprised by today's real news flash."

She peered curiously into the kitchen, made a happy face when she saw the bright red drink, and took it up. "Tell Rebecca, who is wearing nothing underneath."

He let that go. "My father is involved in some way. Maeve and I saw him today."

"I thought your father was dead," she said lightly.

"Uh-huh. Believe it or not, so did Maeve and so does her mother."

"That's got my full attention."

"What would you do if you found out one day that your father, whatever else he was, was a prominent Holocaust denier?"

"Oooh." It was a noncommittal sound, as if a tooth had just given her a twinge.

"Somewhere in his well-before-midlife-crisis my father became an obsessive about race and eugenics and the dangers that threaten the poor overwhelmed white race. Mom was utterly flabbergasted by it all, but she died before it became that big an issue. I think I blamed him a bit for killing her with his new meanness of spirit. I'm not proud of this, Beck, but when I couldn't argue him out of it, eventually I just cut him off. I was going to get married—actually Kathy was already pregnant—and I didn't want him around my family. I told everybody he'd died, and I told him to fuck off. I wanted him away from my family. He bought it, I'll give him that, and he let me pretend to Kathy there was some out-of-state funeral I had to go to alone."

He listened to the ginger ale fizz in the can for a moment, his entire being filling with a burning shame. "I say I didn't want Kathy and Maeve exposed, but really it was me. I just couldn't *stand* him anymore, going on and on about those *ideas*. His ideology was so damn mean that resisting him day in and day out just got me to hating myself."

She came across the room and hugged him.

"Was I wrong to cut him off like that?" Jack Liffey had a terrible sense that everything going on now in this discussion was foreordained, all destined to have a bad end.

"I wasn't there."

"You can be prosecutor, if you want. I think I need to suffer a little here, Beck."

"Jack, counseling girls every day, I learned long ago that sometimes there's just no right answer."

The multicolored kite dipped and spun ineffectually before settling onto the grass, its owner visibly annoyed. The onshore wind that hit the cliff and gusted upward just wasn't steady enough for a kite today.

"They used to do hang gliding off that cliff," Gloria Ramirez told her. "Because of the updrafts. But they banned it when a couple of people fell to their death."

They were in Point Fermin Park, at the southernmost tip of San Pedro, also the southernmost tip of the city of Los Angeles, marked by a lovely old Victorian clapboard lighthouse and a park with a tiny bandshell and an expanse of grass that ended in cliffs. The cliff-side walk high above the Pacific was now truncated by chainlink where sections of the cliff had fallen away. The whole peninsula was like that, yielding slowly to slippage and subsidence, and the unhurried resolve of the pounding surf down below. Without the upthrust of tectonic movement, Maeve thought, the whole land-mass would eventually wind up as smooth as a Ping-Pong ball and about fifty feet under the ocean.

"A friend at school dared me to go skydiving, but I chickened out."

"Good for you." Gloria Ramirez sat across the park bench and extracted their cheeseburgers from the big take-out box. It had probably been three years since Maeve had eaten anything as wicked as a cheeseburger, but after Gloria Ramirez had suggested that the best eats in town came from Tommy's Charbroiler at Twelfth and Gaffey, Maeve wanted to be "one of the girls." Complete with curly fries and chocolate milk shakes.

Just rig me up intravenously with that ol' cholesterol, Maeve thought, but she nibbled at the cheeseburger and, of course, it tasted glorious.

Her companion had unpinned her pigtails to let them fall free, and she was wearing turquoise jewelry, so she really did look Indian. She set out a cell phone and peered at it for an instant to make sure it was on. "I guess you want me to tell you about your granddad."

"Uh-huh. It's a real shock just *having* one all of a sudden when you thought you didn't. And then the one I ended up with . . . wow, that's a pretty bad dream."

"Are you going to go see him?"

"Dad made me promise to wait. He says it's too dangerous right now."

"Um-hmm." Gloria Ramirez glanced up over the enormous bite she'd taken out of the cheeseburger and waited while her mouth worked and worked and finally cleared. "You've got plans to change him, don't you?"

Maeve grimaced as she nibbled at one of the curly fries. She didn't really like the flavor. "Somebody should."

"Hon, in my experience the only time you can change a male is when he's in diapers. This old man is pretty set in his ways. I hear when he first moved downtown there, he wasn't so unfriendly, but gradually his neighbors learned what he was up to and, let's say, a mutual dislike sort of flowered."

"He did seem pretty crusty."

"That's only a little of it."

The phone buzzed and she picked it up. "Ramirez. No, Detective Steelyard is doing that. Get off my back. I'm half day off." She punched off with a disgusted look, glaring, then went back to what she'd been saying.

"Maeve, most cops think I'm a Latina, and they damn well know I'm a woman. I live with a certain level of rude comment and disrespect every day of my life in the department, but your grandfather is something else. I'm not saying he's mean. Nobody's meaner than a street cop. He's openly racist against just about everybody, but it's even more than that. It's not common knowledge, but he's tied in with some groups—all I can say is that they're a real boatload of weasels.

"I'm telling you this for a reason. It's hard to put a dent in somebody who has his own community to support him. You move him an inch and they move him back two inches. Some of his friends are grown-up skinheads, and some are tight-eyed angry professors, but professors of *what* I couldn't tell you. I'm going to swear you to secrecy on this. I learned it from our antiterror unit, which isn't really supposed to exist, but it's watching Declan Liffey along with some other people like him."

"Thanks for telling me."

"I just don't want you to get your hopes up, hon. He may look like a way-past-it old coot, but Declan Liffey is a big frog in a little pond of full-bore racists. He's one of their mentors. An idea man."

They ate in silence for a while, Maeve digesting the food more easily than the information. She'd have to Google Declan Liffey on the Internet and see what was there. Gloria Ramirez disposed of another cell call and then made some stilted conversation about school before Maeve decided to ask her about her own heritage.

"Do you have some kind of pretty Native American name, like Swift Eagle or something?"

Gloria became thoughtful, and it took her a while to think this over. "I found out my real name, Wilson, and some stuff about my mom down here in Owens years and years ago. But more recently I went up to my mom's ancestral territory up around Yerrington, Nevada, and I finally found an old distant aunt. My heavens, Indian women become enormous. All that fry bread and lard. Anyway, she said she'd give me a Paiute name if I really wanted it. I can't remember it now. I found out later it really meant Did-you-hear-a-coyote-fart? or something like that, and I figure she was just having fun with me.

"Wilson is real, though. My aunt swore I was the great-great-granddaughter of Jack Wilson, who was better known as Wovoka. Does that mean anything to you?"

"No." A large Mexican family was strolling along the path at the cliff edge. Clearly, by the evidence of the woman's peasant dress, they were recent immigrants. The father pushed ahead of him a shopping cart padded with blankets that held a boy with an overly round Down syndrome head. The boy grinned and looked around excitedly, but the rest of the family looked grave and indomitable. For the first time the thought struck Maeve that these people were just about as brave as Lewis and Clark lost in the huge West. She thought of the nerve it must have taken for a whole family to cross a dangerous border into a country where they didn't even know the language, bringing along a child with a disability. It was unimaginable to her.

"Wovoka was a medicine man and farm laborer. He had a vision that led to the Ghost Dance in something like 1890."

"Wow, I've heard about that."

"Yeah, the dance spread across the Plains like wildfire, even to the Sioux, or the Lakota, as they call themselves, and Sitting Bull. Their world had already been pretty much destroyed by the white man, and most of the buffalo they lived on were dead. Wovoka's vision said if they did this special dance for three nights and three days, the white men would all go away and the dead braves and the buffalo would come back. They even had special ghost shirts that were supposed to stop bullets.

"Wovoka became a kind of messiah. The government banned the Ghost Dance, of course, since it scared the willies out of the settlers. The Lakota were doing it when the Seventh Cavalry freaked out and slaughtered them all at Wounded Knee. It's so pathetic, really. Just a kind of hopeless gesture of a people who couldn't comprehend what was happening to their world and tried to do *anything* to stop it."

"I don't suppose there were many good ideas right then for getting their land back," Maeve offered.

"No, I guess not."

All of a sudden Maeve's attention was drawn to a congregation of pigeons drifting over a section of the patio nearby, hunting for crumbs or whatever pigeons hunted for. Whenever one bird seemed to find something substantial, they would all make a rush for it on some silent signal. All except one bird, who was hopelessly late every time because he was hopping along on a single leg. Coming right on top of the talk about the Ghost Dance, this poor one-legged pigeon just about broke Maeve's heart.

"Help me," she said.

She and Gloria tore up the remaining burger bun into crumbs, and Maeve got up to deposit half the crumbs on the far side of the patio. When the birds rushed toward the feast, she waited until One-Leg had dropped far behind, and then she made a little circling run to approach the wounded bird, leaving a pile right in front of him. As she retreated, he was able to gorge for at least fifteen seconds before the stragglers noticed and circled back to overwhelm him.

As Maeve came back to the bench, Gloria Ramirez watched her with a pensive expression. "That bird's not going to make it in the long run. You know that."

Maeve found she really liked this woman a lot, and she wanted to say to her, *Don't think I'm just this soppy sentimental collaborator with pathos. I'm more complicated than that, I have my own moments of mischief, and I have been known to turn my back on pain, too, in my own kind of despair.* But she didn't say any of that.

"No I *don't* know that," Maeve said obstinately. "I don't think you should give up on anyone." They both realized that she was really talking about her granddad. I'm hopeless after all, Maeve thought. Just me—ol' heart-on-sleeve.

Dec 17
One should constantly be aware that what one is doing is exceptional and not hide it. It does not matter if you are the only witness. Your acts are testaments.

From a Buddhist text: everything in the world is a marionette show and you must learn to act, accepting that you do not know which strings will be pulled next. Victory and defeat are both temporary, both illusions.

They use the word *gen* for illusion, but I believe there is no negative connotation to the word, as we in the West impute to illusion. *Gen* is what is, the surface of the temporal world, a veil that must be. Merit lies in following the way of the warrior, not in the results.

I am more sure than ever that I am acquiring a worthy nemesis.

Eight

"No No" Boys

He found a place to park, on the marsh side of Culver in front of a little boarded-up restaurant down on the Playa esplanade, and walked back to the wetlands. He had to hop a low fence, with a belligerent keep-out sign that vowed to prosecute him vigorously, before he made his way down a path through tall reeds toward the recognizable tall figure in the distance. Basically, the path was a narrow dike that rose only a few inches above the marsh.

Once away from the road, it was a remarkably peaceful place, though half a mile due west some huge apartments on a bluff loomed over the marsh. These few hundred acres of swamp were about all they had been able to save from the square miles of Howard Hughes property that had once occupied the floodplain beneath the Westchester cliffs—factory buildings where they made helicopters, parking lots, even a little airstrip. All of it now was in the process of being plowed under for the new condo complexes that were destined to jam the 405 solid with commuters forever.

He was startled when, not thirty feet away, a big blue heron unfolded its long wings all of a sudden and flapped once, as it lunged skyward awkwardly to flee from him.

"Take it easy, fella. I mean no harm."

The heron in turn spooked some ducks, who rose in a noisy hullabaloo. Jack Liffey watched them soar and circle, and he simply could not imagine why anyone would want to shoot one of these lovely beings out of the sky. He wished he could invent some form of tiny air-to-surface missiles to strap to their wings to even the odds.

A salty breeze chilled him a little, but it was basically sunny and brisk, another glorious winter day, the best season of the year in Southern California for his money.

"Tony!"

The man gave a broad answering wave, and bobbed beneath the reeds again. As he approached on the dike path he could see that the marshy field was crisscrossed by narrow ditches of clear water, spanned here and there by crude wooden bridges on the dikes. The ditches looked a little too tidy, as if someone had plowed them through the marsh in an attempt to drain it. Far beyond Watanabe, he could see the straight channel of Ballona Creek carrying urban runoff to the ocean. A rock breakwater walled it off from the wider Marina Channel on the far side, where sailboats were tacking back and forth on their way out. The breakwater was like a long nasal septum separating the two waterways for more than a mile. The yachtsmen probably didn't like the heavy metals in the creek any more than Watanabe did.

"Thanks for coming to me, Jack. I'm on the clock."

"I like an excuse to get out here. I was on the wetlands years ago on a case, but those warning signs put me off now."

Watanabe laughed. "Those signs are like ninety-year-old security guards. 'Stop or I'll shoot . . . maybe,' " he said in a quavery voice.

"One likes to honor the environment."

Watanabe rested on his heels, checking some apparatus that dangled from a thin cable over one of the channels.

"How's the water here?"

"The technical term is, 'It sucks.' Don't get any of it on you."

"It can't be that bad. It looks okay."

"It's not getting much better." Tony Watanabe reached into a knapsack and held out to Jack Liffey an opened package of Oreo cookies.

"Is this the antidote?" He took one, and thinking inevitably of his childhood, twisted the two halves apart and licked off the filling.

"Junk food cancels junk water, I wish. I've got some news on your playing card."

"I didn't come all this way for an Oreo cookie."

"I talked to Masako, and she was surprised that I didn't recognize the term 'no no' right away. At one time, she said, any Nisei or Sansei would have known it."

"Refresh my memory about these words."

The squat finally got to him: Tony Watanabe sat down heavily on his clipboard, as Jack Liffey crossed his legs and rested on an offered flap of a canvas bag. It was strange sinking below the level of the reeds, as if cut off from all civilization. The only sound was a faint white noise of traffic, far away, and an occasional airliner throttling back musically as it turned inland after taking off over the ocean. Down low, he could see tiny hovering insects making their way nimbly among the reeds.

"The first generation of Japanese immigrants are called Issei. They came before 1920, when the United States started to pass its anti-Japanese laws. It's odd what those laws did; they made a true generational issue for us. The Issei were mostly young when they came over, and then all of a sudden no more Japanese could come, so we don't have any in-betweens. The Nisei are their kids, the second generation, born before World War II. They're American by birth, but their parents weren't even allowed to apply for citizenship.

"I'm Sansei, the third generation. There's also something called the Kibei. They're Nisei who went back to Japan for a while for their education or just took the culture more seriously. They were American by birth, but they learned to speak Japanese and clung to their Japanese heritage. It's mostly these people the 'no no' refers to."

A big pleasure craft hooted coming down the Marina Channel, probably bleating its displeasure at a sailboat crossing its path. Glancing along the cleared path, Jack Liffey could see it pass seaward, old and square, with lots of dark polished wood and brass, like something Gatsby would show off to Daisy.

Watanabe had craned his neck. "I wonder who owns a boat like that these days," he said.

"If you have to ask you'll never be invited aboard."

Watanabe smiled. "Someone wrote, 'Behind every great fortune is a great crime.' "

"Balzac," Jack Liffey said. "My experience tends to bear it out. I find there are some nice, modest crimes behind modest fortunes, too."

Watanabe pursed his lips. "You know what our crime was, Jack? Believing we were all one big happy family at TBW, the way they told us, and, if we did our work diligently, we had a good job for life."

He reached into the knapsack again with a tissue and offered Jack Liffey a circular pastry, the color of wood and as evenly shaped as a slice of a tin can. When he bit into it, it seemed to contain mashed kidney beans.

"*Imigawa,*" Watanabe explained.

"*Gesundheit.* I'm bitter enough about being laid off, but it was long ago, thank you. Tell me more about the 'no no.' "

"I presume you know about the internment camps where our people were sent after Pearl Harbor."

"Is there an American alive who doesn't?"

Watanabe smiled, but there wasn't much humor in it. "Lots, I'll bet. My family sold or stored everything they owned. They gave up a grocery business over on Sawtelle. I think they got three cents on the dollar for it. I was only a child at Manzanar, four years old, but I remember my bigger brothers playing on a high school football team that only had home games."

Watanabe was digging in the knapsack and finally found the piece of paper he was after. "Early in 1943, somebody decided they'd send a Japanese battalion to fight in Europe, but instead of just taking volunteers, some sadist in the government decided that first they'd ask for a loyalty oath out of everybody in the camps. These were folks who'd been locked up for more than a year by their own country. The Nisei they wanted to recruit were all Americans, but none of their parents could even aspire to citizenship. You can imagine the divided loyalties. There was a lot of anger in the camps, a real uproar. It was remarkable, really, that anybody ever signed on, but most did."

He handed the paper to Jack Liffey, who folded it open on his knee.

"The oath was more like a questionnaire, but only two questions really mattered. Masako was a little girl, too, but she remembered it better than me. I had to download that from the 'Net, the two notorious questions, numbers twenty-seven and twenty-eight."

Jack Liffey glanced down:

27. Are you willing to serve in the U.S. Army in combat and go wherever ordered? Yes   No

28. Do you swear allegiance to the USA and plan to defend it against all attacks by foreigners, and do you forswear any allegiance to the Japanese Emperor? Yes   No

"Some people tried to organize the barracks Masako lived in to vote 'no' and 'no' as a bloc protest. There were plenty of guys who just wanted to go along and enlist, but some of the militants starting calling them *inu,* which means dog or traitor. There also were a whole lot of guys who were perfectly ready to fight for America, but only if the government let their parents out of internment. I mean, really. Would you fight for a country that locked up your parents and wouldn't let them become citizens? It was a real Catch-22 for them. Renounce Japan, and have your kids renounce it, and then have no country at all."

"It doesn't make much sense."

"The really amazing part is that after all the protests—Masako even remembers fistfights—almost everybody decided to go along and vote 'yes yes.' You probably know that the 442nd Regimental Combat Team, made up entirely of Nisei—including my dad, incidentally—went to Italy and suffered more casualties and won more medals than any other unit in history.

"There were some holdouts, though. The army called them troublemakers, and most of them were sent to a high-security camp up at Tule Lake in northern California. Some were really pissed and were even repatriated at their request to Japan. Collectively, they were called the 'no no' boys because of their answers to those two questions. There weren't all that many, and they'd all be in their late seventies or more by now. Does that help you narrow your search?"

"Thanks, Tony. I can't picture an eighty-year-old cat burglar wreaking all this vengeance, but I have a hunch it must connect up somehow."

"Yeah, Masako picked up on the 'no no' right away."

Jack Liffey's legs, tucked under him, were starting to go numb. "I visited what's left out at Manzanar once. I was on a case in the Owens Valley. Do you remember it much?"

He shrugged. "Don't get too worked up with that long face, Jack. It wasn't fair, for sure, for sure, but on the other hand, it wasn't a death camp. The country's tried to make amends. Congress finally paid the survivors an indemnity."

"Sure, and some joker in the highway department has planted a big sign declaring it Blue Star Mothers' Highway right at the camp entrance. Nowhere else on 395, just right there, as if to rub it in that you people were all enemies."

"No kidding? I haven't been up there in a while." He pursed his lips. "Somebody ought to do something about that sign."

"As a friend of mine used to say . . ." Jack Liffey said. The friend was a radical historian named Mike Lewis, whom he hadn't seen in a while. "That's the kind of social problem that calls for a little dynamite."

He stopped at a pay phone on the street near the Japanese American Museum downtown. So much for the old expression about dropping a dime on someone, he thought. It took him fifty cents to get a dial tone, and a lot more to connect.

"Yes," the voice answered warily.

"Declan, is that you?"

"Is this Jack?"

"Uh-huh," Jack Liffey said. "I wanted to make sure you were okay."

"There's a cop car parked out front, but what good is that? There's an alley right behind the house, and the cop appears to be sleeping half the time anyway."

"You could use my condo for a while, Dad. You could have it to yourself. I'm not there."

"I told you what would happen if I left this place vacant. I'd have graffiti on my kitchen walls, and my TV would be in some swap meet the next morning."

At least the old man hadn't thrown around any epithets, he thought. "Well, keep your doors locked and protect your valuables. This guy is coming back, I promise."

The middle-aged Japanese American woman was very kind and kept bowing and making very small, timid gestures, which made him nervous. It left him feeling gigantic and maladroit, like some ham-fisted juggernaut who would break things if he didn't tiptoe. She took him through the exhibits section of the museum and downstairs to a big library, where she filled an oak worktable for him with manila folders of photographs, oral histories, and long lists of names. More than 110,000 people had been deported. There were 10 camps. Manzanar alone held 10,000 people. He learned one thing right away that astonished him.

Right across the channel from the docks where he'd played as a child, at the tip of Terminal Island—where he had seen only tuna canneries and parking lots—there had once been a thriving Japanese fishing town of 3,000 people. Before the war, a sprawling village of Japanese immigrants and a few Filipinos had wrapped around a big square inlet that served as a fishing harbor, just like the "American" one on the mainland.

He stared at one photograph that showed a block of two-story shops, Yoshioka General Merchandise, Eagle Drugs, a liquor store, dry goods, and—he strained his eyes and peered closely—Shoji Market. Beyond were row after row of identical frame houses. Cannery workers and fishermen. The masts of a few boats were visible to one side. An inventory of the buildings that the navy had flattened told him there had been several schools, a cultural center, and two churches—Buddhist and Baptist.

The librarian had provided transcripts of dozens of oral histories that the museum had accumulated. It had been a rough, working-class community—a law unto itself—and Nisei who moved in had had to pick up its rough-and-tumble street games and even a local slang that had grown up there. The grade schools in the village fed into Dana Junior High on the mainland, where he'd gone himself twenty years later. Sports varied from semiorganized street baseball to kendo and judo. One reminiscence talked about massive shoals of kids roaring through the streets playing a variant of kick-the-can. During the Depression, the village survived by swapping its fish for vegetables from the Japanese farmers who grew their crops along the Palos Verdes Peninsula on the far side of San Pedro.

He tried to visualize the town site that lay beyond the big container yards along the channel, and, to the best of his recollection, it was now just a mass of abandoned canneries and vacant lots full of rusting junk. According to the reports, the Japanese had had forty-eight hours to sell and clear out, and some of the fishermen had even been arrested at sea on December 7, plucked off their boats and hauled off to jail before they could even notify their families. The government, every bit as efficient as the Gestapo, had saved a master list of all the families deported from East San Pedro, and he got the polite docent to print out a copy for him. Somewhere, probably not here, there would also be a list of the "no no" boys. Probably deep in some FBI files.

"Thank you very much, Mrs. Nakamura. This was a very sad time."

"Oh, it was a long time ago," she said cheerily. "We are all good friends now."

Not quite all of us, he thought, wondering if there might still be a single "no no" boy on the warpath. Like one of those legendary Japanese holdouts on isolated Pacific islands who had refused to believe the emperor would ever give up. He'd read that the last one had surrendered in the 1970s. "Yes, ma'am."

He tried to bow back to her, but felt like a clumsy giraffe trying to curtsy.

He got home well after the winter dark—not his home but Rebecca's—after brooding helplessly for a while on a mainland bluff that overlooked Terminal Island, as the sun burned down into the hills directly behind him, golding the big cranes and shipping containers over on the island. He had a little trouble getting enough air for a while, but that was just the collapsed lung, and he waited for the breathing panic to subside, as it generally did. He could see where the village had been—the square harbor still existed as a landmark—but the homes and churches and groceries were gone now, leaving a jumble of abandoned warehouses and rusting machinery.

Looking out over the desolate industrial island, he couldn't help thinking about the thousands of Japanese American families the government had broken up in the space of forty-eight hours, and that led him inevitably to thinking about his own father, which only made him edgier and more miserable. It was a closed loop of remorse, and, try as he might, he could not remember paying the old man enough attention when it might have made a difference. He wondered if everybody lived in some relationship to a regret like that that they didn't know how to deal with.

When he came in, just to complete his moral rout, Dicky Auslander was sitting on the sofa with Rebecca. He was clinging to a slim glass of white wine, apparently waiting in ambush. Jack Liffey had been planning to say something to Rebecca about how in winter there was never quite enough light to sustain human life, but he suddenly dropped that line of chat entirely.

"Hello, Jack."

"Jesus, I'm not being cuckolded by my own psychiatrist?" He didn't think so for a minute, but he wanted to see if he could leverage any sort of edge here.

"We're worried about you," Auslander said. "Rebecca's worried about you."

"Hell, *I'm* worried about me. I can't seem to win the lottery, no matter how many tickets I buy." He went straight to the kitchen and got himself a ginger ale. It was the best he could do unless he wanted to go back on the solemn oath to himself about staying off the sauce.

He returned and sat down with a cheerful smile. He was determined that they weren't going to get his goat, though Rebecca was beginning to look very sheepish.

"So. What fun. Lover and therapist gang up on unsuspecting schlemiel."

"How have you been feeling?" Auslander asked.

"Feeling? Look, you're obviously worried that I'm doing some work again. I rest when I get tired. I spent most of today either sitting in a marsh or reading papers in an archive. This case is just talking to people and reading things. I shouldn't have to get into any gunfights."

Loco wandered in and seemed to take his side, flopping down on his feet. He felt grateful to an embarrassing degree.

"You're not ready," Auslander said. "You may not feel it right away, but it's going to catch up with you. You came very close to what we used to call a nervous breakdown, you know."

"I thought we used to call it going flooey up in the second story. Or bailing out the bilge."

Rebecca couldn't help smiling for an instant.

"Or posttraumatic stress. Have you had any crying spells?"

"No," he lied.

"That's good. If you had, I'd want to put you on medication. Stress is your enemy, Jack. I really don't think you can predict where a detective case will take you, and it could blow up in your face."

"I suppose it could." The whole evening was beginning to thin out and grow stale on him, and he could feel himself getting angry. "Why don't you tell me why you're here?"

"Oh, Jack," Rebecca said.

They took him down the hall toward the bedroom. He felt in his pockets immediately, but it was not there, of course, and his heart plummeted to his toes. His own red Swiss Army knife, opened to the big blade, was stabbed through a Happy Kitty playing card and then through his favorite photograph of a smiling Maeve and into the wall above the night table. The card was the seven of one of the Happy Kitty suits, with the now characteristic ink stamp. There was the "no no" in *kanji* and a small inscription: *Stand down*. The knife should have been in his pocket, of course, and the photo should have been on his desk at his own condo, and his heart should have been in the center of his chest, not down under his diaphragm being throttled by a pair of strong hands. This guy was good, almost too good to believe.

He didn't look closely at where the blade penetrated the photo. The threat to Maeve was just too horrible to contemplate, to give any literal play to his imagination.

"In for a dime, in for a dollar," he said grimly. But it did not do much for all the panic he felt.

Low clouds and a chill in the air spoiled the perfection of the morning over the fishing slip. Squid boats with their big outrigger lights were still coming in very slowly, one after another, leaving placid wakes on the slip, having already had their holds suctioned out over on Terminal Island. Grizzled Peruvian and Mexican deck hands jumped to the docks and made fast. Everybody he saw looked exhausted, including the crew working on Petricich's sunk *Sanja P*. There were two big eighteen-wheelers dockside and a strange piece of apparatus between them, like a pump of some sort that issued a fat white hose passing between a small group of men in rubber waders who appeared to be standing on the *Sanja P*.'s deck, maybe two feet under the surface of the gray water. Some proportion of a fathom down, a measure that Jack Liffey could never remember how to calculate.

He found Steelyard at last, in front of one of the trucks, standing and watching beside Ante Petricich as the machinery chugged away. Steelyard used his eyebrows in a minimalist greeting when he saw Jack Liffey.

"The station said you'd be here."

"*Jebi se*," the old man said with a sour face and without looking at him.

"I hope that's a greeting."

"Go fuck yourself."

So much for his relations with this Petricich. A technician was hard at work on the boat's flying bridge, still above sea level, dismounting monitors for sonar and the like to cart them away for safekeeping.

"I assume you heard about the number-seven card," Jack Liffey said to Steelyard. "I called Hollywood Division last night, but they won't find any more fingerprints than you did."

"Uh-huh. Watch this; I've never seen anything like it. They're pumping Ping-Pong balls belowdecks, and this sucker is going to rise like Lazarus."

"*Ja,* when we get her up, we seal the bottom and pump the rest of the water out. *Jebi se.*"

Several wayward white globes had escaped their work assignment and bobbed on the lightly ruffled surface of the slip. A man shouted, and a couple of the work crew grabbed rails and each other for balance. Something belowdecks must have shifted.

"Mr. Petricich. Did you know my granddad Seamus Liffey?"

If anything, the old man's dark eyes seemed to go even darker, and he still wouldn't meet Jack Liffey's eyes.

"He was the secretary of the American Legion post," Jack Liffey continued.

"*Ja,* sure. Everybody knew Seamus. He'd drink every one of us under the table."

"And Steelyard's dad. He was in the post, too."

"He was a whippersnapper, but *ya.* He wasn't eligible for member. He hung around before the war and cleaned up. Suck-up, brownnose." He made no effort to spare Steelyard's feelings, but the policeman didn't seem to be reacting.

"Can you think of any Japanese from this area that you guys pissed off?" Now he had Steelyard's attention. "Somebody who lived on Terminal Island and probably got transported to one of the relocation camps."

"Didn't know no Japs. They kept to themselves. They was all across the ferry. Good fishermen. They started with abalone out at White Point. Shame they bombed Pearl Harbor. *Jebi se.*"

"I don't think those particular Japanese had much to do with it."

The old man shrugged. "Didn't know no Japs. They talked funny. Walked funny, too. All bowlegged and the women made tiny steps like lizards."

"You're the connection," Jack Liffey said. "You and Seamus and Justin Steelyard. You're the one common point in all this."

"Go fuck yourself." The old man turned his back and walked away.

Steelyard was watching, too.

"So Dad was a suck-up at the legion. It fits the profile. A loser if there ever was one, a mutt. He always had some scheme for getting rich, we'd all be living in clover. The one time I saw him after he walked out on us, a whole lot later, he showed up at my door asking for money. Skinny as a rat. And he was trying for last prize in the tooth-to-tattoo ratio."

"My granddad Seamus is only a vague memory," Jack Liffey said. "Somebody who boosted me onto his shoulders when I was three. He died from a piece of rebar upside the head behind a saloon. Good old Shanghai Red's. Remember that place?"

"I can tell you got something to tell me. Let's sit down." Steelyard nodded to Utro's, the same cafe where Jack had taken Maeve. The restaurant's patio was defined by mooring posts and heavy hawsers out front.

They wandered over and ordered coffee, and the friendly waitress greeted Steelyard flirtatiously before scuttling off at an almost invisible gesture from him. Jack Liffey talked about the Swiss Army knife for a bit, then edged into the important stuff. He explained what he'd found out about the "no no" *kanji,* and handed Steelyard a printout of the names of all the residents of Terminal Island in 1941. Three thousand names. "Somewhere in some ancient FBI files there's going to be a list of the troublemakers who voted no and no. Since I don't have any good friends in the bureau, maybe you could ask one of your good friends to come up with that list and cross-reference."

"He'd be eighty by now, at least, Jack."

"It's worth a try."

He wondered how far to trust this policeman, but he had begun to like him. Maybe it was only his hangdog sadness.

"I've been thinking," Jack Liffey said. "This 'no no' guy seems to be focused on families. It could be that the card at my place today is the second one for our family and my dad is off the hook."

Steelyard frowned at him. "Wishful. Does it really look like his usual second card to you? So far the second is always a doozy. Try this on for a theory. The guy starts with a first warning shot to some predefined target, but if somebody gets nosy, he slaps one on Mr. Nose, too. You and me both stuck our noses in."

That sent Jack Liffey's heart sinking another foot. He couldn't get the picture out of his head—ultimately he *had* looked at it—Maeve's open grin with his own blade right through her neck.

"At least I've had both of mine now, as far as we can tell," Steelyard said. "He seems to fuck over the thing you care most about. I think I get that much. Strangely enough, I'm already getting used to the destruction of my layout. Why should I expect different? What have I got? An ex-wife who isn't speaking to me, a kid who went bad, a partner who thinks I'm a pain in the ass, an ulcer that isn't responding to the new drugs, and a sparkling personality that even pisses me off from time to time."

Jack Liffey wasn't sure if he should say something.

"This daughter of yours . . ." Steelyard began.

"Maeve."

"You get along?"

Jack Liffey nodded lightly, as if agreeing too eagerly would be tactless after Steelyard's list of humiliations.

"That's great. I thought nobody got along with teenagers."

"We've had our problems, but things are pretty good in general. I think she saves most of the crap for her mother and . . ."

He broke off. He realized he couldn't say the word stepdad, it was too painful, and he sure wasn't going to say the asshole's name. The man had slapped Maeve once, and that was two times too many for him.

"Christ, I must sound like an ass." Steelyard wobbled his cup a couple of times aimlessly and stuck a dollar under it.

"You've had quite a trauma, I'd say, and I'll bet you haven't got anybody to talk to about it."

Steelyard eyed him almost suspiciously for a moment, as if Jack Liffey were a salesman just getting down to the pitch.

"Fuck it. It's just life."

"Give me a call and we'll have dinner sometime. For old times."

"I don't know how you feel about *your* old times, Jack, but mine may as well be circling the fuckin' drain." He stared at Jack Liffey for a moment, as if trying to figure something out. "I'm gonna go spend some quality time with myself." Steelyard got up and walked away, and Jack Liffey was pleased, just a little, somewhere deep inside to find someone whose gloomy streak made his own take on life seem downright cheerful. Schadenfreude, he thought it was called.

Dec 18

How intoxicating the *Hagakure* is! Here is a true warrior, forbidden suicide after the death of his master, who because he cannot do what he knows is his duty, demands permission to go into retirement and become a monk. It is in this seclusion that his journal is begun. He brings me close to something very ancient, and not just to the values and philosophy of that matchless era of honorable combat in Japan. This awakening stretches back much farther, to the yellow flicker of campfires, to guarding the cave mouth through the night until the *other* is seen approaching in a cold dawn. To the ancient dream of hurting.

Nine

Across the Bridge

Jack Liffey slowed the VW and then had to pull over and stop for what appeared to be a Rose Parade float puttering slowly along Slauson toward him and filling more than half the roadway. It was led by two big motorcycles and a truck encroaching on his lane with a sign that said *Wide Load*. But it wasn't even Christmas yet, he thought. Almost, though. He felt a little tingle of guilt as he remembered, once again, that he hadn't gotten anything for Maeve or Rebecca yet. To avoid that thought he watched the float. Could it actually be for the Rose Parade already? He remembered that the powers that be had wrecked the Rose Bowl, anyway. Now it was set up to please the gamblers and math fetishists, turning a traditional matchup of the Big Ten and Pac Ten into some foul computer-selected national playoff that would put teams like Florida and Nebraska in the bowl but bring in millions in Vegas betting. Not that he cared that much, really. Football was about as important to him as a flower show.

He got a better look at the float as it drew abreast, and what he saw gave him a shock. It was made of flowers, all right, but the dystopic tableau depicted several dead young men lying in front of a burned-out storefront while others crouched within—a shoot-out at the LA Gang Corral. Most appeared to be African American. Even their Uzis were rendered lovingly in some dark silver buds.

"What do you make of *that?*" he asked Maeve.

"Two points, I'd say. But what on earth could it be for?"

"Maybe they're letting the Crips into the Rose Parade?"

"That's two weeks away. The cut flowers would all be wilted by then. Who knows?"

A pickup truck followed with another *Wide Load* sign. "We'll probably never know. And it's better that way. The world I recognize is strange enough."

He was driving Maeve into protective hiding. The knife through her photo had freaked him enough to work on coming up with some way to protect her that she would be willing to buy into. On an earlier case, they had met a famous old civil rights leader and his granddaughter, and Maeve had made a blood sisters pact with the little girl. Ornetta Boyce, two years her junior, had been sent away to school. Working on possible places for Maeve to hide, Jack Liffey had found out that Ornetta was home for Christmas. She was staying with her grandparents, and South-Central LA seemed far enough off the beaten track to be a safe bet. Maeve was keen to see Ornetta again, anyway.

"We write all the time. Remember I saw her last summer?"

Actually, he did. But keeping up with kids was hard, especially when they didn't live with you full-time.

"I saw Bancroft and Genesee, too. They're pretty frail now." Maeve looked sad as she talked of Ornetta's grandparents.

He nodded. "I saw them once. I'm amazed they manage to take care of one another without full-time nursing."

He pulled up in front of a bungalow that was set back above a sloped lawn, and he had the same warm feeling he always had thinking of the couple. Visiting them was like visiting the cloister of some Old World saints: their aura would reach out to enclose and protect you.

Maeve got out and folded the seat forward to get at her overnighter. She'd graduated from her little checkered pasteboard number—its innocence had always stirred a little pang in his heart—to a lumpy Gore-Tex contraption on rollers that looked like it came from Mount Everest Outfitters. The front door banged open, and a shriek announced that Ornetta had seen Maeve. They rushed at each other like diminutive linebackers. Ornetta was something like fourteen now but had grown a lot and filled out even more. He was amazed at how mature she looked.

Bancroft Davis came out onto the porch next. He was on a walker now, but it was one of the new-style ones that looked a lot more like sports equipment, with handlebars and hand brakes and a canvas saddlebag for books and such, as if it came from the same expedition outfitters as Maeve's bag.

"Jack," Bancroft Davis said. "It's a great treat to see you again."

"The pleasure is all mine. That thing looks like it'd be happy to do a marathon."

"It'll have to do it without me." They shook hands warmly.

"How's Genesee?"

"She's inside. Fine, but a little tired." His wife had been in a wheelchair for some time now.

"Hi, Uncle Jack." He got a hug from Ornetta, and then the girls were a blur of eagerness heading away down the hallway toward her bedroom.

"How's she doing in school?" Jack Liffey asked. He followed the old man inside to the living room, with its bleached fifties modern furniture and African artifacts everywhere.

"Straight A's," he said proudly. He smiled with satisfaction as he waved off help and shifted himself gradually into a leather chair that someone had mounted on a box to raise it about eighteen inches and make it easier to use.

The school Ornetta attended, Jack Liffey knew, was called Dunbar Latin, and it was in Washington, D.C. It had been founded in 1807 for the half-white illegitimate children of plantation owners and had sent far more than its share of famous African Americans to Harvard and Yale. The first time Bancroft had told him about the place, he had shown him a photocopy of an old ad the school had placed in newspapers across the South in the early 1800s, disingenuously promising *not* to teach its students to read. But, of course, they had.

Genesee, herself an old Communist, didn't really approve of such an upscale place. But since it got Ornetta away from South-Central LA and its ever-looming troubles, she acquiesced. Jack Liffey wasn't all that fond of private schools himself, but as he was living with a headmistress, what could he say?

"We'd best talk a bit about this danger you said your daughter's in," Bancroft suggested as Jack Liffey took the chair across from him.

"I wouldn't expose you and Genesee if I thought there was a chance in hell the trouble could find Maeve here." He explained about the "no no" boy and the fact that the main targets so far had been physical objects—a sunk boat, a wrecked train set. "I'm told the danger is to what I hold dear, but I own so little of any real value. The problem is, I can't be sure he isn't targeting families."

"That's some profession you got for yourself," the old man commented finally.

"I just fell into it, really. You can't be opposed to finding lost kids—whether they're lost on purpose or not—and getting them out of trouble. And if home is the wrong place to go, I never force them. It's turned out to be a lot better calling than writing boring copy about how to wire up a microwave relay station." Jack Liffey smiled, and took a good, slow, deep breath, as he was doing more often now, running on half his cylinders oxygenwise. "It doesn't *always* get me into trouble."

"I confess to a soft spot for people who work in technology. It always seems to me they're the ones building the world."

Jack Liffey hadn't really thought about things like that in a long time. "It's a great privilege to like your job, and greater still to be able to respect it. I'm thinking of your life's work, Ban."

"Not many are called to be in the middle of the struggle, thank the Lord," Bancroft Davis mused. "It just overtakes you. It frightened me so deeply, so many times, I wouldn't wish it on a single soul." He opened and closed his fingers, watching as if surprised that his hand still worked.

"Genesee and her Marxist friends made a fetish out of the need to struggle. But we were never trying to build a world where people had to fight all the time. I was working for a world where everybody could settle down and go to a job in a nice, comfortable car every day and raise a family." He looked at Jack Liffey.

"I guess I was lucky enough to have some of that. But I couldn't make it last."

They talked for a while longer, but Jack Liffey knew he had to leave soon to meet Ken Steelyard. "May I give my regards to Genesee?"

"She's pretty tired since Ornetta got in. Let me pass her your affections."

"Maeve isn't going to be a burden, is she?"

"On the contrary. She can help us with the chores."

He knew perfectly well Maeve would more than pull her weight. She was a born nurturer and choredoer. He went down the short hall to say good-bye to her and rapped lightly on the door where he heard the murmur of the girls' voices.

"Password!" Ornetta demanded.

He was taken aback for a moment. "Rhinestone animals," he replied finally. It had been the title of the first tale she had ever told him, as an eleven-year-old, wide-eyed, storytelling prodigy. Ornetta was a formidable wordspinner.

She opened the door for him. Maeve was cross-legged on one of the twin beds, looking happy.

"You still telling stories?"

"At school we have story night once a month. It's great—we're preserving our oral tradition."

"That's terrific, Ornetta. I've got to go now, but I want you to save a story for me."

She grinned and took something off a shelf to hand him. It was a little booklet, obviously her school's literary journal, with the title *North Star No. 157.* "I write stories now, too. That's for you."

He flipped to the contents page and found her name on a story called "How the Mule Learned to Tell Time."

"Can I get you to autograph it?"

She lifted her chin. "At Dunbar, we don't be believing in making celebrities out of storytellers," she told him.

"I'll be darned," he said. "Bless you all."

* * *

He tugged hard against the silver tape but couldn't move his enfee-
bled forearms more than a quarter inch from the wooden arms of
his desk chair. It was an old wheelless barrel oak chair and he was
sorry now that he'd never upgraded to a rolling chair because,
while he could still move his feet a little, he couldn't budge the
heavy thing on the carpet. He hoped his asthma didn't kick in
because a big wad of cloth was taped into his mouth and he was
already having trouble breathing through his deviated septum.

For half an hour, Declan Liffey's eyes had not left the apparition
that was hard at work across the room, dressed in a dark black
jumpsuit like some TV ninja. He tried to memorize what he could.
From what little was visible through the holes of the dark balaclava, the man's skin and eye shape said he was some kind of Oriental. Sneaky, like all of them, of course. There was more than one
reason for calling them yellow.

The man had clamped a portable shredder on the lip of the big
garage trash barrel and was methodically shredding every paper in
the room. It was a cheap shredder, good for only twenty or thirty
sheets at a time, so this had been going on for quite some time
now—handful after handful of paper buzzing into strip spaghetti.
The bottom two filing drawers of the cabinet stood open and
denuded now, and the intruder was halfway through the third.

The only duplicate copy of his irreplaceable manuscript was in
the top drawer—good, old-fashioned carbons—but, far worse, the
original was in plain sight on the desk, where he always kept it. He
liked to have it there to add notes as they occurred to him or to
have a quick reread of a particularly satisfying section, marked by
Post-its. He hadn't taken his son's warning seriously enough. He
did his best not to let his eyes drift to so many years' loving work
waiting there, vulnerable as a newborn baby: *The History of the
White Race,* complete from the dawn of time, with only the final
chapter, "Maladaptive Liberalism," waiting to be finished.

The intruder seemed to be serene in his long task, collecting
handfuls of papers from the drawer without hurry and feeding them
deliberately into the buzzing device. That must be how Orientals like

him built the Union Pacific across the Sierras, Declan thought, slowly cutting through solid rock at ten thousand feet. Something in their genes suited them to repetitive and tedious work. They were supposed to be smart, but you couldn't be all that smart if you could tolerate such boredom. And what sort of music or literature had they given to the world? Nothing. It was all copies and imitations, and tinny little cars.

The man got to the top drawer eventually. Declan thrashed and grunted in distress, but nothing could prevent him from stripping off the rubber bands and starting to shred the carbons. The flimsy paper fed easily and, as a result, it didn't take long to dispose of the only duplicate of his manuscript. He dare not let his eyes drift to the original beside the old L. C. Smith upright typewriter.

What was this all about? he asked himself for the umpteenth time. Or could there be any logic at all to the Oriental mind? Was it just random destructiveness, out of envy of the West's superiority? If anything, he'd given the yellow races a more positive assessment in his work than most of the others—industrious and self-sacrificing, disciplined, a culture in which instinct presided over reason. The problem was, they were also derivative and uncreative, always half a step behind the evolution of the white race. Declan had no idea whether the man even knew about the years of work he was annihilating.

He was already contemplating the heart-sinking thought of starting over when the gloved hand reached across him and picked up the manuscript on his desk. He could feel tears rolling down his cheeks and onto the duct tape holding his gag. He mumbled and grunted and tossed his head, but there was only methodical concentration from the Asian mechanism at work in his home. The dark figure went at his task, driven by some destructive impulse beyond any thinking of it. Declan saw the first sheets buzz into fine strips and flutter down into the barrel and clamped his eyes shut for the first time. It was like watching a child violated, a child you had nurtured all its life.

Eventually the buzzing stopped, and an abrupt prickle in his nose snapped Declan's eyes open, some noxious chemical. The ninja figure was emptying gallon plastic jugs of chlorine bleach into the barrel. If there had been the slightest chance of salvaging anything from the shredded strips, it was disappearing into a gluey mass of cellulose and chemistry.

"The Yellow Peril"—the phrase came to him all of a sudden. Jack London and those fellows had been right to worry about the destructive impulses brewing in the East that might sweep over Western civilization and attempt to wipe it out.

The man took a steak knife from the kitchen and drove it through one of those strange playing cards, and then through the side of the plastic trash barrel. At this point the invader addressed himself to the one truly and utterly inexplicable act of the afternoon, something not even the logic of envy and destruction could account for. He emptied the old family china cabinet on the far wall that Declan almost never used, leaving the cloth napkins and old plates and 78-rpm records set out neatly on the carpet. He was obviously very strong, and he braced the cabinet against his hip and lifted the entire thing at an angle by himself, then carried it slowly across the room and out the back door.

The only coherent word Declan Liffey's mind could form for several minutes was *gook*. Just fuck all you gooks, he thought.

Steelyard drove him down to Fish Slip in the plainwrap Crown Victoria, and they parked next to a giant mound of seine net under tarps, where Dan Petricich was talking to his father. The fishing boat had risen from the seabed and was tethered to a big crane on the dock and a large, seagoing tug on its far side, while workmen scrambled over its deck. It looked a bit denuded of equipment and pretty damp, but otherwise fairly sound.

"The crime scene folks will look it over now, but I don't expect much. He didn't leave any clues on dry land. I don't see why he would on a boat."

Steelyard and Jack Liffey sat in the car a while, becalmed by some impulse neither of them could name. In grade school, when both of them had been troubled for various reasons, they had tentatively supported one another, and it seemed to count for something, even though it was more than forty years behind them.

"You getting anywhere with that list?"

"We've been promised the names today."

"I think that old man knows something," Jack Liffey said.

"Every time I touch on a subject he doesn't want to talk about, he starts cursing."

"Do you think you could find your own father?" Jack Liffey asked. "It's just a hunch, but this seems to be about them, not us."

"God." Steelyard gave an inadvertent shudder. "Would I want to find the old man? I don't know. How about your dad?"

"He won't talk to me about anything that matters. I'll make you a deal: you talk to my dad, and if you can find him, I'll talk to yours. There's something about that generation that clams up with their own kids."

"I don't even know if my dad is alive. But it's a deal. I'll talk to Declan."

"Get specific. Push him hard on some very concrete plane. Don't let him slip into rattling off abstractions and types. He's a greased eel in that world. Why don't you have another try with Ante there?"

"Let me do my job my way, okay?"

"Sorry. I'm trying not to presume on all that history we had."

Steelyard smiled ruefully. "Thanks, Jack. You were a good friend in a really bad time."

Finally they got out into the salty, fishy air and walked toward the salvage operation.

Dan Petricich hailed them as they approached.

"Any news on this fucking boatsinker?"

"No. How's the boat?"

"I think we're going to save her. I may need a new GPS unit. It didn't take well to complete immersion. But there's something else."

"Uh-huh."

Jack Liffey could sense Steelyard's professional curiosity gather steam.

"I went aboard this morning when it was first stabilized and looked around."

"I'd rather you waited for the crime scene people." Steelyard glowered.

"Sorry, but listen. Everything was normal except the galley. Some of the *plates* were missing. The metal ones were still there and some old scratched Melmac, but there were a few old plates that had Chinese designs, real china from home, and they're just gone. I almost didn't notice. They were from a set we had for years, and we'd broken so many of them that there was no point trying to use them anymore, so I just demoted them to the boat."

"Where did they come from?"

"I have no idea. They was just always there, even in my childhood. Dad?"

"*Ja?*"

"Where'd that old china come from—you know, the one with the blue designs all over?"

He snapped something in their own language.

"He says we'd have to ask my mother. She's passed on."

Steelyard scowled at the old man for a moment but finally let it go. "Is the boat stable enough so you could get your work crew off for an hour or so? I know we probably won't find anything, but I'd like to have our lab people look around before you paint everything and stomp all over it."

"Sure . . . okay . . . sorry."

Steelyard made a call on his cell and then grabbed Jack Liffey's sleeve and pulled him back toward the car. After they got in, he said, "The old fuck knows something, doesn't he? I'll work on him later. I want to show you something."

They drove back north on Harbor Boulevard to where they could swing around and get on the Vincent Thomas Bridge to Terminal Island. It was a graceful Rust-Oleum green two-tower suspension bridge, like a smaller version of the Golden Gate, but it hadn't been there in Jack Liffey's youth. There had only been the car ferry, and when that stopped running late in the evening and on weekends, there'd been a smaller passenger ferry to bring shift workers home from the canneries. For a nickel each, he and his friends had pushed through the rotating grid gateways on weekends and ridden across the channel as passengers, scampering all over the boat and then hiding under the benches at the far side and riding back for free, over and over. Only much later did he figure out that the crew had certainly known what the kids had been up to and had winked at it all that time.

The fifty-cent tolls had finally paid the bridge off and, unlike the bay bridges up north, the city had dropped the toll completely so it was free both ways now. Steelyard swung off the bridge, past the immense conic hills of coke dust to be shipped to Asia, and on into the old cannery area. The big canneries such as Star-Kist and Chicken of the Sea were gone now, empty shells or razed, their operations moved to American Samoa and other low-wage zones on the Pacific Rim. Some smaller packing plants still seemed to be functioning, but the main part of the island was now devoted to stacks and stacks of shipping containers and an endless bristling of the tall K-cranes that unloaded them.

Steelyard turned down Tuna Avenue where, miraculously enough, there was one cafe that still survived. Then he turned along a broad basin where only a few out-of-town boats were tied up. The only one Jack Liffey could see stern-on had a registry from Seattle. Being down at ground level disoriented him a bit, but he was pretty sure this was the square basin where the Japanese fishing boats had tied up before the war.

Steelyard turned south on a straight street, heading for a big gray building. "That's the federal prison where Al Capone's syphilis ate up his mind," he said.

"I think I knew that once. We joked about it as kids."

He swung to the left around the prison and showed his badge to a Coast Guard officer who lifted the gate to let them enter.

The base was immaculate. There were a few white frame buildings—so clean they looked like a movie set—a dock with a small cutter all set to go in case any Arabs rowed out into the harbor with bombs, and huge expanses of far-too-green lawn. Steelyard drove as far south as he could along the grass to where a stone seawall rising ten feet out of the water formed the southernmost tip of Terminal Island.

"Come on," Steelyard said.

They got out and stood at the seawall to look back into the basin, which was surrounded by small icehouses and packing plants, most of which looked shuttered and abandoned.

"This is the way the Japanese fishermen saw it coming back from the sea," Steelyard said.

"From this far away, it just might still all be there."

"There's a plaque now and a monument, but this view is better."

"Hell, how much of our past is marked by anything at all?" Jack Liffey said.

"Maybe I'd prefer it *this* way. Blast it all flat. It would match some inner feeling."

Liffey looked at the man with compassion but said nothing. Wind blustered against their clothing. Steelyard looked back at Jack Liffey with an expression so lost that he could sense some kind of resigned ghost behind the man's eyes. Steelyard gripped Jack Liffey's shoulder hard. "This is private, friend. Respect it. I've come close to eating my gun three times."

Dec 19 PM
The old man has been paid in full. Paid a little extra, one could say, because the nature of his writing and his life invited it as much as his family's long-past offense.

The span of revenge is endless. A palpable weight all my life, even when you carried it yourself, repeated yourself endlessly, your own merit drowning in the tediousness of your rancor.

You were unfortunate. The *Hagakure* tells us that it is best to pass on through the experience of bitterness when you are young, or your disposition will never settle down. If you become fatigued when you are unhappy, you become useless. You will never be freed from its bondage; the merely appropriate and necessary will dominate what is left of your life.

Every one of these men I confront eases the weight a little. I wonder if concluding this task will leave me weightless and substanceless, without a place in the world any longer. Perhaps the space I occupy will cease to be and the world simply close up around where I had been, as if you and I had never existed. What a perfect Bushido death!

Ten

A Haunted House

Jack Liffey sat in Ken Steelyard's oversized prowl car for the better part of an hour, trying not to feel oppressed by all the angular gadgetry stuck to the dashboard as he listened to the halting, inarticulate revelations that he knew overprocessed and overtight men like Steelyard tended to confess to anyone handy when their egos started collapsing. Seagulls wheeled overhead, and a single pelican dived and dived off the tip of the island. He wasn't much of a consoler or psychologist, with his own problems crystallizing slowly inside him, but he did his best to hear the cop out. He knew better than to offer a lot of glib consolations, some fatuous "purpose in life," but he was sorely tempted to offer the man something.

Jack Liffey remembered that as a ten-year-old, he had usually managed to cajole Steelyard into some form of play that got him to forget his wounding home life for the moment. He had been beaten at home, now and then, but that hadn't been the worst. His stepdad just didn't like him very much. Jack Liffey could see that it was exactly what the stepfather had demanded of poor Kennie Steelyard that he seemed to have become in the end, but at what cost?

"I don't know what to tell you, Ken. Doesn't the department have somebody you could talk to?"

In fact what he kept seeing was the two of them, maybe ten years old, avoiding the long recess, hiding out in the bushes. They had invented a game, wrapping golf balls in white hankies and tying off the neck with rubber bands to make big-headed ghosts. He no longer had the faintest reminiscence of what they'd done with their golf ball ghost puppets in those bushes.

Steelyard glared at him. "It gets out you're seeing a fucking shrink, nobody trusts you again."

"You know, I hate to have to say it, but this is exactly what's making the world such a tough place for you—all these goddamn *rules* that seem to go along with this oaf mentality you cops are always exuding."

Steelyard quickly turned to stare at him, and Jack Liffey glimpsed something almost pensive behind the sudden anger. "What are you fucking getting at?"

"Most of the time you clam up hard, raise your steel armor, like Clint Eastwood on his worst day. When's the last time you let down and unwrapped a little and let something work on your inner spirit? I'm not being religious, dammit. I just mean some basic humanity inside you."

Steelyard looked away, but the anger had left his voice. "I'm not sure I get you. You know I try to watch TV at night to relax, and even the cop shows, they just turn into a big pot of rage for me."

"Kill the TV. Read a book, man. I can give you some books that may make you feel human. Let your mind out of that macho trap. Maybe that's what the toy trains were for, some sort of escape."

Jack Liffey was not a fan of psychotherapy, and this was about as far as he would go.

The man didn't look over but he squeezed Jack Liffey's shoulder, so hard it hurt. "*Read*, huh? I'll give it some thought."

Then Steelyard sighed and turned his cell phone back on. It immediately buzzed angrily at him.

"Eee-yuck!" Maeve had swiped a couple of her mom's nose strips, and they had just peeled them off their noses after the requisite wait. Now they were grossing out on what had been sucked out of their nose pores. The morning light through the window made the little worms of extracted blackheads all too evident.

"Boogerocious!"

They peered carefully at the strips, turning them this way and that in the light, and then discarded the evidence and changed tack to try to decide where to go exploring for the day. There was a lot of the city Ornetta had never seen, but it was the Hollywood stuff that seemed to attract her most, Grauman's Chinese and the boulevard itself and the inevitable Hollywood sign, though she seemed to feel a bit sheepish about it, as if she knew in her heart that there were cultural landmarks more deserving. Maeve had her little Echo, full of gas, and the day was before them, so they could go just about anywhere except San Pedro, following her promise to her dad. Then Maeve had a brainstorm.

"How'd you like to meet a real Native American woman?"

Ornetta looked curious in all the right ways, so Maeve explained the plan. "We'll do Hollywood first and then meet my friend for lunch. She's really super."

"Okay," Ornetta said. "You go, girl."

Her grandfather seemed perfectly agreeable to a mini expedition as long as they stayed well away from San Pedro, of course, or any other areas that might be genuinely dangerous for two young ladies alone. Maeve promised to keep in touch by cell phone, and they started preparing for their outing. They loaded a Styrofoam cooler with four diet Pepsis and two Fuji apples. Maeve knew she had her Thomas map book in the car, and a a box of Gummi Bears. Ornetta brought a little throwaway cardboard camera from the Costco. They were getting more and more psyched.

Maeve called Gloria Ramirez, who told her she could move her day around to take the afternoon off. They agreed to meet for a late lunch in a big marketplace called *El Mercado* in East LA, not far from her house in Boyle Heights. Maeve was thrilled because she had rarely set foot in East LA and she'd just finished a semester of Spanish. Now maybe she could put it to use.

Steelyard peered down into the trash barrel with a dispassionate frown. Jack Liffey had already had a good look. The last three koi from the pool in back had been thrown in on top of a gummy mass of shredded paper that reeked of ammonia and other bathroom chemicals.

"You guys got about five seconds to evolve into something that loves breathing Drāno," Steelyard offered the fish softly.

Actually, the fish were well beyond evolution—as Jack Liffey knew from his peek—motionless, mouths and gills distended, good and dead. The card, held to the side of the trash barrel, said *To defeat the man.* Declan was across the room in his desk chair, rubbing the raw spots where the duct tape had been stripped off and cursing a blue streak, mostly against the Japs, who he was sure were behind the attack, collectively, having waited for it since Hiroshima. *Slopes, dinks,* and *gooks* were words of hate that Jack Liffey had ignored often enough in the service, but obviously, his father moved in circles that had whole lobes of the brain set aside for even more original racial epithets.

"Skibby yellowshitters!"

"Bucktoothed little cocksuckers!"

"Chow Ming Mongoloids!"

"Mustard monkeys!"

"Charlie fuckin' Chans."

He seemed at last to be running down. "You know how many years I worked on that book?"

Steelyard sat on the sofa and opened a notebook, showing very little evident sympathy. "About as many as I worked on my layout," he pointed out.

"You can't equate a major breakthrough in historical scholarship with a stupid toy train!"

Diplomatic as always, Jack Liffey thought.

"What was this scholarly masterpiece called?"

"*The History of the White Race.* It was more than seven hundred pages long and had more footnotes than the *Britannica.*"

"You didn't keep a copy?"

"He got that, too. All the while, your dumbshit colleague sat in his car in front eating doughnuts and never noticed the slant-eyed monkey attacking from the back."

Jack Liffey refrained from reminding his father that he'd warned him several times about moving his valuables out of the house. Given the title he'd just heard, he could pretty much guess what it contained. No loss there. All those footnotes would merely have cited like-minded screeds written by the nutcases holed up in redoubts in northern San Diego County and Idaho.

"We're not baby-sitters, Mr. Liffey. We had a car here watching over you. If the officer hadn't come over to check on you, you'd still be tied up."

"An hour too fucking late!"

"Sounds like you should have accepted your son's offer to get away for a while."

Declan glared at Jack Liffey for the first time. "I don't get paid by the hour to argue."

Jack Liffey wasn't quite sure what that was supposed to mean, but he left it alone. "You're still welcome to go to my place, Dad. You'd have it all to yourself. I'm staying at a friend's."

"What's the point? What's he going to do to me now? Steal my skivvies?"

Jack Liffey shrugged. "It's just an offer."

"Let's go over the perp's actions again," Steelyard suggested. "I want to make sure I've got it all down."

Declan Liffey had calmed down enough to give him a step-by-step account of his ordeal. For the first time, the old man allowed himself to veer away from a single-minded focus on the rape of his manuscript, and mentioned the intruder emptying the cabinet that had been against the northern wall and lugging it away with him. Steelyard perked up a bit and pried out of him a detailed description of the piece of furniture: banged-up mahogany veneer, a rounded front that was called waterfall by antiques buffs, metal handles shaped like Chinese letters.

"The letters mean anything?"

"How should I know? Probably Fuck you, round-eyes. It belonged to my dad. My wife never liked it."

Steelyard fussed around a while longer, but he excused himself when a couple of people from crime scene showed up in their superclean jumpsuits and plastic booties to look for evidence. One of them, unfortunately, was an Asian technician, and Declan glared at her ferociously.

As they walked back to the car, Steelyard seemed lost in thought.

"Any way to speed up the FBI on those lists of the 'no no' boys?" Jack Liffey suggested. "It sure looks like a disgruntled Asian."

"Disgruntled," Steelyard repeated, rolling the word around in his mouth, as if testing several of the flavors it gave off.

"*Very* disgruntled then," Jack Liffey amplified. "Peeved. *I*-rate. Who knows? There's sure as hell a grudge here, and I'm the only one still on this guy's radar, as far as we know."

"The feebs really love it when you call them up and say they're dragging their feet on something you asked them to do. You ever had a lot of luck jamming up the feds?"

"As a matter of fact, I've met good feds, just like I've met good local cops. There're exceptions to every rule."

Steelyard laughed a little, as if he'd softened up some overnight. Maybe it was just getting back on the job after all the soul-searching out on Terminal Island. "I'll call the junior G-men. And *you,* take a lesson and get what you value out of reach."

"There's only one thing I value that much and she's at an undisclosed location."

"I hope you're right, Jack. I worry about this guy. This is not the usual dirtbag from the shallow end of the gene pool. He plans, he comes in under surveillance, he knows what to do to hurt his targets, and then, once in a while, he leaves really skeery things behind like that Special Forces kill knife. He may not have hurt anybody's person yet, but he's had a free run. I have a feeling he might go nuclear the first time he's thwarted."

"Look!" Ornetta had placed her tennis shoe into Humphrey Bogart's shoe impression in the concrete square in the forecourt of Grauman's Chinese, which Maeve noticed was apparently now called Mann's Chinese. As Maeve knew perfectly well, everything in LA ate up its own past every few years, as if what it had once been didn't matter a bit. Ornetta's shoe fit perfectly.

"Wow, he had small feet," Maeve said.

"I guess he was a little guy." She looked around dubiously. They had parked behind Musso & Frank's and walked several blocks to get here.

Hollywood Boulevard was just about the tackiest possible place in LA, but Maeve hadn't wanted to warn Ornetta in advance. Mostly the shops along the boulevard sold T-shirts with pictures of movie stars or little plastic reproductions of things such as movie cameras and skulls and little toilets for use as ashtrays, and also S & M paraphernalia such as spiky collars and whips and black bras with the nipples cut out. In fact, a lot of the local people striding up and down the boulevard seemed to be wearing the stuff.

Except for the gawky camera-laden families from Kansas, who were mostly down by the Chinese Theater at the west end, the boulevard was full of hard-core druggies and bikers and runaways with utterly lost looks in their eyes—a hundred wannabe punk musicians looking for one another. One guy, who was shirtless in the chill of December, bustled past with an angry frown and big half-dollar-size rings in both his nipples. A young woman in leathers lounged sleepy-eyed against a wall, so emaciated Maeve wondered if she would survive the day.

"There's something really wrong going on," Ornetta said. "This place gives me the creeps."

"These kids didn't grow up here. If all you're fed, day after day, is sick dreams about becoming famous, and your parents hate you, what chance do you have?"

"This isn't about *movies*," Ornetta complained. "Almost nothing here is about movies."

"No—but it's full of people whose minds were messed over by the movies."

"Can we go to that other place?"

"El Mercado; sure."

"I know about bad places," Ornetta said, "but I think there's a lot more evil deep in the soul here."

"My dad told me somebody once said if you strip all the false tinsel off Hollywood, underneath you'll find the real tinsel."

A stocky man with a fringed deerskin shirt and a tattoo on his forehead that said *Metal or Death* was striding toward them with the impotent malevolence of a large predator trapped in a zoo. Ornetta wasn't in any mood to laugh at the joke. "Let's book."

As it happened, there was a faxed list of names from the FBI waiting on Ken Steelyard's desk. The list was several pages of names of the Japanese Americans who had declined to make patriotic affirmations in 1942. A clerk-trainee had already painstakingly compared the list to Jack Liffey's roster of the Terminal Island residents and winnowed it down to thirty-one names.

Steelyard had brought Jack Liffey back to the office with him, but he wouldn't let him see the list for some reason. Looking it over with a cursory eye, he was finally defeated by all the Japanese syllables. "I guess we got a new penal code here: BPWO."

"What's that?"

"Being Pissed off While Oriental."

"Has anyone told you the word *Oriental* is relatively offensive these days?"

"Relative to what?"

"Let's say it's somewhere between *Asian* and *gook.*"

"So my partner says, bless her PC heart."

"Why don't we see if anybody on this short list is in the current phone book?"

"I never would have thought of that."

Maeve and Ornetta had just fled south from the hovering menace of Hollywood Boulevard, and Maeve was now driving east across LA on Beverly, one of her dad's many shortcuts she was trying to fix in her memory. She figured his knowledge of LA lore and LA inside info might be her only tangible patrimony, but she didn't really mind. Beverly was a broad avenue that stayed mainly residential until you got near downtown. With half her mind, she noticed how nice some of the old houses were and realized that Rebecca's ritzy school was around here somewhere.

A skinny old man with big wooden wings on his bicycle was pedaling hard ahead of them, leaning into it to tow a homemade fine-mesh chicken-wire trailer chock-full of what looked like old eye-glasses. As she passed she could see that that was exactly what he was transporting. Could he be taking them to a swap meet? One point to me, Dad, she thought.

They left the big houses behind and now were passing shops with hand-lettered Spanish signs and then Korean minimalls as they neared downtown. Where the street split, she decided to go up Silverlake and then take Sunset across downtown. It would keep her north of the worst traffic, and then become the renamed Cesar Chavez Avenue, which seemed fitting for a grand entrance to East LA.

They passed north of downtown LA, right between the abandoned Terminal Annex, which had once been the central post office, and the beautiful arcaded bulk of Union Station. Her father had brought her here several times to drink in the history of the last of America's great train stations, a mix of mission and Art Deco style filled with colorful tile and wrought iron and all that sad ambience of would-be movie stars lugging suitcase up the long, tiled halls on their first arrival into the town of dreams.

Maeve was beginning to worry about which street El Mercado was on. She was pretty sure it wasn't Chavez, which she knew had been called Brooklyn Avenue until recently, from the days when the whole area of Boyle Heights had been Jewish. She thought El Mercado was on First, but wasn't sure and decided it was best to continue on Chavez until she got deep into East LA and then she could circle back on First. If she didn't apologize for it, Ornetta might not even notice she was circling around lamely.

Dec 20 AM
He's coming. I know it. This hunter of children, of men. I feel I must prepare in new ways. He and the policeman were on my island today. They sat and looked back to where your fishing village used to thrive, and they talked for a long time. I sense him drawing the bow against me.

Until now my actions have been simple justice. But I feel a change. His challenge is stirring up the will to hurt.

Eleven

Women Know

"Hamasaki."

Steelyard read aloud as Jack Liffey flipped several pages of the phone book and let his finger run down the names, making no effort to correct the man's pronunciation, Ham-a-SAK-i, which probably should have been something like Ha-MAS-uh-ki, if not Ha-MAS'ki. Americans made only occasional stabs at linguistic accuracy, and in this case it would have been little more than pedantry. The town itself had become San PEE-dro so long ago, and so enduringly, that even the Latinos who lived in it had given up.

"Nope."

"Ozaki, Frank. *Frank*—there's a great Nip name."

Jack Liffey frowned but said nothing about the epithet. "Bingo," he said, his finger stopping halfway down the page. "On Twenty-first Street in the four hundreds. That must be just off Pacific. Not Frank, but Mary. Could be related."

"I don't know what's got into me having you around today," Steelyard said, "but Gloria's taken herself off, so how would you like to come with me, for old times?"

"Sure."

"It violates every department policy I can think of, so keep your mouth very shut."

Jack Liffey mimed zipping his lips.

"If I rub my nose like this," Steelyard insisted, "I want you to leave whatever's going on and go out to the car and wait."

Steelyard punched some code numbers into his phone, probably an I'm-on-the-move signal, after which they trooped out to the parking lot just below the big incinerator stack on the hill.

"I love to ride in these big, wallowy Fords," Jack Liffey said. "You've got some kind of jet engine in here, right?"

"It's called the police interceptor package. It'll catch a Hyundai with one cylinder missing or an old Toyota dragging an anvil. We in the law enforcement community like the elbow room and *traditional* engineering of a full-size American car, which means the power windows break down every week. It does have two hundred horsepower in its big, overweight V-eight engine, but the weeniest BMW six-cylinder can beat it to death on the highway."

"Let's hope we don't have to fight any BMWs."

Steelyard pointed to a row of police motorcycles, all tilted at the same angle on their kickstands. "The poor bike cops had to go over to rice-burning Kawasakis some years ago. Where's the patriotism in that, I say? Okay, Jack, if I'm going to deputize you on this mission, I want you to learn the basic code of the police: *Accept that which you cannot change, especially if it's in large denominations.*"

Jack Liffey laughed politely. He was having trouble discerning any stable mood in the man, but that was probably the point.

Gloria Ramirez found them wandering like dazzled kittens in a *botánica* off in one corner of El Mercado on the street level. The immense warehouse building was chockablock with two levels of shops selling foods and toys and clothing and jewelry, and the walls were beating with crowd noise and insistent *ranchera* music that seemed to emanate from a third level overhead. Maeve had passed *botánicas* on the streets in LA many times, and she'd thought the name was just Spanish for drugstore, but wandering around the colorful aisles, it became obvious that *botánicas* were purveyors of something far more exotic, like Santería, from the Caribbean or wherever, with all its ointments and magic charms and quasi-Catholic icons of saints who really stood for African gods. Maeve ended up buying a little square bottle of yellowish oil that was called Brain-up/Habilidoso, while Ornetta paid four dollars for a bottle called Come-Hither Oil/Aceite de Hechizar.

Maeve could tell that the policewoman was definitely off work, as she wore jeans and a red cowboy shirt, a getup Maeve usually didn't like. It looked great on her, though—tight over her bottom and flattering where her waist narrowed a bit. The policewoman herded them in a motherly way toward a staircase, and Ornetta held their purchases up to the light from a side window to compare them. You could read some Spanish instructions on the backs of the labels, through the amber liquids. "It clear as day, Maevie: you don't trust your brain, and I don't trust my beauty."

Maeve Liffey grinned. "A little edge never hurts; that's what my dad says."

Gloria took the tiny bottles and looked them over skeptically as they waited at a landing for a large family—squat, round adults, a couple of slow-moving grandparents, and more well-behaved brown-eyed kids than you could count—to troop down off the stairs.

"I've learned two things in my lifetime of bungled relationships with men. You cannot make someone love you, but if you're really interested, you can always stalk them like mad and hope they panic and give up." Ornetta laughed as the woman switched to looking at Maeve's bottle. "And you can rely on your brains for about fifteen minutes, and after that it's good to have large boobs."

Maeve was startled and didn't know whether to be offended or not. Her own breasts were fine, almost embarrassing, but Ornetta was two years younger and still developing, and she felt protective of her.

Gloria handed back their magic potions, and they headed up the stairwell. "I'm kidding, girls. Never take advice from other people. Never. They're always much more screwed up than you think. Even me. What do I know? All the important men in my life have been taken away or wandered off in search of younger flesh."

"What do you mean 'taken away'?" Maeve asked as they came around a bend in the stairs into a sudden smell of crushed tropical fruit.

"Cancer, honey. One of them. Another one decided—or maybe learned—that he was gay. I don't know which way's the correct way to think about it. I guess that's okay, but he was really smart and sweet and it makes me worry sometimes that the good ones might all be gay."

"I sure hope not," Maeve said.

"Me, too."

They emerged into the din of a kind of broad, open level that stretched around three sides of the third floor. There were competing Mexican restaurants with competing mariachi bands going full tilt, bawling and strumming and trumpeting at one another. It was hard to talk without shouting. Maeve swore to herself that she was going to work harder at Spanish next semester, though almost all the college-bound kids at Redondo Union High were taking French or German. It was a crime to live in this city and not know Spanish, she thought. It was like being locked out of all the interesting buildings around you.

Gloria Ramirez seemed to have become den mother and seated them near the railing, overlooking the market stalls below. It was marginally quieter there, and once the menus arrived, she leaned close to help order for them in Spanish. They were all having some variation of the standard Norteño-Mex combinations of enchiladas, tamales, tacos, rice, and beans, but Ornetta had insisted on an extra portion of *carnitas*. She said so many African Americans were avoiding pork these days that she rarely got it at school and she loved it. The policewoman ordered a selection of Mexican soft drinks for them all.

Blessedly, the earsplitting bands took a break on the same cue, like going back to their corners between rounds, and they could talk without yelling. The food came right away, and they all sampled the drinks to see which ones they liked best. Gloria Ramirez ended up with the white *horchata,* which seemed to be a kind of rice water that neither of the girls liked, Ornetta had a *Jarritos* soda called jamaica that she said tasted like hibiscus flowers. And Maeve slurped at another *Jarritos,* a guava-based drink that had a weird furry, perfumy taste.

Maeve was so proud of bringing her two friends together that she made Gloria repeat the story of her Paiute ancestor Wovoka and the Ghost Dance as they ate. She knew Ornetta would love it, and then she insisted that Ornetta relate the tale of "The Revolt of the Rhinestone Animals," one of Maeve's favorites. In the back of her mind, Maeve wondered if she might just be testing Ornetta as a weapon she could use against her ornery grandfather. How could anyone resist Ornetta's infectious energy and kindliness? Wasn't everyone good-hearted down deep, just waiting to get over their feuds and intolerances?

Gloria Ramirez seemed to enjoy Ornetta's story, resting her chin on interlaced fingers to listen and smile. She only nibbled at the food.

"I feel lost compared to the two of you," Maeve said. "I've had such a boring middle-class *white* life."

"Be thankful," Gloria suggested. "*Really* colorful is an eight-year-old barefoot Indio orphan selling chewing gum on the streets of Tijuana."

Maeve felt a bit hurt, as if she'd been accused of weeping crocodile tears over her privileged life. "I don't mean anything snotty. You don't really have to go all the way to Tijuana to find people with miserable lives."

The woman nodded. "Yes. Imagine living inside your grandfather's skull," Gloria said. "Day in day out, with all that pointless hatred eating at you."

Ornetta seemed to be listening intently.

"Do you think he's hopeless?" Maeve asked.

"I don't know him very well, but I do know people like him. My own stepparents were pretty sure they knew who were valuable members of the human race and who weren't. I went back to see them when I was grown up, some kind of duty. When I went to college for a year, I pretty much cut myself off. I told them I'd made peace with my heritage, even visited my homeland up in eastern California and Nevada—and they were horrified. They'd done everything they could to make me hate what I was. I have no idea why *anyone* would want to hate Indians so, and then try to make an Indian girl hate herself. But the Paiutes I met don't consider me an Indian because I was raised white. It's funny; I might just be full-blood. It's hard to know who my mom was with."

One of the bands came back and started tuning up noisily.

"Eat up," Gloria Ramirez suggested. "I'm going deaf. I'll take you guys on a little tour of my home. You're in *East* LA now. This isn't LA."

"Super!"

"Here's Twenty-first."

The address was about halfway across town toward Point Fermin—not far, in fact, from the Petricich place.

"This may turn out to be some distant cousin of Frank Ozaki's. You *will* let me do the talking."

The house was one of those sad little stucco bungalows from the turn of the century that suggested the builder was trying for some effect, but exactly what kind was a bit hard to determine. It was symmetrical with a half-round portico dead center in front, held up by pairs of too slim Doric columns. The flat roof had a suggestion of castellations at the corners, and there were little red tiled eyelids over each of the wide-eyed windows.

Jack Liffey followed Steelyard docilely toward the screen door. The unlatched screen rattled as he knocked. A very old, very short woman seemed to materialize slowly behind the screen, at about belly-button level. Her face was so wrinkled it almost suggested another species of life, and her thick gray hair was pulled back harshly, as if by a rake, and tied in a knot the size of a fist on the back of her head.

"Mary Ozaki?" Steelyard said. He showed her his badge wallet.

"Kuichi!" she called behind her. There was a flood of fluent Japanese, and eventually a woman who was not quite so old or so short appeared.

The first woman walked away with mincing steps, carrying a tiny suitcase. She seemed very disappointed.

"I'm Mary Ozaki. My mother," she explained, with a nod

toward the smaller woman. She opened the door, and they entered a small, dark living room. "Fusaye is ninety-six next month. For more than sixty years she's been waiting for the ship that will take her and all the loyal subjects of the emperor back to Japan. Her bags are packed. She's sure they won the war. Losing was inconceivable. We argued with her, showed her pictures of Hiroshima and Japanese troops surrendering, but they were all wartime tricks of the Americans. Then the streets filled up with Toyotas and Hondas, and what could we say?"

Her English was almost accentless, if just a little too precise to seem natural.

"Are you related to a Frank Ozaki, who once lived on Terminal Island?" Steelyard asked.

"He was my husband. Frank passed away seven years ago. Please sit down." Both men sat on a sofa that seemed to puff out dust. "Terminal Island. My, my. I haven't thought about that place in years, and it's only right there." She waved a hand languidly. "Our village was such a special little place. I grew up there. We had our own Japanese slang, our own street games."

As their eyes adjusted, they could see it was a small room, with spindly bric-a-brac cabinets and antimacassars pooling everywhere like deflated ghosts. Steelyard pointedly didn't introduce Jack Liffey. "Could I get you gentlemen some green tea?"

"No, thank you." It didn't appear that this room was used much. "Mrs. Ozaki, was your husband one of the men who refused to sign the loyalty oath during the war?"

She sighed and folded her delicate hands in her lap. For a moment she seemed to go into a kind of stasis.

"There's no problem about it," Steelyard reassured her. "That's all over with. We just need to know we're speaking about the same person."

"You saw his mother, gentlemen. Can you imagine how she would have taken it if Frank had repudiated her and her husband and their country during the war? It would have killed her. They were Issei— first generation—and they couldn't become American citizens under any circumstances. His mother told him over and over that signing that oath would spoil his chances to be asked home for the victory celebration. He knew better, of course, but he got his back up. He stood up in the meeting at Manzanar and said he'd sign it only if they'd let his parents out of the camp. But the government wasn't interested in bargaining. You take an action in a moment of righteous anger and sometimes it stays with you forever."

"Did it follow him after the war?"

"Oh, yes. During and after. Very much. He was taken away from us and immediately moved to a 'troublemaker' camp called Tule Lake, way up near the Oregon border. He carried what he did deep inside. All his friends ended up signing the oath, and most of them went off to the war in Italy and became heroes. I'm sure you know about the all-Nisei unit, the 442nd."

"Yes, ma'am. Did these friends give him problems after the war?"

"It was more himself. I think it was like a sore that wouldn't go away. He kept bringing it up. It cost him several jobs. One in the canneries, then working with a farm co-op growing garbanzo beans up in the hills. He left a print shop and a gas station, he was fired from a nursery. He'd just settle in somewhere, and then he'd pick a fight with one of the war veterans, or one day he'd just start shouting at nothing and walk away from his tools, so I'm told. He was a changed man, I know that. He had been easygoing, but now he was bitter. Eventually he focused all his bitterness on our missing belongings from before the war, even though it wasn't much. They didn't matter to me at all."

"Tell me about that."

"Where we lived was all fishermen and cannery workers. We were so isolated across the ferry, it was like a little Eden all our own. We had our own shops and grade schools, our own community center and celebrations and holidays. We'd cross over to San Pedro for big things like to buy a fridge or the latest dresses, and the older kids took the ferry to school."

There was a burst of yelling in Japanese from a back room. Mrs. Ozaki smiled ruefully. "She's telling you that the new Japanese viceroys of America will be lenient with you if you don't hurt me."

"Thanks," Steelyard said. "I'll tell the guys on the Bataan death march."

Jack Liffey thought the remark was uncalled for, and it didn't seem to be encouraging Mrs. Ozaki any, but he knew to keep his mouth shut.

"Yes, there were atrocities in the war. We can mention Hiroshima, too. I was an American citizen, and I lived three and a half years behind barbed wire in a wood building that could never keep out the terrible dust storms that rose off that dry lake. However, the country has apologized sincerely."

"I'm sorry, ma'am," Steelyard offered. "You people deserved better here, whatever happened overseas."

Their hostess was quiet now for a while, and Ken Steelyard seemed to realize his best stratagem was just to keep his own mouth shut for a while. Jack Liffey was still having trouble connecting this big, short-tempered, outspoken man with the troubled kid with the golf ball in a ghost handkerchief. But there were probably an infinite number of ways of growing up, and they were almost all plausible. The tiny ancient woman now wailed a bit more from deep in the house, but there was no offer to translate this time.

"My husband never owned a boat himself, but he was second mate on a very nice tuna boat and went out all the time. The owner, Mr. Nishimine, was a fair man and always gave Frank a fair share of the catch. Poor Mr. Nishimine was picked up the first day. He turned the boat straight back toward the dock on December seventh, when he heard the news on the radio, and the police were waiting to take him off to prison with all the boatowners. They assumed they were spies. His family had to sell the boat to an Italian family for almost nothing. We were all given two days to clear off of Terminal Island.

"Peddlers came around immediately with their trucks, offering us a dollar for a table, two dollars for a sofa. Most people just sold all their stuff for what they could get, but Frank said he wasn't going to be cheated like that. He had some savings. We took our furniture and dishes and some lovely dolls that his mother had collected and put them in San Pedro Moving and Storage up near Beacon Street."

"Is that the place that's Bekins now?"

"That's it. Frank paid for six months in advance. It was hard to know how long the war would last. His mom insisted America would come to its senses at any moment and beg for peace. Frank's dad just went very quiet and sad and later he died in Manzanar, in fact, just a few weeks before he would have been released. You know, all through our internment, Frank had made arrangements somehow to make the monthly payments to the storage company."

"When he got out of the camp after the war, was he bitter?"

"He was different. It took a while for him to find us because after he voted no, he was transferred. He became very self-conscious after the war. He kept focusing on little things, things that seemed to me side issues. He kept thinking other Nisei were staring at him and hating him. He lost jobs, as I said. Our possessions had all disappeared from the storage company and he made a big fuss about that, though I told him I didn't care a bit. Things kept eating at him. It seemed to me most of it was just excuses to be angry, and it was probably this anger that killed him eventually. A blood vessel in his brain broke."

"I'm sorry. Did you two have any children?"

"A girl who's back East teaching at Rutgers. Joy—she was the older and she teaches social history and has her own lovely family now with a Chinese man. And Joe. Joe—somehow he always went against his father's wishes. I guess it's what boys do. Anyway, American boys do. Frank never really said anything directly, but he certainly disapproved when Joe enlisted for Vietnam."

"Which service?" Jack Liffey interjected, though Ken Steelyard turned his head fractionally and frowned hard at him.

"He went into the army and eventually the Green Berets. The Special Forces. He had a hard time, too, after the war—they called it post-traumatic stress—but not as hard as his father."

"What does Joe do now?" Steelyard asked.

"He's a contractor, a builder. I think it's his way of making up for breaking a lot of things in Vietnam. He's turned out to be a very good man, very quiet, but he's already in his fifties and I just wish he'd hurry and get married." She smiled lightly. "All Japanese mothers wish that."

"Does he have a woman friend?" Jack Liffey asked.

Steelyard turned and glared at him, then rubbed his nose hard. It took a moment for Jack Liffey to remember his orders.

"I have to check something in the car," Jack Liffey apologized and let himself out into the cool afternoon.

Outside, he realized he couldn't wait in the car because it was locked and he didn't have the keys. He drifted to a rail fence at the side of the driveway and sat on the top rail. To the east, he could see down into the outer harbor, where a handful of smaller container ships waited for a berth in the gray, dead water. A sleek, many-windowed sightseeing boat threaded between them, and he almost fancied he could hear the bullhorn voice pointing out the sights.

Much closer to home, he let his eyes run along the driveway at his feet, an old-style drive of two strips of concrete set at the width of a car axle. It led to a detached garage in back that appeared to have been converted into a bungalow. The big sliding wood door was still there, but a curtained window had been let into it, making the door look permanently sealed. There was a well-worn path from a gate at the alley leading to a side door of the garage, where a plastic bag of trash waited for pickup.

He got up and wandered slowly back to the curtained windows of the garage, but he couldn't see in and learned nothing more. He guessed it could be the grandmother's, but something told him it wasn't. There was a *kanji* written tidily on the door—he had no idea what it meant—and a small clay pot beside the single step with a wilted brown stalk. For some reason the little bungalow gave him a chill; it felt like the dead still center of the world. Just being close to it made his cheeks seem to vibrate slightly with foreboding.

He figured he wouldn't tell Steelyard about the bungalow if he didn't notice it himself.

They were sitting on a bench above the concrete banks of the LA River, snacking on *pupusas*—round Central American bread stuffed with cheese and meat—from a tiny storefront restaurant nearby. Gloria Ramirez insisted they slather a spicy coleslaw over their snacks and wash them down with three more exotic soft drinks, this time grapefruit, mandarin, and tamarind.

"This is great," Maeve said. "I've seen signs for *pupusas* for years, even down in Redondo near where my mom lives, but I've never tried one."

"I have to admit a lot of Latino food beats the pants off my culinary legacy," the policewoman said. "You can eat just so much fry bread and jerked venison. You know where we are now?"

The girls shook their heads. They had just had the cook's tour through much of East LA, motoring in the purple RAV-4 past Belmont High, where Gloria told them she had had her first kiss. She was too young to have direct memories of what had been called the Blowouts of 1968, when the students walked out of Belmont and several other Latino schools and took to the streets to protest the inferior education they felt they were getting.

She also showed them where the antiwar moratorium had marched down Whittier Boulevard in 1970 and where sheriff's deputies had killed Ruben Salazar, a *Los Angeles Times* reporter, and two kids. There was a small park there now, called Salazar Park. And down on Olympic they'd walked through Estrada Courts, an endless barracks of two-story public housing, with gigantic dazzling murals on the ends of all the buildings. Maeve especially remembered Che Guevara pointing a finger straight at her and announcing, "We are NOT a minority!!"

Maeve glanced around. Other than a rather nice antique-looking bridge with old-style streetlights crossing the river, it was not a very inspiring place to sit. A trickle of water ran down the middle of the riverbed, feeding some clumpy weeds that had broken through the concrete. There were industrial buildings on the far bank and a bit of puffy-lettered Spanish graffiti here and there.

"Right about here was Yang-na. An old boyfriend brought me here once. That's the Indian village that the first Spanish expedition ran into in 1769. The day the Spaniards entered the village they named the place El Rio de Nuestra Señora de Los Angeles de Porciúnculá." She smiled, as if at a private thought. "The omens were working overtime. The day the Spaniards arrived, they were greeted by a big earthquake. It was LA, after all. Father Crespi, who was the scribe of the expedition, said it lasted about half as long as an 'Ave Maria.' His own primitive Richter scale."

Maeve smiled back. "You sound just like my dad. What happened to the boyfriend?"

She shrugged. "Remember I told you I had a gay boyfriend?" Both girls nodded, trying to encourage her. "He teaches history at Occidental now. When we were still dating, we used to spend every weekend on little expeditions to the historic spots he found. He brought along history books and guidebooks and old maps while I dragged along my criminology texts, which he sneered at."

For an instant, Maeve tried to imagine fixing Gloria up with her father. She had no faith that Rebecca Plumkill was going to last. But her dad was hard to figure out that way. It was hard to know what attracted men in general, and he'd had some of the strangest girlfriends imaginable. It couldn't be just the sex. There were simply things about men's tastes you'd never figure out.

Ornetta slurped at her mandarino. "Have you got any more Indian stories?"

Two dogs played happily in the river bottom, nipping at one another and dancing around.

Ornetta finally goaded her into recounting a tale one of her aunts had told her late at night in a house trailer in one of the Paiute minireservations in the Owens Valley. It was a tale about cannibal giants in armor that the warriors could not defeat. The women of the tribe finally beat them by catching them in a rockslide. "You can still see the red stain beside the highway where the armor rusted away," Gloria concluded. "That's it, kids. There's no moral."

"Well, maybe—You shouldn't eat people," Maeve suggested.

"Women know," Ornetta countered authoritatively. "That's the moral. You got you a cannibal, go ask the women what to do."

Gloria Ramirez laughed. The policewoman glanced upward, as if noticing the sinking of the sun, and took a cell phone out of her shirt pocket and fiddled with it. It rang instantly, and her face went stiff as she listened. "Sorry, Cap. The battery must have died. I just put a new one in." She winked at the girls and listened for a while, her manner going stonier and stonier.

She rang off and looked at them. "Good thing we were well out of the way today. I'm to take you back to your grandfather's, and both of you stay there for now." She glanced at Maeve. "Your father's girlfriend has had some trouble. She's not hurt, but they want you to stay away from her house."

Dec 20 Late
I know they are coming now. I must accept this the way a true warrior greets "it is now."

Twelve

Where Maeve Comes From

"I guess it's a Commie plot," Steelyard said drily.

Despite all the red, nobody seemed to think this was funny.

"Or maybe they thought it was a fire station."

The two detectives from Hollywood Division had already made it clear they were not particularly happy to hand over a case in their area to Steelyard, but the chunky cop in the rumpled brown suit finally took Steelyard aside to fill him in. Jack Liffey was made to wait at the front door of Rebecca Plumkill's bungalow beyond a strip of yellow crime scene tape, where he could still see just about all he needed to see.

Someone had set up an air compressor in the middle of the living room and spray-painted everything, in all directions, a clanging fire engine red. Everything. The rough plastered walls themselves, the oak wainscoting below, the beamed ceiling, the pure wool Berber carpet and the big Oriental rug atop it, her Kandinsky and Goya, her family portraits, other framed red squares that he could no longer identify, the Stickley mission furniture, including the glove-soft leather, a low table full of coffee table books, and a little Giacometti bronze figure on a pedestal. The intruder had even thought to open all the doors of the sideboard so he could paint entire sets of china and crystal, too, as well as the mirror backing.

It was all quite strange and horrifying. The room was so thoroughly evened out into a single color that it suggested one of those museum exhibits meant to focus your attention on the one uncolored item that it was all about. Unfortunately, the only nonred object to be seen was the abandoned air compressor in dull silver, along with a dozen open cans of Sherwin-Williams paint labeled "Red of Reds."

At the moment the only other things in the room not painted red were the police themselves and a runner of brown paper to the door that they had obviously ordered put down. And, of course, the obligatory playing card, the ten of Kitties this time, which was pinned with a Buck knife to what had been a particularly nice Frank Lloyd Wright redwood and stained glass floor lamp near the door. Jack Liffey leaned in to stare at the card, trying to read the message, but then a commotion approached him along the paper runner and he had to pull back.

The local detectives grunted and snarled as they ducked the tape and bustled past him on their way out, none too ready to cede even an inch to anyone. Finally Steelyard wandered over.

"Your dog a sort of ugly little shepherd?"

"Half coyote, actually. He isn't painted red, is he?"

"No. He's drugged, out in the backyard. Your girlfriend is in the bedroom, pretty shook up."

"She put a lot of money and time into fixing this place up," Jack Liffey said.

"The bad news is it's not water-base paint. It's old-fashioned permanent enamel. God knows where he got it, it violates the air pollution laws these days. The Hollywood Division already checked on the compressor and it was stolen last night from Abbey Rents. We know there won't be any fingerprints."

"What's the good news?"

"Nobody's hurt. You think this is your message number two?"

"You're the one said he hits you where it hurts most. Mind if I read it?"

Steelyard gave half a beckon, and Jack Liffey ducked in under the tape to read the tiny scrawl on the card: *Hast thou found me, O nemesis?*

"Sounds like he's choosing you out. Is that biblical?"

"Who knows? At least he didn't go for Maeve."

"Your daughter is safe with my partner right now."

"Ken, let's assume for the moment it's a Japanese American with a grievance about the internment. No, let's go farther and assume it's Joe Ozaki. We know he's a contractor, so he can handle a paint compressor, and we know he had Special Forces training. So he's getting revenge for his poor, embittered father. But why me? Why a woman friend of mine?"

Steelyard shrugged with his eyebrows. "You took an interest in him. Maybe this just says, Back off. Or maybe it means, Grab your sword and come get me. This guy does not seem to mind sending indirect messages through family and friends. Remember, he started with Dan Petricich's son and then he sank Dan's boat, and if this makes any sense at all, it's got to be the granddad he really wanted to hurt. Though I found out today the old man still holds title to the boat. I wouldn't burn out a tube trying to figure this guy out, though. All that displaced anger might just be a sign of somebody who gets signals from the satellites if he doesn't wear his tinfoil hat."

"I don't think so. I'd better talk to Becky."

"I think you're learning that law enforcement is not much as a spectator sport."

He walked down the short hall with trepidation. In the bedroom, she lay flat on her back with her eyes closed, her lips very thin and her fists clenched at her sides. Even catatonic with rage, she was lovely in the tight business suit with the jacket off and the ruffled blouse open one button too far. He closed the door softly. At least the bedroom wasn't painted red.

Jack Liffey sat gently on the mattress and lay his hand on her forearm and saw her eyes snap open, a little panicky, as if she might have been far off somewhere on an anger doze.

"Beck, I'm terribly sorry. If anything I did caused this. . . . I don't know what to say."

She rolled her head a little to look him in the eyes, and he saw once again just how ice green her eyes were. "Jack." She didn't reach out to hold him.

"I won't lie to you," he said. "The playing card out there means this was the guy I've been looking for. He seems to try to wreck what people care about most."

"You didn't have to take this case, did you?"

He shook his head. So it would be a question of blame, he thought.

"I think you'd better go away right now."

He felt a great weight fall through him and hit bottom with a sickening impact.

"Could I help clean things up?"

"I don't think so, not right now. You live in a weird world, Jack. You're some kind of freelance crusader. . . . But I can't see you've got any belief system to go along with it."

"I try to save lost kids. That's a kind of belief."

"I know that. I just don't want to know it right now. And I'm not sure I want to be part of it."

He nodded, the guilt orbiting around him like one of those relentless police helicopters. "I'll take Loco home for a while. We can talk later."

"Thank you, Jack. I'd like you to do that."

He kissed her forehead, aching to hold her, but she didn't respond, and he made no further attempt to touch her.

Out in the backyard, Loco was stirring a little where he lay, but still looked pretty woozy. When Jack Liffey held him, he almost seemed to perk up, but just for a moment. "We're going home, pal. Sorry you'll lose the running space." It occurred to him that of all the victims, the dog might well be the only one able to identify his assailant, not by sight—since the guy always seemed to wear his full-body ninja jumpsuit—but by smell.

Jack Liffey had come straight here with Steelyard so had no transportation of his own. He had to wait in front with Loco while the policeman did his job in the house. At last the crime scene unit showed up in their panel truck. It was the same team he'd seen before. The Asian woman nodded to him in recognition as they lugged their equipment past him.

Ken Steelyard ducked out eventually, carrying his silver-backed notebook, like a hospital chart. Jack Liffey watched him walk away from the house with that slight, unconscious swagger all cops had. It was a walk that said, You might have to explain yourself to me someday, but I will never have to explain myself to you.

"I'll take you to your car."

"Are they finding anything in there?"

He shook his head, and it didn't seem likely he was going to share any more information. "What was the card at my dad's house?"

"I can't remember. Here." Steelyard handed him the metal notebook and he flipped it to a tidy page near the front. It was a hand-drawn grid:

Deuce	Left where Vinnie Petricich was abducted, P.V. bunker (Warning to Petricich family??)	Stay Down	1st?
Trey	In my B&O boxcar with an M-80 (Warning to me??)	Don't get in the way	1st?
4	On dock by the Petricich boat, sunk Throwing knife	The sin	2nd
5	My layout, old half, leveled X-Acto knife	Once the battle is engaged	2nd
6	Stabbed through Declan Liffey's koi Kitchen knife	Fish will not live in water that is too clear.	1st
7	Jack Liffey's home, knifed through daughter's photo L's Swiss Army knife	When you go out any door, the enemy is there	1st

8	Declan's books and papers shredded, fouled with Drāno Steak-knifed to trash barrel	To defeat the man	2nd
10	Rebecca Plumkill (Liffey mistress) house painted red Buck knife	Hast thou found me, O nemesis?	2nd

"The nine seems to be outstanding."

"Appears to be. There must be a reason he skipped a number."

Jack Liffey bridled a bit at the ID *Liffey mistress*. But the entry *My layout, old half, leveled,* written by Steelyard about his own tragedy, seemed so utterly dispassionate that it took his breath away.

"Probably a first shot at someone new, since all the second shots seem to be in."

"Another crony of Ante Petricich and your dad would be a pretty good guess," Steelyard said. "Maybe some old pal who's heard what's going on and is too scared to call us."

"You notice that what the guy writes on the second shots seems to be working out as a complete thought? Except for mine."

"Let's not speculate too much, Jack. I wouldn't give him more credit for method than your ordinary psychopath. The next one might say, Tomorrow is the first day of the rest of your life." He snatched his notebook back before Jack Liffey could befoul it any more with his eyes.

"I'd like to see Maeve, if you could drop me. She can take me back to my car. It's not much out of your way, just off the freeway at Gage."

"I'm not running a taxi service."

"As a friend."

Ken Steelyard seemed about to say something, but subsided as he belted in and started the big car.

"We've got something else now," Jack Liffey said.

"What's that?"

"A witness. He's not a bloodhound, but his nose is a lot better than ours."

Steelyard's eyes flickered across to the groggy dog. "Right, right. When he wakes up, let's take him to see Joe Ozaki." He nodded thoughtfully. "To make it stick we'll need something like a lineup, a smellup. I'll get a couple of Jap cops to volunteer." He reached over and ruffled Loco's neck. "Of course, he might have been darted from long range and not smelled the perp coming. We didn't find any half-chewed T-bones."

"Could it wait until tomorrow? He's out of it, and I've had enough excitement for one day." Jack Liffey had been noticing how short of breath he was. Emotion exhausted him as thoroughly as exertion. It was still a month before the promised date to discuss reinflating the lung. He was experiencing the first throes of depression, too, no matter how hard he tried not to think of Rebecca's voice. Back to his own dismal condo.

"I think the address his mother gave us is just a letter drop, anyway," Steelyard said. "I'll try to track him down through the building department, if he really is a contractor."

"It looks like he can paint," Jack Liffey said.

Just before Steelyard got on the Harbor Freeway, they saw a barefoot man on the embankment wearing a full deerskin tied over his shoulders, the antlers and head dangling behind like a hood. He was selling geraniums that appeared to be wrapped in something like opened condoms. He must have plucked the flowers from some nearby yard. The freeway access lights were on, and there was a long line of cars waiting to get on, but there did not seem to be any rush to buy the geraniums.

They were playing Parcheesi in the living room when Steelyard dropped him off without stopping. Maeve and Ornetta were partnered off against Bancroft Davis and the policewoman. Or maybe they were four separate players. He didn't know if you partnered up in Parcheesi or not. It had been a long time. Loco was still groggy, and Jack Liffey set him down gently in the backyard.

Gloria Ramirez took him aside and said she already had a pretty good idea of what had happened at Rebecca's from a cell call, but she hadn't told the girls. Jack Liffey took Maeve out onto the front porch, and they settled onto an old glider and swung lightly. Maeve could tell something was up.

"I hope this isn't about the birds and the bees, Dad."

He smiled for a moment. She'd walked in on him once with Marlena in what used to be called a compromising position, and later she had joked with him about a whole health science class at her high school devoted to oral sex, presumably to let him know that she hadn't been shocked. But he could tell she had been.

"Do you think the guys are the bees and the girls are the birds?" Jack Liffey asked. "The saying never made much sense to me."

"I think it's just supposed to suggest nature and all that."

"It's the *all that* that causes so much trouble. Have you been dating anyone since Fariborz went back to Iran? I haven't asked in a while."

"We just hang out, my friends and I. No sex now."

"Ummm," was all he could think to say. It was peaceful there in the glider, so he let things stay quiet for a while. South-Central was itself unusually quiet, with only a bit of traffic noise from Vermont, two blocks away, and some happy-kid sounds from small boys playing with a Nerf football up the block. The supertall palm trees on the street were clocking back and forth at the top in a gusty breeze. They all leaned permanently eastward, away from the sea.

"This guy who's been causing all the trouble," he started, "the guy with the Kitty cards. He's made a mess of Rebecca's place. He sprayed red paint on everything. The whole interior and just about all her expensive possessions. She's pretty upset." Wait for it, he thought, here it comes, as Maeve watched him. "We talked a little, and I kind of sense I might not be asked back."

"Fine," Maeve said nonchalantly.

He knew Maeve had always had something against Rebecca, but he had no idea it was this strong. "Easy for you to say."

"Yes, easy for me. She's never been good for you, Dad. She wasn't. She's a snob and a manipulator, and she would have dumped you like a big bag of doorknobs in a minute for some rich bigwig."

That appraisal unsettled him a bit. It was amazing how much antipathy Maeve had built up without him realizing it. "You shouldn't be saying this, you know. If Becky and I get back together, you'll be embarrassed."

"No, I won't. I feel what I feel, Dad. You deserve a lot better than that conceited skinny witch."

"Anyway, I needed to warn you not to go back to Larchmont for now. I'll be staying in Culver City again."

"That's fine with me, but how? Where's your car?"

"I left it down in San Pedro when I rode up to Beck's with the cops. I'll need a ride."

She smiled, but at the same time there was a nearly transparent suggestion of the shifting of some hidden gearbox. She wasn't skillful enough to hide it from him yet, and for that he was thankful.

"Gloria is going back to San Pedro real soon, to go to work. I'll bet you can catch a ride with her."

There was merit in the idea, he saw that. He would just as soon keep Maeve away from the harbor, as far out of things as possible, but something else was afoot in her teenage brain. "Have you got some reason for not giving me a ride?"

"Dad! Check it out. Gloria Ramirez is a wonderful woman. I think you'd really like . . . talking to her. Did you know she's actually a Paiute Indian?"

He started laughing, and the hilarity almost got the better of him, ballooning up into the empty space that so much tension had left behind. His daughter the matchmaker.

"It's a bit soon, don't you think?"

"Keep it in mind."

He didn't want to talk about it anymore—the laughter hurt his lungs. He sniffed the air. "You're wearing a new perfume."

"Uh-huh."

"Reminds me of the sixties. Is it musk?"

"Patchouli oil."

"They're hard to tell apart."

"Not really, but it seems to attract more mosquitoes than men."

"Good; keep it up." He let her swing the glider a few times in silence. He was happy he felt at peace with Maeve. There were probably a lot of fathers and sixteen-year-old daughters who weren't even on speaking terms. "Hon, I know you want to visit your grandfather, but I'd like you to stay out of San Pedro for a couple more days. I think this will all clear up pretty soon."

"Have they caught the guy?"

"They're pretty sure who he is, and it's just a matter of time now. You know, as badly as he's damaged property, he's never really hurt anybody. I know it sounds like a cliché, but I think it might be a cry for help."

"You're not going to try to find him by yourself, are you? To help him out?"

He could hear the disquiet in her voice and sense her disapproval, and it was all he could do to formulate a lie in front of her, but he found that he still knew how. "No, no."

Dec 20 Later
The answers you need to collect always lie where you are least at home. Misgivings surround me now, and they must not. I have only done my duty, I know that. I learn a little of my adversary and I begin to respect him. He shows filial piety. It comes into conflict with my filial piety. So difficult in both our cases.

Tariki suggests reliance on the strength and compassion of the Buddha. *Jiriki* suggests self-reliance. No one has ever reconciled this question. I wonder if the detective and I shall meet and if it will be on the field of arms?

"I want to thank you for looking after the girls. Maeve's a compulsive hugger, but that was a really sincere one she gave you. I can tell she likes you."

"They're both great," Gloria Ramirez said. "Your daughter's a real treat, and Ornetta's something else, really a once-in-a-lifetime girl. I think I regret more and more missing out on that. I love kids."

"You never had kids?"

Her face clouded as she drove the purple RAV-4, and he wondered if he shouldn't have asked. "I had a number of miscarriages," she said eventually. "And now the plumbing's been removed. I didn't really tell Ken how far it all went."

"I'm sorry. Steelyard must be a handful as a partner."

She said nothing, and he realized there were always multiple layers of loyalty at work in any police department. "He's my T.O. But I don't think he has the presence of mind these days to peek around the corner of his own problems to see if I might have any. I'm only saying this because I know you're an old friend of his. He's always talked very fondly of you. You wouldn't think he ever had any other friends at all in school."

"He talked about me, even before these past few days?"

"Yes."

"I'll be damned. We knew each other in grade school, but I thought it kind of ended there. I was no good at sports, and that's terribly important at that age, and Ken . . . well, I swear you'd never know it's the same guy now. He lived in a kind of fragile fantasy world to protect himself. Family stuff. Stepdad, disapproval at home, etc., etc."

It made him feel funny that Ken Steelyard had reminisced about him so much when he'd barely thought of Steelyard for decades. She fell silent, and he reflected on loss and how so many people seemed unable to deal with it. He wondered if he'd always cut his own losses too easily, just let himself walk away. Even losing Rebecca wasn't bothering him that much—though nothing was certain, and it might hit him much harder if it really came home to him that it was a permanent break. He'd certainly taken the earlier split with Marlena hard.

"I think you're straining your nurture genes on Steelyard," he said.

She laughed softly. "I doubt if he even notices."

"You're a Native American." Maeve's clumsy matchmaking couldn't help but interest him a little and he looked at the woman with a different eye. She was in her midforties, with glossy black hair and piercing black eyes, a little stout, but she looked fit—maybe the city required that cops exercise. He imagined there wouldn't be much give if he were to press a forefinger into her taut flank. The thought almost made him do it, and he couldn't help picturing a startled reaction, maybe even drawing down on him with some snub-nosed pistol whisked off her thigh.

She shrugged with one shoulder. "I was adopted and raised thinking I was a Latina. You can't really ever get it all back, but lately I've become interested in who I might have been. My mom was from Lone Pine, but her family was northern Paiute, probably from up near Carson City."

"Native Americans are the only really innocent people in the country."

She made a face. "Indians did some pretty nasty stuff to one another, Jack. You're not really thinking guilt or innocence is inherited, are you?"

"No. But that doesn't mean atonement for what happened is excluded."

"Like affirmative action, you mean?"

"You know, some of the cops I've met—it would take affirmative action to get them into the human race."

She laughed to herself for a moment, but whatever it was, it tailed off quickly.

They were coming down the Harbor Freeway, through the smelly areas around the refineries and sloughs and sewage settling ponds of Carson and Wilmington.

"Indians are in worse shape than blacks, you know," she said. "I've been to two powwows, watching them carefully, and, given all the money in the world and a complete ban on alcohol, I still don't know what you could do to make things right. Everybody enjoyed the dancing—they were probably doing steps that were thousands of years old—and I suppose for some of those folks, at least for one evening, they were out from under the big, smothering weight of the white culture. But you can't dance the Rain Dance the rest of your life. And you sure can't hunt buffalo anymore."

"In my experience," Jack Liffey said, and then he realized with horror that he was about to quote Rebecca Plumkill. He paused, but went ahead anyway, "a lot of the big problems just don't have solutions. People do what they can, and you've got to honor that."

She glanced over at him, maybe actually seeing him for the first time. "I think I can see where Maeve comes from."

Thirteen

Awaken from Dreams

He had to try four stores before he found one, a Rite-Aid along Gaffey, that sold playing cards, ordinary Bicycles in a single slightly soiled box that looked like it had been picked up and fingered dubiously many times. They had a cheap little penknife in a blister package, too. Jack Liffey took his purchases back down to Twenty-first with him and parked two doors up from the house, where he stripped the cellophane to break into the deck. He may as well start with the deuce, he thought. It had the most writing space, too. He had to fight his ballpoint to get it to work on the slick surface, but finally he managed to print:

Let's talk.
Back at 8.
No hassle, no cops.

He carried the scribbled-upon deuce of spades to the converted garage behind the Ozaki bungalow and pinned it to the door beside the *kanji* with a jab of the cheap penknife. He had to admit it gave him a small twinge of amusement. It was a message that Joe, if it was Joe, was certainly going to recognize. But he had no way of knowing whether he'd come back at eight to face a sawed-off shotgun, or an exotic killing knife with finger loops, or just an empty cottage. He had an intuition that it was worth a try to get through to the man, whose acts of destruction had so far been directed entirely toward material things. Of course, it was possible that the occupant of the converted garage was an innocent student from the community college or an itinerant seaman and he would have some red-faced explaining to do. But he doubted it.

Gloria found him hard at work, implausibly, at the one state-of-the-art desktop computer they set aside for detectives. It had Internet access on a T-1 line and its own printer, all on a rolling cart in the corner of the common room they called the Playpen. But woe to him who actually moved it. There was a sign-up sheet full of priority codes, and a column for comments that were largely rude expletives. Steelyard rarely used the computer, and the way he hammered now was a bit too rough, like a boxer asked to stuff envelopes.

"Downloading porn is against department policy," she suggested as she entered the Playpen.

"I never understood looking at pictures of pussies," Steelyard said. "Licking a computer screen doesn't do a damn thing for me. I think we got this Kitty card perp narrowed down, but the guy is damn cagey. He uses one of those commercial postbox houses that's got a regular street address and no box numbers so it sounds like a residence. And he's never slipped up once, all the official glop he's had to fill out in the last five years as a contractor. We'll need a court order to open up their books, but I got me an intuition it'll be a waste of time. I bet he's got another layer or two of security. Anybody this guarded's got something to hide, that's for sure. Take a look at the military record the army sent me."

She sat on the edge of a table and opened a stiff FedEx envelope that contained a very thin file of Xerox copies. She saw a black-and-white photograph of a young, scowling Japanese American, date-stamped April 12, 1968. There was a copy of an index card with the name—Joseph Soto Ozaki, date of birth in 1949, his height and weight, 5-10 and 145. A slip of paper listed his date of induction into the Army—April 10, 1968—and his assignment to basic training at Fort Ord. In the corner of the card was written *census* and *B-57*. There was nothing else, no description of any further training, no record of service of any kind, not even a separation order. One large pink Post-it signed with a scrawl said, *Sorry, folks. I've never seen anything like this. Mice got to his records, I guess. No DD214.*

"Mice, huh," she said.

"*Spook* mice; count on it. One of the knives he used was a K-bar, a Special Forces thing. This guy was probably trained for the Berets and then plucked out for other stuff."

"What's this *census* and *B-57*?"

"I called a guy uptown who knows stuff like that, and he was astonished that slipped through. They're euphemisms. When these guys used the word *census* back then, it was a verb, and what they meant was fingering some population group, killing everybody in the group, and then counting the bodies. 'Census the village elders in District II-A.' It was a funny time, Vietnam."

" 'Funny'?"

"Not funny ha ha, funny peculiar. The B-57 was a designation that was supposedly for guys stuck into an administrative unit of the Special Forces. It was actually for guys yanked off the army books completely for special ops under CIA control. Basically, that means Operation Phoenix."

"What's that?"

"No shit? You haven't heard of it? It was a CIA program to assassinate just about every teacher, doctor, and village official in what they called 'enemy areas' of South Vietnam, every goddamn civilian who might be of any use to the Viet Cong—the 'infrastructure,' as they called it, as if these guys were just a bunch of bridges and roads. The CIA put in requisitions for the nastiest Navy SEALS and Berets and Recon Marines and added some psychopaths of their own. We don't talk about Phoenix a lot these days, but it's pretty much public record that they assassinated about forty thousand civilians.

"Some of these Phoenix guys may be okay back in the world now, sitting happily in a bank or something, but some of them are real scary. I knew a guy once, he spent the war lying in rice paddies breathing trough a straw, his M-16 wrapped in plastic and the barrel taped over. He rose up from time to time and, if some poor medic or village elder was ambling along the path, he shot him. Last I heard this guy was caught up in a lot of S & M out in Wyoming someplace, getting himself bundled up in Saran Wrap and stabbed with burning cigarettes. I can't even guess what shit like that does to your psyche."

"Ken, at the risk of sounding fatuous, I just can't comprehend stuff like this. Maybe it's because I can't imagine a woman doing any of it."

"I can. My wife would have lain years in a pool of snakes and spiders for one clean chance to gut-shoot me. I'm not trying to make some kind of political statement here, Glor. War is dirty, and we were as dirty as anybody. I just want you to know who we might be up against and how this guy gets into houses that have state-of-the-art alarm systems. Nothing is safe from a guy like this."

"There must be another way to go, to find him."

He made one last ham-fisted stab at downloading something and then seemed to give up. "Yeah, I suppose we could stand at Twelfth and Gaffey and stop every Jap who goes into Vons for a loaf of bread. I don't know. He's a licensed contractor, but according to the building permits people, he's had nothing going for months. I already asked for a trace on his mom's phone. I'm not putting a car in front of the house. He laughed at the one we had at Declan Liffey's. We get nowhere underestimating this guy, believe me. Pretend he can make himself invisible and walk through walls."

"What about his Kitty card number nine? I hear we think it's out there somewhere."

"Nobody's reported it. My guess is it's a pal of the other guys, and he's so scared right now he's driving real fast toward Penobscot, Maine."

"Jack Liffey knows something more than he's letting on. Maybe about Ozaki."

That got Steelyard's attention, and he swiveled in the chair to face her. "What? Is he after Ozaki on his own?"

"If I knew, I'd tell you," she said. "What do you know about Jack?"

He sighed. "When we were kids, and I was in a bad way, he gave me the benefit of the doubt and nobody else did. That's worth a lot in my book."

"What else? In general."

"He was a brain, but he never seemed to use it for anything in school. I'd guess he did just enough work in the sixth grade to squeak by. I'm pretty sure he didn't have girlfriends then." He puffed out a breath. "It's a pretty restricted world, Glor, the sixth grade. What else can I say? Neither of us liked kickball or dodgeball. We made up games. We hung out down at the harbor sometimes. We caught crawdads in the park. He said my mom was nice when everybody else was secretly calling her a roundheels because she was divorced and dated guys."

"He told me you didn't have much contact after grade school."

The vice detectives Cole and Buchan looked in the door to the Playpen all of a sudden. "Hi, kids," Cole said. "Oh, nice bra, Sarge."

"What the hell are you talking about?" Gloria Ramirez shot back.

"I watch the ads, see how the straps go and shit, you can never be too observant in the police biz. It shows under your blouse there, a Maidenform cross-your-heart. Women with the big boobs have to go for the real substantial bras."

"Eat this." She raised her middle finger, and they laughed and walked on. She wondered how they'd have reacted if she'd told them two-thirds of her left breast was a saline bag after the tumor came out, but she'd be damned if she'd tell them anything.

"They're just assholes, Glor."

She shrugged them off. "Jack told me you two lost contact."

"Yeah, we did. Junior high upsets everybody's applecart. I don't know about your school, but mine was total hell. From a secure little world with one teacher in the same room all day, we were all of a sudden running from class to class in a big, confusing world, and running alongside what we'd call gangbangers these days, terrified of stepping on the spit-shined shoes of some *pachuco* in the halls. Jack and I weren't in the same homeroom or the same classes. Then I ran away for a while, and I got put back a year. I don't blame him for moving on. I didn't try very hard to stay in touch either."

"I blame him," Gloria said. "He should have watched over you or at least looked you up."

"He had his own problems by then. Don't be such a demanding..." Steelyard seemed to get a sudden idea, and she never learned what noun he was about to use. "Or have you got a crush on the guy?"

"I've got a crush on his daughter, that's for sure. I don't think he knows what a total sweetie she is."

"He knows. Believe me. But let's forget all this personal guff. What makes you think Liffey has a direct line on Ozaki?"

"Nothing specific. But I felt it, I'm sure."

"I don't like it. If it really is Ozaki, Jack's not equipped to front the guy, believe me."

Dan Petricich was asleep, which was noisily apparent from time to time as his rattling snore seemed to shiver the little house. The *Sanja P.* wasn't ready to go out again yet, but his wife told Jack Liffey that he was keeping his sleep cycles tuned to night work. Marin was entertaining Jack Liffey at the dining-room table, steeping a pot of tea that waited on an old round Coca-Cola tray. "You were two years ahead of me. I remember you a little. My friend Cheryl said she always wanted to get into your pants, she was such a hot one." She chuckled.

He remembered Cheryl, all right. "No kidding? I sure wish I'd known. I thought all the cute blondes were unattainable, private property of the Knights."

"You bought all that crud about the Knights? They weren't so great just because they were big jocks. A lot of us liked the smart guys 'cause we knew they were going to be something in life."

"You'd have bet wrong on me. How's your son?"

"He seems to have gotten over that trouble up on the hill, and he's back with his buddies. I don't know why they all have to dress like Zorro."

"I wouldn't worry. Some of them are okay, even into good books and poetry. I think they might be like our beatniks."

She frowned.

"What did you think of the kids who tried to be beats back in high school?"

"I didn't know any, I don't think. You want to know, God's truth, who I liked? I used to get wet just passing Per Houlberg in the halls. God, he was handsome and sweet."

"He was that exchange student?"

"From Århus, Denmark. To this day I remember every one of the twenty words he ever said to me."

"There're always way too many could-have-beens, Marin. I think you've got a good son, and I've got a good daughter, and that makes up for a lot of the backseat groping we never got to do with the people we thought we might have liked."

She smiled skeptically. "I suppose so. I could always use a little groping. Dan sleeps the wrong hours."

If it was an invitation, he wasn't even going to acknowledge it. Someone once told him that the best seducers of women were the guys who were the best listeners. But did women have some sort of radar for a guy like him who was at loose ends? "I really came to talk to Dan's dad, Mare."

"I think Ante's in the workshop. I'll look. But you keep in mind that groping thing."

He smiled emptily, feeling like a fool, as she sashayed out. He'd had almost the same feeling, for just an instant, from Gloria Ramirez. It was just a glance that implied she might be interested, but it filled him with a lot of complex feelings he didn't need. It was by no means certain that Rebecca was a dead issue, and he continued to harbor a lot of fondness for that high-humored sexy headmistress he'd been with for six months now, even if Maeve had never taken a shine to her.

A big freighter hooted out in the channel, reminding him how close the house was to the water. It was a tonic sound that took him straight back to his youth. The sound had once been second nature to him, like a train whistle, he supposed, to somebody from a midwestern railroad town. It summoned up the tar and rot smell of the harbor, the gentle lift and roll of ships at anchor. But, more especially, it suggested to him that other horn, the deep *beeee-oop* of the foghorns early in the morning, walking downhill to school into the damp of a fog so thick that your feet disappeared first, then your legs, until you were swallowed whole by the silent wet hush in which you heard only the occasional shooshing of tires.

Every once in a while nostalgia slapped you upside the head and reminded you that no one ever truly adjusted to the fact of leaving childhood behind. He tried to avoid it, but sometimes it sneaked up. Every moment you lived, he thought, was a small step toward your death.

"So, you want to see me?" The stringy old man stood in the arched doorway with a bottle of beer clutched in one clawlike hand.

"Strange as it may seem. Have a seat."

Ante Petricich set down the beer, and rested the heels of his hands on the table to help himself settle very slowly into a chair, as if his joints needed time to accustom. "Don't grow old, son. It's not worth it."

"Compared to the alternative, it is."

The old man smiled tightly.

"I want to ask you about the American Legion crowd you hung out with. During the war and right after. I know my granddad was there, and even my dad as a little kid. Draw me a picture of the legion hall."

"Go see it yourself. The place's still there today, off Mesa, but it's changed some. Back then there were a couple of pool tables with sloppy pockets, one with some adhesive tape where Tommy Santchi tried a fancy massé shot. And a snooker table that nobody used. Snooker was too tough; those tiny, rounded pockets kick the little balls right back out."

Ante Petricich thought things over for a moment, but something kept him going. "We had one of those bright red Coke chests, though it mainly held Brew 102. That was a cheap LA brand, dead these thirty years now. Or Eastside Old Tap Lager, also dead. There was a podium we didn't use much, except for monthly business meetings. The American flag had a gold fringe. Not many remember that technically that made it a battle flag. One wall was all covered with snipped-off neckties from the men who forgot on casual night, mostly guests who weren't told the rule so they could be ambushed.

"Guys came and went all the time to socialize, play cards, share a few laughs. Women were strictly verboten, except the cleaning lady, and one girls' night a year. The back of the place had a partition for the folding chairs and a little kitchenette. Had a nice Seventh Street Garage calendar with Rita Hayworth on it—you know, the one kneeling with the sweater sticking out. That became our pet, stayed up a helluva long time after the year was used up."

Jack Liffey was amazed that the old man remembered it all in such detail. "Some guys hung out there a lot?"

"Pretty much every night for some, maybe three nights a week for others. It varied. I went to avoid the fights with Sanja when I was in port. The wife, not the boat. She had a tongue on her would bone a tuna with its shock wave."

"Anybody else a regular?"

"Steelyard's dad, Morty, but he took off for greener pastures about Korea time. Morty's wife was more than he wanted to put up with, too, a real nagger. Some other regulars. We had a floating rummy game."

"Any of these rummy players still in town?"

He could see a shadow of suspicion flit over the old man's face, but his urge to dip into his memory seemed to override it. "Robbie Zukor. He must've tipped the scales at three hundred then. He ran a tire shop on Pacific for years, gave it to his son Petros a long time ago. His son got the business squashed when a big Black-O chain store went in down the street, and he gave up. The son shot himself in the mouth in his car, parked out at Point Fermin. That was a long time ago. Robbie's on a walker and oxygen now, and just a shadow of himself, but he comes in from time to time, wheeling his green cylinder behind."

"You've got a good memory."

"Yeah, sure. Funny to think, a lot of those guys, the stuff that's stored in my head is all that's left of them now. Robbie and I put a net load of beer bottles in a tidepool up by White's Point in 1939 and got busy at something and forgot. Went back in 1947 and the labels was gone but the beer was great, crisp and cold. So what's going to happen to that fact when he and I kick the bucket?"

"I know it now."

"Son of a bitch, soon your mind is about all there'll be of old Robbie Zukor."

"Tell me about those plates that disappeared from your boat."

That seemed to do it for the confiding. It was like a roll-down grid slamming closed over a shop window. The old man sipped the beer and said nothing, his eyes wandering the room as if looking for escape routes.

"Memory like yours, you must know something about those plates."

"Who gives a shit about plates? Something Sanja bought at the Newberry's and broke half of."

"I don't think so. There's a mahogany chest of drawers, too, and an old kitchen chair from Steelyard's house. What do you know about them?"

"You can kiss my bony ass, Declan's boy, and get out of my house."

"That's a pretty extreme reaction, don't you think? It's just going to make me more suspicious. Why don't you tell me about it?"

"You can amscray right now. Suspicion your own asshole, for all I care." He got up painfully, abandoning about a quarter of his beer, and walked straight out of the room.

At least he had another name now, he thought, Robbie Zukor, and a pretty good indication that something had happened back then that they weren't too proud of.

Marin came in without her apron, which revealed a plunging sweater, as if to give him a better look, just in case. "Granddad came storming past like a PT boat in a gale warning. Something wrong?"

"He's a bit sensitive about that china that went AWOL off the boat. Do you know anything about it?"

"I inherited it from the great Sanja herself before she passed, but, one by one, we broke the important stuff like the cereal bowls and I went over to some Melmac from Perry's Five-and-Dime. I just told Dan to take what was left and use it on the boat. It's got no value."

"It's got value to someone."

Dec 21 AM

A warrior must face a challenge and solve it lightly, make no great effort, seem to use little energy. If you are resolved beforehand, you will behave with uncertainty. That is why it is essential to study all the possibilities ceaselessly. It is unforgiveable that I made no mental preparations for the card I found on my door, a copy of my own, a taunt, a challenge. It caught me by surprise, and thus I could not treat such a grave thing lightly, as it deserved.

Perhaps I have been walking in a daydream. This is a deep failing that I must remedy before facing this man. Still, I must honor the author of this challenge. I must meet him at the time he chooses. A real man does not fear what comes abruptly, but plunges toward it. Action wakes you from dreams.

Fourteen

Bird of Prey

"Gramps, come help us."

Ornetta had a grin full of mischief as she pulled her head back into the bedroom.

"Are you sure?" Maeve asked.

"He's okay. You can't make my gramps's eyes go pop-the-weasel, not unless you go and open up that whole Pandemonia's box."

It took Maeve a moment to register what Ornetta meant, and then she decided pedants were boring, so she let it be. She might even like it better this way. Ornetta's glory was playing fast and loose with her tales, whatever their roots. Maeve could hear the four rubber tips of his support cane thumping slowly down the hall. "I want to change to bright blue if you're going to go for lavender."

"I want the sparkles, too."

He peered in, and his eyes went straight to their hands. "Whoa! Oh, my lordy heavens!" He labored in and backed the door shut conspiratorially. "Genesee is asleep, but that's so loud it's going to wake her up just looking."

They both wore three-inch acrylic fingernails that Maeve had picked up on a whim in a nail salon in a walk over to Vermont, and, after gluing them on, they'd discovered that the nails them-selves handicapped them so badly that they could barely help one another paint them.

"Gramps, we need your help with the color. We can't seem to hold the brush right."

"Well, I got to sit down for this. I sure hope those aren't perma-nent." He settled slowly into the old stuffed chair with the brown Roy Rogers throw over it, lassos and horse heads and corral fences. Maeve guessed this had been his son's room at one time. His son was dead now—something her own father had discovered almost two years earlier—killed along with his white girlfriend by a group of organized bigots.

"No, sir," Maeve said. "They come off. It's just dress-up."

"Okay, who's up?"

"You go, girl," Maeve offered.

Ornetta knelt in front of him and handed him the lavender nail polish bottle and the spangles. "When it's still wet, you got to sprinkle on the gold."

"This must be what vampires look like. Don't you go biting me now."

"I don't got to bite you to hoodoo you, Gramps," Ornetta said. "I just write your name on a piece of paper eleven times and then stick a candle on the paper and when the candle burn down and start to take the paper, your troubles goin' to begin."

"Whoa, where did you get that from?"

"A girl at school from down in the delta, she full of the old stuff. It don't work, though. I tried it on that man that said the bad words to you at the little store and he still okay."

Bancroft Davis smiled. "Maybe you gave him a slow liver disease."

"Hope so."

"Hold still now, girl. My hand is none too steady." He finished one nail and held an open palm under it as he gently tapped the shaker to spread glitter over the paint. "You're right, it looks great. For dress-up," he qualified.

Maeve stared at his leathery-looking hands and how gently he held Ornetta's. She skootched closer and sat cross-legged, waiting her turn.

"Mr. Bancroft, my dad told me you were a hero during Freedom Summer down in Mississippi."

He smiled some kind of private smile. She expected a modest disavowal, but he was often hard to predict.

"Your dad is exactly right, girl," Bancroft Davis said without a hint of irony. "I was a big hero, big as they come."

He let it sit for a moment as both girls locked their eyes on him.

"You got to be sure what you think a hero is, though, you two hero-worshipers. There's all kinds, some born brave as a tiger and some just too scared to run away. Some people just scared to have people *see* them run away. But, you know, what's most important, you got to have the good fortune, be standing in the right place when the big bad wolf start hassling the little pig."

"I don't follow you," Maeve said.

"We argued round and round all the time about this in SNCC. Some of us said if Mr. Lincoln hadn't signed the Emancipation Proclamation, somebody else would have come along to do it. And I guess that's true, a little. Slavery was going to be stopped sooner or later, it was just so *wrong* and evil. But in 1860, it was only forty years to go to the twentieth century. Think of that. Only forty years. Suppose the might-a-been just for a minute. No Mr. Lincoln, and the twentieth century start up with people inventing cars and airplanes while America is still the only country in the world caught in slavetime." He shook his head.

"People aren't interchangeable, not a bit. You can't go and put Mr. Smith or Mr. Jones in that chair and expect to get Mr. Lincoln. He was right there when he was needed, and we're all lucky for it. Mr. Lincoln went and stood up, just like a lot of boys and girls did in 1963, a hundred years later."

He finished another nail and carefully sparkled it, gripping his pink tongue hard in his teeth while he worked.

"I watched some of these boys from the North like Bob Moses, full of piss and vinegar, but quiet about it, and I learned from them how there just wasn't any otherwise when the time came. I couldn't let them see me back down. I reckon I was lucky just to be there. And I did find how to go still inside so I could sit there quiet at that lunch counter with all those ignorant white boys spitting and shouting hate at us. Not many kids today get the luck to be somewhere important, no matter what they got inside, and I feel sorry for them."

Maeve was in so much awe of him she didn't know what to say.

"Maeve, give me your hand for a sec."

"You're not done with Ornetta yet."

"Not that."

She held out her hand, and he took it in his as if shaking it. His hand was twice the size of hers. The skin was roughened and tough, and his palm felt dry, and he held her hand hard—hard enough that it hurt a little, as if he didn't realize the strength he had.

"Look there." He pointed toward their hands with the nail brush in his free hand. "There's nothing stronger on this whole earth than a white hand in a black hand."

Maeve wanted to say "or vice versa," but she couldn't. She felt herself needing to cry for some reason, her cheeks burning, the feeling pricking the corners of her eyes and then one tear just let loose and rolled down her cheek.

"I'm so happy you two gals are friends."

"Blood sisters," Ornetta corrected.

He went back to painting Ornetta's nails, and Maeve surreptitiously wiped her eyes. It was a long while before she could join their conversation about how hard it must be to work a typewriter or cash register with acrylic nails.

Then all of a sudden the door came open. They hadn't heard the sound of Genesee Thigpen's wheelchair coming down the hall, but it was there now, her hands tight on the wheels. Her eyes took in the scene and then lasered in on Ornetta's long purple spangled nails with a look of wrath.

"You get those things *off* you right this minute!"

"But my momma wore them," Ornetta complained.

Maeve watched them all carefully, and somehow she got the feeling that that may have been exactly the point. Maeve had never heard the full story, but she knew that many years ago, when Bancroft Davis had been a lot younger and stronger, he had flown to New York to rescue his adopted daughter, Ornetta's mother, from either a crack house or a brothel—Maeve could hardly believe such things existed outside of movies. He had failed. The best he'd been able to do was sweep up Ornetta, still a small child, and bring her west. Ornetta only spoke of that time in allegory and folk tale, through a screen of make-believe, as a time of living in a big brick palace with her beautiful mother's many men attendants and a tall knight guarding her.

The old woman's expression softened. "When you two get those evil things off, come help me shuck peas for supper. I'll teach you how to make hush puppies."

"I'm sorry, the dress-up was all my idea," Maeve put in. "The remover'll take them right off."

Ornetta bristled a little but seemed to go along.

"Can I call my grandpa later?" Maeve asked, surprising herself. She said it as much to divert their attention from this fierce focus on one another as out of any desire to talk to him. She hadn't even realized she wanted to call.

"Of course you can, hon'," Genesee said.

"You're a rude old fuck," Steelyard said.

Declan Liffey seemed to stretch his neck, and then roll his head a little, as if working out a kink. "You mean, impolite?"

"And more. Let's come at this another way. I'm not leaving this room until you tell me what happened here during the war that's pissed somebody off so bad and scared all you old farts into conniptions."

The room had been tidied obsessively since his ordeal. All the books were gone, the magazines, and what little had remained of any loose paper. The desk had a brand-new computer on it now, one of those Macs with the swiveling flat screen like a giant shaving mirror.

"Some would say being impolite to authority is necessary. Saying your mind. Truth-telling—a deep human duty."

"Deep doo-doo. Like I give a shit what you assholes think about things. You and your pals *did* something to some Jap in this town that you know you shouldn't ought to 've done and you've been letting it mulch since Truman beat Dewey."

"You like Japs?"

Steelyard wasn't going to get drawn into this. Once you let your subject set the agenda, the interrogation could only go seriously adrift. "The point is what you fuckin' perpetrated, Declan, you and your legion pals."

Declan Liffey went off on a tear anyway, about the Japanese being sneaky and underhanded, coldhearted and unfriendly, vengeful and buck-toothed, copiers and mimickers of everybody else's creative impulses. The old fart would have fit right in at one of the detective lunches, Steelyard thought, though he'd have to shift to a more popular target—say, spades or Mexes. Basically, they trashed everybody but nonhomosexual Protestants, even when one of the detectives present happened to be a spade or a Mexican, he was more or less expected to sit there and keep his mouth shut.

"I don't want to talk about the Japanese, Dec. I want to talk about you and your ballooning guilt."

"You've got to let me demythologize your thinking. You been stuffed with so many half lies. You'll sink in all that shit and never be seen again. You got to get rid of that sentimental claptrap and bleeding-heart stuff about people all being the same."

"Legion hall, 1941. You can fuckin' bottle the rest of your crap and send it out with the tide."

Declan Liffey frowned. "Maybe I got nothing to say."

"Maybe I got no help to give you the next time this ninja shows up."

"What more can he do to me? He's trashed my life's work."

"There's your son and your granddaughter. He's threatened both of them." That gave the old man pause.

"The girl, too?"

"Looks that way. There's a photo of her with a knife through her neck. He seems to go after families."

"They oughta clear out of town and stay out."

"They have, for now. Give me a hint here, Dec. Did you push some Jap around? Lynch him? Beat him up? After Pearl, it was understandable."

For a moment it appeared he might actually be ready to talk, but then the phone rang. Ken Steelyard swore in his head.

The old man eyed the machine for a moment but then answered it. "Yes. Uh-huh."

Ken Steelyard could hear a tiny girl's voice at the other end, though he couldn't take in the words, like a bee in a bottle.

"I'm okay, but I don't think your father wants you to."

The bee buzzed some more, insistently. Slowly old Declan's face took on a defiant air. "Sure, come on down tomorrow."

There was another little sizzle and trill from the bottle.

"Bring your friend, too, the more the merrier." He set the receiver down.

It was not hard to work out. "I doubt if Jack is going to be happy about that."

"Then park your SWAT team in the alley to protect us. I want to see my granddaughter. I've never properly met her. My son cut me off years ago like a pariah dog you kick in the gutter."

Now, why would Jack do that, Ken Steelyard thought sarcastically, to such a pleasant old man? "Wartime, Declan. Pearl Harbor, sneak attack. People are cussing Japs on the street. They're closing down Japtown over on Terminal Island. I imagine you and your legion pals got busy. You know, evening the score for Pearl by beating up little Jap schoolgirls."

The old man sighed. "Most of us then are gone. I was just a kid hanging with the men. Are you going to turn down the lottery if Ed McMahon walks in and tells you you just won? Especially when taking your winnings involves punishing somebody you hate?"

"C'mon, tell me straight."

"I'm not gonna answer. You know and I know that's no fuckin' innocent question."

"I ain't leaving, Dec."

He shrugged. "Shit, it's way past the legal limits anyway. Mike Zorotovich ran the San Pedro Moving and Storage just off Beacon.

What an opportunity, man. All these Japs stored their stuff and then got hustled off to camps. We figured they were going to send them back to Japan. Why not help ourselves to all the good stuff before somebody else did?"

"Break a few padlocks?"

"It didn't work that way. It was one big place back then. Had been an icehouse. They just had ropes around their stuff, with their name on it. Trusting little buggers. It didn't even feel like stealing."

"And after the war?"

He chuckled. "Not even after, man. The whole thing gets real funny here. We pretty much cleaned out the place the week after they dropped off their stuff, but I think the Ozakis went on making storage payments all through the war. Tough titty."

"Go on."

"This guy, Frank Ozaki, straight out of some heavy-duty internment camp for the badasses, he came home and threw a shit fit. Zorotovich wasn't there no more and the guy in charge said he didn't know shit. You know, this Ozaki didn't even go and fight in the war, like most of them. He said he'd rather stay in jail than be a loyal American. Fuck him, you know."

"You did, Dec."

The old man shrugged. "He got a permanent bee in his bonnet about getting his stuff back, but how was he going to prove anything? He even peered in our family's window once up the hill where we lived then and saw the chest and shouted at us from out there on the grass. My old man told him we got the thing at Sears and sent him off with an old forty-five he had."

"You don't happen to have that forty-five anymore?"

"Yeah, I got a bundle of dope, too, and some M-eighties and whatever else the granny state has decided I shouldn't have."

"Granny frowns on anthrax quite a lot."

"I don't have that, neither. But I've got a lot of ideas that granny hates, and that's tough titty, too."

"You and your dad steal anything besides this chest?"

"We got in late and there wasn't much to go around by then. It was like a bunch of sharks in a food frenzy, and we didn't have a truck. We had to tie the chest to the top of Dad's old Dodge. Was a lot of folks to satisfy, you know?"

"Where's the chest now?"

"I guess Mr. Ninja took it away with him. I was a bit preoccupied with other things he was doing to my stuff. Why don't you ask the cop was eating doughnuts out front?"

"You know, Dec, I'm starting to like this Jap. You're lucky he didn't chop off your balls for souvenirs. If you and your pals got any left."

"Jap-loving crud, you are."

"If you only knew."

He had a feeling that being precisely on time would be important for some reason. He waited at the end of the block until exactly three minutes to eight. It had been dark for a long time now because the calendar had hit the dead center of winter, if you measured winter by the shortest days. A few houses on the block had Christmas lights, those dangly white icicle lights that seemed to have appeared all of a sudden a few years ago and instantaneously driven all other Christmas lights out of existence. One roof had a homemade Santa-and-sleigh cutout, but this wasn't the sort of neighborhood that had a lot of money left over for decoration, and it was possible such ornamentation didn't really fit into the Latino conception of Christmas.

He locked the VW, walked up the chilly street to the two-track driveway, and then walked along it to the little house in back that had once been a garage. He could see right away that his knife and message were gone and the front door was ajar, just a few inches, but enough to be unmistakable, intentional.

He stopped at the door, making enough noise on the concrete stoop so he wouldn't startle anyone inside, then checked his watch. Superstitiously, he waited as the second hand staggered drunkenly uphill until it hit the 12, and then he knocked. "Mr. Ozaki. Hello."

There was no answer, but he had a feeling that he wasn't alone. He pushed the door inward slowly, feeling no resistance. The first thing he noticed was his playing card with his message on it lying on a small table by the door, the cheap knife on top of it. It gave him a momentary chill that the man hadn't hidden it away somewhere or thrown it out, just left it there, as if it were basically of no consequence.

"Mr. Ozaki. I'm coming in. It's Jack Liffey."

There was some sort of indirect light in the room, enough so he wasn't too spooked to step inside, and then he stopped in the doorway, easily silhouetted against the outside. Shoot me now, he thought, or forget it. He had the same feeling he had had a few times before, a tickle right in the center of his breastbone, as if sighted down by some new sort of laserscope that made you *feel* the red spot pressing gently against its aiming point. There was no red spot, though, and the sensation was complicated by his labored breathing, with the one lung still shut down.

His eyes adjusted, and he almost jumped out of his skin: there the man was. Jack Liffey's spine prickled all the way down. He hadn't seen him at first because he was in such an odd place. For some reason, he stood on the cushions of the sofa, like a woman in a cartoon who had leaped up there to avoid a mouse. His back was to the wall, which was covered with an ugly vinous flowered wallpaper. He did not seem to be armed, though his head was turned slightly and his eyes were fixed on Jack Liffey like a predator. It was hard to tell, the way he was standing on the sofa, but he looked tall for an Asian, maybe five-ten, and he wore unexceptional chinos and a dark crewneck sweater with shoulder patches, some sort of commando thing from L. L. Bean. The sleeves were pushed up, and his hands were cocked loosely on his hips, the forearms looking strong.

"Good evening, Mr. Ozaki. I'm sorry to intrude, but I think you know why I left you a message. We need to have a talk."

There was still no answer, and Jack Liffey summoned all the self-possession he could muster. He had to keep the tremulousness out of his voice. He had sensed it building up in a tickle at the back of his throat. Silence was a weapon he used himself in interviews from time to time, and he couldn't let himself be unnerved by it. It was a trick he knew well, and it didn't usually get to him. He shut the door behind himself and felt marginally less vulnerable to silhouetting.

He still couldn't work out where the indirect light in the room was coming from, but as his eyes adjusted further, he could see the man clearly, standing there bizarrely in the very center of the sofa, surrounded by all the wallpaper vines, like a large bird of prey perched in some jungle. Everything in the room seemed imperceptibly drawn toward him by his own gravity. It might simply have been that he was positioned in the gloomiest spot in the room, but he seemed to be absorbing light from the air around him, using it up in some way. In fact, Jack Liffey had the feeling the man was slowly drawing energy out of the room, letting everything else go cold and dead with entropy.

"I'm going to sit." Jack Liffey lowered himself onto a stiff chair facing the sofa. It put him at a worse height disadvantage, but he couldn't help that; he had to keep his legs from trembling. "I'm Jack, if you like. I won't call you Joe unless you invite me to. You've done a pretty thorough job of blasting my dad's life's work, as you know." He offered a rueful smile. "I don't really mind that. The world can do without another benighted manuscript about the supremacy of the white race. I can't consider it much of a loss. Good riddance, except maybe for entertainment value."

He knew he was talking too much, but he didn't seem to have any choice. "You did quite a job on Steelyard's trains and the fishing boat and on my woman friend's home, too. You seem to go after what you think people value the most. She did love that place and put a lot of hard work and money into restoring it. Though it really had to be me you were targeting, didn't it? Perhaps you thought the damage would destroy our relationship, she'd blame it on me. Well, I'll be honest with you, maybe it did. Though I had a feeling we weren't going to last forever, in any case. I can move on. You haven't really damaged me at my core, if that was your wish. You did seem to threaten my daughter, too, with that photograph. I hope that was only a metaphor. I really wouldn't take kindly to anyone hurting her. In fact, one of us would have to die if you did. But you haven't actually hurt anybody physically yet, have you? I have a feeling that would violate some code you've set yourself."

He waited to give the man a chance to speak. His only movement so far had been a microscopic adjustment of his head to follow when Jack Liffey sat. His face was expressionless, not even suggesting thought, and his eyes remained fixed, almost unblinking. There was some intimation of mortal fate in his motionless presence, in the immense inertia, the black hole that was drawing in and extinguishing all human emotion around itself.

"I think I've worked out that you have some kind of grievance against a small circle of elderly men, and the grievance seems to extend to their families. I have a little more trouble with that part of it. I imagine long ago there was a slight to your family, some form of cruelty to your parents, maybe. You're too young for it to have been you—I doubt you were even born before the end of the war. It must have been something done to your father, Frank, or your mother, Mary. I'm sure there was plenty of anti-Japanese feeling to go around those days. Does your morality insist that you carry a grudge into the second or third generation? I really can't understand that kind of thinking."

Again, he waited to give the man a chance to explain himself, but there was no reply. His sense of his antagonist was shifting subtly. It was becoming increasingly difficult to think of him as a man at all. He was more a malign voodoo god, with something too fierce in his silent waiting to be purely human. His eyes followed every slight shift Jack Liffey made, and his muscles seemed ready for fast movement.

"Mr. Ozaki. I know you were in Vietnam. I think you were in one of the commando forces, I think the Green Berets, but maybe Navy SEALs, Marine Recon. You probably had to kill your share of people, maybe more than your share. I killed someone once, not in the war, and I think I know some of the strange, sleepy hold it exerts on you. There are people who say you never really recover from that, you slowly become obsessed with guilt. But I think that's just the sentimentality of people who never faced killing. We both know plenty of warriors who have shrugged it off. Some are psychopaths, of course. They don't feel a thing. I don't think that's you, because you've gone to great lengths not to hurt anyone recently.

"There are plenty of ordinary soldiers who came home from

Vietnam with their terrible burdens of memory. They had bad dreams for a while, but they found a way to put it behind them. They were doing what their country asked, after all, and war really is hell, war asks too much of a human being. They weren't bad people to start with, and most of them have healed. Time heals. Love heals. Work heals. The human mind is resilient, it finds a way. I meant well, I loved my dog as a boy, it was all necessary, I'm not so bad, look at my life now. Is this making any sense to you?"

The man breathed palpably, the room so silent that Jack Liffey could hear the breaths in the moments when he fell silent himself, a faint air hiss, as if the man had a slight cold, an allergy, or maybe a problem with his sinuses. His hands shifted slightly on his hips, settled again. But it didn't humanize him. The impression he gave Jack Liffey now was of a total singularity. He was without any parallel anywhere. If there were others even remotely like him, *they* were the copies.

"Were you part of Phoenix? That might have been worse for your psyche, from what I've heard. It doesn't really matter, though, does it? You've been home a long time now, and, for some reason, you've waited and waited until something told you it was time to start evening old scores. That much is pretty clear. My father and his father. Steelyard's father. Ante Petricich. Maybe Robbie Zukor. Don't you want to talk about what they did? Don't you want it *known?*"

Jack Liffey stopped because a police siren had come irritatingly along a nearby block, switched abruptly to its higher-pitched whooping, and now, in the silence, a disembodied amplified voice bellowed, "White Accord, you ran a stop sign! Pull over!"

The announcement must have worked, because all the belligerent noises outside cut off at once. Joe Ozaki did not seem to have noticed the interruption.

"You're taking back things, aren't you? A chest, some china plates. A kitchen chair. Are they in the next room? No, you're too smart for that. You probably don't even live here, at least not all the time. This looks like a motel room, a room with no personality at all. I don't see any signs of use. Are you like those

Middle East dictators who sleep in a different bed every night?"
He had a brainstorm. "Or have you moved back to Terminal
Island, somewhere over there as near as you can get to the site
of the old village? No one's supposed to live there, but that was
your family's home. I'm sure you could find a niche somewhere,
a hidey-hole to make your own."

He waited longer than usual this time, trying to outwait him, but
that was a fool's game. Ozaki was simply not going to talk, not tonight.

"I'd like to hear about your grievance. I like to think I have a
moral code, too." Jack Liffey spoke for a few minutes about losing
his job in aerospace, discovering he had this unexpected talent for
finding missing children. It was unnerving having nothing coming
back—like baring your soul in a confessional and then finding out
that the priest had stepped out for a cigarette break. "Maybe we
could do something about your grievance together."

Jack Liffey glanced at his watch and saw he'd been there almost
forty-five minutes, talking to himself. How strange, he thought. "I
warn you, the cops know your name now, and they'll find you in a
few days, if you have any normal routine at all. I'm not going to tell
them about this place, but they're not fools. I think you may need
me more than I need you, if you have some righteous task to complete. I'll let you think it over. I'll be back here tomorrow night at
eight, and then it's your turn to talk to me."

He didn't wait for the acknowledgment that he knew would not
come. Jack Liffey tore his eyes free from Joe Ozaki's and went out
the door with no departing words. He didn't let himself relax as he
walked up the drive, in case the man was watching, but after he got
the car started and drove a few blocks, he stopped along the road
and let out a massive gasp. The tension had left his hands trembling
against the wheel and his knees shuddering. His one functioning
lung struggled to get back to a normal breathing pace. He had been
near hyperventilating. Joe Ozaki should have been a queen's guard
outside Buckingham Palace, he thought, or perhaps a samurai, legs
apart and arms folded, waiting in front of the paper house,
standing watch unquestioningly for some inscrutable master.

* * *

Dec 21 Late

Nemesis indeed. He is not a stupid man, but he is not self-contained, as a warrior must be. He has little capacity for stillness. He talks far too much. And he speaks more from the mouth and head, not the belly. Doesn't understand that something that is not done in this instant will never be done.

Yet there was something in him that made me wary, something that may prove formidable. He believes he has a moral code.

Fifteen

Duels

"So, the seascape is back," Jack Liffey observed.

The anxiety-inducing abstract painting was gone from the far wall, and the badly executed beach scene had returned to its accustomed place.

"Was that other one one of those novelty paintings done by a chimpanzee?"

But Dicky Auslander wouldn't be drawn. "Have a seat, Jack."

The potted plant was about a foot farther away from the short sofa now, so he didn't have to duck under it. Thanks for small favors, he thought.

"How have you been?"

"Fine."

"Anxiety?"

"From time to time, mostly in the middle of the night. I take one of the tranqs when I have to."

"Everything okay with Rebecca?" he asked lightly.

"Sure."

Auslander looked skeptical. "She called me this morning," he said with a studied neutrality.

"Am I supposed to mail the key back to her?"

179

"She was just worried about you. Apparently your job redounded on her some."

"*Redounded?* You've been doing those 'Word Power' things in *Reader's Digest* again."

"Transferred some of its effects to her."

"I know what it *means,* Dicky. I think Becky's pretty much decided to live in a safer universe than I offer. I must admit her house is badly trashed—quite a substantial redound, in fact—and it did result from my job. A couple of valuable paintings were wrecked, too. Even nicer ones than that sea foam. Maeve never did really take to her, you know, and I've got to trust Maeve. She's got better instincts than me."

Auslander made one of his puckered-up faces. "You really are kind of optimism-challenged, you know that, Jack? Don't you think you're jumping pretty quickly to the assumption that the whole relationship with Rebecca is finished?"

"Why don't you let us work that out? She dropped some pretty broad hints. What I'd like is for you to suggest to Dr. Shaheed that it's time to reinflate my left lung. I'm feeling lopsided and short of breath a lot, and I think I'd like to get back to jogging."

"Isn't that a medical decision?"

"Not entirely. He said it also depended on getting my . . . how did he put it? My psyche back into trim, whatever that means. I feel pretty trim."

"Well, you're not. I don't usually make categorical judgments, Jack. But you're a mess, and if you think your psyche is in fine trim, then you're only hiding some big problems from yourself. You're anxious to the point of detonation, your whole outlook is as brittle as a dry twig, and you're hiding everything away in a cloud of hostility."

"You finally noticed the hostility. I was wondering if I'd have to bring in a bazooka. Dicky, I'm here only because I have to be, you know that. You give me bad marks and they yank my disability, and maybe the feds come and arrest me. I want to turn the page and get on with my life. I think I can be of use in this thing I'm involved with. I don't know if there are higher purposes in life. But this is my purpose, it's what I do. It's the best I can do, and I want to do it."

"Are you *absolutely* sure you can handle what you're doing?" He tented his fingers in front of his chin in that self-satisfied gesture that drove Jack Liffey mad.

"Dicky, there's only one thing in life that I'm absolutely sure of. I'm absolutely sure no woman is ever going to look down in bed and say to me, 'My, what a lovely scrotum you have.' "

In the end, Dicky Auslander had given up and scribbled a prescription for more Ativan and sent Jack Liffey on his way. Dr. Shaheed wouldn't see him for another day, so he had to go on living with the feeling that he was unable to get a single good breath. The VW engine started right away, first twist, one of its glories. He'd had several VWs in his life, and some did while others didn't; in his experience, no amount of mechanical jiggery-pokery would transfer an engine from the one class to the other. It was very good to have some things you could count on.

On the way down La Brea he looked up at the crystal blue winter sky and saw some planes engaged in that newfangled type of sky-writing—*skytyping,* he thought it was called. A rank of five planes flew side by side, and some computer mechanism linking them dot-dashed their smoke trails to spell things out fast. This one had only gotten about halfway: "You do not meet beautiful women at the Laundromat. . . ."

He wanted to know where the beautiful women were, then, but by the time he got home, he forgot to look up again. Loco was waiting for him at the door like a real dog, even scratching and mewling from the inside as the key was fighting its way into the lock. Jack Liffey knelt down to give him a hug. Loco seemed to have finally made the full transition from coyote to dog. He had even discovered that the patio door had been left open six inches for him, and he had deposited a neat pile of dog shit on the morning's sports section of the *Los Angeles Times* left out there for that very purpose.

"Good work," Jack Liffey said. "I'm going to renew your contract, as they say in this town. Right now I have to thaw you some ground round in the microwave until I can get to Pet World. That work for you?" Loco studied the frost-covered Styrofoam package held out to him and didn't seem to object.

They waited in the little Echo for a while as a noisy streetsweeper pulled past on the opposite side of the road, making its scraping-a-dishpan sound. Maeve had hinted to Ornetta that her grandfather sometimes made nasty racial comments, but she definitely hadn't explained that he was actually the generalissimo of all the racists. She didn't want Ornetta spooked. Nor had Maeve suggested to her grandfather that the friend she was bringing was African American. She hoped she was doing the right thing, but she didn't see how anyone, even that crusty old man, could fail to succumb to her blood sister's winning ways.

"Look!"

Ornetta pointed along the road. It was an optical illusion: a big factory had apparently pulled up stakes and was drifting slowly through their field of view, heading for a better location. Two blocks away in the channel between San Pedro and Terminal Island, a giant container ship was skulking silently past, stacked to the heavens with bright green containers labeled "Evergreen." It rode so low that they couldn't see the ship at all below the seawalls, only the huge rectangle of containers.

"I wonder what's in there?"

"Everything from push-up bras to Mickey Mouse telephones," Maeve said. "I don't think we make anything in America anymore."

Ornetta picked up a little brown bear Maeve kept on the dashboard, flipped it over to read the label, and frowned mildly. "We're still the world headquarters of stories and shit."

Maeve smiled. "I'll bet you're right. We've got the movies and music and books and TV. My dad said once that we've ransacked the world for all their raw material in tales and legends in order to colonize the world's imagination." She wasn't entirely sure what it meant, but it sure sounded good.

There was a deep blast of a horn from the ship, and both of them jumped a little.

"Whew, that thing got a voice on her," Ornetta said. "I'll keep my own imagination for myself, thank you."

Finally they got out, and Maeve put on her best brave front, leading Ornetta to the door, where she knocked softly.

"Who's there?" a gruff voice called through the door.

"It's Maeve, Granddad, and my friend. Like I said on the phone."

"Can't be too careful these days," he said, and they heard a chain coming loose and then a whole bunch of locks.

"Whoa, New York," Ornetta observed. "People over there spooked just like that."

"Grandpa had a bad experience. A burglar tied him up and destroyed all his papers and books."

"Whoa," Ornetta said. It had been her favorite word for a day or two, ever since her grandfather had used it on seeing their painted nails.

The door came open, and his baleful eyes stopped immediately on Ornetta's face.

"Hi, Gramps. Mr. Declan Liffey, this is my blood sister Ornetta Boyce."

A strange little smile slowly crept into his features, as if he knew something were being put over on him. "Blood sisters, eh. Hello there, Ornetta." He squeezed Maeve's shoulder and accepted a hug and then put a hand out to Ornetta, who shook it.

"Maeve didn't tell me she was blood sisters with a colored girl."

Maeve started talking fast, hoping to bury the echoes of that phrase he had just used. "Yeah," Maeve said, "we made a pact just before we had to save my dad's life."

"I see. Come in and sit down. Can I make you some tea? Or get you Cokes?"

"Do you have Diet?" Maeve asked.

"I'm sorry, I don't."

"Let's all have tea," Ornetta said. "I don't get to drink it much. My grandma says she doesn't want me to have the caffeine and the tannin."

"Do you think tannin is bad for colored people?"

Maeve cringed, but Ornetta was taking it in her stride so far.

"It's just Grandma's old-fashioned ideas. Tea's not for young folks. I think we're supposed to be having sarsaparilla or something."

"Let's all be old folks," he said.

Maeve was tense as a whip, but so far it seemed to be almost working out. When he left the room, Ornetta turned to catch her eye and whispered, "We got here a Simon E. Legree?"

Maeve made a skeptical face and shrugged. "I don't know." She looked around and noticed now that all his books and papers were gone. She'd been so preoccupied with worry about the meeting she hadn't even noticed. She remembered how crowded the place had been, like the burrow of one of those compulsive hoarders you read about in the paper. "Granddad, what happened? Everything's gone."

"Some Jap in a black bodysuit tied me down and shredded all my papers. It was twenty years' work he destroyed. I'm not sure I've got the sturdy oats to start over again."

"That must be terrible." Maeve had a vague idea what he'd been working on and didn't ask, but apparently he couldn't let it lie. He wasn't like that.

He clattered a bit in the kitchen, probably a teakettle. "It was a history of the white race, all the way back to the Stone Age. You got your Malcolm and your King, Ornetta. I figured I could do some of the same for us white folks."

Ornetta's eyes got busy, and Maeve could practically see her pondering things and finally coming to a decision. Her decision seemed to involve letting things sit for the moment.

"All our history books have been written by ob-FUS-cators," he said. "They tell you how bad slavery was, how guilty we whites should feel. They never tell you that most of the slaves were happy as clams. They had better jobs and better food than they would have had in Africa. Better health care. A chance to learn a trade."

Maeve took Ornetta's hand hard and made a horrified face. She didn't even know what she meant by it, but she was just about ready to run screaming out of the room. Her dad had warned her.

"You think you'd like to be one of those slaves, Mr. Liffey?" Ornetta asked neutrally.

"I don't know. Some days, it seems it might be a pretty good life. No decisions to make, no worries. A lot of friends around, singing and dancing every night."

Maeve gasped softly, but Ornetta shushed her with a big finger wag. Ornetta's face wore a fiercer aspect: she had taken over now.

"It seems to me all civilizations have risen and fallen strictly on their homogeneity," Declan Liffey said. "That's my theory. Everybody likes to live with their own kind, even animals. Just look at your high school cafeteria. I'll bet everybody sits with their own."

"I sit with an Armenian girl," Maeve said defiantly, "and a Latina and a girl whose parents had to bring her away from the civil wars in Somalia. She's the most beautiful girl in Redondo High."

Ornetta shook her head to discourage this frontal assault.

"You must be exceptional. That's not the general experience, I can assure you. Europe was lucky to have a whole string of Nordic invaders waiting in the wings to take over every time the darker peoples sneaked in from the Middle East and North Africa and caused a decline. God bless the Goths and Vandals for sweeping down from the their strongholds to revitalize the European stock."

He strolled into the living room carrying a big tray with a teapot and three delicate teacups. "Nobody has to agree with me. I know I'm an odd man out in this liberal-dominated world, and I'm used to it, but I'm not going to lie to you."

"It's good to know what a body thinks honestly," Ornetta said. "Lots of folks, you're never sure."

Maeve hoped she didn't mean her blood sister. They talked politely for a while about the schools they went to compared to what it had been like in his high school, in the late 1930s. He'd gone to two schools in the midwest, but both had been places where anyone but a Pole or a German or a Bohemian had been an outsider, even an Irishman like himself. There had been no people of color within five hundred miles.

Maeve wondered what it would be like to grow up in such a

whitebread universe. It sure wouldn't equip you for dealing with differences. "Ornetta is a famous storyteller," she blurted.

"Famous?" he said. "At your age? That's a true feat."

"Maeve is just being kind. I had one story published in a magazine."

"And she's been entertaining people with stories over the Internet for two years," Maeve insisted.

"A new electronic Uncle Remus?"

"Well, he was a white man really, but he had a good heart," Ornetta said.

The two of them watched each other for a few moments, like boxers in their corners, wondering if the other knew how to counter certain punches. Finally he offered them his wan smile, which Maeve was beginning to suspect held within it some kind of surreptitious need to feel powerful.

"Can you tell us one?"

"Oh, I do think so," Ornetta said, and this was a new tone, too, as far as Maeve could tell, with a suggestion that she would not be hurried.

They heard another deep hoot from the harbor, and then some answering signal, much weaker, like a child replying to a shepherding parent.

"This is the story of the big grouchy bear and the monkeys," Ornetta announced. "Are we ready?"

Declan Liffey smiled gently. "Shoot, young lady."

"For years, the monkeys were all afraid to move into the big grouchy bear's neighborhood. He was so mean and so big, they just stayed in their own place across the forest. Then, one day, two young monkeys who didn't know any better moved in right next door to Mr. Bear."

As the story went on, Ornetta recounted the monkeys' tentative attempts to be neighborly, which were reciprocated by the big, grouchy bear's snubs and taunts, and Maeve noticed that Ornetta had not once switched into dialect. It was the first time Maeve had ever heard her tell a tale completely in Standard English, as if even a single step into that other world would leave her too unguarded, too vulnerable in some way to the old man.

" 'All right, you monkeys,' growled the big grouchy bear. 'I'll have you over for dinner, but you've got to wash your hands. They're so filthy, they're black.'

"The monkeys looked down at their hands and they were truly surprised. They'd never noticed it before, their hands *were* black as night. Of course, since they moved near Mr. Bear, they were all alone in the neighborhood so they couldn't check out any other monkeys. They didn't remember that all monkeys have black hands.

"So they scrubbed and scrubbed in the stream, but the black just wouldn't come off."

For some reason Maeve was reminded of *The Jungle Book* and the mesmerizing duel of Rikki-Tikki-Tavi the mongoose and the cobra. Not so much by the story Ornetta was telling, but by the real world there in the room. Ornetta and her grandfather seemed just as wary of one another, circling, watching, and she wondered which one was the mongoose and which the cobra. In Ornetta's story, the bear made the monkeys rub their hands with sand harder and harder until they bled, and when that didn't work, he made them scrape their hands on rough rocks for as long as they could stand it. Of course, that didn't work any better. Eventually their hands hurt so much that the monkeys had to stop, and the grouchy old bear turned them away and said if they couldn't get their hands clean, they couldn't eat with him.

"The monkeys were sad for a long time, but little by little, other monkeys moved into that neighborhood until there were hundreds of different kinds of monkeys there, and just only one Mr. Bear. Those first monkeys couldn't help noticing that the orangutans, the chimps, the spider monkeys, and even the howlers—in fact, all their neighbor monkeys—had black hands just like theirs. Their hands were still sore with scars from all the scraping, trying to get the black off, and they started to frown at that big, grouchy bear every time he peeked out his window and saw the changes in his neighborhood.

"Finally they called a congress of the monkeys and said they should invite the bear over to a big dinner party and all make friends. But first he had to make himself respectable, like any good monkey. The monkeys all agreed, so the two monkeys who had moved there first were appointed ambassadors to Mr. Bear.

"One morning, they were ready and they stood on the porch of the big grouchy bear's house and knocked.

" 'What do you want?' Mr. Bear growled through the door. 'I know you two.'

" 'We want to invite you for a friendly dinner party with all the monkeys,' the two first monkeys said. 'But before you can come out here, you got to make yourself respectable, like all of us.' They set a bucket of soapy water and a big razor on his porch. 'No respectable monkey would be caught dead with a big hairy rump like yours. You can't come out in polite society until you shave all that ugly hair off your big bear butt.' "

Ornetta trailed off a few moments at this point. Maeve gulped at her tea to suppress a kind of nervous laugh. She was overwhelmed by the tension, but Ornetta seemed as calm as ever. Her grandfather seemed on the edge of laughter, too, in his own way.

"Well," Declan Liffey finally said, "did the bear go and do it?"

"I don't know," Ornetta said. She wouldn't take her eyes off him. "That's where the story seems to stop for now."

He waited until precisely eight o'clock again, still haunted by the worry that being either early or late by a few minutes would reveal some kind of failing. There was a damp cold off the harbor, and another house in the neighborhood had added Christmas decorations, simple multicolored big-bulb lights along the eaves, a fixture from yesteryear. The door of the garage dwelling in back was standing ajar again, which he hoped was a good sign. He had no idea whether his big bluff would bear fruit. He had tossed down his gauntlet, that it was Joe Ozaki's turn to talk, without any assurance that it would work. He knew perfectly well that there were times that a pure act of will could spread like a ripple in the world around you, to oblige others to acknowledge what you had decided. But that might only work with normal impressionable people. Ozaki was another kettle of fish altogether.

If anything, the room was darker than the evening before. Ozaki was not on the sofa. Jack Liffey waited there a moment in the doorway, willing his eyes to adjust. All of a sudden he saw the man, and the same chill shot through him. Joe Ozaki stood facing him in the dining room at parade rest, this time wearing his black jumpsuit. He had a black watch cap on, too, that looked like it would roll down to make a balaclava and hide his face, but it was rolled up now. Oh, Lord, Jack Liffey thought, here we go. He was determined not to talk first. If it was to be a battle of wills, so be it. He'd wait him out.

"Sit down," a reedy voice finally ordered, after their eyes had rested on one another for what seemed a very long time.

Jack Liffey shook his head. He'd stand as long as the ninja did. Backlighted now with a faint outside glow from the dining-room window, the man looked amazingly thin and lithe. Jack Liffey had a better sense of his height now, maybe five-ten.

"There is nothing outside the immediate moment," the man intoned. The pitch of his voice was a little high, but it was strong and unaccented, used to being obeyed, or at least heard out. "The mind that is pure and lacking complications."

"Oh, I think there's a lot outside the immediate moment, and it's all complicated as shit." He hadn't meant to get drawn into an argument, and he renewed his vow to remain silent. He needed to learn what Ozaki was about.

"All of man's work is a bloody business," he went on, as if Jack Liffey hadn't spoken.

At this point, Jack Liffey realized he could mention Buddha or Yeats or Gandhi or a few other rag ends of man's business that weren't very bloody at all, but he didn't. A ship hooted in the harbor, so close that it seemed to be warning of a collision with the little house. His brain tingled in anticipation of something.

"It might seem to you that Lieutenant Steelyard and Dan Petricich are innocent as individuals, but that's just your Western individualism speaking. Honor inheres in families, as does shame and dishonor. Their families, and yours, participated in the dishonor of my family."

What rubbish, Jack Liffey thought. And we all imported slaves and we all slaughtered the Indians at Wounded Knee. But he controlled his tongue.

"If I run from battle, my ancestors will carry that shame to the ends of time." His voice seemed to shift gear. "You have chosen to challenge me."

It was a flat statement, but it set all the hair on Jack Liffey's neck astir. Had he, in fact? He had thought of it more as offering help, but in Ozaki's strange world, offering help, certainly accepting it, would probably signify a kind of weakness. Real warriors, if there were such things outside the stunted male imagination—and he supposed a Special Forces soldier qualified as a real warrior if anyone did—were probably meant to be self-sufficient and pitiless.

The man brought his hands from behind his back, and there it was. There it was. One of those big horrible serrated killing knives in his left hand. A K-bar. Jack Liffey nearly bolted, but he knew the man hadn't hurt a soul yet.

"As a child I was afraid of knives," Ozaki said, "especially very sharp knives like straight razors. I had a recurring vision of receiving one of those sudden deep cuts into my flesh, like a fish being gutted."

He held out his right arm and ran the tip of the blade down his forearm, laying open a long cut. He let his arm dangle and watched without emotion as blood ran down his wrist, through the webbing of his fingers, and dripped to the floor.

"The idea of a knife fight terrified me in training. But once you accept the fact that you *will* be cut, there are no further barriers. To go into battle, you only need to decide that you are already dead. Morning after morning, you imagine your death, in every possible honorable way. You anchor your mind firmly in death. That is the true victory in the terrain of honor. Earthly victory or earthly defeat is irrelevant, a conjunction of stronger and weaker forces that you have no way to control. Welcoming death is not morbid, it's no more than a question of a different awareness. *Right now* is no different from 'when it will come to pass.' "

He put the knife back into some sheath in the small of his back and turned his gaze to the low coffee table in the room. There was a small book on the table.

"You have made the decision to be my enemy, Jack Liffey. Right now you are not worthy, not because you lack the military skills, but, more importantly, you haven't the proper spirit. A duel with you would not be honorable. Take that book and read it."

Jack Liffey's eyes went to the book, a slim black paperback, but he couldn't make out the title, and he was so rooted in place by dread that he couldn't move toward it, couldn't even lean. When he looked up, Ozaki was gone, just vanished, like a lizard removing itself suddenly from a big rock in the sunlight.

He let out a breath, felt how lopsided his one good lung made him feel, and let his head hang a moment as if exhausted. Finally he roused himself and picked up the book. It was a pristine copy of *Hagakure: The Book of the Samurai,* by Yamamoto Tsunetomo.

Lord, he thought, take this nonsense from off my shoulders.

Sixteen

The Xhosa Delusion

The instant the door groaned open, he emerged angry from the graffiti-scarred elevator into the parking structure. He strode to his car, wrenched open the unlocked door, and then sat hard in a fuming funk. Dr. Shaheed had refused to pump up his left lung, maintaining that it needed another few weeks of healing. Jack Liffey had asked if this was some sort of exact science, the timing of the deflation and reflation of body parts, and the doctor had admitted it wasn't. A few months earlier, in a small closed space, Jack Liffey had suffered the explosion of a powerful bomb loaded with finely milled granite—which the FBI had switched for what was supposed to be powdered plutonium in a dirty bomb. Not only had it filled his airways with silica and collapsed one of his lungs, but it had also ended up putting him into the keeping of these two quacks, Shaheed and Auslander, to continue getting a temporary disability check.

Shaheed explained that intentionally collapsing a lung had been done long ago as a desperation treatment for tuberculosis. The problem was, there wasn't much good information on the proce-dure, and Jack Liffey's pulmonary system had received such a trauma and such a dosing of fine particulates that the doctor thought it would be best to let the left lung rest a while longer. Best to be safe, not sorry, Shaheed intoned, poking his thick spectacles up his bulbous nose with a forefinger. He who hesitates is lost, Jack Liffey quoted back at him, hoping one dim-witted cliché might nullify another, but Doc Shaheed just smiled indulgently.

Jack Liffey knew better than to start the car right away in his foul mood—he might drive straight into a pillar in his rage—and he reached for the little black paperback about Bushido that he'd been reading off and on for a day now. You couldn't take the stuff in large doses, all that macho strut and swagger, the toxic pall of a world slowly suffocating in its own mania for honor. It was like a fantastically bitter medicine that would cure nothing.

> It is better not to bring up daughters. They are a blemish to the family name and a shame to the parents. The eldest daughter is special, but it is better to disregard the others.

He slapped the book shut and banged it on his knee. Nuggets like that didn't help. He wondered what Maeve would make of that aphorism. Still, he puffed out his half breath and opened the book again. He wasn't sure why he had taken on this responsibility, but he felt he should try to drag poor Joe Ozaki, kicking and screaming, out of all this medieval nonsense if he could, before anybody got seriously hurt. Jack Liffey did have a certain reservoir of sympathy for this poor frozen-souled warrior who had obviously become overwhelmed by his need to soothe the wounds he'd carried inside himself for so long. And he was using all this manly gibberish for the soothing. But Ozaki's dark hurt scared him, too. The man was wound so tight that he was obviously capable of serious mayhem at the drop of a hat.

He read for a few minutes more, and the passages seemed to lighten a little, one even speaking briefly of a kind of single-minded compassion.

Then two men in skimpy black bathing suits, racing Speedos, walked toward the VW. It was a dark afternoon in the dead of a California winter, maybe fifty degrees at best, made worse right

there, at least psychologically, by the flat slabs of cold, gray concrete all around, like a manmade ice palace. They passed him, barefoot and as buff as professional bodybuilders, with bulgy arms and
annoyingly narrow waists. One turned around slowly as he walked,
keeping pace backward with the other, as if to check if anyone were
following. Before this man turned away again, Jack Liffey caught a
glimpse of the washboard abs that the TV infomercials that sold
pricey exercise machines were always going on about. He cracked
his window and heard one say, "Archibald insists on weight
training on Sundays, right up to the moment of the contest. But
Exodus thirty-five, verse two, says he should be put to death for
working on the Sabbath."

"Yes, I know."

"I wonder if it means we're obligated to do it."

"It wouldn't be right to let him win by violating the word of the
Lord."

They reached the waist-high wall at the edge of the parking
structure, where it was open to the chill air outside. The first man
cupped his hands as if to pray, and, without hesitation, dived
straight over the wall and out of sight, giving Jack Liffey a sudden
frisson of fright. The second man held back a moment and then followed. This time there was a chilling scream as the man went out
of sight. They had leaped westward, if Jack Liffey's orientation was
right, but he couldn't form a mental picture of what was out there
in the West Hollywood environs. He was pretty sure he had parked
on the fourth floor coming up the spiral ramp, and he had no idea
what they could possibly be jumping into. He wondered if he had
an ethical obligation to check, and maybe to try to save Archibald
from whatever fate they had planned for him, but he figured his
ethical dance card was already full up dealing with Joe Ozaki. He
started the VW engine, first twist, reliable as always.

Maeve's little white Toyota was in the lot at his condo when he got
back, which surprised him, but he was less worried about her now
that he'd met Ozaki and satisfied himself that the man's malign will
was pretty much focused on himself. It was now a duel of wills of

some arcane sort. Well, more than a duel of wills, of course, he thought. Ozaki was well armed. But he was hardly going to meet the man out on the Palos Verdes bluffs at dawn with samurai swords. He would do his best to grasp what was eating at the man's soul and try to defuse it, that was all.

He went inside quietly, and his heart melted as he saw Maeve napping snuggled against Loco on the sofa, her arm casually over the dog's shoulder. Her mouth was open unattractively, and she snored softly. There was a bright green envelope on the tiny table by the door, without a stamp. It was from Becky and hadn't been opened. As silently as he could, he tore it open with his finger and brought out a three-page missive.

Dearest Jack, I think it is best that for a while now. . . .

That was all he needed, really. He folded the letter back up and put it into the envelope. It would take quite a tin ear, he thought, to miss the precise resonances of a "Dear John" letter. There was no need to subject himself to the full humiliation at that moment. He noticed some food brewing in pots in the kitchen and had no idea how long it had been going, so he squatted beside the sofa and rested his palm on Maeve's forehead.

"Hon. Wake up."

Loco stirred first, and his forelegs quivered, some ancestral dream of a hunt, then he writhed around in a predator's panic and woke Maeve.

"Oooh, Dad." She rubbed her eyes. "I was soo far away."

He stroked her head, the touch soothing him probably much more than her.

"My car was parked in this really complicated city and I couldn't find it anywhere."

"I think that's probably a common dream for a new car owner. Or anybody with a sense of responsibility. There's something cooking. I was afraid it might overdo."

"My digital wristwatch will wake me"—she glanced at it—"in five minutes."

He let her shake herself awake for a moment, her eyes becoming progressively less glassy. "I thought you were going to stay over with Ornetta," he said.

"I'll go back tonight, but I asked somebody to dinner and I could hardly cook at their house."

"Ornetta's coming?"

"Not exactly. There's plenty for you, don't worry. You're part of the deal."

"*Deal?* My presence at dinner has been traded for a washed-up southpaw and two future draft choices?"

She grinned. "Exactly. It's Gloria Ramirez. You know, she's really very nice."

His eyes narrowed as he realized what she was up to. "Don't you think it's a bit soon to be matchmaking?"

"What did Rebecca's letter say?"

"None of your business. You should have steamed it open, if it worries you so much. I suppose it's too late to do anything about this dinner."

"Uh-huh."

He gave in to his manufactured fate. "What are you cooking?"

"There's water for pasta. It's the round tube type."

"Penne is the smaller one; rigatoni is bigger."

"Penne. I want to make that thing you taught me with the chicken and mint and Greek olives and stuff."

"Then I better break out a good red wine."

"You have wine?"

"It's from prehistory." He meant from before he quit drinking. "It ought to be pretty well aged. I don't know how well ordinary Chianti ages in the bottle, but she can find out."

"Can I try some?"

He thought a moment. "Half a glass. They do it in Europe, at least in France. I think they water it a bit for kids, but they say it stops a lot of binge drinking later on if you get used to being civilized when you're young."

"Will you be joining us?"

"I don't think so, but don't let it worry you." It was partially the drinking that had broken up the marriage to Maeve's mom, after he'd been laid off from his last good job. Staying off the booze was one of the ways he proved his own willpower to himself—and atoned a bit for what had led to the breakup.

Maeve's wrist alarm went off with an annoying little burr, and she levered herself up and hurried to the kitchen. He went into the back and took a shower, without quite articulating to himself why. He had liked Gloria Ramirez well enough, but anything more than a casual friendship right now was ridiculous, especially since she was a cop. He had no intention of telling her or Steelyard about meeting Joe Ozaki.

"I just learned about the Ghost Dance a few years ago," she said. "It's so strange it's hard to believe it."

Jack Liffey held out the wine bottle and raised his eyebrows. She nodded, so he refilled her glass. He came close to pouring a little into his empty water glass but resisted. The rich red sloshing liquid looked awfully inviting to him. Maeve had done a fine job on the pasta and salad, and he noticed that she was watching them make these near-flirtatious contacts across the ruins of the dinner, watching with a kind of astuteness beyond her years.

"I'm surprised you hadn't heard of it," Jack Liffey said. "But you know, in case it makes you feel uneasy about your relatives, there are other places and other times where people went gaga under the same pressures."

"What do you mean?"

She'd just told him about Wovoka, possibly her great-uncle, a bit mournfully inebriated, apologizing to Maeve for making her listen to the story another time. Almost two-thirds of the Chianti bottle was gone, but Maeve had only had a few sips. It was hard for him to keep his eyes off the plunging loose neckline of Gloria Ramirez's blouse, which seemed designed to invite an exploratory hand. Every time she moved, another angle of cleavage was revealed.

"I read this in anthropology back in college so I'm a little hazy on the facts," Jack Liffey said. "It was before Wovoka, though, I'm sure. But it was almost exactly the same situation—here was a traditional

society that, all of a sudden, found itself facing these damned con-
fident, predatory Europeans who had dropped in on them out of
the blue with guns and new ways of life. This was in southern
Africa—the Xhosa people fighting the British and the Boers to hold
onto their land. By this time they'd been crushed in a whole series
of wars, spears against guns, and their spirit was pretty much
broken. Just like the Sioux, or the Paiute, if you like.

"With the Xhosa it was a young girl who had the vision. She told
her father that spirits had instructed them to kill all their cattle and
burn every last grain of their crops, and the whites would go away.
Then the cattle would come back fatter than ever and the crops
would reappear. Like the buffalo."

Jack Liffey's hand drifted to the wine bottle and he finally did
pour himself half a glass. At his nearest reckoning, he'd had only
two sips in the past seven years. He saw Maeve's eagle eye on his
glass, so he let it sit just to spite her supposed grasp of his weak-
ening resolve under the assault of so much latent emotion.

"So the Xhosa leaders announced what the spirits had said, and
everyone did what was demanded: they slaughtered their animals
and burned all their food stores. Then they built large new corrals
to hold the cattle that would reappear, and granaries for the crops
that would spring up. It became known as the Great Xhosa Delu-
sion. Something like fifty thousand of them died of starvation that
winter, waiting, and the rest were forced to drift helplessly to the
cities on the coast or to the new Boer farms to beg for work."

Gloria nodded sadly. "Sounds like the same thing; you're right."

He did take a sip of the wine. It hadn't aged well in the bottle,
but it still tasted wonderful, tannin and all. He refused to meet
Maeve's eyes. He took a whole gulp and the buzz was almost instan-
taneous, though it was probably just his imagination. He felt
relaxed, strong, wise.

She had another sip, too, which dribbled a little onto her chin.

Then Maeve was stirring. "Dad, could you do the dishes? I
promised Genesee I'd be back before nine."

This was a little too obvious. "How much wine did you have?"

"Two swallows. I didn't really like it. I bet I can pass any roadside test you set me." She showed her glass and it was hardly touched. Then she stood up and remained very still, cocked her head back, and with her eyes closed, bent her elbow like a hinge to touch the tip of her nose precisely with one finger. Probably something she'd seen on *Cops*.

"I'll clean up," Jack Liffey said.

"I'll help, for heaven's sake," Gloria said, and Maeve kissed both of them and was gone before anybody could blink.

They both found themselves staring at the closed door. Maeve's departure had left a big hole in the air in the room, and they hadn't realized how changed it would leave things between them when she was gone. "You know what she's up to, of course," Jack Liffey said.

"But you're already with someone."

"Not exactly. That seems to have collapsed. And Maeve never liked her, anyway. 'Too snobbish.' " He smiled without meeting her eyes. He was afraid to look at her. "Maeve likes people who are down-to-earth. Like you."

He reached for his wineglass, but she laid her palm over it. "Why don't you stop now, Jack." It was ambiguous what she meant. He let go of the glass.

"I don't really need it, I don't really want it," he said. "I think I want you."

"If you're going to make love to me, I don't want it to be the wine."

"Hey, what about you? You're half lit." He eyed the bottle, and it was just about gone. "Maybe I'll figure you only like me when you've had a snootful."

"Oh, let's stop this." She unbuttoned the remaining buttons at the bottom of the vaguely Indian blouse. When it came open he was astonished to see that she wasn't wearing a brassiere. He wondered if she'd had implants. The brown nipples were like doorbells, and he wanted to ring them both.

"Bedroom," he said. "But no handcuffs, Sergeant."

"No, no handcuffs. If you're good."

Ken Steelyard didn't bother bagging the knife and playing card, not yet. They had become so commonplace, and he already knew there'd be no prints. The card was the jack, the next one in the malicious sequence—assuming the nine would ever turn up—and it was stuck into a hatch-cover table that Dick Lammerlaw had painted with ultra-shiny epoxy. It fit right in with all the hand-me-down and beach-combed furniture that crowded the small apartment. The knife was one of the old man's own steak knives, as if the perp were running out of his own knives, or just growing less interested in being outrageous.

"Think back to the forties," Steelyard suggested. "How old are you now?"

"Seventy-nine."

"So you were in town then."

Dick Lammerlaw had a clubfoot in one of those big black shoes you couldn't miss, so he'd obviously been exempt from the draft.

"Yeah, look, I heard about this business. There's some Jap on the rampage with old grievances."

"It's December 7, 1941, Dick. Pearl Harbor day for everybody but the first George Bush. What were you up to?"

"I worked at San Pedro Moving and Storage. It's Bekins now, the one off Beacon Street. I was just an assistant, kept the records."

"What a surprise."

"We wasn't so responsible back then, I admit, but you can't touch me for what we done. Statue of limitations has ran out, you know."

"It's 'statute,' bright boy, and I think you've just had a rude message from somebody who doesn't recognize them. How many of the internees did you rip off?"

A large tabby cat hobbled into the room, spotted Steelyard, and made a wide circuit to get to the sofa where Lammerlaw sat. Something was wrong with the cat, and as it jumped up and settled, Steelyard finally saw what it was. There were six toes on each paw, so it looked like it was wearing catcher's mitts. Seeing the cat gave him a trifle more compassion for Lammerlaw, whose own deformity so far hadn't pushed any sympathy buttons.

"Most of them didn't have no money to store their stuff. They mostly sold their goods for peanuts to all them vultures that drove out there to the island in pickup trucks. Jews and dagos."

"As opposed to the vultures who helped themselves to the storage. You took off two, three families? Or was it more?"

"Just two. And one never came back. You got to understand, things was different then. It was a big open warehouse, and we stacked things sky high in piles and put a name tag on each pile."

"Frank Ozaki was the one who came back, right?"

He nodded.

"What did you get out of it?"

He looked around dubiously. "I don't even have none of it no more. There was a stuffed chair, but it give out years ago and went to Goodwill. A Chinesey table my wife took when she left me. There's a big cookpot I still got, one of those big blue enamel ones. It was too big for any meal for one guy and I got sick of it, so it's in the garage with a bunch of old tools and shit in it. He can have it back, all I care."

"I think it's a little late for that, but you might try putting it out on the porch with a big note on it, 'Sorry, better luck next war.' He just might not kill your cat."

The man glanced down protectively at the tabby and let a hand drift to scratch its ears. "What do you mean?"

"He seems to go after the things people love the most. Assuming you care for this beast."

"Six-pack. Sure. Him and me are brothers in diversity." He bent and gathered the limp cat onto his lap.

Diversity, Steelyard thought. Dick Lammerlaw was not going to win any quiz shows. Steelyard questioned him a while longer, but he already knew the answers. Frank Ozaki had come for his possessions in 1945, after they'd released the last of the "no no" boys from Tule Lake up north. Sorry, was what he'd been told at San Pedro Storage. But he didn't just walk away. He came back at them for years with angry visits, demands, lawsuits real and threatened. He made the connection to all the layabouts from the American Legion and plagued the legion hall, too.

Lammerlaw hadn't been the clerk on duty the day Frank Ozaki signed the goods in, so he told him he didn't know a thing. Must have been this other guy—these ten other guys, all long gone by 1945. Patriots, guys who went off to the war, unlike some.

"You dumb bunny, you think Ozaki couldn't look in your window and see his own stuff in your living room?"

"What's he going to do? Some Jap? Nobody'd listen to him no matter what he did. Judges just sent him packing, there was no proof."

"Well, his son isn't going away, either. He's declared another world war against you bright boys."

Fear entered Lammerlaw's eyes, and he clutched the docile cat to his chest with both arms. "You got to protect me."

"I don't know about you, but I'll do my best to protect the cat."

He was spooned up against her brown nakedness in the rumpled bed, and he could tell by her breathing that she was awake.

"Glor."

"Um-hmm."

"You're not upset?"

"Let's not talk about it right now, Jack. Okay?"

"It was okay, wasn't it?"

She wriggled around to face him, and just feeling so much of her flopping against him started arousing him again.

"Men always think it's something about the sex. It was splendid, okay? You were very considerate. I have plenty of problems, apart from you, to occupy me."

"I understand. If I can help with any of it, I want to."

Her hand came out and rested softly against his cheek. "That's sweet of you, but I might just break your back with my problems. I just don't come easy. I'm a cop twenty-four hours a day. I'm an orphan. My plumbing is stripped out like an old house. One of these breasts, this one"—she pointed to the left one—"is completely rebuilt. *And* I'm an Indian, and I just plain don't have a clue how to be who I am."

Dec 23
I fear he may not be a worthy enemy after all. This is regrettable. I wish I could wrench the great warriors of the 17th century back from wherever they have gone, Lord Kat-

sushige or Samurai Doken or Kazuma, and test myself against one of them. I cannot imagine such lack of discipline: his first act after studying the *Hagakure* is to weaken himself with sex, and with a policewoman at that. He should know it is time to grit his teeth and prepare. I gave him fair warning. I only hope he still has hidden places within his heart that contain the right material. Otherwise I have chosen the wrong bird. And when a hawk has chosen his bird, he has no eyes for any other birds that flock around. He dives straight and true.

Seventeen

Innocence

As he brewed the coffee and put in the toast he could hear the shower running and eventually she came out wearing nothing but one of his dress shirts, a getup he'd always found profoundly sexy. Her hair was wrapped up in a frayed blue towel dug off the bottom of his pile.

"Maeve stocks us with frozen waffles, English muffins, Pop-Tarts, and a few other overprocessed breakfast foods, so I can do better than toast and coffee."

"Uh-uh. Toast. Strong coffee with a little honey. That's it."

"Your wish is my command."

"Really? Go out and wash and wax my RAV-4."

He chuckled. "If you'll stay in that shirt all day, I will." He loved the way it rode peekaboo above her hips as she sat. He gave her a cup of coffee, and some honey in a little plastic bottle shaped like a bear.

"I've got to go in and help Ken this afternoon. I already feel guilty as sin being on half time."

"I hope you don't feel guilty about this?"

"You mean sleeping with you? Not a chance."

She stirred around the parts of the *Times* on the table, selecting the California section, which used to be called the Metro.

"It's always interesting to see which part someone goes for," he said.

"Yeah, I realize most of the cop business is in here. But you'll never guess what I like it for." She flipped it open, causing the shirt-tail to ride up even higher, and he had to busy himself with another cup of coffee to keep from getting aroused.

"Not the editorials?" he said dubiously.

"The letters. I love to read all those forlorn voices coming out of the ether—angry, pained, hurt voices. They're always going on passionately about things the rest of us forget or just take for granted. It's like all the dark corners of the city talking back."

"Or like the old guy downtown broadcasting his warnings about flying saucers into an upside-down ketchup bottle."

She shrugged. "You've got to respect the human voice."

"How come you're a cop?" He sipped his coffee with appreciation. The darkest dark roast possible, like beans rescued from a factory fire, but not before the factory itself was a dead loss.

"How come anybody's anything? No, that deserves an answer. I was having a hard time when I was a teen, and it was a cop who dragged me out of it. It seemed to me—in theory, anyway—that cops were there to help. I know there's a lot the other way."

He got another piece of toast and sat facing her.

"I'll bet you reach for the sports section first," she challenged.

He laughed. "Say that again when you know me better."

This was always one of the best parts, he thought. Getting to know someone new, unaware yet of all their foibles and tales, what they liked in life, what they liked in bed, all the sunny promise of a summer romance. On the other hand, it might be nice if he could settle on one person and not have to go through this periodically. But it wasn't like he hadn't tried.

"Mr. Emmett Rebkovsky of Venice wants us all to know that digital TV is going to be the savior of capitalism," she said, summing up one letter.

He smiled. "A friend of mine says that capitalism is the exploitation of man by man, while socialism is just the opposite."

The word caught her attention. "Heavens, are you a socialist, Jack?"

"I probably was once. Right after the war, when I was in Vietnam Vets against the War. Socialism hasn't had a very good track record, has it?"

"When I was researching my heritage I met some AIM guys at LA State. You know, the American Indian Movement. They said they were socialists, but they couldn't tell me what they meant."

He shrugged. "I suppose they just want the world to be a bit fairer, you know? But I'd like to get there with a lot less of the disruption. Probably skip the killing altogether. Are you still working on your heritage?"

She set the paper down. "For a time I thought all I needed was pigtails and a lot of turquoise jewelry, but I came to see that there were holes in me where I didn't even know I had places."

"You may not be able to get it all back," he suggested, "especially if you never really had it to begin with. I'm supposed to be Irish, but I'll be damned if I'll play at it. A green derby and hanging out in bars, bragging and singing. The hell with that. We're all really mongrels, you know. It's our glory."

She laid her hand on his on the table. "Yeah, alley dogs. Sniffing each other up and down."

"Anytime."

Ornetta hadn't been too sure about Maeve's proposed high-intensity project, described so breathlessly, but had come along in the end. After a string of insistent phone calls, they had picked up Maeve's grandfather and driven him to the Watts Towers in the morning, those strange and wonderful two-hundred-foot-tall artifacts of an era of outsider art, broken crockery stuck into concrete loops and buttresses like some mad daydream of a cathedral. In fact, they had been built between the twenties and the fifties by an Italian immigrant who had hardly spoken English, but they were deeply embedded in black LA now and had an African American art center alongside them, where the three of them had just walked through a show of two series of historical prints by the black artist Jacob Lawrence.

The first series—the human figures all colorful and bold, like construction paper cutouts—traced the migration of blacks out of the South, from dead-end sharecropping after slavery to industrial jobs in Chicago and Detroit. The other illustrated the life of the abolitionist John Brown.

Declan hadn't said much as they strolled along the prints, reading tags, but he'd been game to go along wherever Maeve insisted he go. Ornetta could see that the old man's watery eyes were often fixed on Maeve, this new granddaughter he hadn't even known he had. Ornetta did her best not to identify the old man in her imagination with all the vicious, screeching, hate-spitting racists she'd ever heard about, if only for Maeve's sake, and Uncle Jack's. But her blood sister was going to owe her big time for this.

Now they were sitting in the outside patio of Stevie's on the Strip at the top of Crenshaw, picking at their fried fish lunches. According to Bancroft, it was one of the best soul food places in LA, and it was clean and open, less likely that way to freak out an old white guy unused to crossing the barriers.

A big flat-nosed dog, stretched to the end of his chain, was squatting and glaring at their table, as if well aware that they didn't belong there. Ornetta imagined a lot of the things that Maeve's grandfather wasn't saying out loud padding up on them, too, to stand glowering at them just like the dog. But this reminded her too much of that angry dog pack she and Maeve had once faced to save Maeve's dad, and she couldn't take the tension anymore. She'd eaten about all of the fish she wanted, anyway.

"I'd like to check out a Caribbean music place up the street," Ornetta announced. "I want to see if they've got Soca and Sai Sai. I'll be back."

"Don't get lost," Maeve said.

"I won't. This my town." But it wasn't, and Ornetta knew it perfectly well. She didn't even know if there was a record store up the street. She just had to get away for a while from the brooding tension of Maeve's reclamation project.

Maeve noticed that her grandfather mostly picked the thick batter off the fish. The fish itself was white and light and cooked just about perfect. "You don't like the batter?"

"I love it, but it's bad for my heart." He peered down at what looked like batter-fried acorns on his plate. "I'm not too keen on this stuff, though."

"I think that's okra. It's a lot better this way than boiled, believe me." Genesee made it a lot, and it wasn't the flavor that bothered Maeve so much as the texture, carrying a very high slime quotient.

"What do you think of Ornetta?" Maeve insisted.

"She's a nice girl. Clever with the stories. I'm not really a hater, honey."

"You use some bad words about people."

He made a face. Luckily there was enough traffic noise on Jefferson that it was unlikely they'd be overheard, except by the dog still staring at them.

"Those words—they may not carry all the weight you think."

"They seem pretty heavy to me."

He looked intently at her, some mask of civility seeming to melt away. "I did everything you wanted, Maeve. I've been polite to the little colored girl, I've been to all these nigger places without complaint. You can't ask me to change what I believe inside."

Maeve sat back in her chair, as if struck. "So all day you've been hating being with Ornetta?"

He grimaced. "Look, I know there are individuals that're different. She's nice. Bill Cosby is probably a nice guy. Everybody knows that. The coloreds are still what they are. My life's work has been sticking up for the white man, and a Jap wrecked that now, and I haven't got time to do it all again." The fierce look flickered and softened. "I just wanted to have a granddaughter. Is that too much? I want to do what I have to so we can be friends."

"I'm not sure that's possible," Maeve said, trying to be brutally honest.

"Maeve, I am very pleased I met you and found you. But you know we are probably going to disagree, always, about a lot of things. Just like me and your father. Don't shut me out like he did. Can't we find a way to spend some time together?"

She thought about it. He was such a sad old man. "You've got to watch the words you use. And you've got to respect Ornetta."

He watched her intently, as if waiting for another shoe to drop.

"She's, like, my sister. We made a pact, we're blood sisters, and she helped me save Dad. You know, she gets straight A's at a very good school."

"She's a clever girl. Anybody can see that."

Maeve felt her suspicions gather. "People say trained seals are *clever*. Is that what you mean?"

"Ornetta is smart. Much smarter than most of her people."

Maeve nodded and wondered if she was about to push too far. "Do you think you can try to act respectful of other people who aren't like you, even when it's *not* a favor to me?"

He answered with just a hint of sarcasm. "The thought police now. Maeve, you really shouldn't ask people to change their insides and their private thoughts. I'm going to do my best to be respectful on the outside. And I will think about anything you ask me to think about. That's where we're going to leave it for now. Okay?"

She considered for a moment, wondering if he would ever budge farther than that. His presence made her uneasy now. "All right, Granddad."

He stood up, leaving most of his food. "Now let's go find Ornetta and make sure she's safe."

This time, just to take a new tack, Jack Liffey entered the little bungalow ten minutes early and sat down on an easy chair that creaked under him, trying to make himself as comfortable as he could. He would not play any mind games this trip if he could help it, standing at parade rest or mad-dogging the other man's stare or flapping his arms like a chicken. The house was dark and very cold, and from what he could see, Ozaki wasn't anywhere in evidence.

Jack Liffey looked around at what little there was to see but got no new clues. The vinous wallpaper seemed to have come from another generation, the furniture from the Salvation Army.

As he was trying to make out a grim standard-issue motel print on the sidewall, maybe a mill on a stream, he heard an almost soundless *tunk,* like a small stone that had stood on end precariously for aeons and finally had just worn out and fallen over. Joe

Ozaki stood in front of him, materializing from nowhere Jack Liffey could make sense of. He was in his full black regalia and at parade rest.

"Have you read the book?"

"You going to give me a pop quiz on the Bushi? I'm not playing your game, Joe. I'm not. Be still and listen to me."

There was a slight stir, as if the man were about to depart—how?—but in the end he remained in place.

"You were part of Phoenix, weren't you? Or assigned to the long-range-reconnaissance patrols? Or PRU or ICEX, I knew those acronyms. We invented a lot of words for killing back then. Euphemisms. Dismantling the infrastructure. Neutralizing cadres. Reconnaissance by fire. Free fire zones. Zap. Smoke. Waste. Buckle. H & I. Frag. KIA. KBA. Bust a cap. Even 'go double veteran.' You ever do that?" It meant raping and then killing a Vietnamese woman, but he doubted that fell anywhere within Joe Ozaki's code of conduct. His digs elicited no reaction.

" 'Extreme prejudice,' that was a nice one. You knew better, though. You knew you were plain killing people, not 'lighting them up.' And now you're doing your best to invent a whole narrative to help make sense of what this country turned you into. I feel for you, Joe, but I'm not going to play these games with you. But even if I'm not going to do it your way, I'm your friend, not your enemy, and I'm going to tell you why. You need to know this, so don't just flit away on me like the Green Hornet."

The motionless man seemed to be taking it in. Jack Liffey shivered a little in the cold, and he noticed that he could hear the susurrus of city traffic far better than he should have. He wondered if his senses were somehow being heightened by these encounters. The whole business was far more elemental than he was used to. Certainly his adrenaline was pumping. He was breathing, not well, but just managing, since it was still a near thing relying on a single lung. He imagined a nice sharp K-bar in a sheath on the man's back.

"How could you even pretend I'm a worthy opponent? You've got the discipline and all the skills. All I ever did back in 'Nam was sit and watch radar screens and argue about *Notes from Under-*

ground or *Wuthering Heights* every night with guys just like me. In a blink, you could kill me with a butter knife, you could probably kill me six ways with a marshmallow. I know real samurai aren't supposed to have friends, but you listen to me. You've made the whole city pay attention to you, now pay attention to me.

"You believe in honor, I understand that, even if the brand you admire has gone out of style. But all this stuff that's driving you, the whole Bushido code—you can't just choose it, like a style of dress. It's part of a world that's gone; it needs to have that world around it *to exist.* You can stand out in the tide all day long slashing away at the waves with a samurai sword, but it won't make you a samurai. The world has turned its back on all that. Whether you like it or not, it's dead as a dodo, and there are whole other sets of values now. Even in Japan.

"I know you don't believe me. But before you get upset, answer me just one question: How does your code account for something as simple as human affection?"

Air stirred faintly in the room, and Jack Liffey wondered if it was some ancient Japanese spirit arriving to object to his arguments.

"Bushido just got too heavy, man. Its horns grew too long, its skin too thick, its brains got crowded into those tiny little skulls, and it went extinct. I'm offering a simple friendship that the code you're living by doesn't even recognize."

It was amazing to Jack Liffey that the man remained there taking the harangue without a word. His eyes were fixed, and it was impossible to know if anything was getting through.

"This is the world we've got, for better or worse. We don't have clan honor anymore. What we're left with is personal honor. And the first rule of personal honor is never harm the innocent. The second rule is, when you're overwhelmingly strong and somebody insults you, you walk away. There's even a word for this in your code, isn't there? *Ahimsa.* In fact, you've been following it, at least so far. Whatever my father did long ago, or his father, I've never hurt you, and I offer you my hand as a friend."

Jack Liffey stood up and stuck out his hand ostentatiously, a little too palm-up for a handshake, but it felt better as a welcoming gesture. He watched Joe Ozaki's eyes go to the hand.

"I'm sorry about what the army made you do, or the guys in suits. I don't even like what I did, because I enabled those B-52s and their bomb runs. We can find a way to deal with that, I promise you, but not by relying on a system of dead values. You're not exempt from the modern world, Mr. Ozaki. Here, my hand. Friendship goes a long long way in this world." His arm was getting heavy, but he dare not seem to give up the offer.

"Please. You can always change your mind and kill me later." He smiled, but it was precisely the wrong instant to smile.

Outside there was the abrupt sound of hard braking, several large vehicles arriving at once, and the unmistakable thud-thud of many heavily shod feet hitting the pavement.

"You brought the cops!"

"No, I swear—"

Joe Ozaki did an effortless backflip and passed out the rear window. For the first time, Jack Liffey realized that the French windows had been open and unscreened all this time. Several thoughts besieged him at once, and he realized that every one of Joe Ozaki's seemingly preternatural skills had a logical explanation. Like this one—a backflip through an open window. And no wonder it's so cold in here. And, of course, no wonder I could hear traffic noise distinctly. And how am I going to prove to him I haven't betrayed him? Plus, how the hell did the cops find us?

Just as the chatter of a helicopter arrived overhead and a bright light flooded the room, an amplified voice filled the night: "Joe Ozaki, this is LA SWAT! Your house is surrounded! Throw down any weapons and come out!"

Another thought added itself to Jack Liffey's litany: How the hell am I going to get out of here without half a dozen of these nervous Nellies shooting me to pieces?

Dec 23

"Sergeant, you'd better get with the program here. Now, *today*, 1430 hours."

"Yes, sir. I still need to speak to Mike Osborn."

"Mike Osborn is no longer assigned to debrief your PRU.

Mike Osborn is history. Mike Osborn is a previous war. He is on the Big Bird home. General Abrams has taken direct military command of the entire ICEX operation from the civilians. You report to Colonel Freitag at district, and to me for Bangh Son Southeast."

"Can I see this in writing, sir?"

"No, Sergeant. Tell me: How many VC cadre have you taken care of up to now?"

"I would not know, sir."

"Assuming you were inclined to talk about it, how many would you estimate?"

"I would not know, sir."

"I estimate more than 600 captured, interrogated, and neutralized by you and your PRU colleagues, and another 80 or so on your solo patrols. You enjoy the one-man operations, don't you?"

"Sir, I don't know what you're talking about."

"Late at night, with your face painted black, out there on your own at the edge of some gookville with a silenced Ingram or a K-bar or a simple length of strangle wire. Looking for Tommy Gook. What is the spirit of the K-bar, Sergeant?"

"To kill, sir."

"What is the spirit of the Ingram?"

"To kill, sir."

"Then why are you having trouble with this order?"

"Sergeant McGehee is an American citizen, sir. He is a fine Marine."

"And I'm telling you he's a security risk. He's written secretly to a Democratic congressman and a reporter for the *New York Times*, and he's keeping a detailed journal, not just of his own activities but also of yours and Osborn's, and probably now mine. We've read his journal. In it, he speaks of *U.S. v. Wilhelm von Leeb*. Do you know what that is, Sergeant?"

"No, sir."

"Wilhelm von Leeb was an ordinary Wehrmacht officer who was prosecuted in 1948 for war crimes, specifically for following his orders to assassinate civilian political commissars in the occupied Soviet Union. He protested those orders vehemently to Field Marshal Keitel, Sergeant Ozaki, but in the end he carried them out and he was prosecuted for it."

"We should destroy this journal, sir."

"We can no longer find it, and we cannot trust McGehee. You are to visit Sergeant McGehee this evening in his hooch at the DOOIC and neutralize him. You are to make it look like a VC raid. Is that understood, Sergeant?"

"Understood, sir."

"Are you on board, Sergeant?"

"I am on board, sir."

"Do you protest these orders, Sergeant?"

There was a long pause. "I am an American soldier, sir."

"Very good, Sergeant."

Eighteen

Crossing the Bridge

Declan Liffey was slathering on barbecue sauce, and wherever it dripped, the coals in the rusty old barbecue flared up. They were the fattest sausages Maeve had ever seen. Ornetta was sitting primly on a lawn chair, still being a good sport. They had gotten special dispensation to attend this cookout after Maeve had convinced Bancroft and Genesee that it was a momentous event in the history of the Liffey family. She had a hunch the old man would go the extra mile or two eventually, and she was going to give him the chance. Now, if only Ornetta stayed with the program.

They all wore sweaters in the man's tiny backyard—it was a typical winter afternoon, sunny and in the low sixties. The little koi pond was covered with plywood now, and a gaggle of seagulls circled overhead, squawking away, as if warning her off the whole idea, then heading back toward the harbor.

"Is that kielbasa?" Maeve asked.

"These are *boerwors*," he said. "There's only one place in LA you can get them. They're from South Africa."

Uh-oh, she thought. "Just curious: How come you went out of your way for South African sausages?"

"Why?" he considered, nodding. "Here's why. They're pretty

215

good, that's why. The South Africans call a barbecue a *breifleis*. Over the years I've met a number of South Africans. I didn't like all of them. Originally these sausages were made by the white farmers, the Boers, but I think both blacks and whites eat them now." He raised the grill off the heat so the sausages could take care of themselves for a while and moved over to where the girls were sitting. He swung a plastic chair around so he could sit facing Ornetta, who seemed a little startled. He was pretty spry for his age, and Maeve kept watching him, looking for similarities to her father. There was something about his short bark of a laugh, and the set of his mouth, that reminded her a lot of her dad. And there also was a kind of sorrow he seemed to carry deep inside that he seemed to have passed on.

"Ornetta," the old man said. She regarded him steadily, and it took him a moment to go on. "Maeve says you two are blood sisters."

"That's true." She waited, and when he didn't add anything, she told him a little about how they had met and how together they had rescued Maeve's father from the Abdullah Ibrahim Riot two years earlier.

He nodded. What he hadn't read in the papers Maeve had told him already. "I'm a very old dog, Miss Ornetta, with some very old spots. A lot of my spots run deep on the inside, but they should never ever be allowed to hurt decent individual people. It's difficult for an old man like me to know how some of his ways and his wherefores appear from outside."

For some reason, Maeve didn't quite believe in his sincerity. He still made her uneasy, and she guessed this was all for her benefit. But it was what she'd asked for.

Ornetta continued to stare gravely at Declan Liffey without saying anything, waiting to see where he was going.

"While I cook, would you please tell me another story? Maybe this one can have an ending."

Both the girls seemed surprised, and Maeve remembered how Ornetta had left him hanging last time, when it came to whether the grouchy old bear was going to humiliate himself to appease the monkeys.

"Most of my stories got endings." While Ornetta seemed to consider his request, Maeve went to the kitchen to work on the potato salad according to the instructions she'd copied out of her beat-up old *Joy of Cooking*. She swung the French windows wide open so she could keep one ear on this strange peace conference—if, indeed, that's what it was.

A ship in the harbor booped deeply as it came along the channel, which seemed to give Ornetta a prod.

"Okay. Here's the story of the tortoise and the bear. The tortoise was renowned far and wide as one of the wisest of all the animals. Remember, he beat the hare in that big race? That time he showed how wise he was by sticking to his business. Well, now, Mr. Tortoise, he wanted to become even wiser, so he got him a calabash and started gathering up wisdom wherever he went and tucking it in there. He figured if he kept at it long enough he could soon collect all the wisdom in the world.

"When that calabash was nearly full to bursting, he figured he had collected just about all the wisdom that was going, and he came home and decided to climb the tree behind his house and hang the calabash up there for safekeeping. But every time he tried to climb that tree, holding the calabash in his hand, he'd slip on the tree bark and fall down. Tortoises aren't much good at climbing trees—even with all four hands and feet—but with just three, he couldn't grab on at all."

Declan Liffey went back to tending his sausages, lowering the grill, and Maeve called out the window, "Tortoises don't ever climb trees."

"Hush, sister. So just then, when Mr. Tortoise was trying to climb his tree, Mr. Bear came along and stood watching him. He was a funny ol' bear, with a big, pink, shaved-off rump, but Mr. Tortoise didn't ask about that. Mr. Bear say, 'Hey, Mr. Tortoise, why don't you put a leather strap through that calabash and hang it around your neck so you can climb that tree?'

" 'Damn, you're pretty smart,' say the tortoise. So he goes and does what Mr. Bear says. He puts on the strap and hangs the calabash over his back, and he climbs right up the tree to a nice, strong limb where he can safely hang his calabash, heavy with the world's wisdom.

"But just as he's about to hang it up there, Mr. Tortoise realizes something. He realizes he doesn't have all the wisdom in the world in that calabash after all. He must have missed some, because it was that old bare-fanny bear who told him how to put on the strap and climb the tree. So the tortoise came back down, full of sorrow, and he broke open that calabash on a rock and let all the wisdom back out into the world.

" 'Man,' he say, 'ain't no point getting just *some* of the wisdom. Best to let all God's creatures use it, too.' "

Declan Liffey was turning the sausages as she finished the tale. Maeve had noticed him earlier, smiling privately at the bear's 'shaved-off rump.' Now he was wearing a thoughtful expression, and Maeve hurried out with her bowl of potato salad.

As she arrived, Declan Liffey looked up at her with an unreadable expression. "Thank you, Ornetta. Time to eat, girls," he said.

"Okay, Jack, you can stand up."

He'd been lying facedown in the backyard in front of Ozaki's converted garage with his arms spread out, just as the bullhorn had ordered. There was so much artificial light pouring down on him he was afraid it would leave him with a sunburn.

"Thanks a bunch, Ken." He'd recognized the voice. SWAT seemed to be giving up on Ozaki for now and was apparently turning tactical control back to Steelyard. The high-intensity lights went off, one by one, and the helicopters' hammering sounds dwindled away as the beasts quit their last wide circles and flew off. Jack Liffey boosted himself onto the concrete porch of the bungalow.

"Nice speech," Ken Steelyard offered.

"What?"

Steelyard showed him a small Nagra tape recorder, about the size of a sandwich, like something he'd seen on documentary film shoots. He punched the playback. ". . . . And now you're doing your best to invent a whole narrative to help make sense of what this country turned you into. I feel for you, Joe, but I'm not going to play these games with you. But even if I'm not going to do it your way, I'm your friend, not your enemy, and I'm going to tell you why. . . ." He shut it off.

"Where was the mike?"

"Just an ordinary phone tap. We could turn the line on any time we wanted to pick up the room ambience. It wasn't just you who figured he came back to this place now and again. We may not be quite as lame as you think."

Gloria Ramirez was there, too, behind Steelyard. She looked a bit shamefaced. She made what might have been a kind of private apology to him, with a nod and a brief grimace, and he let it ride.

"Wish you'd've let us know you'd been meeting him," Steelyard said. He didn't look friendly. "In some people's eyes that could make you an accomplice after the fact. Abetting a fugitive."

Jack Liffey set his hands beside him on the stoop but seemed to have lost all strength. Ken Steelyard gave him a hand to help him to his feet. "He hasn't hurt anybody yet," Jack Liffey said. "I was hoping I could head him off before he does, but you've spooked him now."

"I'm not too keen on your definition of 'hurt,' Jack. He's done a lot of lasting, very destructive damage. Not the least of which was to *my train layout!* Do you know where he's actually living?"

Jack Liffey shook his head. He looked around and was shocked when he saw in the crowd gathering on the street beyond the end of the Ozaki driveway, his own father, plus Maeve and Ornetta. "Excuse me a moment."

He walked up the driveway to them, ducking under the yellow crime-scene tape. "What the hell are you all doing here?"

"We were having a barbecue two blocks away, and we heard the commotion," Maeve said. "What are *you* doing here?"

It took him a moment to digest that, and he glanced at his father.

"It's okay, son," Declan Liffey said. "We're all fine. The girls are safe."

"This is too much to take at one sitting," Jack Liffey said. "Are we all pals now?"

"Something like that," Maeve said. "At least, we're doing our best."

Everybody was keeping secrets, he thought, and all with the best of intentions. "Take care of them, Dad. I hold you responsible."

"Haven't you always?"

Their eyes met, but that was as far as reconciliation was going to go that night.

Gloria Ramirez walked up to them now and hugged the girls herself. Then she put her hand on Jack Liffey's shoulder. "Ken wants you."

"Sure."

"I'll make sure a car takes them home," she said.

They walked back up the driveway side by side. "And how are you?" Jack Liffey asked her.

"Confused. Emotionally."

"I hope so. I miss you."

Then Ken Steelyard descended on them. "Jack, we think the guy's on the island. We talked to an FBI profiler. He thinks the guy has a sentimental bent, of a peculiarly male sort, anyway. What that means is it's likely he'd build himself a nest somewhere near the old Jap village."

"Japanese," Gloria corrected. Steelyard was oblivious.

"That's going to be hard to do," Jack Liffey said. "We were over there. Where the town was is just a bunch of decrepit canneries, all locked up now, and big, empty lots full of junk.

Steelyard shrugged. "I think he's over there."

Jack Liffey thought about it for a moment. "Yeah, you're probably right."

"That's in our favor, because it means the only ways on or off are the Vincent Thomas Bridge from San Pedro, the Henry Ford from Wilmington, and the Gerald Desmond from Long Beach. You've got to drive, or you stand out a mile. There just aren't any pedestrians on those bridges."

"Ken, there are other ways."

"Okay," Steelyard allowed. "He can swim the channel, like one of the harbor seals, but that's pretty conspicuous. And anybody in that water better have a good skin doctor."

"There're little boats, which he could stash anywhere," Jack Liffey said. "And there're other ways still."

"Like what?"

"Think Recon Marine, Ken. No, think Green Beret. He has a way to get there and back unseen, believe me. He probably has two ways. He's good, so let's not underrate him. He got past your alarms."

"Get in the car. We're going to have a look."

The SWAT cops were lovingly repacking all their state-of-the-art equipment into the niches of their black van. They were the American metaphor, Jack Liffey thought: overequipped and underbrained. But, all in all, he figured America didn't really need a metaphor. Jack Liffey got in the backseat of the big beige Crown Vic with Steelyard driving and Gloria Ramirez in the seat he and his school friends had called shotgun.

"We could probably be even more conspicuous in that SWAT truck, if you wanted," Jack Liffey said.

"This is what we get," Steelyard said. "When they issue beat-up Toyotas for camouflage, I'll ask for one."

They headed up Harbor and then over the Vincent Thomas Bridge toward Terminal Island. "I take it you want to use me as some kind of bait."

"That's the general idea," Steelyard admitted. "You seem to have developed a rapport with the guy."

"I tried, but I don't know if it got very far. I don't know if the modern samurai allows himself rapport."

"What's being a samurai mean practically?"

Jack Liffey shrugged. "Honor is paramount. Following a lot of prescribed rules that dictate what warriors do and don't do. But really . . . I only have a few clues what it all means to him."

He stared back at the big green suspension bridge as they came down into the industrial wastes of the island. He couldn't help himself: "In the movie *Heat*, Robert De Niro calls it the *St.* Vincent Thomas Bridge."

Steelyard chuckled. "Old Vince, the long-serving congressman, would like that, wherever he's buried."

Ahead of them were the onion domes of the sewage treatment plant. Beyond them lay a vast network of conduits running overhead, containing conveyor belts for moving petroleum coke. This system carried the powdery stuff, even finer than coal dust, from the black mountains down by the railhead out to the farthest shipping docks of Pier 200, which had just been built far out into the harbor on new landfill. The town had been promised that the coke deposits would all be covered over, but they never had been, except for the conveyor belts themselves. When the wind was right, a fine grit blew off the black mountains at the railhead to lay a film over every flat surface in San Pedro, from the channel to the Palos Verdes Hills.

They took a hard right off the bridge and then drove into a warren of streets through old industrial buildings, brick and corrugated iron and Art Deco stucco. Fenced lots held rusting railcar wheels and abandoned boxcar-size containers, snowlike piles of the big Styrofoam coolers they packed fish in, and locomotive-size hulks of abandoned machinery that could have been anything. He was reminded of Steinbeck's description of Cannery Row in the early 1940s.

Most of the fenced lots had fiercely bright antitheft lights on high stanchions, to suffuse the area with that eerie perpetual day—or perpetual evening—that you found in Las Vegas. The car eventually came to a big square basin of gray oil-slicked water where out-of-town fishing boats were docked, some of them Japanese long-liners and others from all over the west coast. Steelyard stopped at the edge of the basin, which was maybe a quarter mile across, and they could see more of the same all around the bay—more dead warehouses and abandoned canneries. Seagulls squawked as they circled, and a big pelican or two perched on the pilings, as if posing for tourists. But there were no tourists.

"It would take an army to search this mess," Gloria said.

"We have some advantages," Jack Liffey said. "He's alone out here at night, and the place is lit up like a football field."

"There's plenty of dark spaces between the goalposts," Ken Steelyard said.

"We have another advantage," Gloria pointed out. "There's only one minimart and cafe on the island, right back there."

"You going to stake me out like a goat in front of the cafe and wait for him to come for me?" Jack Liffey asked.

"That's an idea," Ken Steelyard said.

It turned out that they did pretty much that: they sent him into the Harbor Lights with an old photo of Joe Ozaki. It had been blown up from a news shot and he was in a business suit, but it was a pretty good likeness. Coincidentally, the counterman at the cafe was a tall Japanese American, too. The place had a small deli section full of junk foods and a few staples, and an eating area of battered tables.

"Hi; I'm looking for one of your customers." Jack Liffey showed the counterman the photo. "Joe and I bought a lottery ticket together, and I owe him half the winnings."

The man glanced suspiciously at the photo and shook his head. "Don't know him."

This seemed highly unlikely, as it was the only place to obtain food on the entire island.

"If he comes in, tell him Jack has his money."

He showed the photo to a few workmen eating at the tables, but they just shook their heads no. One shrugged and said something negative in Spanish. Then Jack Liffey bought two packets of fiery hot peanuts and went back out to distribute them to the cops.

"Next time send me in with a neon vest. That would make sure they remember me."

"They'll remember you. You don't look much like a fisherman or anyone else with an excuse to be over here this evening. Oh, my God, my mouth's *on fire*." Steelyard spit his jalapeño peanuts out the window and hurled the cellophane tube after, but Gloria Ramirez chewed up hers happily.

"I think I know one of the ways he's coming across to the island," Jack Liffey offered mildly.

"How?"

"I kept my eyes open. Drive back that way."

Steelyard did as asked, making several turns in the tangled industrial wasteland and one false attempt down a dead end, where he had to back out. He parked under one of the first big abutments of the suspension bridge. Jack Liffey pointed up. A ladder ran up the concrete abutment, with a safety hoop around it, the ladder leading to an open catwalk. It would be a serious maneuver to shinny around the shoulder of the concrete pier where there was no walkway, but then it would be child's play to step-slide along the giant I-girders under the roadway to the next abutment. The lowest rung of the access ladder was thirty feet off the ground, but that wouldn't prove much of a hindrance for their ninja. He'd have a ladder somewhere, or a grappling rope.

"Damn," Steelyard said. "How long do you think it would take him to cross the whole bridge underneath?"

"An hour? Forty minutes? He'd be virtually invisible up in the superstructure."

Steelyard sniffed. "So much for the guys blocking the bridges and the three guys with the image-stabilized binoculars I've got watching the channel for suspicious-looking harbor seals."

"You're mobilizing an awful lot of resources for this poor guy. Maybe we should just let him burn himself out. What do you think?" He glanced at Gloria. He was trying not to think of how sexy she looked undressed.

"They can't back down now. It's the cop code," she explained. "Why do you think there's a real car chase on TV three times a week in LA?"

"He sent me another card, Jack," Steelyard said. "Didn't I tell you? The queen of that goddamn suit, and his note said I'd already had my game and lost. He told me to be a good sport and quit now or he'd have to neutralize me. Remember that word? This card was stuck to my headboard with an unfired five-fifty-six-millimeter cartridge he'd hammered into it somehow. That means he's got an M-16 or something like it."

"Hell, Ken, he's probably got missiles and Claymores, but he hasn't used any of them."

"The night is young," Ken Steelyard said.

"We're staying the *night*?"

"We're here for the duration, Jack, and you're drafted. You're the one who started talking to him, offering your friendship. I'm giving you the chance to try to save him from suicide by cop. We got a field office with cots and supplies in that place two blocks up from the cafe, calling itself a cat food research center."

"Please, Jack," Gloria said. "Help us stop him before he hurts somebody."

When he thought it over later, he had to admit to himself that some part in his decision was played by the thought of staying near the policewoman.

"I'll have to call Maeve to get her to feed my dog."

She offered him her slim cell phone.

Dec 24 Late
I was obviously mistaken to treat them as honorable adversaries, even him. No more words. Too late for words.

Nineteen

Am I Ready?

"We don't really know for sure he's on the island," Jack Liffey said.

The three of them had motored slowly around the eerily deserted streets for two hours, getting the feel of the entire island—and incidentally, Jack Liffey thought, displaying him in the passenger seat, where they'd moved him. Overripe bait. Pier 200, a giant new container terminal, had just been completed out into the bay, and farther east, almost as much work was going on building China's new container terminal on the flattened naval base. But apparently the work wasn't urgent enough to go to double shifts, as both sites were quiet as the grave—this particular night, anyway.

Gloria Ramirez had brought along some more background information she'd dug up on Terminal Island. It was a weird place, in civic terms, and always had been: two ports side by side, two cities, Los Angeles and Long Beach; two tax and customs districts sharing the one artificial island, which had been built out of landfill in the early twentieth century on the site of two tiny islets that had been called, heavy with omen, Rattlesnake Island and Dead Man's Island. The site had only been chosen as LA's port after a near shooting war between competing railroads, with the despotic Collis P. Huntington and his Southern Pacific Railroad insisting that LA's port be built fifteen miles west of downtown on land he owned in Santa Monica. At the same time, two other railroads insisted, just as fiercely, that a free port be built in the marshes to the south.

Eventually the marshes and the channel were dredged out, a huge breakwater built, and the natural little islets extended and reshaped to become Terminal Island. The harbor was about as artificial, Jack Liffey thought, as everything else about Los Angeles. But he rather liked it that way, this wonderful fraudulence that meant people didn't take things, or themselves, too seriously.

They'd had a beer at the cafe to wind down, and, at closing time at ten, they'd been shooed out by the owner. They took one last drive around, with everything shut now, and parked at the cat food research facility that Steelyard had commandeered as home base.

"Shit," the cop said as they got out and approached the building.

"I guess we know now," Gloria Ramirez said. If they hadn't been sure Ozaki was on the island, they knew now.

The door of the office had a playing card stuck to it with a simple drawing pin. It looked like the king.

I grow tired of fighting, but I cannot spare those who challenge me.

Steelyard went straight back to the car and flicked the button on his radio mike a couple of times. Then he changed his mind and hung it back up.

"He'll have a scanner," he said to no one in particular and took out his cell and hit a speed dial button. "Yeah, Captain. It's Steelyard. He's here, all right, left us another card on the command post. Once the last workers are off, can you get our teams to lock down all the bridges until dawn? And have them watch the *undersides* of the bridges, too. Let's not let him shinny out on the superstructure. And keep watch for swimmers, or suspicious trails of bubbles. And any boats, obviously."

There was a long pause. "We don't need a posse, Dave, but you could have a chopper standing by if you want. We can handle this. He's not going into hiding. He's coming after us."

He shut the phone with a flourish, as if cutting his boss off in midsentence. "No little dink fucks with me," he said. "I don't care what color his beret was."

"That's not a helpful attitude," Jack Liffey said. "You're just pushing Joe to the wall. He's not so little, by the way." He looked at Gloria for help.

"How about the LAPD's negotiating team?" she suggested.

"How are they going to talk to him, scatter pinochle cards from a chopper? This is none of their business. *I* want him."

He had his key in the door to the little building before she yelped. "Stop! Booby traps!" He scowled at her and pushed the door open.

"If he's going to hit me with a daisy cutter or a Claymore, so be it. I figure him for a man-to-man kind of hitter. All that samurai honor stuff."

Jack Liffey nodded. "I doubt he'll use anything that isn't face-to-face. He'll give you an even break, at least in *his* mind. I'd guess he's well past punishing his dad's old enemies. He's only after us because we're getting in his face. On the whole, I'd rather be in Vegas."

"Have you got a gun?"

"I don't carry a gun. I don't even have a detective license. What would I do, pistol-whip runaway kids?"

"Bully for you." Steelyard bent down and pulled a little .38 snub-nosed revolver out of an ankle holster and held it out to him. "You are hereby deputized."

Jack Liffey looked the little pistol over as if it were a large dead insect. "This is, like, accurate to maybe fifty feet?"

"It's better than throwing rocks at him."

"Put it back on. It's yours. It'll only get me hurt."

Steelyard shrugged and snapped the pistol back onto his ankle. They walked together through the wreck of the office, studying Ozaki's handiwork. The three old canvas army cots had been sliced to ribbons, as had a big plastic-laminated map of Terminal Island tacked to the wall. Papers from a filing box were strewn everywhere, torn and mangled. Two pairs of binoculars had their lenses shattered, and a strange piece of apparatus, like a big toaster with a telephoto lens, was mashed out of shape. "That was a heat imager," Steelyard explained. "You can see a body right through a wall. Took a lot to get my captain to borrow that from the spooks. They'll be pissed."

After the tour of the three rooms that were to have been their command post, there was little they could find left in usable condition. Some army MREs—meals ready to eat. A bottle of water. It was just possible that the foam mats meant to soften the cots could be chivied back together on the floor, even after a bad slashing. And, strangely enough, there was a small porcelain decanter of Tsuru Japanese whiskey sitting in the middle of the back room. Like a peace offering—or maybe a thumbed nose.

"Nobody touches that," Steelyard said.

"I don't drink," Jack Liffey said.

"It's late. I'm tired. I think I'll have some," Gloria Ramirez said, going into open revolt.

Maeve wasn't sure what she felt about her grandfather. Obviously he was trying hard, but there was a closed door to his inner world—his dog spots, as he put it—and he wasn't offering her a way past it. If he was really as bigoted as her father thought, he would hardly be getting along so well with Ornetta, yet Maeve still sensed that he was condescending to both of them, as if he had to appease a couple of trained animals to effect an escape.

She let herself into the condo, unlocking to the noise of the hysterical dog on the other side of the door. Loco leaped joyously onto her shoulders.

"Down, c'mon, down, boy. You'll get fed, honest."

When the dog persisted, she settled onto her knees, wrestled one arm around him, and stroked his breast, down between his forelegs, as her father had shown her. He'd told her it was a universal soothing action for canines—even ones that were half coyote—and it seemed to work. Loco settled onto all fours and seemed hypnotized into swaying back and forth.

She laughed softly, imagining using the same stroke to pacify her grandfather, and seeing him sigh and settle back on his haunches to sway a little and gush cheerily about all his former hates: "Ohh, love those Mexican Americans. Black culture is so rich. Gays are *sooo* stylish." Yet he made her uneasy, and she was sure contempt simmered inside him.

"I wish we could help Dad, Loco, but I don't see how we can. He said on the phone you were to get a special treat. That's his guilt speaking, but you know that, don't you? I guess it means I thaw the T-bones in the freezer. Let's figure out something we want in exchange from him. Maybe make him take his own father to dinner."

Gloria Ramirez had drunk most of the little bottle of Japanese whiskey and was now squatting and tearing apart plastic pouches from the MREs, naming the foods as she found them.

"Cheez Whiz, dry crackers, some kind of chicken noodles." She was discarding as fast she opened.

"I think you're supposed to heat the entrée," Jack Liffey said. "Those things have a pretty good reputation, especially if you grew up on C rations. Ham and motherfuckers, I'll never forget those—that was ham and limas. Nobody would trade you a dead rat for those."

Ken Steelyard was sitting on a second crate of MREs in the corner, cradling his pistol and trying to think. Gloria found some kind of food bar called a "Hooah!" and began nibbling on it. Jack Liffey squeezed the soft cheese out of a plastic tube onto a cracker and took the whole thing in one bite.

"If you kids are through playing with your food, we have to address what to do."

"This is your war now," Gloria said. He could hear a bit of slurring in her voice. "I take no responsibility for this childish duel. We should have retreated from the island long ago and called in a tactical search team."

"They'd clomp around like a bunch of Dickless Tracys, and he'd either get away in the confusion or slaughter them all." Steelyard must have been thinking of calling for some kind of assistance, though, because he took out his cell phone, turned it on, listened, and stared evilly at it. "No dial tone."

The policewoman handed her phone to Jack Liffey while she tugged greedily at the packaging of a big burrito she had found, and he pressed the "on" button. Nothing happened. In a few moments a little amber LCD display lit up on the screen: *No signal*. He passed it on to Steelyard.

"How the hell has he done that?" Steelyard complained.

"He's knocked out the cell tower on the island."

"We're line of sight to at least three other repeaters on the mainland."

"Maybe he's found a way to jam the local carrier signal. I said, don't underestimate this guy. I'm sure it's too much to hope any hardwired phones in this building are working. Maybe you should check the radio in the car."

Steelyard killed the lights and studied the world outside through the venetian blinds on the front window for a long time before venturing out. He was soon back.

"Shit on a stick," he said. "All four tires are flat, and nothing works. The doors won't even open."

"I've seen this movie," Jack Liffey said.

"I surrender," Gloria said. "Let him take me prisoner. You can trade me for some real food and another bottle of this Tsuru."

"What movie?" Steelyard glowered.

"Well, it might be *Rio Bravo*, or it might be *Assault on Precinct 13*," Jack Liffey said. "They're basically the same movie. Though in both of those, there were a lot of bad guys, not just one. Did you find an ace on the car?"

"No."

"That's good. It's his last card. I'd say, when you see an ace, kiss your ass good-bye."

All of a sudden, they felt a faint rumble in the floor, like a subway train passing deep underground, though there were no subways on Terminal Island, and as yet no night trains either.

"I hope he doesn't have an Abrams tank," Jack Liffey said.

"That's strange. Once that guy shut the cafe, there shouldn't be a soul on the island but us and him. Not counting the prison, which is locked down. I had the bridges blocked."

"Well, there's some kind of machinery running. Maybe somebody's night-loading a ship."

"I like it," Steelyard said. "It could help us if there's normal activity."

"Right now I'd like a helicopter out," Jack Liffey said.

"I might, too, but how do I call for it? Set the building on fire?"

"It's a thought."

"Last time I talked to the captain, I asked him to seal the place off and let me handle it. I must have caught this from you. I thought I could talk Ozaki in, and a bunch of leadfoot SWATS trotting around—hut-hut-hut—would just spook him."

The next sound was a sudden snuffle and then the dull thunk of a soft weight going over slowly, followed by a snore. Gloria Ramirez was keeled over, asleep on the floor. The innocent look she wore reminded him almost unbearably of the way she had looked in his bed, and he wanted to snuggle up next to her, rest his arm over her, and sleep this horrible night away. "We could hide until morning," Jack Liffey said. "I saw a couple of places when we were cruising around."

"No, I want to bring in this guy. Nobody is Superman."

"Except Superman. Think about it, Ken. Is this just payback for breaking your model train? Man, you and I may have played together in grade school, but I don't want to die for your train layout."

For a moment they both watched Gloria Ramirez sleeping. Her hands were palm-to-palm and tucked under her cheek, like a child miming sleep, and her breathing had settled into a soft gasp and flutter. Jack Liffey desperately wanted to kiss her.

"I'm a cop," Steelyard said. "Bringing him in is my duty."

"Forget the cop shit for a moment. He's got us trapped in here. He knows where we are, and we haven't got a clue where he is. I don't know what you did in the Big 'Nam, but I reckon he's got martial skills you've never heard of. What are you carrying?"

"Glock nine-millimeter. I've got a spare magazine in a pouch on the shoulder holster. There's an AR-15 in the trunk of my car out there."

"Want to bet? You've also got your ankle backup, that Chief's Special thirty-eight, with six shots. As far as we know, he's got a sniper rifle with night vision, a bazooka and a mortar, and probably an F-16 warming up. And he could hurl all that in the channel and still kill us both in a second with a piece of old Styrofoam. He might be in the next room right now."

Involuntarily they both looked at the dark doorway.

"Ken, he didn't seem to me to be a bad guy, but he's been nursing his father's hurt all his life. People can back off their own fights, but his father isn't around to give him permission to back off. I don't have any idea what that kind of obsession does to you. If they'd picked up all the Irish and put them in concentration camps, maybe I'd be pissed off, too. You know, I'm sure the furniture was never really the point. It was just something to focus on. He wanted his dignity back. He wanted to be respected. He wanted to respect *himself* again."

"That's a long time ago, Jack. We can't do anything about that."

"You had a lousy childhood. Can't you see how you might have gone bad?"

"Oh, I see it perfectly. I see the day the McGreevy boys almost enticed me into breaking into a car that looked abandoned up in the hills near Miraleste. But I didn't do it. It was wrong."

"So instead you emptied your mom's purse, put all your possessions on a Greyhound to Fresno, and decided to run away. What were you, thirteen? We don't always make good choices."

"The guy's a loose cannon, and it's my responsibility."

"He'll be just as caught if SWAT finds him in daylight tomorrow. He's playing warrior, and he's got himself all twisted up inside to justify it. You're just giving him the adversary he wants. I tried to befriend him, but I don't think it got through. I don't think his world can handle friendship."

"This is my friend." Steelyard indicated his pistol.

"Damn it, Ken. He can *trump* you. It's dark out there, and dark is his element." He pointed at the sleeping Gloria, whose forehead now had wrinkled up in worry. "Look at her and see if it doesn't remind you of the value of life. There's something about her that's completely outside this haze of hormones you and I walk around in. I don't want to go down in a blaze of glory tonight, whatever cowboy movie you're acting out."

"I thought I could count on you, Jack."

Jack Liffey thought about it for a moment. "You can't. Not for a death duel."

Steelyard unstrapped his .38 and slid it across the floor. Jack Liffey slid it right back. "I don't want a weapon."

Steelyard set his hand on it. "You sure?"

"I'm sure."

"Fuck you, then, Jack. I'm *ready*." Ken Steelyard snapped the snub-nose back into his ankle holster. "I told you he wasn't Superman."

Steelyard went to the cobwebbed water cooler in the corner, removed the empty water bottle, then tipped the sheet-metal base onto its side. He tugged out of the base a disassembled deer rifle and a big Starlite scope. "I'm Superman." It took him only a few seconds to assemble the rifle.

"I can see like daylight with this. He can run around in those black PJs all he wants, and I can still punch his ticket. Am I *ready?*" he shouted at Jack Liffey.

"Huh?"

Something a little spooky had come into his eyes. He stood, slung the rifle over his shoulder and grabbed Jack Liffey's shoulders and shook him. "Am I ready? Come on. Say it, damn it! I'm ready! Say it *now!*"

"You're ready."

"Damn straight. I'm glad we cleared that up. I'm *ready*. Now I'm going outside. Just part of the process. You can cower in the corner until he comes for you, if that's what you want. Or spend your time fucking Gloria, if you can wake her up. I'm going out the back with my Jap-killer. You might want to lock the door behind me."

Maeve drove back to Brighton Street, and the whole family was still up. The lights on the Christmas tree were on. "I think my dad's in trouble," she said bluntly.

"What can we do?" Bancroft said.

"I don't know."

"Let's talk it over," Bancroft said. "Maybe we can figure something out together."

"Go to channel nine," Ornetta said. "They always got the car chases and stuff."

Twenty

Where Does Honor Stop?

Jack Liffey followed Steelyard to the back door, where the big man turned back and smiled. "What did that Indian say? Today is a good day to die."

"Please don't do this," Jack Liffey said.

Steelyard snorted. "We *have* the ordnance, we *have* the manpower, we *have* the motivation." He winked at Jack Liffey. "That's sure some awful shit, isn't it?"

He slipped out, and Jack Liffey locked up after him, trying hard not to speculate on the man's suicidal tendencies. He stared at the little brass knob. He had no idea what the cheesy Kwikset deadbolt was worth against a pro; probably not much. Or Steelyard's deer rifle and night sight, for that matter. He figured Ken Steelyard was prone to overrating the importance of technology, just like the LAPD, just like the whole country. He'd vote for skill every time.

Jack Liffey went back into the front room and knelt to pat down Gloria's body with a kind of guilty abandon. He found the pistol on her hip under her jacket, in a little leather holster hooked over her belt. He took it away from her and hid it in the toppled water cooler, which seemed the official gun repository. Then he shook Gloria's shoulder after kissing her once on the cheek. It took a moment, but she shivered and sat up all at once. "*Jesus,* what?"

He put his hands on her shoulders. "Time to come back to the world, that's all. Nothing's happened. Yet."

Her eyes were unfocused for a few moments more, and then she began to seem more like herself.

"Jack, God, I'm sorry." She looked around. "Where's Ken?"

"I don't know how much slack to cut him anymore. He's gone off on his crusade."

She shook her head and took out her cell phone, but it still had no dial tone. "What are we going to do?"

"Do you know Morse code?"

"Are you nuts? Nobody knows Morse code."

"Well, I know SOS. Dit-dit-dit, dah-dah-dah, dit-dit-dit. We can rig up a light in the front window and interrupt it with something . . . the venetian blinds or that cardboard on the floor. If anyone onshore is watching, they'll see it. That's worth a try for a few minutes. After that, I don't know."

He found a gooseneck lamp on an empty desk in back and brought it into the front room. With the lay of the buildings and the big bridge abutment to the west, there was no chance of a direct line of sight to the police station, or even to the shoreline in San Pedro. But there were hundreds of houses up on the hill that could see him, hundreds more than when he was a kid and the whole slope had been weeds and secret climbing trails and garbanzo beans—the hill where, at age twelve, he had stepped on what felt like a garden hose until it wriggled under his foot and then rattled at him and he had run more than a mile home with visions of that snake wriggling right behind him every step of the way. It was all houses now along the flank of the hill—rich people, horsy people—but you couldn't stop the world just to suit your nostalgia.

He plugged in the lamp, pointed it out at the hill, and, feeling rather silly, began fanning the cardboard in front of the bulb, short-short-short, long-long-long, short-short-short.

"Do you think anyone will see it?"

"It's a pretty distinctive signal if somebody does. Half of them are yachtsmen up there. They ought to figure it out."

"I should be out there protecting my partner."

"He left you behind on purpose."

"Where's my pistol?"

She must have just noticed.

"Ken took it," he lied. He had a feeling that being weaponless might be the best protection against a samurai warrior. Her little 9-millimeter was not going to be much good against whatever the Special Forces could produce.

Just then he heard a gunshot, and his heart sank a foot. It echoed a few times between the warehouses. He wasn't an expert on typing gunshots, but it sounded like a rifle. "Oh, Jesus."

"Jack, we've got to do something."

"That's what I'm trying to do. Try your cell again. Try it in the back room. Try any phones you find."

In a few moments she came back, shaking her head disconsolately. "No good. The regular phone's dead, too." She stood beside him at the window.

"What about the radio in the car?"

"Ken said the whole car was bugged, and the doors won't open."

There were two more shots, one after another, roughly the same quality as the first and about the same distance away. Maybe four or five blocks, he guessed. He decided there was an immense epistemological difference between hearing one isolated gunshot and hearing several more shots a bit later. A solo gunshot might have been a sniper hitting his target unexpectedly, but now you knew either he wasn't hitting or the target was shooting back.

"Poor Ken," he said. "If he didn't get the guy with his first shot, he's had it. Do you think they'll hear that on the mainland?"

"I don't think so. The wind is out of the west, and it'll blow any noise out into the harbor."

Then the power in the room went out, right in the middle of a long O on his semaphore. She gave a gasp. "Let's get away from the window," he told her.

He closed the blinds, and the only light now filtered into the room through a curved window of wavery glass bricks in the corner. They sat side by side against an inner wall and listened for any more signs of the battle outside.

"We've got to do something, Jack. We'll never be able to live with ourselves if we just hide here."

"I'm kind of at a loss."

"God," she said, all of a sudden. "It's Christmas Eve."

"Yeah, I got myself together enough to stop and buy Maeve a color printer and I haven't even had a chance to wrap it. I'm sorry, I didn't get you anything. This was kind of sudden."

"Me neither." They kissed, but it was only for a moment and rather chaste.

"Okay, you wait here," he said finally. "You're a cop, which makes you a legitimate target. I'm just a civilian, and he knows me. I'm going to stand under that streetlight out front and show I have no weapons, and maybe he'll talk to me."

"The idea frightens me to death."

"Well, it doesn't thrill me, but I've read his book about the samurai code, and I don't think it's within the code to kill an unarmed man, whatever I represent to him. I get to be a man of peace tonight. I think it even runs in my character."

She clung hard, but finally she had to let him go.

One TV camera had set up on the bluffs at Sixth and Harbor looking across the channel, where it was about three hundred yards wide over to Terminal Island. There was a channel nine logo on the big camera, so it wasn't even a network affiliate, but, after all, it was Christmas Eve, and the heavy hitters were probably all at home. A blandly handsome man in a ski jacket was doing a stand-up, saying into a microphone that the police weren't allowing helicopters to overfly the island, because there had been warnings that a renegade Japanese American they were calling the Samurai Green Beret was rumored to have a Stinger missile.

There was yellow tape everywhere, keeping people back. After they'd checked the television news reports, Maeve and the Davis household had agreed that the only thing for them to do was drive down to the harbor. Nobody was giving any names on the air, but Maeve knew for sure her dad was on that island they'd sealed off. Bancroft insisted on taking his big Buick, and it was Ornetta's idea to pick up Declan Liffey on the way. Neither of the girls told the older folks anything about him except that he was Jack's father.

It took Declan almost a minute to recognize his well-known driver. "My heavens, you're Bancroft Davis. You were bitten by those dogs in Mississippi."

"Yes, sir, I was."

Genesee turned in her seat, her eyes fierce as hot coals. "He was near killed three times. Some Klansmen wannabes caught him once by himself and took him out on a levee and put a gun to his head."

Ornetta and Maeve eyed one another, holding their breath and gritting their teeth.

"That dishonors all white people," was all Declan Liffey said.

Policemen with waving flashlights wouldn't let them stop on the freeway where the ramp toward the Vincent Thomas Bridge had been blocked off by police cars and sawhorses. So they had to exit on Harbor and drive along the channel to the low cliff, parking next to the old ferry building, where they could see up the slope to the TV camera plus a crowd of rubbernecks. Maeve had just read *Day of the Locust,* and she recognized Nathanael West's thrill chasers, drawn to any break in the common run of life. She pressed her way uphill to a police post at the top of the cliff where they had a fancy telescope on a tripod, giving them the best view out over Terminal Island. An area was roped off with more yellow tape that said *POLICE LINE—DO NOT ENTER* over and over. Maeve called to one of the policemen over the tape. "My name is Maeve Liffey. Is my dad, Jack, out there?"

An older officer in a suit strolled toward her. "Your father is Jack Liffey?"

"Yes, sir."

"My name is Captain Adler." He held up the yellow tape to let her in.

"This is his father and some friends of his." She indicated the others struggling up the gentle slope behind her, Declan and Ornetta pushing Genesee in her portable wheelchair, and Bancroft doing pretty well in his walker. Adler frowned at the whole group, but nodded slowly and let them all duck and enter the area of grass behind the tape.

"Stay right here at the edge, all of you. We think your father may be over there, miss. He's with a senior police officer and his partner. At the senior officer's request, we've sealed off the bridges to prevent trouble. The last thing we need is a lot of people running around out there in the dark. Unfortunately there's a skeleton crew loading a coke carrier out on Pier Two Hundred. We're trying to get permission to go in and evacuate them, but we've lost communication with the island."

"What about ham radio to the ship?" Maeve said.

Captain Adler raised his eyebrows to acknowledge her insight. "You're a bright kid. It's a different band from our units, but we've thought of that. The harbormaster is trying to raise them now. The ship is only loading, and it's quite possible they're not manning their radio room. There's no reason to believe anyone is in any danger. Please just wait here. We'll let you know if anything develops."

He moved back toward the telescope, where half a dozen uniformed officers waited, taking turns peering into the lens, swinging the big telescope back and forth and talking into various kinds of walkie-talkies and the pack sets attached to their shirts.

The slope was just too steep for a wheelchair. They lifted Genesee out and set her gently on the grass. Ornetta knelt to make a backrest and put her hands in a protective way on her grandmother's shoulders. Maeve watched this, and then went up to her own grandfather and put her arm around his waist. He seemed surprised, but rested a leathery hand on her shoulder.

"Jack's a tough cookie," he said.

"He's been beat up a lot since you knew him," Maeve said. "I think he needs help. Liffey and Liffey Investigations."

The old man glanced down at her. "You stay right here, young lady."

"I meant in general."

* * *

The streetlight directly across the road from the cat food research facility seemed to be the only one on the street operating, though there was a glow from something on the next block. He wondered if leaving this one light on, like killing the cell phones, could be attributed to Joe Ozaki. Jack Liffey just didn't want to frighten himself with too much reference to superpowers. He stood in the cone of yellow beneath the cobra-necked streetlight, his opened empty hands in plain sight, and once in a while he called out. He decided not to use Steelyard's name in case the man was still alive out there. No sense giving him away.

The way the coastline curled around here, the mainland was due west of the island, and a chilly wind came off the land. You could see Christmas lights outlining the eaves of almost all the houses on the flank of the Palos Verdes Hills. A few seemed to have fancier displays that were hard to interpret from so far away but probably were the usual sleighs and mangers and angels. Time for the Magi to show up, Jack Liffey thought, this very night, bearing their frankincense and myrrh. And some police backup.

Now and again he glanced discreetly across the street, where there seemed to be a small disturbance in the slats of the pulled-down blinds, Gloria Ramirez peeking out at him. There was a fair amount of ambient light as his eyes adjusted. To the north, there were tall yellow security lights shining down on the huge container yards and the holding lots for import cars that were parked nose to tail, with opaque paper over their windows, Suzuki after Suzuki, Mitsubishi after Mitsubishi. The distant lights gave the air a faint glow, and drew an eerie orange radiation off the underside of a solid cloudbank.

"Come on, Joe! I want to talk to you!" His voice carried between the buildings, muddied a little by its echo. The only other sound was the moaning and sighing of the wind and that faint, low rumble from the machinery he'd heard before.

"There's still time to fix this! You're a war hero!" he shouted.

Just as he was about to give up, he noticed what seemed a thickening in the darkness in the very darkest provinces of the road, maybe two blocks ahead. It wasn't exactly a thing he saw, more a small lopsidedness he sensed in the night itself, an occurrence, the way scientists spoke of a disturbance in space-time, a bending of gravity. No matter how hard he looked, it did not resolve itself. Then the hair on his neck stood up as he saw that the phenomenon seemed to be moving, very slowly, toward him. Gradually he made out a complex shape, but it was bigger than a man and more angular. He had to fight a dread that pulled him hard toward the meaningless safety back inside the building with Gloria.

Eventually he heard a whine on the cold air and made out a squarish shape of some sort. Had somebody sent a robot, one of those bomb investigators? Then he saw it was an ordinary forklift puttering slowly toward him. The fork was down, and something irregular sprawled across a palette that joggled toward him about a foot off the ground. The machine whirred into the outer edge of his circle of light, and, though he didn't want to acknowledge it, it was pretty clear that the burden on the palette was an inert Ken Steel-yard, his distinctive Redwing boots hanging off one side of the wood and his head off the other. His chest was dark with what must have been blood. There was no rifle.

The forklift came to a stop twenty feet away from him and switched off. Joe Ozaki stepped out of the driver's seat in his black jumpsuit. As they stood facing one another, a whiff of the acrid propane exhaust reached him on the Christmas Eve breeze.

"I hope he isn't dead," Jack Liffey said.

"He's dead. He tried to kill me."

Jack Liffey stared hard. There was no movement from the blood-stained form slumped on the old palette. Jack Liffey hadn't seen all that many dead people in his life, and he gave the body his respectful attention. Good-bye, old friend, he thought. I knew you a long time ago. I forgot you for a while, but I'll remember you now.

"None of this was necessary," Jack Liffey said.

"Just where do you think the line is drawn where honor stops? He challenged me. He came here after me. He fired the first shot. I had no choice."

"You're expert enough at martial skills. You could have disarmed him or incapacitated him."

"It was time. Liffey, you've challenged me, too. And the woman in there."

That gave him a chill. "She means you no harm. Don't worry about her, worry about me."

It was the first time he'd ever seen Joe Ozaki smile, just for an instant, like someone dismissing the transparent threats of a child. "She's watching us right now," Ozaki said.

"She and I are both unarmed. I saw to that. I'd like to hear a definition of honor that includes killing the unarmed."

His adversary eyed him, almost with curiosity. "You don't know it yet?" The man thought for a moment, his whole body stiffening into the misnamed "parade rest" posture. "Honor means to be resolute, to be desperate, to be nearly insane with strength of mind, to do things in the right way so that you manifest the good that resides in your entire ancestral line."

"I don't understand any of that."

"Have you ever been caught in a bad rainstorm? If you run from house to house, trying to stay under the eaves, the method will be useless and you'll still get soaked. But if you set out already decided that you'll be soaked, you can walk like a man and still do your duty to your father and his fathers."

"My father is a racist shithead. Do I really want to honor him?"

"Then you have a problem."

"Maybe you and I could honor one another. It's Christmas Eve. I'm not a believer, but I respect a lot of those values. Just look up at the hill and see all those lights meant to represent hope and forgiveness and maybe a kind of second chance in life."

Ozaki didn't look. "Honor does not turn on and off. I've studied this carefully. Where would you have me turn it off? At noon yesterday? Do I forget the early 1900s, when my ancestors were brought over here as farm labor? Do you want to turn it off in 1905, when the California progressives came up with the expression 'Yellow Peril' and formed the Asiatic Exclusion League? Even the sainted Jack London was a member.

"Or how about 1906, when a mob in San Francisco stoned a group of scientists who had come over here from Tokyo to study the effects of the earthquake? Or 1910, when Asian immigration was completely banned? Or 1913, when we could no longer buy land in America? Or 1915, when we were no longer allowed to catch seafood off the Washington coast? Or 1922, when an American-born Japanese woman would lose her citizenship if she married a Japanese man?"

"It's not a very nice record, Joe. I know that. Hell, the Irish were mistreated for a long time, too. To say nothing of the blacks and the Indians."

"We haven't even got to 1942, when my parents were thrown out of their home and interned at Manzanar. Or 1943, when my dad refused to take the loyalty oath as long as his mother and father remained in a prison camp. Or 1945, when my dad found out all our possessions had been stolen and then ended up fussing about it for the rest of his life, infantilized by his own weakness and shame, like some poor child who's had his toys stolen. This was my *father*. Where does honor stop, Liffey?"

"You've made your point. Just by stirring up all this ruckus. It'll get into the papers. If you go on killing, your point will be forgotten, and the whole story will just become psychobabble about another Vietnam vet who went berserk."

"Honor has nothing to do with the newspapers, Liffey. You've got to understand that much."

"Your idea of honor says kill *me*? Somebody who offers to be your friend?"

"You challenged me. You stuck a card to my door. You came over here with my enemies to help them. I can't let that go." His hands came into sight from behind his back—empty, thank God—and one went to his breast pocket, where he pulled out something small. He let it flutter to the ground at Jack Liffey's feet. He hardly had to look. He knew it would be the ace of that strange Japanese deck of cards.

"I have no weapon. And I won't touch one."

Joe Ozaki indicated the shadowed form lying across the palette.

"That one has two pistols and a rifle. The rifle is under him. Feel free, Liffey."

"I don't want them."

"I'll give you and the woman fifteen minutes to run. Who knows? You might make the bridge in that time."

"Don't do this. I want to help you."

Joe Ozaki couldn't just disappear this time, backflipping through a dark tear in the universe, but he turned and walked rapidly away, and the night was so dark and his black catsuit so dull that he became invisible very soon. Jack Liffey looked involuntarily at his watch. It was five after nine. At least he would live until nine-twenty.

Twenty-one

Hamster Run

"If we go for the bridge, he'll get us." Jack Liffey stood with his back pressed to the closed front door, watching the way calculation played across her face. He wondered if all that calculation was getting her any farther than he was managing. "He might just let us go," he went on, "but I'm not willing to bank on it. He's killed now, and that changes a lot of things. I can't get a handle on what he thinks he's going to have to do about us to earn his Bushido merit badge."

"Shouldn't we go out and get Ken's guns?"

"If we arm ourselves, we're only challenging him to kill us. I have no doubt he can do it, with or without. Okay, here comes an idea."

Whether it was the short nap she'd had or the shock of Ken's death, she seemed completely nonplussed. He took her hand, warm and rough and a little damp, and she let herself be towed toward the back door, where they waited a moment, just as Ken Steelyard had.

Turning the bolt ever so slowly, he opened the heavy door cautiously onto the alley. Cool, turbulent air billowed in around them. A dark cloudbank overhead reflected what light there was, looking like a kind of rippled chocolate. They stepped out and immediately got a strong whiff of fish on the breeze. Across the alley there was a two-story mountain of white Styrofoam boxes, the size of foot-lockers. Whole fish had once been packed in them. He was tempted to burrow into that lumpy white hill and try to play possum the rest of the night, but he didn't think they would get away with it. And he had a terrible vision of Joe Ozaki setting the boxes afire to flush them out.

"Feel that vibration in the ground. I think it might be some of those big cranes out at the pierhead. I think there're longshoremen working out there, and we'll be safer if we try to get among them."

He'd felt the tremble in the floor inside, but out here it had become the faintest audible rumble, mechanical and characterless, impossible to assign to anything you knew, the sobbing of a machine deep in the earth. In fact, the vibration came to him most strongly in the sensitive metal plate he carried in his head from an earlier accident, like a primitive sounding board for a pre-human sense.

"I think it's this way."

They hurried southeast, away from San Pedro and the bridge, toward the new piers and the raillines across the huge landfill that the port authority had been building for years.

"Merry Christmas Eve, Jack."

"I keep forgetting." He had an urge to look back briefly at the Christmas lights on the hill, but he didn't. There was no indication of the holiday on the island, certainly not in this dark alley, where they picked their way around puddles and trash.

"Christmas never meant much to me, but I always wanted it to," she said. They found themselves talking in short snatches so they could stop to listen for suspicious sounds on the air. "It was like I was looking in at the holiday through a thick glass window. It was something other people enjoyed."

"Maeve loves Christmas. She loves the giving. I have a vague memory of loving it like that as a kid."

Was that a noise? They were both silent for a while, and then it came again, the wind rush of a bird, then a distinct flap of large wings. If it was up there, he couldn't see it.

"Maeve's mom was different," he went on. "Before Maeve was

born, she used to go away for the week by herself and pretend
Christmas didn't exist. Something in all the commercialism and
fake festivity got to her."

"Maybe that's what I need. They say it's suicide season for single
people."

"I'd like to give you a good Christmas, Glor, if we make it to
tomorrow. You deserve it." Saying that gave him a small rush of
emotion on top of the fear.

Then he banged his shin hard on something that was virtually
invisible at his feet and swore. They kept their eyes down now, at
the hardpan that was suddenly littered with abandoned engine
parts and long-rusted pipes rising at angles to threaten their ankles.

"You're a truthteller, aren't you, Jack?" she offered all of a sudden.

He wasn't sure what she meant. It might have been yet another
complaint about his being a pessimist in the teeth of trouble, so regularly anticipating the worst. Both Maeve's mother and Marlena
had been at him about that, but it seemed to him the only responsible attitude. "I don't know. Rigid rules always trip you up in the
long run," he said.

"You know, a word spoken as meant contains twice the energy
of a lie—that's what my adoptive mom always said," Gloria
offered, and he had to think about that. If only it were true. They
detoured far to one side of the alley, skirting a broad puddle of oily
water that filled a depression.

He took an awkward step over a high curb as they came out into
a long, dark, paved road that was penned in on both sides by chain
link. Beyond the fence, across a weedy expanse to the north, there
was a gigantic floodlit construction of green and red cargo containers, the colors so pure they looked like LEGOs that had been
stacked into ten-high formations by an overly-officious governess.
A siren wound up far behind them on the mainland, sounding forlorn for a few moments as its waves of sound spread across the
nearly deserted island like a gas, and then fizzled off.

Straight ahead, along the road, it was a different world. He
turned his attention to the white pipelines that ran overhead on
girder supports, the pipes apparently fat enough for a man to stand

upright inside them. They climbed at a shallow angle from one gray tower to another, trending south, but never low enough to snag a truck that might pass underneath. There was a whiff of the toy world here, too, with the Tinkertoy tubes a pristine white, supported every fifty yards or so by a rickety Erector set cradle painted playroom yellow. A ladder led up each cradle to a bright red door in the conduit. The nearest of the pipelines, two blocks ahead of them, had flashing yellow lights all along it, like feral eyes winking slowly against the dark. He guessed that the lights meant something was functioning, the conveyor inside was running.

"What are those pipes?"

"I think they cover conveyor belts for petroleum coke. It's like powdered carbon. I've read it's a leftover from the oil refineries, but obviously somebody has a use for it. Maybe they burn it in Japan."

The rectangular gray towers every quarter mile or so were like the guard towers at the corners of a castle keep, still more strange suggestions of the playtime world. He guessed that they were way stations or distribution forks. Tubes entered each tower near the top, while one or two new ones—at a much lower level—connected to still other towers. It all made up acres of a fairyland of mysterious passageways, leading to the new piers where the giant ships waited.

"It's always reminded me of a hamster run," she joked wanly. "But for hippos."

He laughed softly, liking her more and more. The vibration and rumble had swelled, and the tubeline with flashing amber lights was just ahead of them.

"Jack!" She froze, staring at something just at the curb. An upright wooden pole, tall as a basketball hoop, held a sealed metal box at head height that had no discernible purpose.

"Ah, shit," he said, a chill taking him.

Stabbed to the pole was the ace of kittens, the very card that he had already seen flutter to his feet, or another like it. It was pinned there by some strange star-shaped implement that he guessed was a martial arts throwing device. He had never seen the Hong Kong chop-socky films—they weren't to the taste of any of the women in his life—but the existence of throwing stars and nunchakus and the like had leached into the general culture. He checked his watch: nine-fifteen. Only five minutes of grace left from Joe Ozaki.

"I guess we're not outwitting him," he said. "Unless he's planted these all over the island to spook us."

He looked around. Five more minutes wouldn't take them anywhere near the big ship that he could see far out at the end of the conveyors, from this distance a long, low toy boat docked more than a mile away under bright lights. Perhaps they could play hamster, he thought.

"You think we can get over this fence?" he asked.

"I'm game."

He made a stirrup with interlaced fingers, and she stepped into it with a sensible ripple-soled shoe. He boosted her to the top of the fence. Luckily there was no barbed wire. She hung over on her belly and reached a strong arm down to him. Tugging against her pull and scrabbling his toes against the chain link, he got himself up to belly height like her.

"You've got arm strength," he said.

"When the gods start you out, everybody gets one virtue."

"I can think of more than one," he said, his voice choking against the pressure on his stomach. But there was no time for flirting now, and they leaned forward over the fence until, passing equilibrium, they pushed off and tumbled to the gravelly earth on the other side. He had twisted his ankle a little, but not so much he couldn't pretend it hadn't happened.

"So far, so good. Now up the ladder."

The throb in the earth was much stronger here, but the instant he clamped his hand onto a rung of the cold steel ladder, he knew he was connected to its source. It was eerie and frightening, a machine powerful enough to send out vibrations that disturbed the earth. He remembered once laying his hand against a massive cold aqueduct pipe, twice his height, and shivering with all that unseen power, just out of sight. He started up first. About ten feet up there was the beginning of a safety cage encircling the ladder, and then, for some reason, a small landing about two-thirds of the way up.

"I hope you're not afraid of heights," he said.

"Not my phobia. Spiders."

The second flight of the yellow ladder took them onto a small landing that crowded them against a bright red door. It was numbered 32, and there seemed no lock.

"Hamsters," he said. "At least he can't see us once we're inside."

They leaned together to one side to give the door room, and it came open with difficulty, heavily sprung so it would close securely. Along with a sudden increase in the sound, there was an exhalation of black dust that rolled over them out of the darkness. Jack Liffey coughed, retching once from deep in his good lung. He stuck his head inside and saw that there were ventilators overhead every fifty feet or so and that they admitted just enough light for him to see faintly. Right at his ankles, at the door, he could see the heavy V of the canvas conveyor belt grinding along, piled chest high with an endless charcoal gray snake. He reached out, and it resolved itself to black coke dust flowing over his hand. Gloria wormed around the door, and now it rested against their backs, pressing them both hard forward. The belt ran only inches from the wall of the surrounding tube, and if they jumped onto that moving pile of dust, there would be no getting off until the conveyor reached its destination, wherever that might be. He thought of those towers ahead where there appeared to be a drop to a lower level. No choice now, he thought.

They looked at one another and held hands. His watch said it was nine-nineteen, and he could imagine Joe Ozaki lining them up in the crosshairs of some high-tech rifle.

"I think we've got to do it," he said. He drew his lapels over his nose and mouth, barely able get a breath in the choking air. He saw that she had yanked a corner of her blouse up across her mouth, too, inhaling through the cotton. Something deep inside him resisted any move forward: the coke was so much like the dust that had collapsed his lung in the first place that his body hair stood on end with loathing. The trouble was, he could see no way around this.

"On three," he said.

"Aw, hell." She tugged him in before he could count, and they were abruptly sprawled across the yielding, puffing, choking hillock of black filth, yanked forward as they found themselves embedded in the snake. The door slammed behind them, taking most of the light with it. He could feel that the coke had been lightly dampened, but it didn't hold down enough of the dust to keep him from feeling a little panicky. Lozenges of faint glow were projected below the ventilators, gliding along the top surface of the mounded coke like spirits. He brought up the tail of his shirt to breathe through, fearful that his other lung might shut down at the shock.

"I was trapped down a well as a child," he managed to get out, his voice echoing weirdly off the metal wall, which seemed quite thin. He couldn't say more, since even the thought sent him rigid with a sense memory of the terror he'd experienced back then, seeing only one tiny eye of light far above. He rolled onto his back, then sat up to get his face as far from the coke as possible as they rumbled along.

"I hope you've got a plan," she said. She coughed a few times herself. "I think I've got a case of prickly heat."

"That's fear," he said. "Don't you know what it's like?"

She didn't answer. They rode in silence for a while, joggling a little now and then as the conveyor passed over irregularities or rollers out of alignment. It was funny, but he figured at least he had a good lung in reserve. If he wrecked the working one, they could always reinflate the other. Maybe we should all shut down one twin of the organs we had in pairs. Keep a kidney in reserve. An eye. One brain lobe. He was just trying to figure out if there were two livers or one big one when Gloria Ramirez found his hand and held it tightly.

"Yeah, it's fear."

Then there was a thump, like a small hammer on the outer metal tubing. A pencil of light appeared about ten yards in front of them, hinting at a billow of dust and tracing a bright spot on the coke rolling past. As they neared the light, he could see metal tabs torn inward at a small hole in the tubing. Nice shot, he thought, and a pretty spooky job of timing their progress along the conveyor. Superstitiously, he tried to squirm away from the bright finger, but there was no way, and it passed first across her arm, illuminating her shirt briefly, and then across his belly. They both looked back to watch the spot drift away behind.

"He's reminding us he's still there," Jack Liffey said.

They rode on a while with no further shots. He could feel, or maybe only imagine, the gradual rise, and he began to wonder what they would meet when they came to the tower. There was a permanent ache in his lung now from the powder, a tightness across his chest. He studied the conduit walls, and at every rivet and irregularity, he could see a fur of the powder.

The vibration changed noticeably under them, got rougher as if they were nearing a drive motor or some sort of transition. "I think we'd better get ready for something."

Not too far ahead, the circle of the walls seemed to disappear into a faint radiance, as if the conduit opened into a different dimension.

"That's got to be one of the towers," he said. "Let me get ahead of you."

He wormed over her, briefly enjoying the contact with her body but regretting the billow of coke dust he sent up. The coke was starting to penetrate his socks and trousers and neck, gritty and dry and irritating. His eyes focused hard on the glow ahead of them, the circle of faint light expanding gradually, welcoming them into another world. As they got closer, he could see the peaks of powdered coke on the conveyor dropping away like a river going over a falls, and there was a steady *shish* sound, growing in volume, like a giant hand dragging through a sandpile.

"Uh-oh."

He got up on his hands and knees, facing the opening that was approaching inexorably. To the right, down low ahead, there was a slight disturbance in the uniformity of the glow. The light was so weak it was hard to know what it was, but anything was preferable to a sudden drop . . . into what? His imagination supplied a forest of spikes pointing upward down below, then, perversely, an upturned shark's mouth. All at once, he pictured his job in 'Nam: he would watch the radarscope day after day for planes suddenly winking off, hearing cries for help on his earphones, and then dispatching first an A-6 ground attack fighter for protection, followed by a rescue chopper that would drop a nylon line and Stabo webgear for the downed pilot to climb into. He longed to see a nylon line dangling there at the end of the conveyer, with a big swivel hook he could grab and snap onto his belt.

The small outcropping to the right of the conveyor became clearer, and it was almost as good as a chopper dust-off.

"Take my hand!" he called. "There's a catwalk! Get ready to jump right!"

He suddenly spasmed into a bad coughing fit but did his best so suppress it. What irony if they lost their chance to a fit of coughing! It would have been easier to pull off with both his hands available to catch onto whatever the catwalk offered, but he clung to hers.

They rumbled closer to the drop-off, section after section of the coke mound plummeting away, and he could feel a cool mist on the air, like a light rain. The catwalk had a railing that ended close to the conveyor, so if he could hook the railing with his free arm he could swing her up behind him. But he would have only one chance for the grab.

"I see it," she said. Her voice was dead calm.

When the time came, he panicked a little when he pushed off hard and the yielding coke gave suddenly under him, nearly sabotaging his lunge. He missed the railing with his hand but flung his whole arm around it from the far side and caught it painfully in the crook of his elbow. He yanked hard on her arm behind him and felt her launch herself past him to get her chest onto the gridded metal of the catwalk. Immediately she gave him an extra tug that saved the day and pulled his torso up, beside her. They hung there on the dead edge of the catwalk on their bellies, just as they had on the fence, and he felt the coke pouring over his legs, trying to drag him down into some abyss he didn't even want to see.

She recovered first and squirmed up onto the catwalk, wriggling past him. She squatted and tugged hard on his free arm with both hands. Working inch by inch, she finally got him completely onto the walk, and he lay there for a time trying to catch his breath, moisture prickling all over him.

"I should have let you jump first," he said. "You're stronger."

"We made it. That's what matters. Look down there."

He crept forward a foot to put his head over the edge of the walk. There was just enough light from a series of ventilators to see the dark coke spilling into a huge mound far below, where two big metal screws fed the coke dust into other openings. Only one screw was turning, but, rotating or not, the big metal screws were not something you wanted to fall onto.

He rolled onto his back to look upward and saw white plastic pipes and fine sprayers. Presumably they added just enough moisture to keep the coke dust manageable. The catwalk continued around the inside of the tower to a red door, just like the one they had entered, and on to a ladder that led down to a small platform exactly between the screws. He let himself cough long enough until his good lung seemed to have the strength to carry on, and it was a relief to enjoy the relatively damp clear air under the misters.

"Like it or not," he suggested, "I think we've got to take another ride."

"You're probably right," she said. "We know he's tracking us."

As if her words had summoned the Devil himself, an angry fist slammed into the metal tubing right behind them, answered by a slap on the concrete block wall across the tower. A fuzzy rod of brighter light extended out into the silo through fine billows of dust, right where the conveyor spilled its load. Joe Ozaki was timing his shots with uncanny accuracy. Now there was the faint comfort of being inside the concrete block silo, but soon. . . .

"He seems to know everything."

"You talked to him. What's he like?"

"I can't say. Not really. He didn't seem like a psycho, but he's pretty eerie. He's feeding on his father's grievances, and I suspect there're his own feelings from 'Nam, too—we'll never know what that did to him. But it's all mixed up now with his own crazy brew of Bushido philosophy. The thing is, he's trying to kill us, and none of this matters now. We've got to go."

They had all settled onto the grass to wait, and the crowd below them had grown and grown as the local TV station went on broadcasting, with a breathless reporter offering meaningless updates like one of those police chases that the TV choppers followed relentlessly, at least three times a week, along the LA freeways.

Ornetta was whispering in her grandfather's ear, and Maeve wondered if it meant she was explaining to him Declan Liffey's life's work.

"O come, all ye faithful . . ."

Voices rose in the air as a group down the slope began to sing Christmas carols. It frustrated the TV reporter, who'd been rabbiting away about the "protocols" for dealing with barricaded suspects that he'd just gotten from one of the cops. He gave up for the moment, invoking the spirit of the day and holding the microphone out to the carolers.

Bancroft Davis shinnied very slowly down the slope several feet, working his hips and arms painfully, until he was right next to Declan Liffey. Maeve was on her grandfather's far side and watched the old black man lean in to whisper to him. "I lost my son," he said gently. His voice was amazing, since, with all the singing and chatter on the hill, Maeve could still hear his baritone clearly.

"A year and a half ago I hired your son to find out the truth for me. He did. He found out that Amilcar and his fiancée had been dead for some time, murdered in a fit of rage by a group of thugs after he mouthed off at them. I'm afraid Amilcar never learned the transforming power of nonviolent love. I wish I still had him so I could convince him about Martin Luther King and Jim Lawson and Bob Moses, but these were always just names out of the past to him. He never saw how love and forgiveness transform hating."

Declan Liffey did not respond to the old black man, but his face was twisting and flexing in a rictus of some terrible emotion.

"I guess you could say I lost my son, too," Declan Liffey whispered into the night. "I wish I could have him back." Maeve could see his shoulders give a shudder, and then she realized that the warping and crumpling that she had witnessed in his features was his own peculiar surrender to grief. He started to weep, and Bancroft turned his upper body to hold him just as Maeve fell against his other side and hugged him, too.

"I'm still me," Declan Liffey insisted softly. "Inside I'm still me."

Maeve was crying, gulping a little against the musty jacket her grandfather was wearing. Down below she could hear the crowd go on singing their hymns, with a number of people obviously la-la-ing away when they didn't know the words.

They stood side by side on the small landing between the two big screws. They were impressive, all right—corkscrews the size of dump trucks. One of them was static but the other was turning over slowly, digging coal dust out of the damp mountain and spiraling it toward a conveyor that was moving west. There was just room to slip between the top of the rotating spiral and the roof of the conduit, but there was nothing to grip, no way to get up there.

"Not one of your great forms of public transport," he said. "For humans, I mean."

"I bet, statistically, it's very safe. Probably haven't had a single passenger accident."

He chuckled despite himself. "When you're right, you're right. I'll give you a big boost over the screw onto the conveyor."

"Then how do you make it?"

"A leap and a prayer."

"Jack, the last time we did something like this, not fifteen minutes ago, you admitted I was stronger. Let me give *you* a boost. I can make this on my own."

She flexed an arm for him like a Gold's Gym muscleman, and he actually felt it. It was startlingly strong, the whole upper arm hard as a tree, and he knew, too, she was a good ten years younger than he was.

"Jesus, you must pump iron. Okay, it's age before beauty," he conceded, and a laugh racked him with coughing for a few moments.

He positioned himself at the edge of the short catwalk, squatting and bobbing to get some spring in his legs. He tried not to look at the big screw that was turning over slowly only a few inches from his nose, making crunching and hissing noises where it churned through the coke. But he had to look up to judge his leap, the blunt steel spiral blade whisking past, stirring little eruptions and boils in the surface of the coke pile, as if small animals warred beneath the surface. There was muscle of a sort in that giant screw, an almost malign force. It was quite capable of crushing an arm against the conveyor. But if you timed it right and got a good leap, there was just room to get over.

He felt her hands against his bottom. "Wait for three this time, for Chrissake," he said.

"You count it."

He didn't even want to think about what it would mean if she couldn't make the leap through the gap after him.

"One . . . two . . . THREE." He pushed off hard with his legs, and she shoved, and his chest scraped the steel a little and his knee knocked hard at the top of the device but he dropped on the far side face-first into the choking pile of coke. Something tweaked his foot briefly, and more coke was deposited on top of him. He pushed off the rough canvas and erupted out of the mound of coke, sputtering and coughing. He rested on his knees, spitting coke dust, and as soon as he got his eyes open, he looked back. She was silhouetted against the slight glow in the tower, bobbing a little, as if working up her courage.

"*Come on!* You're strong!" He could hear his voice bang and echo its way down the long tube, and he went on spitting out grit.

The opening looked treacherously small from this angle, but finally he saw her make a leap for it. In midair he saw her jolt sideways with great force, like a rag doll hit by a hammer, and her course shifted noticeably. One of her legs had clearly slammed against the giant screw as she came over, and then she kicked against something. She had fallen through into an odd posture, freezing that way as the machine shoveled piles of coke over her. With a real shiver of horror taking him, he crawled and fought his way back toward her as fast as he could, his knees slipping and sinking.

Only a leg showed. He dug her out and tugged until she was lying on her back, conscious but grimacing in pain.

"Where is it?"

"Leg."

In the intermittent faint pools of light from the ventilators, he saw a great tear in her long navy blue skirt, and then a gash deep into her flesh where she had caught her left leg on the device. She might have some injury, too, from the first jolt he had witnessed, but that would have to wait.

"Maybe I wasn't stronger," she offered in a strangled voice, as if she couldn't quite get her diaphragm working.

"That blow would have snapped my leg off," he said.

He didn't like the way dark, thick blood was oozing out of the cut on her leg. He dug out his Victorinox and pried open the little scissors. The spring that reopened them at each snip had given up the ghost years earlier, and it was a long, aggravating chore to take a half-inch bite into her skirt, stop and pry the blades open again, then take another bite until he had enough to grab to tear strips for a tourniquet. He tied a wad of cloth hard over the wound, and it seemed to slow the seepage. He had no idea how bad the coke dust would be for an open wound, but there was no way to avoid it. It was everywhere. He felt it in his hair and crotch and shoes, even working its way into his eyes so he had to keep looking for a relatively clean patch somewhere to wipe them.

Once he was done with his ministrations, Jack Liffey turned his attention to getting the two of them off the conveyor again at the next tower.

"Grip my hands," he ordered her, and she did. "Pull, *pull*. Okay, your arms are still strong. We'll make it." And after a while, "I'm not leaving you behind for the Indians."

She smiled weakly, and he started to say something but went into a coughing paroxysm. This time it took him over completely. The convulsing went on and on, and he had to flop onto his back to try to stabilize some of his bucking and kicking and to keep from hurling a body part into the small gap between the conveyer and the metal wall, where he'd do himself some real damage.

Then, all of a sudden, he felt some internal part of him rip from the exertions. He could feel it instantly, as if his rib cage had torn from its mountings. He shouted out at a fiery pain, and then felt a dizziness, as if he'd taken a whiff of some intoxicant. In one more bout, the coughing seemed to blow itself out and left him becalmed in some strange universe. He lay and breathed very slowly, bringing his shirt over his nose and mouth. His breathing was odd, lopsided in a new way, but it was serving better than it should, and he realized all at once what had happened.

"I was hoping to save you for later," he said aloud. She was up on an elbow, fretting at him with those wonderful, dark eyes, black with no centers.

"I think my bad lung just popped, reinflated itself," he explained for her. He smiled. "Sorry, Doc. I beat you to it." It felt strange, like walking hard on a leg that you had grown used to favoring. The extra air was exhilarating, even with so much dust around. He hadn't felt dizzy-drunk like this in a long time.

"Air is good," he said.

"Jack!"

There was a rasp of danger in her voice, and he forced himself to sit up on the traveling black mound. There it was ahead, that same faint round radiance approaching, a featureless entry into another tower. For just an instant he pictured the two of them tumbling off the edge, plummeting in the cataract of carbon dust straight toward two giant screws, both grinding away. He pushed the image away. If they made it onto this catwalk, assuming there was a catwalk, they wouldn't be doing any more conveyors, that was for sure. There would be a red door out of the tower, and they would just have to risk the goodwill of Joe Ozaki.

He pushed himself onto his knees. All his thrashing had managed to dislodge a lot of coke and give them a shallow plateau. "Can you get onto your knees?"

"I'll try."

He could hear her stirring behind him over the light rumble of the machinery.

"*Oooh,* that hurts. I'm up."

"Give me your hand." She clung to the one he offered, slippery with dust, and there wasn't a drop of sweat to help with the grip, every bit of moisture absorbed by the powdering of coke. She took his wrist in both her hands, relying on him. This time he was planning to thrust his free arm through the railing and catch it in his armpit, grabbing for anything he could, and then use all his strength to try to hurl her up onto the catwalk. But he didn't see how he could do it if her legs couldn't push off and give him some help.

"I need all the kick you've got left in you," he said.

"I don't know about my left, but the right's willing."

"Piece of cake," he said. His eyes never left the opening, and he inhaled to air himself out, full-lunged for the first time in months. The O of pale luminescence widened slowly like the iris of a lens, and he was relieved when he made out the edge of a catwalk on the right, just like the last tower. "I can see the railing. We're home free."

"I'm scared, Jack. I'm feeling weak."

"One last heave. Hang on like fury."

He kept drawing in those big, satisfying breaths, not used to both lungs yet, and he heard a whimper of pain behind him. He realized the blood loss was catching up with her, and he just hoped she didn't go into shock.

The conveyor began to shudder beneath them as the opening drew steadily closer. He felt one annoying hammer in his knees, a roller well out of alignment with the others.

"Get set!"

He had his left arm thrust out in front of him, anticipating. He grabbed, misjudged, and felt the steel rail hit him hard above the elbow, but his hand flailed around for something to grasp just as support fell away beneath his knee and he started to drop. A wave of panic took him over as it became clear neither of them had the strength for this maneuver.

"Push hard!"

Then some inexplicable force sucked them up, some giant magnet above that grabbed them both and yanked them aboard the catwalk. He couldn't believe she had that much power in her legs, but he lay for several moments enjoying their safety as the panic abated. When he moved his head slightly, he saw blacked-out tennis shoes, and then a human shadow in a ninja suit, backing away cautiously.

"Thank you, Joe," Jack Liffey said softly. As far as he could tell, Gloria had passed out.

"There is no distinction to be made between the battlefield and one's own kitchen," Joe Ozaki said in one of his gnomic riddles. "Courage is present or it is not."

"I'll take the kitchen," Jack Liffey said. But he wasn't sure whether he'd said it aloud. He was too dazed.

"All time is within us now."

The dark figure came close again and squatted down to handcuff Gloria Ramirez to the catwalk railing.

"I require you to come with me," Joe Ozaki intoned to Jack Liffey.

Twenty-two

The Coldest Day in History

One of the cops barked in surprise, his eyes pressed hard to his big, electronically amplified night-vision binoculars. Others, in the crowd below, holding vigil with their own binoculars, seemed to be reacting to something, too.

He showed up first as a tiny figure trotting hard along the approach ramp that curled onto the bridge. It was only because the bridge was at an angle to them that they could see him at all. Like any short suspension bridge, the roadway rose steeply, so he would remain invisible to the line of police cars blocking the shore end until he crested the middle, which was still half a mile ahead of him, two hundred feet above the channel.

Even at this range, Captain Adler could see there was a lot of blood on him, and he wouldn't let Maeve look.

"He's moving okay," was all he would say after he'd shouldered the uniformed cop aside to take the binoculars himself. Then he grabbed the uniformed cop and used the packset microphone on his shirt to alert the police cars at the barricade and scramble an ambulance.

"Just a precaution," he tried to lie, but she wasn't fooled.

* * *

Joe Ozaki had led Jack Liffey down a metal staircase that circled the inside of the tower and then out a door where they had to jump about three feet to the ground. Jack Liffey was worried about Gloria Ramirez, but he comforted himself that a last look seemed to show that her bleeding had stopped and she was breathing regularly.

"It doesn't have to go this way," Jack Liffey said.

"Of course it does." There seemed a tremendous energy pent up in the man in the jumpsuit—he almost vibrated with it—but Jack Liffey couldn't identify the source. "Follow now."

Despite his fear, Jack Liffey took a deep inhalation of the outside night air with both lungs and couldn't help glorying in the sea air, even with its overtones of oil sump, coke dust, and rotting fish. He wondered if he'd ever take breathing for granted again, but he guessed that the novelty would soon pass and, within a few minutes, he'd stop thinking about it—if he was still alive in a few minutes, of course. He again could see the Christmas lights up on the big ranch houses on the Palos Verdes Hills, a gesture of celebration from a faraway world.

"I don't suppose Christmas means anything to you," Jack Liffey said.

"Does it to you?" The man's voice was tight now, as if his vocal cords were stretched to near breaking.

"Sure. All the exciting wrapped gifts. The smell of the tree. That enormous anticipation as a child. Nothing very religious, except you can't really escape the mangers and Magi."

"My father was a Baptist. Can you believe it? He adopted the religion of the people who ruined his life."

"So what about all those Buddhists in Vietnam? Did you do them proud?"

He stopped in his tracks and stared hard at Jack Liffey. "You know nothing."

"I know you did what you thought was your duty. Even me, and I just sent codes over a radio."

"I used a knife," Joe Ozaki said. "It was very personal and direct. Can you visualize lopping the end off a Christmas ham at one blow?"

"I'd rather not. What do your samurai books say about some poor warrior who gets stuck with an evil master? You know, a master who makes the poor guy go against his code of honor?"

"The situation is not supposed to arise."

"That shows how realistic the code is."

"I did things. That's my business."

"Talking to a friend can help you let some of it go." He felt fatuous, like some sheltered advice columnist trying to soothe someone with real trouble—two missing legs, a terminal disease, serious jail time—but he didn't know what else to say.

Joe Ozaki was leading him eastward from the tower, back toward the village, but, at the same time, toward a low building not far away, boarded up and surrounded by rusting machinery. A seagull gave its sad, shrill cry in the dark. Jack Liffey had thought birds weren't supposed to cry at night, but he didn't know why he thought that. The chocolaty rumple of the cloud cover was still reflecting the orange security lights on the northern flank of the island.

"DIOOC intel interrogated the villagers that I took prisoner," Joe Ozaki said abruptly. "I stopped taking prisoners when I realized that they never survived the process."

"*Process*. You guys had some really quaint words," Jack Liffey said drily. "So in the end you disobeyed your orders out of a sense of humanity."

"It was better just to kill them."

Jack Liffey wanted to offer him a crumb of respect, some last shred of integrity, but he worried the man was well past anything like that. "Look, life threw you a curve. You did the best you could with two bad choices."

Joe Ozaki looked up at the clouds, as if there might be some reply there, but maybe he was just looking. "There is always an honorable choice."

"That's not my experience. There's the devil and the deep blue sea."

"There is always seppuku."

"That's what we call hara-kiri, isn't it?"

"Seppuku is the formal Chinese word, but it is the word the

Bushido used." Joe Ozaki stopped and turned to face Jack Liffey, then drew a crude sword out of his waist. It wasn't one of those long, shimmery, steel samurai swords, all elegant weaponly perfection. It didn't even have a handle. It looked like a raw, sharpened length of a car's leaf spring. The man held it by a wad of paper tied to one end.

"Man, I am not going to sword-fight you," Jack Liffey said.

"Of course you're not. You offered to be my friend. You're my kaishaku."

"What's that?"

"In Europe it might be called a second."

Jack Liffey didn't want to face the obvious. "Who are you going to fight?"

His companion only smiled a tight smile and beckoned him between what might once have been two large diesel engines, now just rust and decaying rubber hoses. What looked like a boarded-over door on the low building opened easily. They went inside, and Joe Ozaki lit a kerosene lantern. It was a strange room that the lamp revealed, like a jigsaw puzzle with most of the pieces lost. A lopsided china cabinet stood against one wall, and stacked on one shelf were a handful of plates and cups. An old rocker, losing the stuffing from its seat. A ladderback chair. A cooking pot. A Japanese wall hanging of split bamboo, with the image of a heron. All of it appeared generations old, rescued from thrift stores. Or rescued, Jack Liffey realized all at once, from thieves.

"You've reassembled your father's possessions." This was Joe Ozaki's nest on the island.

"What little remains, merely fingers pointing back at his life. Don't mistake the fingers for the life. All this is of no value whatever."

From a side room he retrieved a lacquered tray with several objects on it and a chest. He took them both outside, and Jack Liffey followed to watch him set them both gently in a cleared rectangle about the size of a double bed, against the side of the building. High streetlights along the road nearby cast a faint, even illumination over the smoothed soil. He went into the building once more and brought out a low, tippy-looking bench, no taller than his ankles, which he set before the tray. He sighed once, as if something was now complete.

Joe Ozaki stripped off the top half of his black jumpsuit to show a chiseled bare back with flanks that narrowed impossibly to a tiny waist. There was a long-healed wound running the full height of his back in a scar with crude stitching dots on either side, as if his spine had been surgically removed. On closer inspection, a section of the scar near the bottom still seeped a little, as if it had never healed.

He opened the chest and took out a folded white kimono. Very slowly, Joe Ozaki worked himself into the kimono with what seemed a kind of ceremony. A lot of preparation had gone into this playground, and Jack Liffey still didn't want to acknowledge to himself what it meant, though inside he knew.

"Can we talk about this?"

"Talk is past. I've made a mess of my life. Let's hope we may be given another."

"We all make a mess, Joe. I know I have. Mess is just being human. You want to know the great big hole in your Bushido philosophy? It's so big you could drive a bus through it."

That got the man's attention, and he stood very still, listening, the breeze fluffing the loose white robe like a giant, flightless bird.

"It's all duty and blame and pride. I told you before—there's no place in it for ordinary human love or forgiveness or mercy. It can't even cope with a simple act of human weakness without touching off some absurd spectacle of self-destruction. What good is all that inhuman rigidity?"

"It preserves a sense of honor in the world."

"You think that goofy novelist Mishima was honorable when he killed himself up on that roof at the military school? Wasn't it because Japan wouldn't renounce its pacifism? The whole country dismisses him. They call him a crank."

Joe Ozaki held out the two-foot-long sword. "This is yours. Hold it by the paper. Traditionally you must hold it out of my sight until it is needed. It has no virtue or quality as a weapon. When you are through with it, discard it, for it will be tainted."

Jack Liffey looked down at the crude knife he had been handed.

He'd almost withdrawn his hands to let it drop, but the aura of ceremony had been too great, the pure force of the man's will. The
blade looked quite sharp for two-thirds of its length, and a sheaf of
handmade rice paper was tied around the last third of the steel,
where the haft should have been.

"Joe, I beg you."

"I must compose myself now. Stand to my left, please."

The man spread his arms and, in one movement, sat gracefully
on the low bench, crossing his legs in front of him. He bowed to the
tray and picked up black chopsticks to eat some pickled vegetable
from one of the little bowls. Then he took two sips of something
from a tiny cup. Jack Liffey could smell alcohol on the air and
guessed it was probably sake. A bird passed overhead, like an
omen, and it gave a shrill, sarcastic cry, a crow. A night of far too
many birds, he thought.

"Joe, please tell me what's happening."

"You will know what you need to know."

Joe Ozaki picked up a bamboo brush and gently pulled a sheet
of paper toward himself on the tray. He made a number of false
starts and discarded several sheets before beginning to write. Jack
Liffey leaned in to read.

He dipped the brush repeatedly in a bowl of black ink to pen an
elegant, vaguely Asian-looking script. Obviously he had never
taught himself *kanji* or even the phonetic *katakana,* because his
poem was in English and in Roman characters.

> **At night both**
> **Good and bad die**
> **Under the bruised eye.**
> **Night's our reward, our counterweight,**
> **One crow asoar,**
> **A confessor for**
> **Rumors of the coldest day in history.**

A chill swept through Jack Liffey as the other man took two
more sips of the sake from the small, reddish-clay cup and then

finished it off with his head thrown back. Then he leaned forward and, one after the other, tucked the long lapels of his kimono under his knees on the earth to hold his head forward.

"Joe, I beg you . . ."

"You will see your duty, Jack Liffey. No creature must be permitted to suffer." He untied the plain belt and opened his kimono in front so his muscled belly was bare. He reached to the tray where Jack Liffey had not noticed another knife, shorter than the one he held behind his back, this one also handleless but pointed. Joe Ozaki wound the blunt end with sheet after sheet of the rice paper and then gripped it with both hands and brought the blade around toward himself.

"Joe, don't don't don't. You have too much to live for." The hackles on Jack Liffey's neck rose. He considered pushing the man over, grabbing for the knife, but he knew how strong and determined Ozaki was. He'd just make a mess of things.

The man bowed low once, made some short prayer, and Jack Liffey hoped against hope that it would stop in some elaborate joke right there, or maybe only a kind of ritual mimic of seppuku. Then Jack Liffey's whole body jolted with the electric shock of what he witnessed. The man had yanked the knife straight into his belly. It was all in one motion and accompanied by the obscene butchery sound of steel through meat, plus a suppressed whimper at the end. Jack Liffey was frozen in place and couldn't move. He couldn't see the small blade any longer, but by the motion of the man's arms he could make out a hard, horizontal cut from left to right, a pause, and then a desperate tug upward.

Reflexively, he closed his eyes on the horrible spectacle, praying something would happen to undo these moments, but he couldn't keep his eyes closed for long.

The way the man's kimono was tucked, he rested in a slight forward bow, rocking a little. A kind of groan came from Ozaki's throat, and he set the bloody knife down gently in front of him. In the half light in front of the kneeling figure, Jack Liffey seemed to see something spill out of the man, but he couldn't look, couldn't concentrate. He felt himself yawning, his vision narrowing to a tiny cone. An avoidance of any thinking, only a kind of mental idling.

"Now, Jack Liffey. Strike my neck. The pain is great."

He was paralyzed. He couldn't believe he was actually standing there holding a ritual killing knife. The thought of hacking off someone's head was just out of the question, yet this man was obviously suffering terribly.

"I can't do this, Joe. Can't you just shoot yourself?"

"This is the way it is done," he said with immense patience, gritting his teeth.

"This isn't fair."

"I am already dead. What are these on the ground? These are my intestines. Take your swing. Try to strike hard enough to cut through the spinal cord, but not so hard that you completely remove my head. That is the way it is done."

Jack Liffey sensed a trembly panic spreading through him. He felt the weight of the big blade dangling from his hand. How could he do this obscenity? But how could he let the man suffer?

"Jack Liffey, *now,* please."

A police car brought him to the command post at the hillside park above the old ferry building. He had already told an ambulance driver where Gloria Ramirez was handcuffed and about her injuries. Captain Adler helped him out of the car, making a face at the blood on his clothes.

"I'm afraid Ken Steelyard is dead," Jack Liffey said. "So is Joe Ozaki. I think Gloria Ramirez will be okay."

"She's being seen to."

"I'll be okay, too," he said numbly, "and five billion other souls. Christmas Eve."

Maeve managed to squeeze through the surrounding ring of officers and ran to hug him. "Daddy!"

He was startled by her voice. He looked up and saw Ornetta tugging his own father uphill, stringy and frowning, as if she'd adopted the old Nazi as another blood relative. It didn't really make any sense to him, but his mind was already far into overload.

Adler offered him a pint bottle of J & B. Jack Liffey looked at it for a long time but finally shook his head. "I've already broken too many rules tonight. Have you ever done something you thought you could never do?"

"Passed the captain's exam the fourth time I tried."

Jack Liffey smiled for just an instant. "I have no context for tonight. Christmas Eve."

"Christmas proper," he corrected. "It's twelve-thirty. You look pretty tired, fellow. Why don't you save the talk for back at the station."

"Uncle Jack! Here's your dad." Ornetta had finally made it through the crowd, towing the old buzzard behind, and Declan Liffey stood there, watching him sheepishly. The old man reached out and put a hand awkwardly on his son's shoulder. In a moment he took it back and surreptitiously wiped it off on his pants. Blood was everywhere. "It's real good to see you, Jack. We were all worried."

"Thanks, Dad." Despite the surrounding of family, he felt utterly bereft. Something had returned him to childhood, if just for that moment. And only his mother would have done for comfort. He felt trapped in some dark, unchanging moment, and he just wanted the cops to lead him away and punish him. He had desecrated Christmas. And probably Bushido, too.

It wasn't fair, he thought, to be suspended between two moral codes, believing in neither one.

A few days later he found himself alone in a spartan two-man cell in the new Twin Towers jail downtown, having missed Christmas altogether and unable to make bail on the charge of involuntary manslaughter. Ridiculous charge, he had thought as the DA announced it to him. Involuntary was the one thing it hadn't been. Bail—he might as well pray for a white Christmas. Any zeros beyond two put the figure out of the question for his bank account.

He'd had plenty of solitude to think about what he'd done, or been forced to do, and still hadn't found a way to return to a sane and normal universe. He watched his fingers drum on the steel table, trying to figure out if his own will was working them.

The weird stainless steel cell wasn't helping much, like something carved out of a single block of ice. The table and bench combination, the one-piece toilet, the shelf bed belonged to a very strange, shiny, austere world. But what made him most uneasy was the fact that the tiny slit window with wired glass showed him nothing but a concrete block wall, and he had no way of orienting himself in the universe. Even a few stars would have done it, or a glimpse of one of the downtown buildings, but it was like coming unglued from the earth. It was a habit he had picked up long ago and couldn't break: he always kept a compass and a simple altimeter in his car so he would know roughly where he was on the surface of the earth and which way he was facing.

After two days of solitude—mostly footsteps and harsh voices during the day, and wet coughs, groans, and rage-fed cries all night long—he had three visitors, one right after another. First, a reasonably polite guard who looked about fifteen came to fetch him. They were all trainee sheriffs. The boy brought him down to a barren room that contained a brushed aluminum table and two chairs of the same stuff that looked like they had just been delivered from the same world that had invented his cell.

He sat with his hands folded docilely and waited for a long time, and then the weasely little balding man he recognized as his public defender came in. The fellow made a display of his hurry, like a doctor annoyed that you were bothering him with a simple cold. He slapped open an aluminum briefcase and consulted the papers in it, probably trying to remind himself of Jack Liffey's name.

"How's it going, Jack?" he said emptily as he read something. "You been one-H before, I bet."

"If that means in jail, I have. I've even been in an army guardhouse. But I never really get used to the—what is it?—*resource deprivation*. I would be delighted to get out of here."

"I think I can get her to settle for assault, with some supervised probation time. Is that a go?"

"I helped kill a cop-killer. They should be giving me a medal."

He shrugged. "The whole thing should have been HBO—that's handled by officer—right there on the scene. But they've got a flea up their ass about a big mercy killing case at a nursing home. Time served and checking in with some squarehead once a week ain't bad, Jack." He held up an eight-by-ten photograph to peer at it,

made a sour face, and put it back in the briefcase so Jack Liffey
never saw it. "Jesus, man. You made a mess."

Jack Liffey was glad the PD hadn't felt like sharing the photo. It
was vivid enough in his recollection. When he'd finally worked up
his nerve to do what he had to do, realizing there was no way out,
he hadn't wanted to make a bad job of the coup de grâce, so he had
hit pretty hard, but the crude knife had been sharpened so well that
it had almost severed poor Joe Ozaki's neck. The head had yanked
back at the blow, his mouth jolted into a strange grin, and then the
head flopped forward, as if hinged, which, as he was to learn later,
was exactly the way it was all supposed to happen. In Bushido
code, only criminals had their heads fully severed.

"Get me as off as you can."

"Sure, Jack. Sorry it didn't go easier, but you seem to be a bit of
a shit magnet on this one."

Later that afternoon, he was taken down an elevator to a different
area, a big room with a lineup of bank teller cages. He was sat down
behind a glass window inches thick. A telephone handset hung from
a partition.

In a moment, he was grinning ear-to-ear as Maeve settled onto a
stool on the other side, looking very earnest. Her mouth started
moving, but he couldn't hear a thing, and he had to rap on the glass
and point to her own handset.

". . . Daddy, it's so horrible seeing you like this." Her voice
was like a fly in a bottle, buzzing far away. She said she wasn't
fond of his denim getup either, with a number where a pocket
should have been.

He didn't want to upset Maeve any more than she already was,
so he went for a little Damon Runyon humor. "Da mouthpiece sez
he can bribe da judge and spring me outta dis joint."

She made a pained face. "Don't joke, Daddy. This is really, really
awful. And they're probably listening."

"More power to them. We're making a deal for probation. The
lawyer's pretty sure the judge will go for it." It took some doing
before she was convinced he wasn't just mollifying her.

"I want you out *now*. You know, I could go to Becky and ask her for the bail money. She's got plenty in the bank."

"Absolutely not. Just have patience, hon."

To change the subject, he asked how Ornetta was doing. For some reason she got a sly look. "I've been staying with Gramps since Christmas and, you know, he's trying fairly hard not to be his old self. He keeps saying he's the same inside, believes the same things, but I know he's changing. By the way, Mom is pretty pissed at you for telling her that your father was dead."

"Kath would have loved his Sambo routines and all his greedy-Jew stories. And all his theories about light-skinned people being the acme of evolution. Not to mention his plan for sterilizing the mud people for their own good. Or maybe it was just *most* of the mud people—we always needed to keep a few to do our dirty work."

Maeve seemed to get impatient. "I'm *sure* he's changing, Dad. Ornetta visits us and he really seems to like her."

Every bigot in the world had one black friend, Jack Liffey thought. It didn't mean a thing. He thought of all the years he had argued and cajoled and shouted at his father without leaving a dent in all those fortressed beliefs. He also thought of the essays he'd had his friend Chris Johnson download from the Internet only a few years back, just to get a look at his father's most recent rants, essays Jack Liffey had soon discarded, held at the corners by two fingers, like something the cat had killed and left at the back door.

"Well, hon, I sure hope you're right. I have a terrible feeling he's just a lonely old man putting on a big front to please you, but I'll give him a break. You've got magic power in you, I won't argue that."

"It's Ornetta with the magic."

"So does she."

"Last night she told us all a story about—" The phone went dead suddenly, and he was left staring at her lips moving happily on the other side of the glass. He loved seeing her so close—her mobile, emotional face; her skinny, vulnerable arms; a certain determined set of her lips, just like her mother's—and he didn't want to interrupt her, so he went on watching. Finally, a deputy appeared behind her and tapped her on the shoulder.

She kissed her hand and held it against the glass. He reciprocated, though it was not very satisfying.

Late that afternoon Gloria Ramirez came to the bars outside his cell, leaning on one wooden crutch. She had on a knee-length black skirt that revealed a long plaster cast on her leg. The other leg looked great—muscular and shapely. Her police wallet with its badge hung from a plastic cord around her neck.

"They say you'll be out tomorrow."

"Hope so. Chipped beef on toast is not my idea of a gourmet snack."

"If that's the worst—"

He waved it off. "Sure."

"We found Joe Ozaki's journal. I'll try to fix it so you can read it if you want."

He got up off the built-in bench to get a better look at her. She looked great there, even in the dim light. "I guess I'd like to read it. You know, he might not have gone over the edge if Ken hadn't been pushing him so hard."

She nodded. "We call it suicide by cop—pushing cops into killing you. Maybe this was the opposite, you know? Suicide by perp. Ken had his own trouble. But he didn't keep a diary."

"Steelyard knew he was outmatched. I'm sure he gave Ozaki no choice. Ken admitted to me that he'd tried to eat his gun a couple of times."

"Damn. I didn't know."

"What we have is two tragedies colliding. That's the nut, really. I liked Ken, but I liked Joe, too. His country sent him to Vietnam and made him into a first-rate warrior, but they never told him anything that could make sense of what he was sent to do. And that Bushido crap he stumbled onto just made it all worse." Jack Liffey shrugged. "He grabbed it because it was Japanese and seemed to give his life some meaning. Race is always a lie, always."

"Really?"

"I believe it. We're just humans. That guy, he'd have been better off watching *Shane* and *High Noon*. Do your best. Keep the peace.

Love the schoolmarm. Never shoot a guy in the back. And don't hurt the civilians. That all works. He stuck himself with a philosophy so brittle it couldn't deal with forgiveness, or forgiving yourself, or even with the friendship I offered. Bushido broke him."

"Jack, this is such *guy* stuff. No woman would do all that."

He nodded. "You're probably right. The heart beats the head every time."

"Come here," she said in a throaty voice.

He came toward the bars.

"Put your hands on the bars right here. And here."

He did, and she pressed her breasts against his hands. "Get out soon."

"I'm doing my best."